The Birthday Girls

Pauline Lawless

POOLBEG

This novel is entirely a work of fiction. The names,
characters and incidents portrayed in it are the work of the
author's imagination. Any resemblance to actual persons,
living or dead, events or localities is entirely coincidental.

Published 2013
by Poolbeg Press Ltd.
123 Grange Hill, Baldoyle,
Dublin 13, Ireland
Email: poolbeg@poolbeg.com

1 3 5 7 9 10 8 6 4 2

A catalogue record for this book is available from the British Library.

ISBN 978-1-84223-549-2

Printed and bound by
CPI Group (UK) Ltd, Croydon, CR0 4YY

www.poolbeg.com

Note on the author

Pauline Lawless is the bestselling author of four previous novels: *Because We're Worth It, If the Shoes Fit, A Year Like No Other* and *Behind Every Cloud*.

From Dublin, she now lives in Belgium and spends winters in Florida, which she loves. It is the setting for her fifth novel *The Birthday Girls*.

For more information visit her website at www.paulinelawless.com.

Also by Pauline Lawless

Because We're Worth It

If the Shoes Fit

Behind Every Cloud

Acknowledgements

This bit is harder than writing a book. There are so many people who have shown me support and encouragement in writing not just this book but my previous four also that I never know where to begin to thank them. Well, actually, I do!

To all at Poolbeg, Kieran, Ailbhe, David and especially Paula Campbell for believing in me and giving me this wonderful opportunity.

To the best editor any writer could have, Gaye Shortland, who improves every story with her sharp eye for detail. Thank you!

To my daughter, Ciara, who keeps me on the straight and narrow as I write, telling me where I've gone wrong and setting me on the right path again. Your help is invaluable. Love you.

To my friends in Florida, who make me feel like a real author and to whom this book is dedicated, thank you all.

To JM, as always, with love.

And lastly to the most special people of all, my readers. You have made this all possible and your kind messages and support mean a great deal to me. I hope you enjoy this book as much and I would love to hear from you on my website at www.paulinelawless.com.

To all my dear friends in Florida – you know who you are – who give me so much support and encouragement with my writing and who are also great company and fun.

Chapter 1

"I absolutely refuse to be forty," Angel declared, her voice strong and determined, "so I won't be taking part in any fortieth celebrations next year. Please don't be angry with me, Lexi, but I have always said that I planned on staying thirty-nine forever." She reverted to her normal little-girl-voice as she continued. "I'm truly sorry, honey, but this coming November will be my very last birthday."

Angel was a diva – a full-blown, over-the-top, Hollywood-style diva. She had been for as long as Lexi had known her, which was all of thirty-five years. She was almost thirty-nine now and as dramatic as ever as she made her announcement. The emotion in Angel's voice was palpable on the other end of the line. Lexi sighed. Angel had often said her thirty-ninth birthday would be her last, but no one had really taken her seriously. Now it was apparent that she had indeed meant it, thereby wrecking Lexi's plans for a fabulous slap-up fortieth, the following year, in Guatemala.

"Well, if you're really serious –"

"Oh, I am," Angel insisted. "I'm sorry, sweetie, but I just

can't go there. I hope you understand. It would be the death knell for my career. God, if word got out that I was forty, I'd never be offered another part." She sounded appalled.

Lexi thought she was overreacting. Lots of Hollywood actresses were still working well into their forties.

"Well, in that case the four of us had better try and get together for our thirty-ninth as it will be our last birthday together," she responded glumly. "Doesn't leave much time though – it's only six weeks away."

"I know, but I was thinking that we could all come to Florida, to your place," Angel suggested breathlessly. "That would be just fabulous. Could you arrange it, Lexi?"

Angel had been born with that knack of being able to wind everyone around her little finger and Lexi, as always, was unable to deny her anything.

"Okay," she reluctantly said. "As Thanksgiving falls the Thursday after our birthdays, maybe we'll make a week of it. What do you think? Do you think Mel will be able to come?"

"I'll make sure she does," said Angel. "Could Brenda get over for it, I wonder? Seeing as it is our last?"

"I don't know. Leave it with me. I'll see what I can do."

"You're a pet – I love you!" Angel cried, blowing kisses down the line.

Lexi rang off with a heavy heart, disappointed that her plans for Guatemala were dashed, unless Angel changed her mind by next year, which was possible, but unlikely. Ah well, she thought sighing, things could be worse.

* * *

She rang Brenda right away but it went to voicemail. Lexi hated those bloody things. She found it hard enough to talk on the phone without talking to a disembodied voice. She hung up without saying anything and decided to wait until 1 p.m. to call, which would be 6 p.m. in Ireland and a good time to get Brenda in. She had intended going to her studio to paint but Angel's phone call had scuppered that. She was too agitated now to produce anything worthwhile so decided to go for a walk on the beach instead.

* * *

Brenda was very surprised to hear her old friend on the other end of the line.

"Lexi, is that really you? Is everything okay?"

"Fine, sweetheart, just fine. How are you?"

"I'm grand. There's nothing wrong, is there? I'm just surprised to hear you. I know how much you hate the telephone."

Lexi laughed. "There's nothing wrong but it is an emergency of a sort, I suppose. Angel has decided that this will be her last birthday so it looks like we won't be having a fortieth, at least not all four of us together. She's asked me to have everyone here to Florida for our thirty-ninth. Is there any way that you could get over for the third week in November?"

Brenda hesitated. "Well, the kids are all away so that wouldn't be a problem but . . ."

"I would like to offer you your flights, as a fortieth birthday present – seeing as how we won't be having one – if you'd accept. It just wouldn't be the same if you weren't here."

"Oh, Lexi, that's very generous of you! I would so love to go. I'm feeling very down at the moment, suffering from empty-nest-syndrome I suppose. Carly, my baby, went away to college in Limerick last week. I can hardly believe it! I'd love to get together again with all of you but I'm not sure Bob will agree to my going."

"Oh I'm sure you'll be able to persuade him." Lexi smiled to herself. "It's Thanksgiving so we can have a whole week here celebrating and maybe you and I could have a few days in New York the following week. We could stay with Mel. What do you think?"

Brenda could hardly believe her ears. She'd always longed to visit New York and to visit Florida would be heaven. This was an amazing opportunity. She'd have to manage it.

"Leave it with me. I'll see what I can do," she said excitedly.

"Let me know as soon as you can. It would be wonderful if you could come, Brenda. I'd so love to have you here."

Brenda's heart beat wildly as she replaced the receiver. How generous of Lexi, who knew that there was no way on earth Brenda could afford to pay for the trip herself, to offer her the flights as a gift. Money had always been tight and now with the economic crisis and three of the children still at university, it was a struggle to make ends meet, let alone take off on a holiday to Florida. She desperately wanted to go. It would be great to get together with Lexi, Angel and Mel for a whole week. If only she could persuade her husband, Bob, to agree to it. Unfortunately, she wasn't at all sure that he would.

* * *

She made Bob's favourite dinner and even bought a bottle of wine – a rare occurrence these days – hoping to soften him up. After they'd finished eating she broached the subject of a possible visit to the States to meet up with the girls.

"Florida? Are you serious?" He looked at her aghast. "You know we can't afford that."

"It won't cost us anything. Lexi is giving me my flight as a birthday present and I have some money saved from my Avon sales." Brenda had started selling Avon cosmetics when the children were little so that she could make a few bob to buy those little extras they needed. To her surprise she'd enjoyed being an Avon Lady and had built up a loyal clientele over the years, many of them becoming her friends. She'd continued with it even when the kids were gone and, although her earnings were not huge, she'd managed to put a little by each week. She'd been saving it for a rainy day – now she was hoping to spend it on a sunny one in Florida. "I really want to go," she persisted, determined not to give up without a fight.

"For how long?" he asked sullenly.

Brenda decided to go for broke. "Two to three weeks. There's no point going all that way for just a few days, is there?" She held her breath, waiting for his response.

"I suppose not," he muttered, finding no reason to oppose it. As long as it wouldn't cost him anything!

She breathed a huge sigh of relief and didn't dare mention a possible jaunt to New York. She knew he'd never agree to that. She felt bad deceiving him, but she wasn't really. It wasn't definite yet anyway, just a possibility.

* * *

On a high, she tried later to initiate lovemaking but as usual Bob wasn't interested and turned away from her, feigning sleep. She lay awake, wondering where it had all gone wrong. They'd been married for twenty-two years and, with five children to raise, they'd never had much time to think about themselves or worry about their marriage. But now, with the kids gone, Brenda had begun to question her life. She had given unselfishly to others all of her life: as a daughter, sister, wife and mother. She loved them all, naturally, but she felt badly in need of some TLC herself now. She'd been so busy taking care of them all that she felt as if she had lost herself. She longed to find herself again and she hoped this holiday might help her do that.

Being on their own since the last of the kids had flown the nest had also brought home to her just how much she and Bob had grown apart. Maybe a break from each other would be a good thing. She turned her thoughts to the forthcoming trip, unable to sleep with excitement.

* * *

The four women went back a long way, back to their very first day at school, in fact. It was a day that would be etched in Brenda's memory forever. The teacher had put the new pupils together according to their birth dates and, as the four of them had birthdays within days of each other, they were all put sitting at the same small table. They were excited but a little nervous and shy, as most kids are on their first day of school, except for Angel of course, who was in her element with this new audience of admirers.

Brenda had felt dowdy and plain beside the other three and was quite in awe of them. She was particularly drawn to Lexi who was quiet and gentle and had a sweet, kind face. Her hair was a halo of unruly red-gold curls which hung down her back and she had soft brown eyes which lit up when she smiled, which was often. Brenda was fascinated with her and her accent which she later discovered was because her mother was American and Lexi had been born in the States and had lived there for the first three years of her life.

Angel was exceptionally pretty with long silky blonde hair and blue eyes and a cute nose that turned up at the end. She was outgoing and extrovert and a right little chatterbox. Brenda could still recall every detail of the beautiful blue dress Angel wore on that first day and the blue ribbon that tied back her hair. She was the prettiest girl Brenda had ever seen and she longed to be her. Even back then, Angel had acquired the knack of batting her eyelashes and using her big blue eyes to get whatever she wanted. And she did! No one could resist her – not the other pupils and not the nuns. She was adored and petted and the envy of the whole class.

Mel was another kettle of fish entirely. Her hair was jet black and tied back in pigtails. Her eyes were so dark that they appeared almost black, or maybe they just gave that impression because of the scowl she continually wore. She could have been pretty, if only she'd smile. For a long time Brenda was almost afraid to talk to her. Lexi was the only one who seemed to see past that and had taken Mel under her wing, otherwise it is doubtful that she would have made many friends.

Brenda remembered how ugly she'd felt in her cousin's hand-me-down dress which was way too big for her. She was also as timid as a mouse and felt overwhelmed by the others. Lexi understood this and reached over and took her hand, squeezing it gently. Brenda smiled gratefully at her as her fears receded. She loved Lexi from that moment on.

Strange but, thinking about it now, Brenda realised that their characters really hadn't changed all that much since that first meeting.

Angel was still a chatterbox and was a famous actress in Hollywood. She was as vivacious and beautiful as ever – with a little help now from the best plastic surgeons in LA.

Mel was still unhappy even though she was now a very successful businesswoman in New York. She was still driven and never satisfied despite the fact that she was now a partner in the most prestigious law firm in New York and highly respected in the legal world. Brenda suspected that Mel regarded her as a failure and thought that she hadn't achieved anything. Raising five children would not be considered an achievement to Mel's way of thinking.

As for Lexi – well, she was still gentle and loving and the glue that held them all together. She was still happy in her own skin and had a wonderful outlook on life. She only saw the good in other people and was loved by everyone who met her. When any of them were in trouble it was Lexi they ran to and somehow it never seemed quite as bad when seen through her eyes. She reached out to people and spread sunshine wherever she went. Her three old school friends would have been lost without her over the years.

* * *

Brenda was dying to call Lexi first thing the following morning but had to wait impatiently until one o'clock due to the five hours time difference. With shaking hands she dialled the Florida number.

"Hi, Lexi, it's Brenda."

"Calling with good news, I hope?" Lexi sounded apprehensive.

"Yes, yes, I can come." Brenda's voice was high with excitement. I'm so thrilled."

Lexi whooped with glee. "Brenda, it's fantastic that you can make it. I'll book your flights right away. I was thinking of bringing you via New York so that you can fly home direct from there. You'd like to visit New York, wouldn't you?"

Would I what? Brenda thought. "Oh, Lexi, that would be heaven," she squealed. "I've always longed to visit New York. Are you sure Mel won't mind my staying with her?"

"Course not. I'll fix it with her," Lexi replied confidently. "You won't have a problem staying those extra few days, will you?"

"No, I told Bob it would be two to three weeks."

"That's decided then. Hopefully Angel will persuade Mel to come and we'll all be here together for Thanksgiving which will be wonderful. I'll contact my travel agent now and have the tickets sent on to you. It will be great to get together again – like old times."

"It sure will. I'm really excited about it. This thirty-ninth birthday is going to be the best birthday I've ever had."

Lexi laughed. "Well, I'll do my best to make it so. You coming is the best birthday present I could have."

Chapter 2

Angel knew that Lexi was disappointed when she'd told her that there was no way she would consider having a fortieth birthday but Lexi, true to form, had rallied round and agreed to organise a party in Florida for their thirty-ninth. A party was just what Angel needed right now. The very thought of approaching forty was depressing her as she peered in the mirror to check for any new fine lines around her eyes.

She had called Mel as soon as she'd come off the phone from Lexi but as usual it went to voicemail.

When she wasn't working, Angel's day usually started around noon with a mug of coffee – not decaf, she couldn't stand that stuff – or more likely, especially if she was hungover, a glass or two of champagne with orange juice. That always lifted her as she checked her iPhone for messages. She lived in hope that one would be from her agent offering her the role of a lifetime – a fabulous script with her in the starring role. She constantly cited other actresses such as Jennifer Anniston, Sandra Bullock and Halle Berry, who at the same age were still hot and even winning Oscars. If they could do it, so could she. Anything was possible in Hollywood!

Then she would settle down at her computer to read her emails. Most of them were rubbish but this could just be the day she would hear of some project coming up with a part for a thirty-something blonde. Hollywood ran on rumour so it was important to keep one's ear very close to the ground.

With a second mug of coffee in hand, the next thing she did was check her dating site to see if any eligible blokes had winked at her. She had not dared put a real photo of herself up there as there was a good chance she might be recognised so she'd put one of another blonde up instead.

If she liked the look of any of the men who winked at her she might flirt back and forth in the hope that one of them might turn out to be the gold nugget amongst all the mud and sand. She knew it was unlikely but she was always optimistic. She had met some nice guys on there though unfortunately most of them were married at the time. But, as she was fond of saying, "How long do marriages last in this town? Whoever is married today could be available next week!" She did meet her third husband on a dating site and my God, what a tosser he turned out to be! She refused to think about him. It would only bring her down for the whole day.

She did have a live-in boyfriend at the moment, Will, who was about to become live-out very shortly, although he didn't know it yet. He was sixteen years younger than Angel, which was nothing in Hollywood, but she'd discovered that, hot as it made her look, pandering to the whims of a penniless twenty-three-year-old could be very tiring, not to mention expensive. He wanted to party all night, drinking champagne that she paid for, and then stayed in bed all day. She regularly bemoaned the fact that unfortunately there was only one Ashton Kutcher! Will hadn't worked a day in his life and she knew he probably never would, as long as there were foolish women like her around to support him.

After she checked the dating site, it was more coffee and then she went on Facebook to see what all her friends were getting up to. She had hundreds of friends – too many, she often thought – but it just wasn't possible to drop them. She knew that people got very upset when you did that. She did. Then it was on to Twitter to catch up on all the news there. She only read the @connect now – the tweeters who had mentioned her. She doubted there was anyone on earth who had the time to wade through 375 tweets every day. She knew that she should unfollow some of them but then they'd unfollow her and she was trying hard to reach 5,000 followers. She was very nearly there. If she just followed another forty people or so, they'd follow her back and she'd make it. If by any chance she should land a plum role then that would go up to gazillions, just like Demi Moore, whom she followed. People loved to follow big stars.

Angel sighed, thinking back to the time when she'd been a mega star, famous all over the world. She was twenty-four then and newly arrived in Hollywood when she'd landed a major role in the most popular TV show of the day. Those were halcyon days when she'd been an A-lister and feted wherever she went. The show had lasted for eight glorious years and she'd been bereft when it had ended. She'd landed a plum role in a movie about Marilyn Monroe shortly afterwards, thanks to her resemblance to the famous star, but unfortunately the movie had bombed. She'd worked pretty constantly since then but only bit-parts. A further big movie role had eluded her but she never gave up hope. Sadly, there'd been no Twitter around when she'd been a star.

Sometimes she wondered if maybe Lexi had the right idea shunning all this modern technology. One thing for sure, Lexi would never find the time to paint if she were to try and keep up with the social network.

All of this took until about four thirty every day when, if

she was lucky, Will might condescend to put in an appearance. She had lunch then which was usually an egg-white omelette or some salad leaves. Angel was a serial dieter, like every other actress in Hollywood. Of course, she drank the best part of a bottle of wine with it. She read somewhere that there were no carbs in white wine and carbs were the real enemy.

She was excited at the thought of hanging out with the girls again. They'd been best friends all of their lives but it had been a while since all four had met up together. The last time was three years ago and then only for a night. She, Lexi and Mel all happened to be back in Ireland at the same time and they'd met up with Brenda. What a night that had been! Even though they hadn't all been together since their combined thirtieth birthday, six years before, it was as if they'd never been apart.

Both she and Mel had been down to stay with Lexi for quick breaks, but never at the same time. Lexi sometimes travelled to New York in connection with her art and met up with Mel but as she hated Los Angeles – Shallow Town, she called it – Angel didn't see as much of her as she'd like.

Brenda was a little out of the loop, being the only one left in Ireland and of course it wasn't easy for her, with five children like steps of stairs. When they last met she seemed happy enough but her life was a constant struggle. Bob had a taxi and Brenda said he now earned less than he did seven years ago. So much for the Celtic Tiger! Three of her children were at university and living away from home which took every cent they had. Angel could never live like that, no matter how much she loved a man. She thought Brenda was a saint!

* * *

Mel rang back an hour later.

"Sorry, missed your call, I was in a conference."

Angel threw her eyes to heaven. When was Mel ever not in a conference?

"What's up?" Mel asked impatiently.

"Well, as you know, I will not be having any more birthdays so Lexi has agreed to host our last birthday party in Florida. You absolutely have to come."

Mel laughed. "So she's finally accepted that you plan to stay thirty-nine forever?"

"Yeah. Can you make it?"

"Gee, don't know if I can. We're crazily busy here. When is it?"

"Thanksgiving week."

"Hang on a sec while I check."

Angel heard her turning the pages in her diary.

"Well, I can make a couple of days – but a week? I don't know. Leave it with me."

"She's invited Brenda to come over for it."

"She's what?"

Angel heard the surprise in her voice before a huge clatter almost deafened her.

"Sorry, I just dropped my phone," Mel explained. "Can Brenda afford it? I thought they were struggling financially."

"Don't worry – Lexi will find a way. Anyway, isn't it fantastic? The four of us together again for a whole week!" Angel squealed excitedly.

"Well, I could certainly do with the break. I'll call you when I get home around nine. Okay?"

"Jesus, Mel, you're working yourself to death. What time did you start this morning?"

"Six thirty. Why?"

"You'll kill yourself." Angel shook her head in disbelief. "Mel, you have to come. I need you there."

"Okay, okay," Mel said resignedly. She knew Angel would keep at her until she gave in. "But only for a couple of days.

Have to rush now, sorry. I've got another meeting. Byeee!"

"Bye," Angel started to say but Mel had already hung up.

"What a life!" Angel said aloud as she replaced the receiver. Mel had sounded stressed. She would kill herself working. Hopefully she could make the party. It wouldn't be the same without her. She obviously needed the break and a week in Florida would help her relax and chill out. Angel knew that once she got her there she would convince Mel to stay the whole week.

* * *

Lexi rang Angel the next day. "Wonderful news! Brenda is coming for the party."

"That's great. I'm looking forward to seeing her again."

"What about Mel? Did you talk to her?"

"She said she'd come but maybe only for a couple of days. But I'm sure once we get her there we'll be able to persuade her to stay the week."

"That girl works far too hard."

"She's nuts. She never takes a holiday and for what?"

"I know, but that's Mel. She's always been like that," Lexi remarked dolefully.

"Isn't it great that Brenda can come?"

"Yes, I'm really looking forward to having her here. God love her, she's earned it. I must give Mel a call. How was she today? She was very stressed out the last time I spoke to her."

"She still is. It looks like we all need this break."

It amused Angel that Lexi had never lost her Irish accent which was even more accentuated over the phone. Both she and Mel had embraced the American way of life with open arms and could now be mistaken for natives, but not Lexi. She had been almost paranoid about keeping her Irish identity.

Angel sometimes regretted that she had been so quick to lose her Irish accent. Colin Farrell – what a dish – hadn't, and what success he'd had, Dublin accent and all! Well, too late to do anything about it now, Angel sighed.

* * *

Mel was thinking about Angel's phone call as she rode a taxi home that night. She doubted she could take a whole week off although she'd had no holidays at all this year. She was feeling so very tired and stressed and had begun to wonder if this was all life had to offer. She had no love in her life – heck, she didn't even have a dog or cat to welcome her home at night. She couldn't remember the last time she'd had sex and sometimes feared that she was turning into a dried-up old prune. Sure, she had a fantastic job and a fabulous apartment on the Upper West Side of New York. She was now a partner in the most prestigious law firm in New York and made pots of money but what good was that if she had no time to spend it and nobody to spend it with?

Arriving home, she reheated one of the soups from the 2nd Ave Deli that substituted for dinner most evenings and had just finished it when Lexi rang. To Mel's surprise, she appeared to be as excited as Angel about the forthcoming birthday party. Lexi was usually very laid back about things. Mel supposed it was probably because Brenda was coming. Those two were always as thick as thieves. It would be nice to be together again for a whole week but she honestly didn't think she could take that much time off. However, she'd certainly make it for the party.

She felt that old fear in her stomach again, thinking back on her childhood. She was unfortunate in that both her parents had been teachers and had very high expectations for her. They were teachers first and foremost and could never leave their teachers' hats behind them at school. They saw Mel and her brother more as 'pupils' than as their own offspring. They were brilliant teachers but as parents they sucked. Everything was geared towards academic success, which was very tough on Mel and her older brother. He rebelled against their Dickensian regime and ran off to London after his Inter Cert. Mel wasn't sorry to see him go as he'd always teased her unmercifully but it did mean that she was now unfortunately the sole focus of her parents' attentions.

Her teen years were miserable. Her parents exerted constant pressure on her to be the best which was difficult for her as she was only an average student – certainly not as bright as Brenda or Lexi. Even Angel, who was much more concerned with boys and how she looked than with studying, sailed through all her exams without a worry.

Mel watched longingly as the others went to parties and discos, wishing with all her heart that she could join them. "There will be plenty of time for partying when you've finished your education, young lady," her parents would say, setting her some more Irish or maths tests to do. It was then that she started to hate them. She didn't have her brother's courage to up and leave. If it hadn't been for her friends, Mel knew that she would have committed suicide. She'd often considered it but somehow Lexi and Brenda had managed to see her through the bad moments. They were both very supportive and, if they hadn't been there for her, she was sure she would not be alive today.

Angel had scarcely been aware of Mel's misery. She was too busy having fun. The ease with which she attracted boys fascinated her friends. Watching her flirt and tease them left Mel feeling more inadequate than ever. She was always tongue-tied in their presence and never knew what to say.

Things hadn't changed much since then! Angel still had every man she met falling in love with her and Mel still had a problem connecting with them on any level or letting any man close. She had done so once but it had ended disastrously.

By contrast, Angel had sailed through life petted and pampered by one and all. She'd been christened Angela but by the age of three months she was such a beautiful baby that her besotted, doting father started calling her Angel and the name stuck.

They lived in a beautiful big house on Kenilworth Square, which was the posh end of Rathmines, and they all loved going to Angel's house for tea. Her mother was very beautiful but aloof and not very friendly. It was always Angel's father who was there at parties and who seemed to be in charge. They had lots of servants who did all the cooking and cleaning so her mother could go to lunches and dinners, so Angel told them. Her father was very wealthy – a developer, Angel informed them – although none of them knew exactly what that was.

Everyone adored Angel. She was so pretty and lively and all the other girls wanted to be her friend and be invited to her parties. To Brenda, in particular, Angel resembled a princess who lived in a world that was a million miles from hers.

Brenda's world was a three-bedroom council house in the poorer part of Rathmines where she lived with her parents and seven siblings. All through secondary and even primary school, Brenda had had it tough because she was the eldest of the eight children and had to shoulder a lot of responsibility. Her mother was lazy and very fond of the drink and so Brenda had practically raised her younger brothers and sisters. In spite of this she found the time to study and was the brightest student in the whole class. How she had ever managed to get straight A's in her Leaving Cert and win a university scholarship was a miracle. The others couldn't help but admire her for that. She certainly got no help at home.

Lexi's home life was the most balanced of them all. Her father was a doctor and they lived in a lovely house on the Rathgar Road. Her mother was forty when Lexi arrived and her parents called her their miracle baby. Lexi was very laid-back and easy-going and a bit of a dreamer. Nothing fazed her and she took everything in her stride. Her parents were very nice and down-to-earth which was probably why Lexi was so grounded. She was very artistic and excelled in art class and it was no surprise to any of them when she went on to be a successful artist.

She still painted and regularly had exhibitions in New York and London. Her paintings now sold for exorbitant amounts and she was quite famous.

Chapter 3

The four of them were still the best of friends when the time came to leave secondary school. Angel was prettier than ever and had all the boys chasing her. She had lost her virginity in fifth year and was very casual about it all. Lexi was much more circumspect and more interested in art than boys. Mel was scared of boys and would have been terrified of getting pregnant because her parents would have killed her but, as she had never even kissed a boy, that wasn't likely to be a problem.

Brenda had started going out with Bob when she was fourteen. He had left school after his Junior Cert and, though he wasn't the sharpest knife in the drawer, everyone thought he was ever so cool. He was devilishly handsome and oozed a raw sexuality that reminded them of Elvis Presley. Most of the girls at school had been mad about him but he'd only ever had eyes for Brenda. Mel and Angel wondered at the time if they were 'doing it' but Brenda never said. She might have told Lexi, as they were very close, but Lexi never said either. Unfortunately, they found out soon enough.

It happened the night they were out together at a disco celebrating the end of their Leaving Cert and school years. For once Mel's parents had agreed to let her go. It was during a lull in the music that Brenda broke down in tears.

"I'm pregnant," she whispered, so low that the others thought they'd misheard.

"You're what?" Mel asked, shocked.

"I'm going to have a baby," she said, louder this time, her cheeks streaked with tears.

"Oh, my God!" Angel cried. "Is it Bob's?"

"Of course it is," Brenda replied, shocked that anyone would think otherwise.

"You poor dear," Lexi comforted her, putting her arms around Brenda who was sobbing her heart out.

"What will you do about it?" Mel asked, thinking of abortion or adoption or . . . she didn't know what really.

It was just such a shock to them all. Brenda was only seventeen, with her whole life ahead of her.

"We'll get married as soon as we can," she whispered.

"But what about college?"

"Oh, even if I win a scholarship my parents could never afford to keep me in college," she'd stated simply. "I'm lucky I got to stay on for my Leaving. Mam wanted me to quit after my Junior Cert and help out with the kids but Dad insisted I go on."

"Brenda's mother is a silly cow," Mel had said afterwards to Lexi. "And now here goes Brenda, just like her mother, married at seventeen!"

"And shackled with a baby shortly after her eighteenth birthday," Angel remarked, wrinkling her pretty little nose in distaste.

Lexi tried to persuade her to consider adoption but Brenda wouldn't hear of it. Mel was furious with her. She suggested to Brenda that she might have an abortion. Brenda was horrified. She loved Bob, she insisted, and wanted to be his wife and have his baby. There was nothing any of them could say to change her mind. But they couldn't help thinking – what a waste of a life!

* * *

Brenda and Bob were married six weeks later. The wedding reception was bizarre with Brenda's brothers and sisters running around the place like crazy and her mother drunk as a skunk. It was held in the local GAA club and her three friends were uneasy, hoping that she wasn't making a huge mistake. Bob was a hunk and a right charmer but unimaginative and way below Brenda's level of intelligence. Despite that, she appeared to be blissfully happy. Mel could never understand that husband-wife correlation or why some marriages worked and others didn't.

When, four months later, they visited her in Holles Street Maternity Hospital and saw how thrilled she was with her little daughter, they felt a bit better about it, but neither Angel nor Mel thought it would last. Lexi was much more optimistic.

Although Mel didn't get the university scholarship that her parents had hoped for, she did get good enough results to study law at UCD. College was a whole other ballgame and she loved it, free of her parents at last. She found law fascinating and to her delight her parents had no idea what she was talking about. They were slowly but surely losing their control over her.

Angel was studying drama at Trinity and Lexi had enrolled in the College of Art and the three of them met up regularly in the Buttery in Trinity. Angel and Lexi were sharing an apartment – a tiny flat really – and Mel would have given her right arm to have moved in with them, but her parents wouldn't hear of it. She visited their place often and was never happier than when she was hanging out with the girls there.

They all felt sorry for Brenda who was busy having babies while they were living the carefree student life. However, she seemed happy with her lot and they could see she was absolutely crazy about Bob and he about her.

Lexi constantly pointed out that Brenda was a wonderful mother and, in fairness to her, Mel had to agree. Her kids were very bright and were doing brilliantly at school.

"Thank God they've inherited her brains and not Bob's," Mel commented uncharitably to Lexi the last time they'd met, when she'd heard that all Brenda's kids had gone to university.

"Yes, but you have to admire how she has worked her butt off to give them the opportunities she never had," Lexi responded.

"I don't doubt it but I still think Brenda was mad to have sacrificed her own life for her husband and kids. As I'm so fond of saying, we have only one life and it's up to us to make the most of it," Mel replied smugly.

She'd been taken aback when Lexi had retorted sharply, "And what are you doing with your life except working your way to the grave?"

Mel had been speechless. Lexi, whom she still adored, had never spoken harshly to her before. She rarely spoke harshly to anyone. It rocked Mel back on her heels and that was when she had begun to take stock of her life.

Lexi was right. Work was her life. It was what she was good at. Business she could handle, with aplomb, but relationships and real life – that was another matter! Maybe at the end of the day Brenda was the most successful one of all.

Chapter 4

Lexi was delighted with the way her plans were going. It had been too long since they'd spent any length of time all together and she hated to think of their friendship disintegrating in the hustle and bustle of modern life. She was especially pleased that Brenda could make it. She looked forward to hearing all about her children. Lexi was godmother to her eldest daughter, Alex, and she'd been touched when Brenda had named her Alexandra, after her. She was determined to show Brenda a great time and give her the holiday of her life.

Lexi was worried about Mel and was hoping to have a heart-to-heart with her while she was visiting. She felt guilty that she had not made the effort to go to New York more often to visit her but on previous trips Mel had always been so busy that Lexi felt it only added to Mel's stress to have a houseguest.

She could never forget that awful time at school when Mel had been suicidal. It was all her parents' fault, of course, driving her relentlessly to succeed. Lexi had hoped that when Mel moved to New York she would finally be free of them but that hadn't happened. No matter what she achieved, it was never enough and meanwhile Mel was letting real life pass her by.

Lexi hoped to convince her that, for her own sake, she needed to change her lifestyle and that life was too short to be spending it trying to satisfy her parents. How awful to think that otherwise intelligent people could mess up their child's head and life!

Mel had said she could only stay until Wednesday but Lexi hoped that, as Angel said, once they were all together and having a wonderful time, she'd change her mind and reschedule.

Lexi was also worried about Angel and the ridiculous hang-up she had about turning forty. Of course she lived in LA, which more or less said it all. Nobody could live there and still be in touch with reality. The fact that she became famous and a household name when she was in her twenties and was the star in a hit sitcom hadn't helped. In fairness to her she still kept in touch with the three of them, even through all the madness of being a big Hollywood star.

Angel showed a brave face to the world but Lexi knew that beneath it all she was a little-girl-lost and deeply insecure. She'd been through a lot – failed relationships, divorces, betrayals, yet she always appeared to bounce back, smiling and optimistic, certain that the next man would be the one.

Angel had never lost the joie-de-vivre that captivated everyone who met her but even she couldn't keep age at bay forever. Nobody could – so why try? Lexi knew it was easy for her to say – an artist doesn't have any pressure to stay looking young – but still she wished that Angel could be happy in her own skin, and body. She planned to try and make her see sense, if she could.

She had explained to Marvin, her friend – she felt

awkward using the term 'boyfriend' at her age – that he would not be able to stay over during the time the girls were in situ. He usually stayed over two or three nights a week but he understood that she'd rather not do that while her friends were there. He had never met them but Lexi had talked about them a lot and he was looking forward to meeting them.

Lexi was hoping to finish up her current painting before the girls arrived so that she would be free for the week. She wanted this to be the best birthday they'd ever had. God knows, it could be the last for any of them.

* * *

Brenda was looking forward to Skyping her daughter, Alex, to tell her about the forthcoming trip. With all five kids living away from home, Skype was her lifeline to them. The week after Alex graduated from UCD with a nursing and midwifery degree she was on a plane to Africa, to Sudan, to work with Goal. It was something she'd always wanted to do.

Her first few weeks there had been very difficult as she tried to come to terms with the devastation the drought and famine had wrought but she soon settled in and just got on with it, doing what she could to help. Due to the shortage of medical staff she often worked eighteen-hour days. Brenda was extremely proud of her.

"Hi, darling, how are you?" she said, noticing how tanned Alex was since the last time they'd spoken.

"Great, Mum. I've been out working in the field, travelling to various towns, for the past two weeks and it's been wonderful. The people are so pleased to see us and I feel we are really making a difference to their lives."

"You look tired, sweetheart."

"I am but it's been worth it. I can rest up tomorrow and

then I'm back in the hospital on Sunday again so it's not too bad." She smiled reassuringly at her mother.

"Make sure you take care of yourself. The last thing you want is to get sick."

"Don't worry, Mum," Alex smiled, "I'm as strong as an ox. How are you? Any news?"

"Well, yes, I have some brilliant news. Lexi has invited me to Florida to celebrate our fortieth birthday in November and I've decided to go. Lexi is flying me out as a birthday present. I'm so excited." Brenda knew she was grinning like a Cheshire cat.

Alex gave a whoop of joy. "That's fantastic! Good old Aunt Lexi!"

"Hey, enough of the 'old' if you please," Brenda admonished her, waggling her finger at her eldest child and grinning.

Alex giggled. "But did you say fortieth? It's only your thirty-ninth, isn't it?"

"Yes, but Angel refuses to be forty, so as it's our last birthday – all four of us together – Lexi thinks we should celebrate in style."

Alex pealed with laughter. "Angel is a howl, isn't she? But she's great fun," she added, grinning. "Oh Mum, it's wonderful that you're going to Florida. You deserve a holiday and you always have so much fun when you all get together. I'm thrilled for you."

"Thank you, darling. It's as if we're all schoolgirls again whenever we meet up. I'm as excited about this trip as you were when you went on the school trip to Paris that time. Do you remember?"

"How could I forget? I couldn't sleep for nights beforehand."

"Yeah, well, my trip is over a month away and I'm having

a problem sleeping already. I'm so looking forward to it."

"What did Dad say about it?"

"Well, you know him. As long as it doesn't cost money he's okay with it."

Brenda tried to keep her voice upbeat but she guessed Alex wasn't fooled. She knew her father too well.

Diplomatic as always, Alex changed the subject.

"How is Megan? Have you talked to her lately?"

Brenda rolled her eyes to heaven. "I spoke to her last Friday and she and Sheena were still in India and planning to travel on to Nepal next week." Brenda's second daughter, Megan, had also graduated that summer – with a first-class degree in journalism from DCU – and was off travelling the world with her best friend shortly after. "But you know that pair," she went on. "They could change their plans at any time depending on who they meet up with."

Alex giggled at the truth of this. Although they were like chalk and cheese she and Megan were very close. There was, after all, only a year between them.

"She said she'd Skype me tomorrow if she can get access to the internet," Alex said. "I do hope she does."

"You can be sure she'll manage it, by hook or by crook. You know Megan," Brenda laughed. "Nothing stands in her way."

They said goodbye, both thinking of Megan with a smile on their faces. Like Angel, who was her godmother, she had that effect on people. Brenda promised to Skype Alex from Florida to let her know how things were going.

* * *

Lexi surveyed the house with satisfaction. Everything was ready at last for her guests. Marvin had been a great help.

He'd decorated the garden and it looked magical with fairy-lights in the trees and lanterns around the pool. She expected they'd spend quite a lot of time out there as the weather was perfect and not too hot. The house was spic and span and the bedrooms were all ready.

Marvin took her out for a meal in their favourite restaurant the night before Brenda was due in and they made gentle love afterwards. As she lay in his arms he rubbed her back in the way she loved and she realised with a shock that she would miss this over the next couple of weeks.

As if he could read her mind, he said, "I'm going to miss you, you know. I've kind of got used to these nights together."

"Mmmmm . . . ." she replied, loving the way his hand was moving up and down her spine. "Me too."

It was true. They were very comfortable together. He often finished her sentences for her and generally knew what she was thinking before she even said it. He was also a wonderful companion.

"Do you think we could maybe move our relationship up a notch when the girls are gone?" he asked.

This knocked her for six. Lexi was very happy with the status quo and she'd thought Marvin was too.

"Don't you think we have the perfect relationship just as it is?" she asked him, not sure how to react.

"You know I love you and I was thinking that maybe we could make it more permanent – perhaps start a family." He looked at her, his head cocked to one side.

"Start a family?" She looked at him in shock. "I'm almost thirty-nine, Marvin. Don't you think I'm a bit old to be having a baby?"

"Nonsense! I've read about celebrities having babies well into their forties these days."

She was flustered. This was the last thing she had expected.

Marvin noticed her hesitation and didn't press her for an answer.

"Let's talk about it when you get back from New York," he suggested.

Lexi was relieved.

She lay awake for hours afterwards thinking about what he'd said. She'd felt their relationship was perfect as it was. She liked to think of herself as a free spirit and yet she would hate it if Marvin was not in her life. They played bridge together, went for long walks on the beach, their sex life was very satisfactory and he understood her need to paint. She loved him but was she in love with him? Certainly not in the way she'd been in love with Gianni who would always be the love of her life. She didn't think there was room in her heart for another love like that. Maybe one only got to enjoy that privilege once in a lifetime. Yet maybe one can love again but differently, she thought. As for having a baby, she knew that was out of the question. She could not risk getting pregnant for fear that she would lose the baby as she had lost Alessandro. How could she go through that devastating pain again? She tossed and turned and finally drifted off to sleep having decided to put Marvin's proposal out of her mind until the girls were gone and she was back from New York. She had enough on her plate at the moment without worrying about her relationship with Marvin.

Chapter 5

Brenda had to pinch herself to make sure she was not dreaming as she saw the buildings of Manhattan loom into sight through the aircraft window. The whole trip had felt surreal from the moment she'd boarded the flight in Dublin. She felt it was not her making the journey – it was someone else. The fact that she hardly recognised herself in the mirror was probably a factor. Her mousy brown hair, which used to hang limply on her shoulders, was no more and in its place were honey-blonde highlights and a brand new cropped style.

She'd lost over a stone in the past five weeks and was now wearing the Earl jeans that Lexi had given her three years ago. To her mortification she hadn't been able to get into them then and they had hung in her wardrobe, unworn, for the past three years. She couldn't believe it the day before when they had slipped on smoothly without even having to lie on the bed to zip them up!

Thanks to Brenda's sister Jean, who owned a hair and beauty salon, she no longer had bushy eyebrows and was now sporting long gel nails which were so gorgeous that she couldn't resist admiring them every ten minutes. Was it any wonder she felt like someone else?

JFK airport was so enormous that she was afraid she would lose her way. She collected her case and then made her way from Terminal 4 to Terminal 7 where she checked in for the flight to Tampa. Pleased with herself she went into a café and ordered a hotdog which was delicious. When in Rome, she told herself. She resisted the urge to buy any Big Apple souvenirs as she would be spending a few days in the city before she left for home.

* * *

The flight down to Tampa was over before she knew it and as the monorail took her to the arrivals hall at Tampa Airport she was impatient to see her best friend again. She spotted Lexi immediately, standing tall amongst the crowd, looking gorgeous and more attractive than any of the other women there. She was wearing a vividly patterned halter-neck top and a matching sarong-type skirt which showed off her smooth olive skin to perfection. She also had a flower in her hair and was wearing jewelled sandals on her tanned feet. She was waving wildly, three balloons floating above her head.

"Welcome, welcome!" Lexi cried, wrapping her in a bear hug and then they were both crying and laughing at the same time.

As she hugged her, Brenda was taken aback to feel how thin Lexi had become. She'd mentioned in one of her letters that she had lost weight but Brenda didn't expect it to be quite so much. Lexi had always been a big girl but now she was model-thin.

"I'm so happy to see you and you look terrific!" Lexi exclaimed, standing back to have a good look at her dear friend. "You've lost weight and what have you done to your hair? I love it. How was your flight?"

Lexi's hair was still long and curly but Brenda noticed that the red-gold now had some silver strands through it. Lexi never worried too much about her appearance or bothered with make-up but she didn't need to. Her face was tanned and glowing and she still had the same sweet smile and kind face that Brenda loved. She also had an innate sense of style and could throw on any old thing and with a tweak here or there, or an accessory or two, manage to make it look amazing. Brenda, who envied this talent of hers, figured it was because she was so artistic.

They linked arms as they weaved through the airport, the balloons fluttering above their heads. People turned to smile at them but they were too busy talking nineteen-to-the-dozen to take much notice.

"How was the trip? Are you tired? Was Bob okay about your coming here? How are the kids? Has Alex settled down in Sudan? I do hope she's not working too hard."

Brenda laughed at this barrage which gave her no time to answer. "I had a fantastic trip and I'm feeling exhilarated," she replied. "The kids are all fine and Alex is doing great. Hopefully, I'll be able to Skype her when I'm here and you'll be able to see her too."

"Skype?" Lexi asked, looking mystified.

"Just wait and you'll see."

The warm air caressed her face as they exited the airport. Thinking of how icy cold it had been in Dublin that morning, Brenda sighed with pleasure. "Feel that heat," she cried. "It's pure bliss."

Lexi laughed. "I'm so used to the heat that I'm always surprised when someone comments on it. In fact it's a little cool today, for November."

"You call this cool? You should be in Dublin," Brenda cried, envying her this gorgeous climate.

Lexi had a problem getting the balloons to stay down in the back of her Escalade so she released them to the sky. They laughed as they watched them fly away over the car park.

"I'm so happy you were able to come," Lexi told her as they exited the airport.

"Not half as happy as I am to be here," Brenda answered, meaning every word of it.

She was amazed at how relaxed and casual Lexi was about driving in the manic traffic. There were flyovers and flyunders and a six-lane motorway – highway Lexi called it – and Brenda closed her eyes as the huge trucks and the biggest cars she'd ever seen zigzagged from lane to lane in front of them. It didn't seem to faze Lexi who zigzagged with the best of them. Twenty minutes later they passed through a cute little town called Dunedin where Lexi pulled in to a bakery to pick up some stuff she'd ordered earlier.

Brenda sank back into the luxurious leather seat, determined to embrace everything about this country which already had her under its spell.

They drove over the causeway bridge, admiring the wonderful view of the Gulf of Mexico as Lexi pointed out the luxurious yachts in the marina at Clearwater Beach. Suddenly they were entering the large gates of Lexi's home and Brenda caught her breath at the palm trees lining the driveway and the beautiful white house that rose up before her.

"Oh my God, Lexi, it's a mansion!" she cried, awestruck at the opulence before her.

"Oh, it's very modest by Floridian standards," Lexi replied laughingly. She parked the car and as they got out a small dark young woman came out to greet them.

"This is Maria, my housekeeper." Lexi introduced the smiling woman who gave a little bow.

"Welcome, Miss Brenda," she said with a Latino accent.

A housekeeper? Brenda thought. Lexi had never mentioned anything about having a housekeeper. A dark-skinned attractive man appeared from around the corner of the house.

"And this is Pablo." Lexi grinned, seeing her surprise, "Maria's husband. He takes care of the garden and the car and just about everything else around here."

He smiled and bowed also and took Brenda's case which, as per Lexi's instructions, was practically empty. They moved into the large high-ceilinged foyer and Brenda looked around in awe.

"You never told me you lived in a house as grand as this," she said to Lexi accusingly, noting the elegant columns and marble floors.

"Come on, I'll show you round." Lexi was amused at her friend's obvious amazement. She led her up a winding staircase and into an enormous living-room with French windows and a balcony which overlooked the sea. It was stunning and decorated in beautiful pastel shades.

"It really is too big for one person but I love it here." Her father had bought it for his retirement but her parents didn't get to enjoy it for long because her mother got Alzheimer's and then her father passed away. She stayed on after his death to nurse her. There was nothing to keep her in Europe after she lost her husband and new-born baby. Then when her mother died two years before she decided to stay on. "I'm happy here and the light is wonderful and don't forget I was born here and have American citizenship so it somehow seemed like a good place to settle."

Brenda squeezed her hand, remembering how death had robbed Lexi of Gianni and Alessandro and then both her parents in quick succession.

"It's beautiful here. I don't blame you," Brenda exclaimed

as she was led out through the French doors to the terrace, below which was a large infinity pool. It was truly magical.

"I've asked Maria to make us margaritas so that you can unwind before I show you to your room," Lexi said as they plonked down in the luxuriously cushioned sun-chairs. "I can pull the awning out if you wish to stay out of the sun?"

"Are you kidding?" Brenda cried, lifting her face up to the sun. "I'm starved of sunshine. I want to catch every last ray of it."

From the terrace she could see the white sand of what Lexi told her was Clearwater Beach and beyond that the blue water of the Gulf of Mexico.

As Maria placed the drinks in front of them, Brenda sighed. "This is heavenly. I feel like I'm in a movie. It's surreal."

"It's real and I'm going to make sure that you have the best holiday of your life," Lexi assured her, patting her hand. "Now tell me all your news."

Brenda didn't know where to begin. She gave her news of Alex as they sipped the delicious drink and Lexi beamed with pride at her goddaughter's achievements.

"And Megan? Tell me about her travels."

"Well, she and Sheena have been in India and plan to hit Nepal, Thailand, Vietnam, Cambodia and Malaysia – on their way to Australia and New Zealand, or so they say."

"She always was an adventurous little thing," Lexi said laughing. "You must be very proud of her."

"Oh, I am. I admire her very much. She's incredibly brave – she has no fear whatsoever of the unknown. My biggest concern is that she will want to stay in Australia and that I'll only see her every few years when she returns home for a holiday."

"Don't think about that until it happens. It may never come to pass."

"I hope not. I couldn't bear it!"

Brenda could feel herself relaxing, whether from the cocktail or the warm sun she couldn't say.

"And the twins?" Lexi asked as Maria placed two more drinks in front of them.

"The twins . . . what can I say? Well, boys are easier, aren't they? You don't worry about them as much as you do girls. Ryan is the business and computer brain in the family and is studying International Business in Derry. He has another year to do. I know he's having a great social life but he's passed all his exams so far so we can't complain. Bob and Ryan don't get on very well." Brenda eyes clouded and she shook her head sadly. "Ryan is far too ambitious for Bob's liking. Good as Bob is, no one could ever accuse him of being ambitious!"

Lexi secretly agreed with her but kept mum.

"Bob gets on much better with Dylan who is the opposite of his twin. He's a dreamer and without Ryan always pushing him that extra step, I guess he'd be happy to just drift through life."

"He hasn't changed much then," Lexi interjected. "He was always a gentle little boy. What's he doing?"

"He's studying Psychology at Queen's in Belfast. He could have done it in Dublin but chose Belfast to be closer to Ryan. They're joined at the hip that pair – even though they're fraternal twins of course, not identical."

"You're so lucky to have them. You must be very proud of them," Lexi said wistfully and Brenda knew she was thinking of the baby she'd lost.

"I'm sorry, rabbiting on about them like this. It's very insensitive of me."

"No, no, I love to hear about them. It's fine. Nothing will bring Gianni or Alessandro back. I've accepted that. It's my lot in life," she said resignedly but her eyes were clouded with pain.

Brenda remembered how devastated Lexi had been at that

time. She and Gianni had been so much in love and thrilled to be expecting their first baby when they were involved in a horrific accident which left Gianni dead and Lexi unconscious. Eight hours later her little son Alessandro was born prematurely but he only lived for twenty-four hours. She had watched as he'd fought for his little life, willing him to live, but his little body couldn't survive and he went to join his father. Lexi was inconsolable and poured her grief into her painting. Brenda and Mel had supported her as best they could but nothing would bring her loved ones back.

"They say time heals everything but it doesn't, not much. I used to wish I'd died in the car with Gianni but then I'd never have got to hold my Alessandro. I must be grateful for small mercies."

Brenda reached out and squeezed Lexi's hand.

"Enough sad talk," said Lexi. "Tonight is a night to be happy. Isn't that a beautiful sunset?"

Brenda sighed. "It's magnificent."

They watched in silence as the big ball of fire sank into the ocean, both of them happy and relaxed.

"Now tell me about Carly. She left school this year, didn't she?"

"Yes, can you believe it? My baby – already at university! Carly has such a sweet nature that everyone loves her. She's the sporty one of the family, excelling at everything from athletics to gymnastics and everything in between. She's in her first year studying PE in Limerick. She's completely focused and it looks like she might make the next Irish Olympic athletics team. She's Bob's pet and he is more proud of her athletic prowess than of any academic achievements but I always made sure that they all studied hard to become the best they could be. I didn't want them making the mistakes I made."

Brenda grimaced and Lexi reached over and took her hand. "You've done a fantastic job. I'm so proud of you!"

"It means a lot to me to hear you say that. But, you know, it's weird The kids have always been my priority, been my whole life really, and now all of a sudden they're gone. It's very disconcerting. I hardly know what to do with myself. Empty-nest-syndrome, I guess." She grimaced again.

"I can imagine. Maybe you could get a job?"

"In Ireland? These days? You've got to be kidding. They say people with law degrees are clamouring for jobs in McDonald's. But I've done all the stages of Computer Studies and I've been studying French so you never know. Maybe things will improve and then . . . who knows?"

Lexi beamed at her. "You always were the brightest one of the four of us. What does Bob think of all this?"

Brenda smiled ruefully. "Not a lot, I'm afraid. He thinks study is a waste of time at my age. We've had quite a few rows about it." She tried to avoid Lexi's eyes.

"How are things between you? You don't seem as happy as I remember. Do you want to talk about it?"

"Not right now, maybe later," Brenda answered, her eyes clouding over. She looked at her watch. "I promised I'd call him to let him know I arrived safely. Is that okay?"

"Of course. There's a telephone in your room, you can call him from there. I'm being selfish. You must be dying to freshen up," Lexi jumped up. "I was so anxious to hear all your news that I couldn't wait. Come on, I'll show you to your room."

Brenda followed her to her bedroom which was huge – four times the size of their bedroom at home. It was decorated in white and yellow and there were French doors opening onto a balcony which overlooked the sea. It was beautiful. There were two walk-in closets and an enormous marble bathroom with a big Jacuzzi bath.

"Oh how wonderful!" Brenda cried. "I can't wait to sink into that gorgeous bath!"

"It's so refreshing to have someone who takes a bath here. Americans only take showers," Lexi laughed. "Have a nice long soak. There are lots of lotions and oils in the cabinet so enjoy it and when you're ready, come down. We'll have aperitifs by the pool then – a nice respectable hour! Most Americans are already at dinner now. They invite you for five o'clock aperitifs, dinner at six thirty and home in bed by nine. Can you believe it? I do sometimes miss the civilised European habit of eating late. There's the phone," she said, pointing to the bedside table. "The prefix for Ireland is 011 353. See you later, sweetie, enjoy your bath!"

Brenda sat down on the edge of the bed and dialled home. It seemed strange to hear the phone ringing in her living-room back in Dublin while she sat in these luxurious surroundings.

Bob answered eventually and his voice sounded gruff.

"Hello, it's me. I'm here safe and sound in Lexi's. Is everything okay there with you?"

"You do know it's almost midnight here, Brenda?" His voice was sullen and she could tell that he'd been drinking.

"I'm sorry, but by the time I got here and then had a chat with Lexi and gave her all our news . . . well, you know how it is."

"No, I don't know how it is. I'm not swanning around in Florida."

She could hear the resentment in his voice and knew there was no point in continuing the conversation. "Well, I just wanted to let you know I'd arrived safely and say goodnight."

"Goodnight," Bob replied gruffly and then he hung up.

Brenda felt the tears come to her eyes. Why could he not be happy for her? Sighing, she replaced the receiver. She was determined she would not let Bob spoil this holiday for her. She put him out of her mind as she ran the water and poured luxurious oil and bubbles into it.

Chapter 6

After a delicious bath Brenda went downstairs, glowing and relaxed looking.

"That was fantastic. I never have time to soak in a bath at home. It's usually a quick shower for me. I could have stayed in it forever."

"Well, you have all the time in the world here. Make the most of it."

"I will. The house is just gorgeous. It's so spacious and full of light. You must love waking up every morning in this beautiful home."

Lexi realised guiltily that she never thought about it much. She took it very much for granted. Seeing it through Brenda's eyes made her appreciate how beautiful it was. Brenda gave her the sausages and black pudding that she'd asked her to bring with her from Ireland.

"I also bought some Irish bacon and potato cakes as well as some Lyons teabags and Tayto," Brenda said, handing them over.

"Oh my God, Tayto!" Lexi cried as she put the other stuff into the fridge. "I miss them most of all." She opened a packet on the spot and started crunching on them. "Nobody makes crisps like Tayto," she sighed happily.

They moved down to the pool terrace where the garden looked magical with the fairy-lights and lanterns reflecting off the green water of the swimming pool.

"This is so beautiful," Brenda cried, looking around appreciatively.

"My favourite sound," Lexi said, as she popped the cork on a bottle of champagne and poured the lovely pale gold liquid bubbles into long-stemmed glasses. "*Fáilte romhat!* See, I haven't forgotten all my Irish," she laughed. She raised her glass to Brenda. "Here's to a wonderful holiday and birthday and to old friends!"

"To the best friend any girl could ever have!" Brenda replied and raised her glass to Lexi who thought that the sparkle in her friend's eyes matched that in the glass.

They sipped the champagne and chatted quietly, catching up on all that had happened since last they'd met.

"I will have to paint for a couple of hours in the morning, I'm afraid, as I need to put the finishing touches to my latest canvas," Lexi said. "I hope you don't mind. I thought perhaps you'd like to chill out at the pool and rest after the long flight."

"That sounds perfect to me. I can't think of anything I'd rather do and I can work on my tan at the same time. I'm so pale in comparison to you." Brenda held out her arm which was indeed milky white. "You go ahead and paint. I'll be fine. I have a really good book to read and it will be bliss to be able to read uninterrupted."

Lexi understood. She was like that too when she got into a good book. She just wanted to be left alone.

"Then tomorrow afternoon we'll go shopping in Clearwater Mall. It will be an eye-opener for you to see how cheap everything is here in comparison to Ireland."

"So I've heard. I can't wait to go shopping here."

"Then tomorrow evening I thought we'd go to the Beachcomber restaurant, which is great. You'll like it. We go there a lot."

"We? Is that Marvin and you?" Brenda asked.

Lexi found herself blushing. To cover it up she reached for the champagne bottle and refilled their glasses. Brenda wasn't fooled.

"Is this getting serious?"

"Well, he does want to take it up a notch but I'm not sure that I want to. I'm pretty set in my ways."

"What's he like?"

"Well, I was thinking of inviting him and his brother, Troy, who's staying with him at the moment, for drinks tomorrow evening to meet you. What do you think?"

"I'd like that very much."

"Fine. I'll give him a call after dinner."

Maria announced that dinner was ready and they climbed up to the upper terrace where she served the Lobster Thermidor that she had prepared.

"Wow! This looks delicious! I've never had lobster before," Brenda admitted.

"I hope you like it," Lexi said as she poured the chilled Chablis. "This lobster comes from Maine which has the best lobster in the world and Maria is a great cook. If it wasn't for her I'd forget to eat half the time. I get so wrapped up in a painting that nothing else matters. I go into a world of my own."

"Mmmm . . . it is delicious," Brenda said as she tasted it. "Maria certainly has done it justice."

* * *

"I'm dying to see Mel and Angel again," said Brenda, between mouthfuls of the chocolate mousse dessert. "How are they?"

"Oh, what can I say? Mel is working far too hard, as always. She doesn't have a life outside of her work and is stressed out all the time." Lexi shook her head. "She's still smoking like a trooper and I worry about her, honestly I do. I would so love her to meet someone nice."

"She did have someone a while back, didn't she?"

"Yes, but that bit the dust. I don't know why as she was really crazy about him. They were even talking of marriage. She's never told me why they broke up but she was very depressed after that which is why she threw herself into her work like a maniac."

"Poor Mel! I'm looking forward to seeing her again."

"Me too. I do hope she'll stay for the week. The break will do her good."

"And what about Angel?" Brenda asked as Lexi topped up their glasses.

"Angel? Well, there's no fear of her getting depressed over a man. She seems to bounce from one to the other like a hippity-hop ball. The latest news from her is that she's become a cougar."

"A cougar?" Brenda looked puzzled.

"Yeah, it's the latest phenomenon in Hollywood. It describes an older woman who takes a much younger lover."

Brenda looked at her disbelievingly. "Angel has done that?"

"I'm afraid so. You know she's quite desperate to stay young and I suppose he makes her feel that way. All the stars are doing it, she tells me. I worry about her a lot too. She's very fragile, you know, under all that bravado."

"Really? I've never thought that," Brenda said, stifling a yawn.

Lexi stood up. "Forgive me, you must be exhausted. You've had such a long day."

"Yes, and I was so excited I didn't sleep a wink last night. I think I'll hit the sack."

"I'm so glad you're here," Lexi told her as they hugged goodnight.

"Me too," Brenda replied, trying but failing to smother another yawn.

* * *

The following morning, after a delicious breakfast on the terrace, Lexi headed to her studio and Brenda changed into her bikini. Then, armed with her book, fluffy towels, a sunhat and sun lotion, she stretched out by the pool. It was paradise!

The sun was very hot but slathered with Factor 25 she toasted her body, slipping into the beautiful pool to cool off whenever it got too much to take. Meanwhile Maria plied her with iced water and cold fruit drinks so that she wouldn't get dehydrated. She suspected Maria was under strict instructions from Lexi to take care of her. By eleven thirty she felt it was time to get into the shade and it was there Lexi found her, snoozing gently.

"Come on, lazybones! Time for lunch," Lexi called out, tickling her feet playfully.

"Heavens, did I fall asleep?" Brenda jumped up, coming awake with a start.

Lexi laughed. "Don't worry! You're probably still a little jet-lagged and tired after your trip. Come on! Maria has prepared a lovely salad for us."

And lovely it was, with succulent prawns and scallops. Brenda had never had scallops before either but didn't want to appear like a total bog-woman so kept mum about it. They were yummy.

After lunch they drove across the causeway again to the Clearwater Mall. She'd been expecting a huge indoor shopping mall, like Liffey Valley, but instead she found a series of individual stores spread out over a very large area.

"What do you do if you don't have a car here?" she wanted to know.

Lexi laughed aloud. "Oh, my darling girl," she spluttered through her laughter, "everybody here has a car. One couldn't survive in Florida without one."

"Amazing!" Brenda observed, dumbstruck.

The next three hours flew by as Lexi introduced her to Ross, the low-cost outlet store. The price of the clothes, shoes and bags there blew her mind. She figured she would have paid at least ten times more in Dublin for the lovely Ralph Lauren dress she found and the fabulous shoes that were only $12 a pair. Brenda was not a big shopper and definitely not a designer nut but at those prices she reckoned even Mother Teresa would have lost it. She also spotted an emerald-green silk dress on the clearance rack which cost an unbelievable $15. It fitted her to perfection and it too went into her trolley.

"You're becoming a true Florida girl," Lexi remarked as she saw Brenda choose some shorts and halter tops and two bikinis.

"If you can't beat them join them," Brenda laughed.

She saw beautiful towels and bed-linen and would have bought the lot if Lexi hadn't stopped her.

"Take it easy. It's only your first day. You've got two whole weeks to shop."

Brenda grinned foolishly at her. "Sorry, but everything's so fabulous and so cheap."

She saw gorgeous things for her girls too but Lexi persuaded her to wait a while until they'd visited Burlington and the Ellenton Outlets. They deposited the bags in the car and then moved on to Target. This reminded Brenda of Dunne's Stores back home except that everything was about quarter the price. She finally understood why hordes of Irishwomen crossed the Atlantic every year to shop. The difference in price between Ireland and the US was ridiculous!

Exhausted yet exhilarated, she returned home with Lexi to prepare for the evening ahead.

* * *

Brenda soaked in another heavenly bath and was so happy she felt like singing. "God, I can't remember the last time I felt like this," she said aloud. She'd had a wonderful day – like something out of a movie, she thought.

Reluctantly dragging herself out of the bath, she towelled herself dry and, sighing with pleasure, rubbed body lotion onto her glowing skin. Slipping on the Wonderbra that Lexi had insisted she buy, she then stepped into the red Ralph Lauren dress that felt like a second skin.

"Is this really me?" she asked her reflection in the mirror. She had a cleavage for the first time in her life and the silk jersey clung to her body giving her curves she'd never had before. Her skin was already turning a golden brown and her eyes were shining. She looked better than she ever had before and . . . well . . . sexy and hot – her three daughters' favourite words. She giggled as she twirled in front of the mirror, happy and excited with this new woman she'd become.

Lexi looked up as she came downstairs. "Wow!" she exclaimed, giving a low whistle, and Brenda was gratified to know that she had not been imagining that she looked great. "You look sensational!"

Brenda blushed, delighted with the compliment. She had never, ever, been told that before.

They were sitting on the upper terrace sipping mojitos when Maria came out, accompanied by two handsome men. Lexi kissed them both and made the introductions. Marvin was younger than Brenda had expected, in his mid-forties, she guessed. She had expected him to be older, perhaps because Lexi had said he was an art dealer or perhaps because she had the notion that everyone in Florida was retired and therefore old. Marvin was most definitely not in that category. She found him quiet-spoken and even a little shy which endeared him to her. She noticed his long elegant fingers and wondered if he painted himself. He had the gentle look of an artist and was the perfect man for Lexi, slim with dark, slightly greying hair and . . . well, elegant was the best word to describe him.

Troy, his brother, was the opposite of the gentle laid-back Marvin. Larger than life, he was very tall and athletically built and exuded an energy that was palpable. He was also extremely handsome, deeply tanned, with longish blond hair and very blue eyes. It was obvious that he spent most of his time outdoors. Lexi had told her that he was a keen sailor and ran a very lucrative yacht business. He smiled at Brenda as he took her hand in a firm grasp. She saw a look of admiration in his eyes that shocked her. It had been a long, long time since any man had looked at her like that. Not since Bob, all those years ago. She pulled her hand away and was mortified to feel herself blush. He smiled at her, his eyes never leaving hers.

At that moment, luckily, Maria arrived with a jug of mojitos and they all sat down as she poured.

"*Santé!*" Marvin said, as he raised his glass to them.

"*Sláinte!*" the two girls replied in unison, both of them erupting in laughter.

"What's that?" Troy asked, mystified.

"It's the Irish way to say 'health'," Lexi explained.

It took five minutes and lots of laughter before Troy was happy with his pronunciation of it.

"*Sláinte!*" he saluted them after the second mojitos had been poured.

"*Sláinte mhaith!*" Brenda said as she raised her glass to him.

He groaned. "Now what does that mean?"

"It means 'good health'," she explained to him and another Gaelic lesson ensued until finally he'd got it right.

"Could you two excuse us for a moment?" Lexi asked. "I need Marvin to take a look at some lights that are not working down by the pool."

They moved off together down the steps to the pool level.

"Do you live here too like Marvin?" Brenda asked.

Troy told her that he had lived in New York for most of his adult life but had now decided to relocate to Florida. He was down here house-hunting at the moment.

"The winters up north are too cold for my liking and I'd also like to move closer to Marvin."

Brenda heard his voice soften when he spoke of his brother.

"Both our parents are dead so there's just the two of us now," he explained. "Besides, I like the Florida lifestyle. It suits me better."

"I quite like it myself," she laughed.

"Have you ever considered moving here?"

"Good Lord, no, I couldn't possibly."

"That's a pity," he remarked, looking deep into her eyes. "Why not?"

"Well, I have a husband back in Ireland for a start . . ."

"Would your husband not like to live here?"

"Bob move here? God, no! Are you mad?" She laughed at this preposterous idea.

"Are you happy with him?" Troy asked in a low quiet voice. He leaned forward in his chair and steepled his fingers, looking at her very intently, a small frown creasing his forehead. She was a little taken aback by his bluntness and hesitated as she tried to answer truthfully, as much to herself as to Troy. He saw her hesitation.

"Oh Brenda honey, life is much too short to spend it with the wrong person," he said gently, shaking his head.

To her embarrassment she felt the tears come to her eyes. "If only life were that simple," she replied.

"It is. It truly is," he stated with a faraway look in his eyes. "I found that out a long time ago."

She wondered what he meant. "How about you? Are you married?"

"I was. Got divorced after two years," he replied, his voice sad.

"Any children?"

"Lord, no! That would have been a disaster."

She didn't enquire further not wishing to appear nosy but she'd love to have heard more.

He was very entertaining and easy-going and slowly she relaxed in his company. She found herself drawn to him and when he accidently touched her hand she drew back as if she'd had an electric shock. Troy made her feel attractive and desirable, feelings that were alien to her. She found it very exciting and figured it must be the mojitos!

She was relieved when Lexi and Marvin came back. Troy was way too disturbing for her peace of mind.

Shortly afterwards, the taxi arrived to take them to the restaurant.

As they said goodbye, Troy invited them to spend the following day on his yacht.

"Sorry, we'd love to but Mel and Angel are flying in tomorrow," said Lexi. "Maybe another day? I'm sure the girls would love it."

"It would be my pleasure," Troy answered, looking straight at Brenda.

She felt herself blushing yet again.

"Just let me know when," he said as he kissed Lexi goodbye.

"I really hope to see you again soon," Troy whispered to Brenda as he took her hand to his lips. The look in his eyes sent a tingle down her spine.

Chapter 7

Brenda was very impressed by the Beachcomber and the elegant décor. She was also intrigued by the tray which the waistcoated waiter placed before them when they'd sat down. It contained four small bowls which he said were their special relishes.

"This one is beetroot," he explained, pointing to the bowl, "and here you have fig and mango, sweet pepper and onion and some salted herrings."

They were accompanied by some salted crackers.

"How lovely!" Brenda said as she dipped a cracker in the beetroot relish.

"Don't they bring you a relish tray in restaurants in Dublin?" Lexi asked.

"I wouldn't know," Brenda replied simply. "We never go to a restaurant as fancy as this. The only time Bob and I go out for a meal is for birthdays and our anniversary and then we always go to the local Chinese. Bob loves Chinese. Eating out in Dublin is just not affordable," she explained.

"Yes, I discovered that last time I was home and we went to that place on Stephen's Green. You remember?"

"I do indeed. You wouldn't let me see the bill but I guessed it must have been almost €200 for the two of us."

"I was happy to do it but you're right, the restaurants in Dublin are a rip-off."

After the relish tray they both had the Gulf shrimp which came with delicious fresh-baked assorted bread. Brenda saw the prime rib beef being served at the table next to them and her eyes were out on sticks when she saw how enormous it was. Lexi ordered the sole and suggested Brenda order the house speciality of deep-fried chicken and when it arrived she swore it was a whole large chicken and, delicious as it was, could only eat less than half of it. What with the salad and vegetables that were included, she couldn't attempt any of the desserts. When she asked for a doggy-bag to take the chicken home, the waiter looked at her not knowing what she was talking about. Laughingly Lexi explained that what her friend wanted was a 'to-go box' and he promptly brought her a Styrofoam box into which she put the chicken and the remainder of the delicious walnut bread.

She insisted on paying and when she asked for the bill, Lexi intervened and grinning said, "She'd like the check, please."

"I'd better swot up on American jargon as they don't seem to understand me at all," Brenda laughed.

She was completely shocked at how little the meal had cost. She marvelled at how they could produce such a wonderful meal for so little money. If only they could do the same in Dublin!

* * *

Lexi was seated at the table the following morning when Brenda came down for breakfast. She could see that Brenda was truly blossoming in the Florida sun and already had a lovely golden glow that had been missing when she'd arrived two days before. She'd never seen her look so vibrant in all the years she'd known her and she could see from Troy's reaction the previous night that he had been very taken with her. Even Marvin had noticed that which in itself was unusual as he was not normally aware of male/female interactions.

There was no doubt that Troy was very attractive and charismatic and she could see how Brenda responded to him. Lexi knew from what Brenda had said the evening she arrived – or rather from what she hadn't said – that things were not going too well with Bob. They had been so much in love and devoted to each other that Lexi had thought their marriage would always be rock solid but life was not always straightforward, was it? Angel and Mel had both been convinced it wouldn't last and were surprised that it had lasted as long as it had. Lexi hoped they were not going to be proved right as it looked like there might be trouble on the horizon.

Her thoughts were interrupted by Brenda who appeared on the terrace wearing a pink halter top over a pair of cute white shorts.

"Beautiful morning," she greeted Lexi as she came over to her.

"It's always a beautiful morning here," Lexi laughed.

"Happy birthday!" Brenda said, bending down to kiss her. Lexi was the oldest by one day, then Mel, then Brenda and finally Angel.

"Thank you, dear," Lexi beamed. "Another year older!"

"'What's another year?'" Brenda sang the line from the Johnny Logan song. They both laughed. They were only eight years old when he'd won the Eurovision with that song and they'd watched it together in Angel's house. It had been a favourite of theirs ever since. Today was Lexi's birthday but they'd decided that Monday would be the joint celebration.

Brenda drank the orange juice that Maria had just squeezed and declared that she'd never drink orange juice out of a carton again.

"I'm telling you, if this keeps on, I'll definitely be looking for my green card."

"You'd never leave Ireland!" Lexi exclaimed, shocked.

Brenda sighed. "I don't see how I could. Bob certainly wouldn't entertain it. He's very set in his ways. But if I was on my own I would certainly be tempted."

Lexi heard that note of unhappiness in her voice again. "You know I'm here to lend an ear if you want to confide in me," she offered.

Brenda pressed her lips together but said nothing. She'd expected Bob to call her that morning to apologise but he hadn't.

"Now to work! I've only got about another couple of hours to do before I wrap up this painting. I'd like to know what you think of it." Lexi checked her watch. "I should be finished about noon. Why don't you work on that tan and I'll get Maria to bring you down to my studio and we can have lunch there."

"Oh, that would be lovely." Brenda clapped her hands. "I'm dying to see where you paint."

"Great! See you then, honey."

* * *

As arranged, at noon Maria and Brenda made their way down to the studio which was tucked away in a corner at the bottom of the garden.

"Good timing – I'm just finished." Lexi smiled as she wiped her brushes. Maria set the lunch down on the small table on the shaded patio which was nice and cool.

"Thanks, Maria. That looks great. You can go now and

we'll take care of it ourselves."

"*Gracias, señora,*" Maria smiled as she left. "*Buen provecho!*"

Brenda looked around the studio in awe. "This is great, so bright and spacious."

"Yes, I had it designed to let in as much light as possible."

Brenda looked at the painting Lexi had just finished. "It's lovely, so lifelike. What a beautiful girl!"

"It's a young girl I met in Guatemala. She's an indigenous Indian I found on the shores of Lake Atitlan. The Mayans are the most fantastic people you could imagine, Brenda. I fell in love with them instantly."

"They're certainly beautiful," Brenda said, as she looked around at all the other paintings propped up against the walls.

"Gosh, these are fantastic, Lexi. They're so vibrant and colourful."

"I'm glad you like them. They're for an exhibition in New York next summer. Guatemala is a wonderful country. I did hope to take the four of us there for our fortieth but, well . . ."

"Maybe Angel will have changed her mind by our fiftieth and we can go then?"

"I'll believe that when I see it."

They both erupted with laughter.

* * *

After lunch Lexi locked up her studio and they headed back to the house to get ready to drive to the airport to collect the girls. She gave a last check to their bedrooms and bathrooms. All perfect.

Brenda hummed quietly as they headed into Tampa. They parked the car and headed down to the airport arrivals hall, eager to see Angel who was arriving thirty minutes before Mel.

Chapter 8

Angel was relieved to see the buildings of downtown Tampa come into view at last. She had hoped to sleep on the flight down but even after two whiskies, she still couldn't manage it. She popped a polo mint into her mouth so that Lexi wouldn't smell the whisky on her breath. Lexi was a mother-hen and had expressed concern at Angel's drinking the last time she'd visited her in LA but Angel had assured her that she was only a social drinker. That wasn't strictly true of course but Angel felt that life was so difficult these days that she needed all the help she could get.

As the plane came in to land she checked her reflection in her compact mirror and was horrified at the dark circles under her eyes. Damn! More Touche Éclat needed. She swore she went through this concealer quicker than a smoker through a packet of fags. Luckily, that was one bad habit she'd never acquired. Smoking was far too damaging to the skin and ageing.

She made her way through to the arrivals hall, aware of the admiring glances she was getting from women as well as men. She was hard to miss in a yellow figure-hugging dress, vertiginous nude platforms and a huge yellow Hermes bag draped over her arm. Her long blonde hair was swishing behind her as she walked and although she was wearing huge Jackie O sunglasses some people recognised her and asked for her autograph. She smiled graciously as she gave it to them before striding into the arrivals hall.

She spotted the girls immediately.

"Lexi! Brenda!" she squealed as she ran towards their smiling figures.

"Angel, it's so good to see you!" Brenda cried, throwing her arms around her.

Angel could hardly believe her eyes. Was that Brenda? My God, she looked fabulous! Cute honey-blonde crop cut, tanned glowing skin – what had she done to herself? She looked hot and sassy and very young. Angel felt quite jealous.

"Welcome to Tampa. It's great to see you again." Lexi gave her a hug.

"Hey, girl, what diet have you been on? You've lost a ton of weight. You'll have to give it to me," Angel exclaimed, hugging her back. "What have you done to yourself, Brenda? You look fabulous. You seem to be getting younger instead of older. I want your secret too."

They linked arms as they went down the escalator to collect her luggage.

"Three cases, for just a week!" Lexi exclaimed as they took Angel's Louis Vuitton luggage off the carousel.

"Well, you know me. In California we change five times a day!"

"Yeah, well, you're in Florida now. Not much call for designer gear here. Bikinis and shorts, that's about it."

"Oh, go on!" Angel cried, punching her playfully in the arm. "You never know who I might meet. I might find my handsome prince here and if so I certainly want to be dressed to impress."

"What happened to your toy-boy?" Lexi asked as they made their way to the car.

"Oh, he's still there but there are lots of other fish in the sea," Angel responded brightly. "How is everything back in good old Dublin then, Brenda?"

"Oh, same old, same old," Brenda grimaced. "Nothing very exciting ever happens there."

Angel heard the despondent note in her voice and caught the look Lexi threw her. She wondered what was up. She never did think that marriage would last although it had survived over twenty years now. Angel wondered how Brenda could have stuck with one man for that length of time. Three years had been the longest relationship she'd ever had.

"And how's Megan? She's such a good goddaughter. I've had several cards from her, from places I can't even pronounce. Quite the little adventuress, isn't she?"

Brenda laughed and gave her the latest news from Megan. They deposited Angel's luggage in the car and as they had thirty minutes to wait till Mel would get in, Lexi suggested they go for a coffee. Angel would have much preferred a drink but was afraid of Lexi's disapproval if she suggested it. Lexi was a 'six o'clock, time for a drink' kind of person whereas she was more of an 'it's five o'clock somewhere' kind of gal. Well, variety was the spice of life. If they were all alike, life would be very dull.

Angel had never noticed how green Brenda's eyes were before. They were like emeralds now, glowing and bright. Her tan and newly blonde hair had accentuated them and she had really fine cheekbones which Angel had never noticed before either.

They chatted away – well, Angel did most of the chatting. She was aware of it and wished she didn't talk so much. She would love to have been the quiet mysterious type and envied women like that. Sadly, she was born a talker and couldn't change no matter how hard she tried.

Before they knew it, it was time to go and collect Mel.

* * *

Mel was exhausted as the plane touched down at Tampa Airport. She hadn't been to bed the previous night, instead finishing off a report that was overdue and tying up loose ends for her PA. Luckily she'd got a few hours' kip on the flight down. One of the joys of flying business class was that there were no kids screaming or kicking the back of her seat. She could not wait to land as she was simply gasping for a cigarette.

* * *

Mel looked every inch the businesswoman as she strode purposefully to the arrivals hall. She was pulling a monogrammed black Tumi cabin bag and had a matching computer bag slung over her shoulder. She wore a beautifully-cut black trouser suit over a white shirt and her shiny black hair was cut in a severe bob. She looked intimidating and was reading a text as she entered the arrivals hall. She looked up from her iPhone to find her three friends standing, grinning broadly. Amid hugs and kisses all round she noticed how great Brenda was looking.

"Wow! You look amazing," she exclaimed, as she held her hands and took a step back to look her up and down. "I love the hair. You look so healthy."

"More than I can say for you," Angel piped up. "You look a wreck!"

"Thanks, sister." Mel punched her in the arm playfully. "Actually, I am wrecked. I feel like I could sleep for a week."

"Well, you can sleep as much as you like while you're

here," Lexi told her, reaching for her pull-along bag. "Do you have any other luggage?"

"No, that's it."

"See?" Lexi grinned at Angel. "It is possible to travel light."

Angel groaned. "I don't know how you do it. It must be genetic."

"C'mon, I'll expire if I don't have a cigarette soon." Mel ignored Lexi's shake of the head and linked her arm as they headed for the car park. "You've lost weight, Lexi. Have you been dieting? You don't need to, you know. You're slim enough."

"No, of course I haven't been dieting," Lexi replied irritably. "When did you ever know me to diet? I just don't seem to have much of an appetite lately."

"Have you been to the doctor?"

"Lord, no. You know how much I hate doctors. I don't feel sick, just tired."

"Join the club!" Mel commented as they reached the car.

While Lexi paid for the parking Mel lit up and the others waited patiently while she sucked in the nicotine as fast as she could.

"Will Mel's case fit in the boot?" Brenda wondered.

"The boot?" Angel asked, puzzled.

"She means the trunk," Lexi explained grinning.

"God, even the Irish here don't understand me!" Brenda cried, shaking her head.

They all laughed. Angel had become so American that she'd forgotten what they used to call it in Ireland.

Mel stubbed out her cigarette and they all piled into the Escalade and suddenly it felt like old times. Within minutes they were laughing and teasing each other as they'd always done. Lexi thought how amazing it was the way you could reconnect with true friends so easily, even when you hadn't met for years.

They chattered all the way home each of them fighting to be heard. It was always difficult to get a word in when Angel was around but they gave it a damn good try.

As they crossed the Clearwater causeway Mel could feel the stress melt away. To hell with work, she thought. It didn't seem quite so important now as the beautiful Gulf of Mexico came into view. She'd earned this break and she was damn well going to enjoy it.

* * *

They arrived at Lexi's house and both Mel and Angel made a dash for the bedrooms.

As they ran up the stairs they could hear Brenda ask Lexi, "What's going on?"

"They both want to bag the best bedroom," she replied laughing. "That pair have done that everywhere for as long as I can remember. They're like two kids."

Brenda couldn't believe it and laughed aloud with her.

Mel in her sensible loafers got there first with Angel teetering behind on those ridiculous platform stilettos.

"Tough luck!" Mel turned to Angel who had finally made it up the stairs. "Brenda bagged it before us." They collapsed laughing. The incongruity of two grown women behaving like that wasn't lost on them.

"Outfoxed this time, girls. Brenda's got the best room!" Lexi called out as they came back downstairs.

"Oh, I don't mind moving," Brenda offered and Angel's eyes lit up hopefully.

"Nonsense, you were here first. That was always the rule. First in gets the best room," Lexi insisted.

"Absolutely!" Angel acceded, realising it was a no-go. When Brenda and Lexi turned away she gave Mel the fingers. Mel stuck her tongue out at her and then they both collapsed laughing again. Things hadn't changed much since they'd been in first grade. It was great being back together again.

Chapter 9

Brenda had forgotten just how much fun they'd always had when they were together. Fun was something that had been missing from her life for a while and she revelled in the laughter and exuberance that they generated as a group. She felt a little shy at first but after two margaritas she relaxed and found herself joining in the banter.

Angel and Mel both wanted to know what the kids were doing and Brenda felt very proud as she told of their achievements.

"Well, I have to hand it to you. You've done a fantastic job with them. I daresay Bob had very little to do with it," Mel commented bluntly.

"Oh, he's very good with them," Brenda replied gallantly, not wanting to be disloyal to her husband.

"You know, we never thought your marriage would last," Angel remarked, warranting a frown from Lexi. "But I have to say you've surprised us."

"So says the thrice-divorced expert!" Lexi noted drily.

Angel burst out laughing. "You have me there."

"And now that you're a cougar, how is your new toy-boy?" Mel asked coyly.

"I do so hate those labels," Angel exclaimed. "I'm an independent, sexy woman and he's my younger lover."

"Okay, independent, sexy woman, c'mon and dish the dirt on your hot younger lover then!" Mel demanded.

Brenda was relieved that the attention had been deflected from her marriage as Angel and Mel sparred with each other, the way they'd always done.

"Oh, he's fine, fine – exhausting, to be honest with you."

"I can well imagine it," Mel commented. "A twenty-three-year-old stud would exhaust any woman!"

They all laughed. "Yeah, well, it's obviously not long-term," Angel admitted. "In fact I'm hoping I might meet a nice guy down here."

"Someone less exhausting, I presume," Mel teased.

"Well someone with his own income preferably," Angel retorted, tossing her head so that her long blonde hair swished from side to side.

"Oh, God! Watch out, men! Go hide!" Mel cried as Angel swatted her, grinning.

Angel kept them all entertained with gossip of Hollywood and listening to her talk Brenda thought how exciting her life had been in comparison to her own dull, boring one. Had she been crazy giving up her life for Bob? She'd never have had the kids of course, and she wouldn't change that for the world, but if she was honest she and Bob weren't happy now. She'd changed and she'd outgrown him. However, she was too scared to think about it too much as then she would have to face the problem so she blocked it from her mind.

She'd expected Bob to ring her to apologise for his rudeness on the phone the night she'd arrived but she hadn't heard a word from him since.

* * *

They had dinner out on the terrace where Pablo and Maria cooked up a fantastic barbecue. Brenda could see her hard-lost pounds piling on before her very eyes but it was all so delicious that she couldn't resist it.

Angel kept up a monologue throughout the meal, which was easy as she barely touched her food. Brenda noticed that her forehead wasn't moving when she talked or laughed. She understood why when Angel started telling stories about her Botox doctor.

"You've had Botox?" she asked her.

Mel hooted with laughter. "Botox and the rest!" she cried. "Brenda, you're such an innocent. Everyone gets Botox nowadays and fillers and plumpers. We get them done during our lunch break."

Brenda was shocked and turned to Lexi. "You don't do that, do you?"

"Not in a million years would I allow them to stick a needle in my face," Lexi stated. "I'm happy as I am."

"Our Lexi doesn't need it," Mel observed fondly. "She's a natural beauty."

"It's different here in Florida," Angel explained to Brenda. "Everyone in LA gets it done. It's the Botox capital of the world!"

"So sad!" Lexi declared.

Brenda was inclined to agree with her. Mel was constantly puffing on one cigarette after another and it was obvious to the others that she was as tense as a tightly coiled spring. However, after a couple of glasses of wine she did appear to relax and Lexi was relieved to see it. Although Angel had eaten practically nothing she made up for it with her alcohol consumption. Brenda began to understand Lexi's concerns for the two of them now.

Nothing was ever as it seemed, was it?

* * *

After dinner they moved inside and Lexi revealed her plans for the week which sounded very exciting. She proposed a relaxing day on the beach or by the pool the following day so Angel and Mel could chill out and adjust to the Florida lifestyle.

"I've booked a table in Shephard's for tomorrow night. It's a buffet restaurant overlooking the beach. It's relaxed and casual and I think you'll enjoy it."

"Sounds good to me," Brenda said.

"Is that the place with the music outdoors overlooking the beach?" Angel asked.

"Yes, that's the one," Lexi replied. "You've been there with me before, haven't you?"

"Yeah, the music was great and the cocktails divine." She threw her eyes to heaven.

"Count me in so," Mel laughed.

Lexi then told them that she had also booked them into the local spa salon on Monday for some pampering in preparation for their combined birthday party that evening.

"It's my treat," she announced.

"Gosh, I've never been to a spa salon before," Brenda admitted.

"You're joking!" Angel exclaimed in a shocked voice.

"'Fraid not." Brenda shook her head.

"I don't believe it! Where have you been hiding yourself?" Angel cried, her words slurring.

"You'll enjoy it," Lexi assured her, frowning at Angel for being insensitive. "They do a great massage there. It's very relaxing."

"That's exactly what I need right now," said Mel.

Lexi looked at her sympathetically. "It will do us all good and it will be fun. Get us in the mood for our birthday party. After that we'll play it by ear. Troy has invited us out on his yacht one day and I thought we'd take a trip down to the Dalí museum another day."

"Great! I hear the new museum is fabulous," Mel interjected.

"It is. Thursday of course is Thanksgiving and we'll celebrate here with turkey and all the trimmings."

"You're doing a good job of tempting me to stay till then," Mel commented ruefully.

"But of course," Lexi grinned at her. "And finally, I think we can't let Brenda go home without experiencing Black Friday."

"Oh no!" Mel groaned.

"Do we have to?" Angel asked.

"What's Black Friday?" Brenda asked mystified.

"It's the day after Thanksgiving when America goes crazy shopping," Mel explained. "It's nuts. Prices are slashed everywhere and the shops open at midnight and you wouldn't believe the pandemonium."

"At midnight?" Brenda exclaimed, finding it hard to believe.

"Yes, and you should see the crowds. Every shop is packed with huge queues at the cash desks all night long," Angel added.

"You can't find a parking space – at 3 o'clock in the morning – can you believe that?" Mel asked.

"You're not serious!" Brenda cried open-eyed. "That is something to write home about. Shopping has become the leisure pursuit in Ireland now but I don't think even we would do that," she chuckled. "And you want us to go out shopping at midnight, Lexi?"

"Well, maybe not at midnight, especially not after Thanksgiving dinner, but the sales go on the whole weekend."

"That I can take," Brenda told her enthusiastically.

"Count me out," Mel said.

"Me too," Angel concurred.

"You're both chicken!" Lexi laughed. "Don't worry, Brenda, I'll take you shopping."

* * *

They had a great night and Lexi observed that she hadn't laughed so much since the last time they'd all been together. She'd been worried initially that Brenda would be lost between the two strong personalities of Mel and Angel so she was pleased when, after a couple of margaritas, Brenda had held her own and hadn't let them intimidate her. Sometimes it was hard to get a word in edgeways with that pair around. The evening had been great fun and she hoped that the rest of the week would go as smoothly.

* * *

The following morning when Lexi came down for her swim she was surprised to find Mel sitting on the terrace with a cup of coffee and a cigarette. She was on her laptop.

"Good morning and happy birthday!" Today was Mel's birthday. "Did you not sleep well?"

"I never sleep well." Mel grimaced.

"Oh Mel, you're going to kill yourself if you go on like this. I'm really worried about you, you know. You work far too hard. You really have to rethink your lifestyle. I'm concerned for you."

"I know and I appreciate that but it's so difficult to switch off. I'm just so stressed out all the time. It's a rat race out there, you know."

"Well, this is your chance to get away from it all. Why don't you put that laptop away and come for a swim with me?"

"I'll probably drown! I haven't been swimming for yonks."

"Well, come on, put that away and go get changed and join me in the pool."

"Okay, okay, I surrender," Mel laughed, closing the computer and stubbing out her cigarette. She went upstairs to change and fifteen minutes later came down. She smoked another cigarette before finally joining Lexi who was busy doing laps in the pool.

Mel was still in the pool when Lexi got out and as she towelled herself dry Lexi admired Mel's sure strokes as she cut through the water. She had always been the most athletic of the four of them. Lexi showered and dressed and when she came back down was surprised to see Mel still in the pool, floating lazily on her back. She finally joined Lexi on the terrace, shaking the water from her dark hair.

"I've forgotten how good it is to swim," she observed as she towelled herself dry and slipped on her bathrobe. They moved up to the upper terrace where Maria had set out a delicious breakfast buffet of cold meats, cheese, fruit and yogurts and brought them a jug of freshly squeezed orange juice and coffee.

"What! No Irish breakfast?" Mel asked, pretending surprise. "I'm hungry after that swim."

"I only make that on special occasions. We'll have one on Thanksgiving, if you stay for it that is."

"I'm only kidding. I never eat breakfast. I just have coffee."

"You really must take care of yourself, Mel. Your health is the most important thing you have. You should look after it."

Mel sighed. "I know, I know. You're right as always, Lexi."

Knocking back her juice she leaned back in her chair and turned her face up to the sun. "Oh, this is bliss. I'm beginning to think you have the right idea, Lexi. This is the life. Maybe I should leave New York and move to Florida. I'd have no problem getting a job here. The sunshine is so relaxing that it's hard to be stressed out for long."

"I'd love it if you were here."

"If only!"

"Then I could keep an eye on you and make sure you take care of yourself."

"Yes, Mama," Mel replied and they both burst out laughing, remembering how they all used to say that to her whenever she doled out advice to them at school.

"You're still a mother-hen, you know that?" Mel smiled as they got up to help themselves to breakfast.

Lexi was pleased to see Mel filling her plate.

When they were sitting down eating Lexi leaned forward and looked at Mel intently. "What is it you want from life, Mel?"

"I don't know. I was just thinking this morning, when I couldn't sleep, that even though I've achieved everything I ever wanted, I've really got nothing at the end of the day."

"You certainly have proved yourself but you're not happy, are you?"

"No, I'm not. When I hear about Brenda's kids, I realise that she's achieved something far better than I ever have."

"Would you have wanted children?"

"I didn't think I did but the old biological clock is ticking away and knowing I'll probably never be a mother makes me sad."

"You could always adopt a baby."

Mel laughed harshly. "What agency would consider giving me a baby, working the hours I do?"

"You could always change that. I guess you've made enough money to retire by now. It's a thought."

"Yes, money wouldn't be an object but I'd be terrified that I'd be a bad mother. Mmmm . . . this ham is delicious, I think I'll have some more." She got up and helped herself again.

When she sat down Lexi continued.

"All pregnant first-time mothers worry about that, I guess. I know I did, though I never got the chance to find out." Her voice was sad.

Mel reached for her hand across the table. "Oh, Lexi, I'm sorry. I shouldn't go on about babies when you lost yours so tragically."

"It's okay. It's good sometimes to talk about Alessandro. Not a day goes by that I don't think of him and wonder what he would be like if he'd lived. He'd be eight years old now."

Mel squeezed Lexi's hand and searched for words of comfort but there were no words for something so devastating. Brenda appeared just then, breaking the sombre mood.

"Good morning, you energetic people. I saw you swimming earlier from my bedroom window. Gosh, but you're both very fit," she observed admiringly.

"Don't believe it. Appearances are deceptive. I'm as unfit as a couch potato," Mel said, making a face.

"Well, you looked pretty good to me. You were always very sporty. Happy birthday, Mel!" She kissed her friend.

"God, don't remind me. Thirty-nine today!"

"What's another year?" Lexi and Brenda chorused together. They all laughed.

"Mmmm . . . that breakfast looks delicious," Brenda observed.

"It is. I'm stuffed." Mel patted her tummy.

"Help yourself," said Lexi, pulling out a chair for her.

"This is the life, isn't it, Mel?" Brenda commented as she went to the buffet with her plate.

"It sure is," Mel agreed. "I was just saying to Lexi that maybe I should relocate here."

"Could you?"

"I could if I wanted to, I suppose. It would be a demotion from where I'm at now but I'd certainly have no problem getting a job."

Brenda sighed. "You're so lucky. I'd live here at the drop of a hat, if I didn't have Bob at home, I mean."

"If you leave him and move here then I'll move here too," Mel proposed.

Brenda laughed. "Not a chance but it's a nice dream all the same."

"Oh go on, the two of you," Lexi cried, shaking her head. "You're just tantalising me."

"Any sign of Angel?" Brenda asked.

"You must be joking! She's not exactly an early bird. I reckon we'll be lucky to see her before noon," Mel laughed.

"*Plus ça change . . .!*" said Lexi, shaking her head.

After a leisurely breakfast Lexi told them that she had some shopping to do. They both offered to go and help her but she shooed them off to the beach where Pablo set them up with lounge beds and parasols. Still no sign of Angel.

Chapter 10

Lexi arrived back home just before noon and was helping Maria put things away when Angel surfaced. Her face was make-up free with her hair tied up in a ponytail. She was wearing a long T-shirt and flip-flops and without her heels and other accoutrements she looked extremely young and vulnerable.

"Good morning, am I late for breakfast?"

"A little," Lexi responded, thinking that Mel would probably have replied, 'Only three or four hours.' "What would you like?"

"Oh, just coffee would be great. I never eat breakfast anyway."

"Oh my God, you girls!" Lexi exclaimed, switching on the coffee machine. "Mel said the same thing but she ate a great breakfast this morning. Are you sure you won't eat anything?"

"No, I'm sure. Where is she by the way, and Brenda?" Angel asked, looking out at the pool.

"They're on the beach. Do you want to join them?"

"God no, I hate the beach! All that bloody sand, not to mention baking in the sun which is sooo ageing." She wrinkled her pert little nose.

"But you have a great tan," Lexi observed.

"That's fake, Lexi. Nobody has a real tan these days. It's bloody suicide for your skin."

"Oh, I see. Well then, if you don't want to take the sun you can give me a hand making some cheese straws for the party tomorrow."

"Sure, no problem. I just need to go online first." She hoisted herself up on the kitchen stool as Maria poured her coffee. She looked no older than she had done fifteen years before. Lexi couldn't understand her fixation with staying young. She was still stunningly beautiful and as irresistible as ever.

* * *

Lexi was left to make the cheese straws on her own. Three batches had been removed from the oven and two loaves of brown soda bread were baking away and still Angel was playing away on her computer thingy – an iPad, she'd called it. Lexi shook her head in disbelief and wondered what on earth she could be doing on it. To Lexi's horror she had also consumed eight cups of coffee in that time.

"Angel, have you any idea how much caffeine you're pumping into your system? It's no wonder you're on a high all the time."

"I know," Angel replied sheepishly. "I run on coffee."

"It's not good for you, you know. Why don't you drink decaf?"

"Yeuch! Can't stand the stuff! I'll cut back, I promise."

Lexi sighed. She didn't believe a word of it.

Angel was relieved to see Mel and Brenda come into the kitchen and distract Lexi. They were both pink and glowing

72

from the sun and they had wet hair.

"Have you been swimming in the sea?" Lexi asked.

"Yes, it was wonderful, wasn't it, Mel?"

"Simply divine," Mel agreed.

"God, how can you bear the beach? All that sand getting into all those private places?" Angel cried, wrinkling her nose in disgust.

"Don't be such a sugar-baby. You're far too pampered," Mel retorted.

"And I aim to stay that way, thank you very much."

"Girls, girls!" Lexi reprimanded them fearing another sparring session.

"So what have you been doing with yourselves?" Brenda asked.

"Well, I've been baking while Her Ladyship has been tapping on that yoke for almost two hours."

"I've been reading emails and on Facebook and Twitter," Angel said, pretending to look aggrieved.

"Oh, I wanted to ask you," said Brenda. "Could I Skype Alex at some stage? I promised her I would. She wants to wish us all a happy birthday."

"Of course, honey."

"It's better if she does it from my laptop," Mel suggested. "The picture will be bigger. I'll go and get it."

"Can it wait till after lunch? Maria has it set out for us on the terrace," Lexi pointed out.

"Oh no, not in the sun!" Angel wailed.

"Don't worry, baby, the awning is up. No sun will touch your delicate face," Mel teased her in a babyish voice.

"Okay," Angel said hopping down off the stool. Still, she went to get a big sunhat and huge sunglasses just in case.

* * *

After an extended lunch Mel went up to her room to get her laptop as Brenda texted Alex on her mobile telling her to log on to Skype. Eventually they were all set and Brenda was delighted to see Alex's face, smiling and happy on the screen.

"Hi, Mum, how are you? Did you arrive safely? How is it and how are Aunt Lexi and the girls?"

"Fantastic, darling! It's beautiful here and Lexi and the girls are all here with me and in great form."

"Hey, you've got a tan already."

"Yes, I've been lolling about in the sun since I came."

Lexi couldn't believe her eyes. To think that Brenda could see her daughter who was on the other side of the world. It was quite amazing.

Brenda moved over on the chair and beckoned Lexi to sit down beside her.

"Hi, Aunt Lexi, how are you?" Alex said.

"I can't believe this. This is incredible. How is it possible to be able to talk to you like this?"

"That's modern technology for you."

"It must be very expensive."

"No, it's free. That's the great thing about it."

"Well, I never!" Brenda and the others smiled at Lexi's wonder.

"How are you, darling? Are you happy out there?" Lexi asked.

They chatted for a few minutes as Alex told her all about her life in Sudan.

"Hi, Angel and Mel," said Alex as she spotted them bend down over Lexi's head, waving and blowing kisses. "You look like you're all having a great time."

"Oh, we are, honey. It's great to be here together. We're having fun."

"And lots more to come," Mel added.

"Well, I hope you have a fabulous birthday. It's so good of you, Aunt Lexi, to have invited Mum over. I know how much it means to her."

"It's lovely to have her here." Lexi was getting quite emotional. It was wonderful to be able to talk to her goddaughter who was so far away in Sudan. She said goodbye and handed over to Brenda once more.

When the call was over Lexi bombarded them with questions as to how this Skyping worked. They explained it to her and she was mesmerised by the whole thing.

"Maybe there's something to be said for modern technology after all," she admitted.

"Just think, if you had a computer you could Skype us all," Brenda pointed out.

"Yeeesss, it's a thought. Maybe I'll look into it but I'm afraid I'm not very good at technical things."

"I'm sure Marvin would help you," Brenda suggested.

"Sure. He's pretty good at that kind of thing. I'll talk to him about it."

After lunch Lexi went up for a lie-down and the three girls got their heads together.

"Angel and I have been racking our brains trying to think what we should get Lexi for her birthday," Mel said to Brenda. "I think we've just found the perfect gift for her. A laptop! What do you think?"

"Brilliant idea!" Angel agreed enthusiastically. "But why not the latest iPad 5?"

"Those things are much too complicated. I think a laptop would be better."

"Mel is right. The simpler, the better," Brenda agreed.

"Okay. I suppose it would put her off if it was too high-tech," Angel conceded.

"Are they very expensive?" Brenda asked. She had brought

Lexi a book on Irish Art but wanted to contribute to the laptop as well, if it was not too pricey.

"No, we should get a good one in Walmart for about $300."

"You're not serious!" Brenda exclaimed. "I was checking prices out at home in the summer sales because we could really do with a new one. Our computer is very slow – it was a hand-me-down from my sister – and a decent laptop would have cost at least €500. I needn't tell you I gave up the idea pretty quickly."

"Everything is ridiculously expensive in Ireland," Mel observed, winking at Angel.

Angel copped on immediately. They had also been trying to decide what birthday present to get for Brenda but had no idea what she might like. They didn't think Brenda was a designer-bag-type and had more or less decided to get her a gift voucher for Macy's. A laptop was a much better idea, especially if she needed a new one.

"I'd like to share in Lexi's present if that's okay with you two," Brenda said.

"Of course. It can be from the three of us. Won't she be surprised! We'll need to get to Walmart before the party so that we can present it to her then."

"How will we manage that?" Angel asked.

"I'll say I want to go buy something for my PA tomorrow morning," Mel proposed, "and you guys offer to come too."

"Great idea! That's agreed then. Good work, girls!" Angel cried, high-fiving them.

"One for all and all for one!" Mel exclaimed, pleased with what they'd decided.

* * *

Brenda had still had no word from Bob and was damned if she was going to call him and risk the reception she'd received the last time they'd spoken. She guessed he was sulking but was determined not to let him spoil this time with her friends. She was disappointed in him. If the shoe had been on the other foot she would have been happy for him to be with his friends. She put him out of her mind.

Chapter 11

That evening they descended on Shephard's and sipped margaritas as they watched the glorious sunset from the terrace above the beach. They then moved inside the restaurant where an enormous amount of food was set out for the buffet. Brenda had a tough time deciding what to choose and even agreed to try some oysters which Mel told her were delicious. She didn't like the look of them and they tasted even worse than they looked so she offloaded the rest on to Mel's plate.

"They're delicious," Mel insisted.

"They look and taste like snot," Brenda replied, sending Angel into peals of laughter.

After the seafood course Mel nipped outside for a cigarette. Making her way down the steps to the beach, she sat on the lowest one and lit up. In the gathering dusk she couldn't see much but was aware of someone sitting on a rock a short distance away. She saw the glow of a cigarette and felt an immediate affinity with this person. She'd begun to feel like a pariah what with all the anti-smoking propaganda she had to endure every day.

"It's nice to see I'm not the only one polluting my lungs and the atmosphere," she addressed the stranger.

"All this politically correct shite does my head in," a deep male voice replied but she could tell from his tone that he was smiling. His voice was low and mellow and she was surprised to hear his Irish accent.

"You're Irish?"

"Ah Jaysus, how can you tell?"

"I'm Irish too."

"You are? You sound more posh-American to me," he remarked.

She laughed. "Well, I guess I've been here too long then. Nearly seventeen years. I'm from Dublin."

"Jaysus! You don't have any trace of a Dublin accent. What part of Dublin?"

"Rathmines."

"Ah, that figures. Sure southsiders never speak with a Dublin accent."

"I gather you're from the northside then," she observed sarcastically but she couldn't help grinning.

"Yeah, Castleknock."

"Ah! That's why you sound like Colin Farrell."

"He's cool, isn't he? We went to the same school. He was a few years ahead of me. Did you see him in the film *In Bruges*? Bleedin' great, he was!"

Hearing him talk, Mel felt herself being catapulted back to Dublin. Dubliners had a very unique way of talking. She loved it. She'd also taken note of the fact that if he was younger than Colin Farrell then he was obviously younger than her too.

"Yeah, it was a brilliant film and both he and Brendan Gleeson were terrific." She smiled as she thought of it.

He got up from his rock and she could see that he was very tall. He quenched his cigarette with his fingers then placed it in an empty cigarette box. Not a litter lout then, throwing it on the beach. She liked him for that.

"Jack Molloy," he said, stretching out his hand as he came towards her.

"Mel O'Brien," she replied, shaking his outstretched hand. He had a firm strong handshake. In the moonlight, she could see that his skin was pale and he had long black curly hair. He moved very languidly.

"What are you doin' here?" he asked her.

"I'm down staying with a friend. There are four of us. It's our birthday."

"All of you?"

"Yes, we were all born the same week."

"Jaysus, you're jokin'?"

"No, I'm not. Today's my birthday actually." She blushed, surprised at herself for telling him that.

"Well, happy birthday, darlin'."

"What are you doing here?" she asked, anxious to change the subject, afraid he might ask her how old she was. She just stopped herself in time from saying 'doin'.

"I'm a singer. I have a gig over there in the bar overlooking the beach." He jerked his thumb in the direction of a thatched cabana on the boardwalk from where came the sound of disco music. "I'm workin' my way through all fifty states. Only six left to go," he told her proudly.

"Wow!" Mel was impressed.

"Is there a Mr O'Brien with you?"

"There is no Mr O'Brien. I'm here with my three girlfriends."

"You're not gay?"

She laughed. "Definitely not."

"Thank God for that. You never know these days."

"I'd better go back. We're having dinner here. Nice to meet you," she said, getting up to go back inside.

"Hey, why dontcha come over later and have a listen. I'll be on my break at ten and we can have a drink. Bring your friends if you like."

"Maybe I will," she smiled at him.

* * *

"Where have you been?" Angel enquired as Mel sat down again at the table.

"I met a cute guy from Dublin who is a singer in the bar here. He's working his way around all fifty states."

"My oh my, we can't let you out of our sight for a minute," Lexi teased.

"That's more Angel's style," Mel countered but she was grinning. "Anyway Jack asked us to go over and listen to him later. He seems like a nice guy."

Lexi heard the unaccustomed softness in her voice and looked at her with raised eyebrows. They'd definitely have to go and check this guy out.

* * *

After the main course Mel slipped out for another cigarette. Instead of going down to the beach she strolled along the boardwalk to the outdoor bar, attracted by the strumming of a guitar.

She stopped short, out of sight, as the haunting sound of James Taylor's old song 'You've Got a Friend' filled the air. Jack was perched on a high stool, hunched over his guitar, his eyes closed. Mel stood transfixed and felt the music flow over her. His voice was low and gentle and rich with feeling and it struck a chord deep inside her. As he finished she slipped away, his song still with her. She felt drawn to him and knew she had to meet him later.

* * *

When they'd finished their meal Mel casually suggested that they adjourn to the beach bar.

"Yes, let's go and hear this Dublin fellow you met," Lexi agreed.

Mel was excited as they made their way across the boardwalk. Quite a crowd had gathered, attracted by his singing, but luckily a group was leaving and vacated a table which Angel grabbed. Jack was between numbers. He spotted Mel and gave her a wave. She smiled and waved back.

"Mmmm . . . he is dishy," Angel observed.

"Yes, he is rather gorgeous," Lexi agreed.

"You said he seems like a really nice guy too," said Brenda.

"Yeah, I think so," Mel replied.

"Ooohh, you'll have to introduce me," Angel said, patting her hair.

"Not bloody likely! I saw him first," Mel retorted sharply.

Lexi and Brenda were taken aback by her tone. Angel pouted but didn't pursue it.

They ordered a round of cocktails as Jack took up his guitar again.

"This next song is for a lovely lady who hails from my home town, Dublin. Happy birthday, Mel." He looked straight at Mel as he started to strum and then the strains of the beautiful Roberta Flack song, 'Killing Me Softly With His Song', filled the air.

You could have heard a pin drop as all conversation ceased and everyone fixed their eyes on the soulful singer. His voice touched everyone in the audience, not least Mel who felt tears come to her eyes. Brenda saw it and squeezed her hand. All of them felt the power of his music and when he finished clapped and cheered loudly.

Mel knew that he was indeed 'killing her softly' with his song. She wondered what it would be like to make love to him and was shocked at her thoughts. She'd never thought about a man like that before. His music seemed to have cast a spell over her. The crowd kept calling for more and when he had finally finished, he put away his guitar and came over to greet her.

She introduced him to the others who complimented him on his singing and she could see they all found him very attractive.

Mel ordered another round of cocktails and a beer for Jack. He sat up on the stool beside Mel, his thigh brushing hers, which sent shivers through her body. Angel was gushing with praise but he didn't take much notice of her. This pleased Mel more than anything. Up close she could see that he had startlingly blue eyes that were solemn when he was serious but when he smiled they twinkled and a dimple appeared in his right cheek. Over those blue eyes he had the longest black eyelashes she'd ever seen which made him look incredibly sexy. It was obvious that the others also found him very attractive too and were charmed by his personality.

"So, Mel tells me youse are all here for a big birthday party."

"Yes," Lexi told him. "It's tomorrow night. If you're free we'd love you to come, wouldn't we, girls?" She looked at the others for confirmation.

"Ooooh, yes," Angel cooed.

"That would be great," Brenda said enthusiastically. She really liked this down-to-earth Dubliner and sensed the chemistry between him and Mel. Gosh, but he had damn sexy eyes.

He turned to Mel. "Would you like me to come?"

"I'd love you to come," she replied, her eyes shining.

"Well, I'm workin' but I could get off early. I should make it by nine, if that's not too late."

"Not at all. Better late than never," Lexi smiled at him. "And maybe we could even persuade you to sing for us."

"My pleasure, ladies." He gave a mock bow. "And now I'd better go back and sing for my supper. Are you stayin' a while?"

"I'm afraid we're leaving now," Lexi said. "I've a lot to do tomorrow."

"What about you, Mel? Could you stay on a bit? Shame to go to bed before your birthday's over." He grinned at her.

Mel was exhilarated. "Is that okay with you, Lexi?" she asked hopefully.

"Of course, as long as Jack sees you home. I take it you'll walk back along the beach?"

"Yeah. Thanks." Mel smiled at her gratefully.

"Great! I'll take good care of her and see her safely home, don't worry," Jack assured Lexi, grinning as he put his arm around Mel's waist.

Lexi fished in her bag and handed Mel two keys. "This is the key to the beach gate and this one is for the back door," she explained. "Just make sure you lock both of them afterwards. And, Mel – have a wonderful time," she whispered softly as Mel gave her a little hug.

Angel, who was quite drunk by now, wanted to stay too but Lexi took her firmly by the arm and, saying goodnight, marshalled her out the door. Brenda was delighted for Mel and blew her a kiss as she left, giving her the thumbs-up.

* * *

After another few margaritas, Mel was quite tipsy by the time Jack came to the last number.

"This one's for Mel," he said softly as he launched into

Roberta Flack's 'The First Time Ever I Saw Your Face'. Mel's heart melted as he looked into her eyes as he sang. When it was over he said goodnight, packed up his guitar and came to her.

"Let's go," he said gently, taking her hand. Leaving his guitar with the barman who was a friend of his, he led her down to the beach. They sat on the rock he'd been sitting on when she'd first seen him and he lit two cigarettes, handing her one. He put his arm around her shoulders and they smoked in silence, their bodies close together. There was no need for conversation, they were perfectly in tune.

When they'd finished, he pulled her to him and kissed her softly. He kissed like no one had ever kissed her before, not that she was an expert in that area. Then, taking off their shoes, they walked hand in hand along the beach. The moon formed a path along the water and the night was warm and balmy. Mel felt that this was as close to Paradise as it was possible to be. She'd never been very good at small talk with men but Jack was different. She was relaxed and easy in his company as he told her of his travels. He'd visited just about every country in Europe and Asia.

"Don't you get tired travelling all the time?" she asked him.

"God, no. I love it. I couldn't bear to be tied down anywhere. I guess I must have gypsy blood in me somewhere."

"Won't you ever want to settle in one place?"

"Not if I can help it," he said with a shudder. "No, when I get through in America, I'll be off to Australia and New Zealand. I think I'll like the life there. They say it's very relaxed and easy goin'. What about you? Don't you want to travel?"

"I'm too busy working." She grimaced.

They had reached the Sandbar restaurant and sat down on the wall there to have another cigarette. He put his arm around her and pulled her close which sent a thrill through her body once more. She was acutely conscious of his masculinity and when he kissed her again, she felt her body responding. She knew, without doubt, that she would make love to him if he so wanted. When they'd finished smoking he stood up and pulled her to her feet. Then they walked on, arms around each other's waists, as he quizzed her about her life. Try as she might she couldn't make it interesting.

"Jaysus, that would be my worst nightmare, tied to a job like that. How do you stick it?"

She shrugged her shoulders. What could she say?

"Were you never married?" he asked, turning to look at her curiously.

"I'm married to my job."

"No children so?"

"No, that's my only regret. It's too late now."

They had almost reached Lexi's gate when he stopped and pulled her to him and pressed his body against hers. She felt his hardness and was excited to know that he wanted her too.

"I really like you, you know," he whispered huskily in her ear.

Then he took her face in his hands and planted little kisses on it. Her body ached for him and as he caressed her she found herself responding with passion to his touch.

It seemed like the most natural thing in the world to make love to him, right there on the sand. Mel was oblivious to the world, not thinking of the sand in her hair or that anyone might see them or the fact that she was having sex with someone she'd just met. All she could think of was the pleasure of their lovemaking. She gave herself up to it completely and her orgasm, when it came, was the most delicious, explosive sensation she'd ever experienced.

Afterwards she clung to him, tears streaming down her

cheeks with the sheer emotion of it. He held her close, murmuring her name and kissing her tears away. She lay wrapped in his arms never wanting to leave and when, a little while later, he started caressing her once more, her passion flared instantly and they made love again, more gently this time. Mel had never felt anything remotely like it before and it was almost daybreak when she was finally able to drag herself away from him.

"You're pretty special," he murmured as she brushed the sand away.

She felt a warm glow at his words.

"See you tomorrow night then?" he said softly as he took both her hands in his.

"You will come, won't you?" she asked nervously.

"I promise. If you promise we can sneak away alone for a while," he grinned.

"It's a deal," she smiled as he gently kissed her goodnight.

He waited until she'd let herself into the garden before he turned and walked back the way they'd come.

Letting herself into the house quietly, she crept up the stairs to bed where she relived every moment of the last few magical hours. She couldn't believe what had happened. She barely knew him and yet it had seemed so right. She knew she should have felt like a slut but she didn't. She felt exhilarated and womanly and blissfully happy. Instead of feeling guilty, she felt liberated. She couldn't wait to see him again. It was the best birthday she'd ever had, thanks to this handsome stranger with the mesmerising blue eyes.

Chapter 12

The day of the big birthday party dawned. Lexi had just finished her swim when Brenda arrived down to breakfast.

"I hope our Mel had a good time last night," Brenda remarked as they sat down together.

"I reckon she did. She's usually up at cockcrow but there's no sign of her yet."

"I really hope so. Jack seemed like a nice fella and was definitely into her in a big way."

"Yes, I liked him too," Lexi agreed. "Mel needs a little fun in her life and I think Jack might be just the person to supply it."

Mel finally put in an appearance at nine o'clock and blushed when the others started teasing her.

"Good morning, beautiful, and how was your evening or need we ask?" Lexi grinned at her.

"Very nice," Mel replied noncommittally as she helped herself to eggs and bacon and hash browns.

"God, I'm ravenous," she exclaimed as she loaded her plate.

"All that exercise last night, I suppose," Brenda teased, grinning.

Mel blushed and swatted her playfully as she sat down to the table.

"Jack seems really nice," Lexi remarked. "I do hope he can make the party tonight."

"I hope so. He promised me he'd come," Mel replied, blushing again. She refused to say any more about him but they weren't fooled. She seemed very relaxed and in high spirits.

"Will you still be heading home tomorrow?" Lexi asked.

"No, I think maybe I'll stay on. You're right, Lexi. I need to chill out and have some fun. It's about time I took some time off."

Lexi threw a triumphant glance at Brenda as she patted Mel's hand. "I'm delighted to hear that, sweetie."

"Where's Angel? Isn't she up yet?"

"No, and I warned her that she'd have to be up earlier today. I made an appointment at Sharmaine's Spa Salon for one o'clock. I'll get Maria to give her a shout."

Angel arrived down shortly afterwards which was much earlier than she usually surfaced. She was looking grumpy and much the worse for wear as she headed for the coffee pot. She barely spoke to the others and was obviously suffering a hangover.

"Could I have the car for an hour, Lexi? I need to do some shopping," Mel asked.

"No problem. The caterers are coming shortly so I'll be tied up for a while and won't need it. I'll ask Pablo to bring it round for you."

"Great! Perhaps you'd like to come too, girls?" Mel said to Brenda and Angel.

"If Lexi doesn't need us to help," Brenda replied, looking to Lexi.

"No, no, go ahead. This place will be crazy with the caterers running around. Go and enjoy some shopping. Just don't forget you have to be at Sharmaine's for one o'clock."

"Don't worry, we'll be back in plenty of time," Mel assured her.

"You two go on without me," Angel said. "I need to read my emails and stuff."

Mel threw her eyes to heaven. Typical Angel, backing out when she'd said she'd come! "Okay, Brenda, let's go," she said, throwing Angel a dirty look.

*　*　*

"I can't believe how cheap these are," Brenda exclaimed as they checked out the laptops in Walmart. "How do they do it?"

"Because they don't have the Irish government loading excruciating tax on them," Mel replied caustically.

"At that price I might buy one before I go home," Brenda confided. "I'll wait and see how much money I have left at the end."

Mel smiled at her. "Good idea!"

They chose a laptop for Lexi and while the staff were gift-wrapping it Mel suggested that Brenda take a stroll around the store and she'd meet her back at the car in thirty minutes. Brenda was pleased with the opportunity and Mel then ordered a second laptop for her and secreted them both in the car, happy with the way it had gone.

They arrived back before noon to find the house buzzing with florists and caterers. Maria had prepared sandwiches for them which they ate by the pool so as to keep out of the way. Angel, as she did every lunch-time, polished off the best part of a bottle of wine on her own. It had become obvious to the

90

other three girls that she was drinking far too much. Mel was convinced that she was also drinking secretly in her room but didn't want to worry Lexi by mentioning it. She knew she would have to tackle Angel about her drinking before the week was out.

"I'm not coming with you to the Spa," Lexi informed them as they prepared to leave. "I'm tired. I'm going for a lie-down as I want to be fresh for the party."

"Ah, Lexi, that's a pity. Are you sure?" Brenda asked, looking at her closely.

"Dead sure. Honestly, I would prefer go and rest but you guys go and enjoy it."

* * *

"I'm worried about Lexi," Brenda confided to the others as they drove to the salon. "She seems to tire very easily. I don't ever remember her being like that before."

"No, she's always had lots of energy," Mel agreed.

"I expect it's having us all here together," Angel said. "That's a lot of work for her."

"Indeed. She's used to having a quiet life with her painting and now we three have descended on her, creating havoc and turning her life upside down," Mel remarked.

"Yeah, I suppose it's natural that she'd be tired," Brenda agreed.

She put it to the back of her mind as she succumbed to the pampering of the next three hours. She enjoyed it so much that she resolved to treat herself from time to time in the future. American women certainly knew how to pamper themselves. She left the salon feeling like a million dollars.

* * *

When they got home Lexi was waiting for them with a bottle of champagne on ice and some tasty appetisers. They had decided to exchange birthday gifts before the other guests arrived for the party.

"How did you enjoy the Spa treatments?" Lexi asked Brenda as Mel and Angel headed upstairs.

"Fantastic! It was a wonderful present. This whole week is glorious. I can never thank you enough, Lexi," Brenda replied, her voice full of emotion. She gave Lexi a quick hug before going upstairs to get the gifts she'd brought from Ireland for the others.

Back downstairs, they set the presents out on the table. Maria poured the champagne and handed each of them a glass.

"Happy birthday, girls!" Lexi toasted them.

"Happy birthday, everyone!" they chorused raising their glasses to each other.

Lexi was overjoyed when she unwrapped her laptop but not as surprised as Brenda was with hers.

"Oh my God! A laptop!" she gasped. "Thank you so much, girls. I'm speechless!" Brenda hugged them both. She shyly gave Mel and Angel a silk scarf with Celtic designs which they both said they loved and then presented Lexi with a book on Irish Art. Mel had bought Angel an evening bag and Angel in turn gave her a leather briefcase. There was much oohing and aahing as they admired their gifts and thanked each other.

"And thank you, Lexi, for this wonderful week and also for the spa treatments," Mel said, raising her glass. "To Lexi!"

"To Lexi!" the others joined in.

As they sipped their champagne and nibbled on the titbits, Pablo came into the room carrying some paintings.

"I have a special present for you all, seeing as it's our last birthday together," Lexi announced.

She took the paintings from Pablo and they crowded around her, amazed to see that they were paintings of the four of them as children, each painting slightly different. Mel could see that they were based on photographs that Lexi's father had taken at her eighth birthday. Mel had one of those photos in an album she'd brought with her from Ireland. They'd all been dancing and were holding hands and laughing gaily as they faced the camera. She'd loved that photo as she'd been happy and smiling too, just like the others. Angel stared at one painting, recognising it from the photo her father had kept in a frame on his desk till the day he died. Brenda also remembered the photos and was touched by the gesture. The paintings were stunningly beautiful and the girls stared at them in admiration. They were so lifelike that it brought tears to their eyes, each of them remembering that innocent time.

"Oh Lexi, this is too much," Brenda said, hugging her tightly.

Mel and Angel followed suit amid tears and thanks. It was the best present any of them could have had, unique and sentimental and something to treasure. Only Lexi could have thought of it.

They were all on a high as they finished the champagne and went to get dressed for the party. It had the makings of a fabulous evening.

* * *

Brenda was tempted to call Bob, if nothing else than to tell him how angry she was with him. He knew their party was tonight but she still had no word from him. Well, to hell with him, she thought, as she showered. He was being childish. She would not give in and call him. Let him sulk!

Chapter 13

Brenda and Mel came down the stairs together.

"You look terrific, Brenda," Mel said linking arms with her. "I've never seen you look so good. No one would believe you have children in their twenties."

Brenda blushed with pleasure at the compliment. She was wearing the emerald-green silk dress which exactly matched the colour of her eyes and accentuated her honey-gold skin.

"I can return the compliment. You look very chic indeed."

Mel was every inch the sophisticate. Her black bob was shining and she wore a simply tailored, black Stella McCartney dress with a white panel down the centre. It suited her to perfection and gave her curves where she didn't have them. It was mid-thigh and showcased Mel's wonderfully long shapely legs. She looked downright sexy, perhaps because she had an inner glow and softness about her that had not been there before. That hard edge was gone.

"Thank you. I'm really excited about tonight." Mel's eyes were shining brightly.

"Looking forward to seeing Jack again?" Brenda asked.

"Oh yes. I can't wait," Mel admitted, blushing prettily. It was true. Every minute of the day had seemed like an hour as she anticipated meeting him again. She hoped they'd get to make love later. She shivered with pleasure at the thought. She looked at her watch. Only two hours to go till she saw him again.

"Ooh la la!" Lexi cried as they came down into the foyer where the guests would arrive and be received by the girls. "You both look fabulous." She noticed that Mel was glowing and wondered if Jack was the cause of it. Was it possible they'd made love? Lexi was not one to moralise or judge others and if Mel was happy then so was she.

"You're looking pretty fabulous yourself," Mel replied. Lexi was looking very striking in a bright yellow linen pantsuit.

"You look wonderful," Brenda agreed. "That colour really suits you. Is there anything we can do to help?"

"Not at all, the caterers have everything under control. Just relax and enjoy your party."

The young guy who was the barman for the evening appeared with a tray of cocktails and the girls all chose margaritas. They had just toasted each other when the first guests started to arrive.

Marvin and Troy were the first. Brenda thought Troy looked even more handsome than she remembered. They were followed by a couple from Lexi's bridge club and also a sculptor and a potter from the Artist's Co-Operative that she helped run. Her good friend Sandy, who ran a craft shop in Dunedin was next to arrive with her partner, who was a writer. They were closely followed by Lexi's gay friend Randy and his partner who both worked in the Dalí museum in St Petersburg. It was an eclectic and diverse group which augured well for an interesting night. Brenda tried to remember everyone's name but it was difficult.

Introductions over, the guests stood chatting as the barman passed around drinks. The evening looked set to be a great success and Brenda found everyone charming and friendly. The Irish considered themselves to be the friendliest nation on earth but she discovered that these Americans could give them a run for their money. Of course, almost everyone she met claimed to be of Irish descent!

They had almost finished their drinks but there was still no sign of Angel. Lexi came over to the two girls a worried look on her face. "Have either of you seen Angel?" she asked. "I wonder why she's not down yet?"

"Waiting to make a grand entrance no doubt," Mel replied caustically.

No sooner had she uttered the words than Angel did exactly that. She shimmied down the stairs, her blonde hair a mass of curls and her body poured into a figure-hugging, low-cut, off-the-shoulder red dress which showed rather too much of her amazing breasts. It also showed quite a lot of slim thigh and her feet were encased in the most divine red shoes that Brenda had ever seen. They were platforms with what must have been five-inch heels and they had a jewelled cuff around the ankles. She looked sensational and as glamorous as any star on the red carpet. Conversation stopped and all eyes were drawn to her as she sashayed into the crowd, a bright smile on her face.

"Angel, honey, I was getting worried about you," Lexi said going forward to take her hand. "Come let me introduce you."

"What did I tell you," Mel hissed out of the side of her mouth.

Brenda couldn't help smiling. "She certainly knows how to make an entrance," she whispered back.

They could see all the men clamouring to be introduced to

this goddess and Brenda was dismayed to find that Troy was one of them. She saw him take Angel's hand to his lips as he flashed a smile at her. She, in turn, batted her eyelashes and smiled at him seductively. Brenda felt a quiver of jealousy run through her as she watched Angel flirt outrageously with him. Naturally he would fancy Angel. What man wouldn't?

"Bah!" Mel retorted. "Sometimes she gets on my goat." She was more than a little concerned that Jack would be seduced by Angel just as the other men present appeared to be.

People had started to move out on to the pool terrace where the bar had been set up. Brenda and Mel joined them but then Mel went down into the garden for a smoke.

"You look ravishing tonight. Do you know that dress is the exact emerald of your eyes?" said a voice behind Brenda.

She turned to see Troy smiling at her and she blushed at the compliment.

"Well, I thought I looked okay till Angel put in an appearance. She puts us all in the shade, I'm afraid."

He raised his eyebrows and smiled sardonically at her. "Ah yes, Angel. She's something else."

"Yes. She's very beautiful," Brenda observed as she looked inside to see that the lady in question was now talking to Marvin.

"I didn't say that," he replied. "I think you look very beautiful tonight."

Her self-confidence had taken a down-turn when she'd seen Angel but, with his words, her confidence returned. She wouldn't go quite as far as to say she felt beautiful but she did feel young and attractive and her spirits lifted. Troy was good for her ego which was feeling pretty bruised, thanks to her husband's behaviour.

"Your glass is empty. Let me go get you another drink," he said, moving away towards the bar.

Brenda was perturbed to see Angel come out on to the terrace, her hand possessively on Marvin's arm. She was flirting outrageously with him too and he appeared to be enjoying it. Mel came over to speak with her.

"Oh God, do you see what she's at?" she hissed in a low voice. "We have to get her away from Marvin."

"How can we?"

"I don't know but I don't want to see Lexi hurt." She left to go and tackle Angel.

"What's the matter?" Troy asked as he came back with her drink. He could see that Brenda was uneasy.

"Oh, Mel is worried that Angel is going to seduce your brother."

Troy threw back his head and laughed. "Well, Marvin is a big boy but I see what she means. He is rather naïve and innocent when it comes to women."

"We just don't want to see Lexi hurt."

"Neither do I. Come on, let's go rescue him!"

They ambled across the terrace to join the group and as they did Mel took the opportunity to grasp Angel by the arm and pull her aside.

"What the hell do you think you're playing at?"

Angel stared at her, her big blue eyes open wide. "What do you mean?" she asked, all innocence.

"I mean that Marvin is Lexi's boyfriend and you should leave him alone."

"Don't be ridiculous! We're only having a bit of fun." Mel heard the slight slurring of her voice and guessed that she'd been drinking in secret before the party had started. Angel pulled away from her grasp. "Anyway, I don't think Lexi's all that serious about him," she said, pouting.

"That makes no difference. Just leave him and go find someone else to seduce."

"Like the lovely Jack, if he ever arrives," Angel sneered.

Mel felt like slapping her but restrained herself, clenching her hands by her sides. She prayed that Jack wouldn't fall for Angel's wiles.

Angel stalked off and joined the others.

Lexi, having seen the altercation, came over to Mel.

"What was that all about?" she wanted to know.

"Oh nothing. I was just telling her to stop trying to seduce every man in the room."

Lexi laughed. "Don't you know Angel has to have every man in love with her?"

"Why? Even when he's with another woman? It's disgusting."

"Don't be too hard on her, Mel. She's very insecure. She doesn't mean any harm."

"You think not? Don't be too sure," Mel retorted in a bitter voice.

Lexi had no time to reply as her neighbour, Kenny, had just arrived and came to greet her. She introduced him to Mel. He barely glanced at her as he shook her hand before turning back to Lexi.

"Who is that ravishing creature in the red dress?" he wanted to know. "I feel like I've seen her somewhere before."

Mel threw her eyes to heaven as Lexi tried not to laugh.

"That's Angel Flannery, the actress. Come – I'll introduce you." She led him over to where Angel stood with Marvin, Brenda and Troy.

"Angel, I'd like you to meet my friend, Kenny."

"What a perfect name for such a beautiful vision," Kenny declared, taking her hand to his lips. Angel looked him over and dismissed him straight away as too old for her. Kenny couldn't take his eyes off this ravishing woman and was thoroughly mesmerised by her.

Lexi then introduced him to Brenda – he already knew Marvin and Troy – but after a cursory hello he quickly turned his attention back to Angel. Kenny was certainly in his sixties but he was a handsome virile man and although Angel had no interest in him she enjoyed his obvious admiration and couldn't resist flirting with him.

Brenda watched her in action. It was no wonder that she could ensnare men so easily. Not only did Angel resemble Marilyn Monroe in looks, she oozed the same sex-appeal and vulnerability that had men flocking to her like bees to a honey-pot. Brenda guessed she'd been born with it and couldn't have changed even if she'd wanted to, which she clearly didn't.

* * *

Troy was hovering over Brenda solicitously making sure her glass was never empty.

"Please, no," she eventually said. "These cocktails are lethal. If I have another one I'll never make it to dinner. I would love a glass of water though."

"Sensible girl," Troy grinned. "Unfortunately your friend Angel isn't too concerned about that."

Brenda looked across the room to where Angel was talking and laughing rather too loudly.

"Oh God, I'd better go and see if she's okay."

She moved over to Angel who when she saw her, cried out, "Brenda, honey, come and tell these lovely people all about the first day we met!" She was slurring her words and Brenda realised that she was half-pissed. "Brenda can remember everything even though it's thirty-five years ago. Isn't she amazing?"

"Angel, I need a word with you." She turned to Kenny and

the other people he was with. "Would you excuse us for a moment, please?" Taking Angel firmly by the arm, she took her aside. "Angel don't you think you should ease up on those cocktails? They're very strong."

"Hell no, it's my last birthday party! Don't tell me you're getting as sancti . . . sancti . . . nomious as Mel," she said accusingly as she wrenched her arm free. She went back to the group as Brenda looked at Troy and shrugged her shoulders. When Angel was in this mood there was nothing anyone could do. Brenda was relieved when Lexi announced dinner was about to be served. She was happy that Angel would now at least have something to soak up the alcohol.

Chapter 14

As it was a very warm evening Lexi had decided they would eat outside and they all climbed the steps to the upper terrace which looked truly magical with candles glowing on the table and around the balcony. As they took their places Brenda was relieved to see that she was seated beside Troy with Marvin and Lexi on her other side. Jack would be there in time for the main course and would be seated between Mel and Angel, who were on the other side of the table. Kenny was seated on the other side of Angel.

There was a buffet set out on a long table which was manned by two waitresses and Brenda had never seen such a fabulous selection of seafood. She piled her plate with scallops, shrimp, crab and lobster, wondering how she would have any room for the main course.

"I could get used to this lifestyle," she whispered to Mel who was standing behind her.

"Enjoy it, honey. Lexi has certainly pulled out all the stops."

"I'm a bit worried about Angel. She's really pissed."

"I just hope she doesn't ruin the party," Mel replied.

Brenda was surprised at the vehemence in her voice.

Mel saw that Angel only had a couple of shrimp on her plate but was knocking back the wine twice as fast as anyone else. She caught Brenda's eye as the waiter refilled Angel's glass yet again and raised her eyebrows. Brenda shrugged helplessly. There was nothing they could do about it. Mel was glancing at her watch every few seconds and looking towards the French windows, willing Jack to walk through. Eventually, her wish came true and he arrived. Mel jumped up and went to meet him, her heart hammering as he grinned at her.

"I'm so glad you're here," she told him, her eyes glowing.

He kissed her and hugged her tight. "Me too. You look terrific," he said, standing back to look at her. She felt a thrill as his eyes devoured her and then, holding hands, she led him over to say hello to Lexi.

"I'm so glad you could make it, Jack," Lexi smiled as he kissed her on the cheek.

She introduced him to everyone and called for the wine waiter to pour him a glass of wine. Mel then took him over to the buffet.

"Holy mackerel! I've never seen so much gorgeous food."

She laughed as he piled his plate high.

"Jack, sweetie, aren't you going to give me a kiss?" Angel pouted prettily as he sat down between her and Mel. Then she leaned into him, giving him a bird's-eye view of her cleavage.

"Hello Angel." He turned to kiss her on the cheek.

She deftly moved so that his kiss landed smack on her open lips. He pulled away as Angel smiled at him seductively and then pealed with laughter. She continued to flirt with him while he ate, constantly leaning into him. He was conscious of her breast brushing his arm and her thigh pressing against his. He tried to ignore her but it was difficult. Mel was furious.

Angel really was going too far this time.

"Let's go for a smoke," Jack whispered to Mel when he'd finished eating. They made their escape as the hot food for the main course was being set out on the buffet table.

"My God, what a woman!" Jack exclaimed as they made their way down to the pool level. He lit up two cigarettes, handing one to her.

Mel was dismayed. "She is very sexy," she admitted, upset that Jack had fallen for Angel's tricks.

"She certainly likes to flash her tits."

"You like them that big?" Mel asked, looking down at her own small breasts.

"I much prefer yours," he said, reaching out to caress them. "Hers are fake. Gimme the real thing any day!"

Mel reached over and kissed him. "You've made my day."

"Do you think we could change seats when we go back?"

"You don't want to sit beside Angel?"

"God no! I want to enjoy my dinner without havin' her tits in my face all through it."

Mel was delighted and hugged him before they ran back up the steps to the party.

Angel was very put out when Mel sat down beside her, separating her from Jack. "Spoilsport!" she sulked.

"Just leave him alone!" Mel muttered.

"You're jealous," Angel accused her, glaring at her angrily.

"And you're drunk!"

* * *

Lexi had outdone herself with the food. There was prime rib and stuffed pork alongside poached salmon and chicken wrapped in prosciutto as well as numerous vegetable and pasta sides. They all agreed that it was a splendid meal and the wine waiter was kept busy, not least refilling Angel's glass.

The dessert trolley held every dessert imaginable and Mel laughed as Jack took a bit of everything then tucked into it with gusto. He really had an amazing appetite.

Finally, it was time for the birthday cake which was wheeled out, candles blazing. It was in four tiers, all the same size. Each tier had one of the girls names iced on it and ten candles around the circumference except for the top layer which had Angel's name on it with only nine candles. Brenda and Mel laughed when they saw what Lexi had done. Angel was too far gone to notice.

The champagne corks popped as everyone stood around the cake and toasted the four birthday girls. Angel was just about able to stand up and Lexi and Brenda had to support her as the others sang 'Happy Birthday' and the girls blew out the candles. Then Lexi and Brenda both led Angel inside and up the stairs where she collapsed on her bed and within seconds was passed out.

"I'm really worried about her," Lexi confided to Brenda as they undressed Angel and put her under the covers.

"Me too," Brenda agreed. "Isn't there anything we can do? She'll kill herself if she keeps this up."

"Yes, indeed. Poor Angel. She has no family and we're her only friends. We have to do something. Let's discuss it tomorrow," Lexi suggested.

They went back down to join the party.

* * *

Mel and Jack had escaped for another cigarette while the girls were escorting Angel to bed.

"That Angel is one fucked-up lady," Jack said as he handed her the cigarette he'd lit for her. She loved the way he did that.

It was somehow a very intimate gesture as it was when he kissed her and blew a little smoke into her mouth. He was so different from anyone she'd ever known and she longed to make love to him again.

"She's on a self-destruct course, you know that?" he continued.

"Gosh I hope not. I know she has developed a drink problem –"

"It's more than that. She needs help. I saw so many women like her in LA. They're all fucked-up there."

"I suppose it can't be easy there, especially if you're in the movie business."

Jack drew her close. "Let's forget about her. Do you think you could come back to my place tonight?"

Mel nodded. There was nothing she wanted more than to spend the night with him. "I'd like that."

"Good! Then I don't have to take you down to the beach and ravish you in the sand."

She laughed, happy and excited at the prospect of another night of love.

They returned to the party at the same time as Brenda and Lexi.

"How is Angel?" Mel asked them.

"Out for the count," Lexi replied. "We really have to talk about her drinking tomorrow and see what we can do to help her."

"Yeah, she needs help, that's for sure," Mel agreed.

"Well, Jack, are you going to sing for us?" Lexi smiled at him.

"Sure thing, Ma'am," he grinned. "I'll go get my guitar."

He left them to go get it and Mel turned to Lexi. "Isn't he divine?"

Her eyes were glowing and Lexi felt a little disquieted. She hoped Mel wasn't falling for him because from what he'd said over dinner, Jack was not the marrying type – nor even the settling-down-for-a-short-while type. He'd spoken of his plans to travel to Australia and New Zealand after he'd finished visiting the fifty US states. Definitely not husband material but she didn't want to burst Mel's bubble.

"Yes, I really like him," she replied and it was true. He had a very charming manner and made you think you were the only person in the world when he was talking to you. She didn't blame Mel. He was very attractive indeed, and sexy.

Pablo had lit the outdoor heaters as it was getting a little cool on the terrace as they sat down to listen to Jack. Everyone listened spellbound as his haunting voice filled the night air. He sang some Irish songs – in honour of the girls, he said – and when he sang Mary Black's 'Song for Ireland', they clapped and cheered in appreciation.

"This last song is especially for the birthday girls, Lexi, Brenda, Angel and Mel." He then launched into Johnny Logan's 'What's Another Year?' which seemed a fitting tribute.

The party finished shortly after and the guests departed one by one, thanking Lexi profusely for a wonderful night.

"Do you mind if I spend the night in Jack's place?" Mel asked her shyly.

"Of course not. Go and have a good night and be happy."

"Thank you, Lexi. I will." Mel turned to a smiling Jack and gave him the thumbs-up.

Mel ran upstairs to change and grab her overnight things. She was back in a flash, a broad smile on her face.

"Could you be back by ten tomorrow morning as I thought we might go down to the Dalí museum in St Petersburg?"

"Sure, I'll be back by then."

She and Jack gave Lexi and Brenda a big hug before they set off hand-in-hand.

* * *

"Well, that was a success I think," Lexi said as she kicked off her shoes and stretched out on the sofa. Marvin sat beside her and rubbed her feet.

Brenda sat with Troy on the sofa opposite them and she would love to have been able to have Troy rub her feet which were aching from her new shoes but of course that was out of the question.

"And now for the post mortem," Lexi said. "I think a party is not complete until we've had the post mortem."

They all laughed and then ensued a discussion on the guests and conversation of the evening. They avoided all mention of Angel. Lexi was grateful for that. She didn't want to end the night on a downer. Tomorrow was time enough to tackle that problem.

"Kenny is a lovely man, very interesting to talk to," Brenda observed, "but I noticed he was drinking a different wine to the rest of us. Why was that?"

"He's a recovering alcoholic so he only drinks non-alcoholic wine."

"Oh, I'd never have guessed that about him! He's such a gentleman."

"Alcoholism knows no boundaries, unfortunately. It affects people from all walks of life."

"He's a great guy," Marvin said. "I also really like Mel's fellow. It looks like she's fallen in love with him."

Lexi looked at Brenda and they were both thinking the same thing: God, I hope not!

* * *

The following morning Lexi was a little later than usual in the pool and was just getting out when Brenda appeared on the terrace above.

"With you in a sec," Lexi called out as she wrapped her bathrobe about her.

"Well, good morning. You don't look like you were up till the wee small hours last night," Brenda greeted her.

"Believe me, I felt it before my swim but I'm feeling awake at last. Happy birthday, hon," she said, kissing Brenda.

"Thank you. I feel like every day is my birthday this week."

"Yes, it's pretty prolonged alright," Lexi laughed. "And why not if it's to be our last?"

"It was a great night. I wonder how Angel is feeling."

Lexi grimaced. "Not too good, I imagine. We really have to talk to her about her drinking today. I'm not looking forward to that conversation."

"Me neither but it has to be done. It is worrying. I don't suppose she'll surface anytime soon?"

"We won't see her before lunch, that's for sure," Lexi replied. "I had hoped that we would go down to the new Dalí museum this morning but I think maybe we should leave it for another time."

"Good idea! I'm quite happy to chill out here today. We can't very well go without Angel and Mel's not back yet anyway, is she?"

"No. I do hope she had a good time. I think I'll give her a call and tell her she can spend the day with Jack if she wishes. No point in her rushing back here if we're not going to the Dalí," Lexi said, reaching for the phone.

Mel answered sleepily.

"Hope I'm not disturbing anything," Lexi began, grinning at Brenda.

"Lexi? No, I was sleeping. Gosh, what time is it? Did I sleep out?" She jumped out of bed to reach for her watch. "Am I late?"

"No, sweetie. I'm just calling to say that we've postponed that trip for another day. Angel won't be in any fit condition to go so if you want to spend the day with Jack, that's fine."

"Are you sure you don't mind?"

Lexi heard the relief in Mel's voice.

"Not at all. You have a good day. We'll see you for dinner."

"Thank you so much, Lexi. You're an angel!"

"I hope not. One Angel is enough in this house."

They both laughed.

"Well, she seems to be happy," Lexi said to Brenda when she'd hung up. "I'm so glad. I just hope she doesn't get too involved with Jack. I don't want her to get hurt."

"No. I gather he's a bit of a gypsy. I heard him say last night that travelling is in his blood."

"Well, as long as Mel sees it as a bit of fun," Lexi said, biting her lip. She had her doubts about that unfortunately.

Marvin rang as they were having breakfast. When he heard that they were not going to St Petersburg he offered to come and collect her new laptop so that he could download the apps she would need. He also invited the four of them over for a barbeque that evening which Lexi said would be lovely.

Chapter 15

Mel was in seventh heaven. She and Jack had spent the night making love. Now as she lay in Jack's arms she thought that she had never been so happy. The only cloud on the horizon was that it would be over at the weekend unless she decided to stay on for another week which she was very tempted to do. She pushed it to the back of her mind as she looked forward to a whole day with Jack.

She would have been quite happy to spend the day in bed with him but, after making love once more, Jack carried her out of the bed and into the shower as she giggled uncontrollably.

"C'mon, you hussy! You have me exhausted. It's a beautiful day and we're goin' to make the most of it."

They showered together and despite his exhaustion he took her once again, the water streaming over her as she climaxed. It was the most fantastic thing she'd ever experienced. He towelled her dry and she wallowed in his tenderness. Dressed at last, he took her for breakfast and she marvelled at his appetite as he demolished bacon, eggs, sausage, hash browns and fried potatoes followed by pancakes and maple syrup.

"I have to keep my energy up for you, you demanding woman," he grinned at her as he cleared his plate and finished her pancakes.

After breakfast Jack stopped off at a Publix supermarket and came out with two large bags before he drove her, in his banger of a pick-up truck, to a house along the bay. There he introduced her to his friend, Kris, who took them around to the back of the house where a boat was moored.

"I did as you asked," Kris said, grinning as he handed Jack the key.

"Have a good day and don't do anything I wouldn't," he added, winking at them.

"Thanks, mate," Jack clapped him on the back.

As Jack led her on board, Mel asked, "Do you really know how to drive this thing?"

"Steer, Silly Billy, steer. One drives a car and one steers a boat."

She blushed, giggling. "Where are you taking me?"

"To a deserted island where it will be just we two and we'll swim in the turquoise water."

"But I don't have a swimsuit."

"You won't need one, sweetheart," Jack replied kissing her before steering the boat out into the Gulf.

It was the most perfect day Mel had ever spent. To her surprise Jack was an accomplished sailor. He was an enigma, this man. Was there nothing he couldn't do? She was falling in love with him and she couldn't help herself. They sailed out to a tiny island and disembarked.

He immediately stripped off his clothes and stood naked, totally at ease and unembarrassed as he let the hot sun warm his skin.

"Come on," he said to her. "Aren't you coming in for a swim?" He ran naked into the crystal-clear turquoise water.

She stood feeling awkward and then, looking around to make sure there was no one else around, she too stripped off and ran self-consciously down to the water's edge to join him. The water was warmer than she'd expected and she dived in and swam out to him. It felt exhilarating and very sensuous to be swimming naked and she felt as free as a bird.

Jack took her in his arms and started caressing her and kissing her body. It was wildly exciting. He then lifted her up so that her legs were around his waist. She was so hot that she thought she was going to explode. He must have felt the same because he took her right there and then as the turquoise water lapped around their naked bodies. She almost died with pleasure. Then he carried her out of the water and lay her down gently on the fine sand. They were both breathless. Mel thought she'd died and gone to heaven. She never wanted to leave this magical place.

After they'd dried off in the sun, Jack carried an icebox from the boat and, handing her a cool beer, spread out a picnic of bread and dips with shrimp and chicken wings, followed by fresh pineapple and grapes.

"Not exactly what you're used to," he said, biting into a chicken wing.

"It's the most romantic meal I've ever had," she replied, kissing him, tasting the salt from the sea on his lips.

They sat wrapped together in a huge beach towel as they ate. Then Mel lay down with her head in his lap and he fed her the grapes and pineapple. She was totally naked but it felt like the most natural thing in the world. Her previous inhibitions had disappeared. She would have stayed there forever but sadly the day had to end and they were both quiet as they headed for home.

"That was a very special day," Jack said as he pulled up at Lexi's house.

"I'll never forget it, as long as I live," she told him and she knew it was true.

Neither of them wanted to part but eventually he had to leave and, missing him already, she walked in to meet her friends.

* * *

Brenda had been in bad form all afternoon and Lexi knew it had something to do with Bob. Although Brenda had received calls from her kids and family all day long, wishing her a happy birthday, Lexi suspected that Bob was not among the callers. Eventually, while they had been relaxing alone by the pool in the late afternoon, Lexi asked her outright.

"Have you heard from Bob today?"

"No. I can't believe he's being this childish. It's ten o'clock at night in Ireland now but he still hasn't called to wish me a happy birthday. That's the first time in twenty-five years that's happened." She sounded glum.

"Tell me about it," Lexi said, reaching for Brenda's hand. Although they were all close, Lexi had always had a special bond with Brenda. She was the sister Lexi never had and she loved her dearly.

"Where do I start?" Brenda wondered. "I loved Bob so much but we seem to have grown apart over the years. I was so occupied with the kids and my younger brothers and sisters that I didn't notice, or if I did, I was just too busy to do anything about it." She grimaced. "That was probably a big mistake."

Lexi patted her hand. "How could you have, with all the responsibilities you had on your shoulders?"

"I guess. Bob never was great with responsibility and he

didn't have the ambitions that I had for the children. I wanted them to fulfil their potential, something I never did, but Bob didn't understand. We had endless rows over it."

Lexi was heartbroken for her.

"To be honest, I feel like I've outgrown him and I can't see any way forward. We're just two different people now from the people we were twenty years ago. I never thought I'd say it but I guess we married much too young."

"I don't know what to say. What are you going to do about it?"

"I don't know. I'm so afraid. He doesn't want to make love to me any more and he won't talk about it. I can't even remember the last time we made love, it's been so long." Brenda felt the tears come to her eyes as she voiced her worst fear.

"Oh honey, I'm so sorry," Lexi said sadly, taking Brenda's hand. "That must be difficult."

"It is. Our sex life was always good and I'm missing it now and feeling frustrated all the time. I wonder if it's my fault that he finds me undesirable and unattractive. I miss the intimacy. It's as if there's a huge chasm between us and I don't know how to bridge it." She swallowed hard, trying not to cry, but it was difficult and a tear slid down her cheek.

"That's terrible and trust me, you are desirable and attractive. Troy certainly agrees with me there."

Brenda smiled. "He has boosted my confidence, I have to admit."

"It sounds like you and Bob don't communicate any more which is the most important thing in a relationship. You absolutely have to get him to talk about the problem."

"I have tried but it's hopeless. He adamantly refuses to discuss it. I will try one more time but if he won't communicate with me then I guess our marriage will be over. I can't go on like this."

"All I can advise is that life is so short, you must live every moment to the full."

"You know, Troy said the same thing to me the first night we met."

"He's right. I, more than anyone, know how quickly it can be snatched away."

"You certainly do," Brenda replied as she wiped a tear away. "Why is life so damn difficult?"

"I really think you have to thrash this out with Bob as soon as possible. You can't let it fester on like this."

Brenda nodded. She knew Lexi was right.

* * *

Mel returned home to find Lexi and Brenda in a sombre mood.

"What's up?" she asked, worried that something had happened while she had been having such a wonderful day.

"Nothing to worry about . . . well, I mean, it's just Angel. She refused to get out of bed at all today. I tried to bring up the subject of her drinking but she wouldn't listen," Lexi explained. "She's in a bad way, Mel. She needs professional help but I don't know how we can get her to go for it. Brenda and I are so worried about her."

"Oh lord! Sorry I wasn't here to help."

"You couldn't have helped. No one could get through to her, the state she's in. She's been sleeping all day."

"I'm not surprised after all she drank last night. Is there nothing we can do about it?" Mel asked in a worried voice. Yes, she'd been really angry with Angel last night but they'd been friends for so long and if Angel needed help then she could count on her.

"I don't know. We'll have to put our heads together and come up with a solution."

116

"Well, you look like you had a good day," Brenda observed, changing the subject.

"I did. I had a wonderful day. Today's your birthday, Brenda. Happy birthday! I hope you had a great day."

"Every day's a great day here," Brenda replied, smiling. "But I suspect you had an even better day," she remarked, noting Mel's tanned skin and the glow in her eyes.

"It was like a dream. The best day of my life," Mel admitted breathlessly.

"I hope you're not falling for him, sweetie. I don't think Jack is a guy to be tied down," Lexi warned.

Mel didn't reply but looked downcast which made Lexi fear the worst.

"Well, go and get changed quickly," she instructed Mel. "We've been invited to Marvin's for a barbeque in fifteen minutes."

"Oh great! But what about Angel?"

"No, she won't come. She's taken some sleeping pills so I reckon she'll be out for the count till morning. We'll have to decide what to do about her tomorrow. In the meantime you'd better go get changed or we'll be late."

"I expect to hear all about today in detail later," Brenda said as they stood up.

"Ooooh, you'd never believe it if I told you," Mel pronounced as she skipped out and ran up the stairs.

"I can well believe it!" Lexi called after her, grinning.

"Lucky Mel!" Brenda said enviously as she left to go upstairs and grab her bag.

Lexi looked after her worriedly, a frown on her face. Lordy, she thought to herself as she waited for them to come down, this birthday week is turning into something of a nightmare. Things were not going according to plan. Angel's problem would have to be dealt with immediately and then there was Mel's inevitable heartbreak when she and Jack would have to say goodbye. There was no way that was going to work out! And it was now obvious that Brenda's marriage was in trouble. If only things were as straightforward now as they'd been when they were kids! Life had been so simple then.

* * *

Thinking over her conversation with Lexi, Brenda decided, on the spur of the moment, to call Bob. She checked her watch. It would be eleven in Ireland now.

She dialled the home number with trepidation. It rang and rang but there was no reply. She tried his mobile number but it went to voice message. She hung up without leaving a message. Where the hell was he?

* * *

Mel checked in on Angel who was, as Lexi had said, out for the count. Mel spoke to her softly but Angel did not respond. When Mel saw the bottle of Ambien on her bedside table she understood why. It was the strongest sleeping pill available and was also addictive. There was also some Prozac. She wondered if Angel was taking them regularly on top of alcohol. If so, then her friend really was in trouble. She debated whether to mention it to Lexi and Brenda. Better leave it till tomorrow, she decided.

They left for the barbeque, Lexi having left instructions with Maria that she was to call Marvin's number if Angel should wake up.

* * *

The three girls linked arms as they made their way up Marvin's driveway.

"Wow!" Brenda exclaimed as she spotted the mansion rising up before her.

"Wow again! My lord, Lexi, that is some house!" Mel cried.

"You just think it's huge because even the largest apartments in Manhattan are like a shoebox in comparison to the houses down here and they're more expensive!" Lexi laughed.

"I'm not surprised Troy wants to relocate from New York to here," Brenda remarked.

"Maybe he has a point," Mel agreed as Marvin answered the door, an apron over his shirt and jeans.

"Welcome, lovely ladies," he bowed as he showed them in. "Aren't we missing someone? Where's Angel?"

"She's not feeling well and went to bed," Lexi told him.

He didn't say anything but raised his eyebrows. In a way he was relieved. It would be more relaxed and easy without her. A true diva, she clearly thrived on drama which could be very tiring at times. Marvin preferred the quiet life. He led them through the house to the lanai out back where Troy, also wearing an apron, was bent over the barbeque.

"What is it with men and barbeques?" Brenda asked as he kissed her cheek.

"Yeah, they don't know how to boil an egg but won't let anyone else get a look-in when it comes to cooking outdoors," Mel declared.

"I'm not complaining," Lexi said, sinking into the soft white leather chair.

* * *

It was a brilliant night and there was much laughter and fun as they enjoyed the delicious barbeque the two guys had cooked up. They had grilled rib-eye steaks and corn-on-the-cob, served with loaded baked potatoes which they explained to Brenda meant butter, sour cream, bacon bits and cheese.

"My God, how fattening!" she cried, yet she ate every morsel of them as they were so delicious.

All this was accompanied by Troy's signature salad which they all agreed was unique. He took the teasing with good humour.

When Marvin heard that Mel had spent the day with Jack, he said, "You should have brought him along. There's more than enough food here."

"Ah, thank you, Marvin, but he couldn't come. He's working this evening," Mel told him.

"Maybe, if he's free tomorrow, he'd like to come out on the boat with us," Troy suggested.

"Uh-oh, sorry, Mel, I didn't tell you that Troy is taking us out on his yacht tomorrow," Lexi explained.

"Thanks anyway but Jack has plans for tomorrow. He's promised to help a friend paint his boat," she informed Troy, grateful that he'd thought to include Jack.

* * *

When they'd finished eating Mel went out on to the beach to have a smoke. She texted Jack: **Thanks for a wonderful day. Wish you were here. Love, Mel.**

Meanwhile, Marvin had taken Lexi into the house to show her what he'd done with her computer and Brenda found herself alone with Troy.

"It's so great to have you here tonight," he said, taking her hand. "Happy birthday, sweetie."

Brenda blushed prettily. "How did you know it was my birthday?"

"Ah, a little birdie told me," he laughed. He then produced

a velvet box from his pocket and held it out to her. "This is a little something I got for you."

She was taken aback. "Oh, I feel embarrassed now. You really shouldn't have –"

"I wanted to. Please take it," he said, pressing it in to her hand.

She opened the box and gasped when she saw the gold chain with the small palm tree hanging from it. In the centre of the palm was a lustrous green stone.

"Oh, I couldn't possibly accept this," she stammered.

"Of course you can. It's a small birthday gift and I hope when you're back in Ireland you'll wear it and think of us here."

Brenda was overwhelmed. She had a lump in her throat as she said, "This is the nicest thing anyone has ever given me. Thank you." She reached forward to give him a kiss on the cheek but somehow they ended up having a real full-blown kiss. She pulled away breathlessly, shocked at what had just happened but aware of how much she'd enjoyed it. Seeing the desire in Troy's eyes she knew he felt the same way but she quickly came down to earth with a bang. Okay, so Bob hadn't so much as called her to wish her a happy birthday but he was still her husband and getting involved with another man was wrong. Flustered, she excused herself and ran to the bathroom. Breathing deeply, she tried to gather her composure and after a few minutes managed to calm down. She was shocked at her behaviour but even more shocked at the passion that kiss had aroused in her. Troy made her feel sexy and attractive again and kindled feelings she'd thought were gone forever. There was no doubt she and Bob had problems but getting involved with another man was not the way to fix them, however attractive he was. Still, it was exciting to feel alive and desirable again. It made her realise that the time had come to address the issues in her marriage.

Luckily, when she got back, the others had returned and it was time to leave. She avoided Troy's eyes as she said goodnight. When she got home she tried to call Bob once more. She didn't care that it was now three o'clock in the morning in Ireland. She rang him anyway, thinking that at least he'd be home now. However, once again the phone rang and rang with no reply. She replaced the receiver angrily. Where on earth could he be at this hour of the morning? Frustrated and lonely she went to bed but sleep evaded her. All she could think of was the fire in Troy's kiss and the longing it had awakened in her.

Chapter 16

Lexi was more than surprised to see Angel appear the following morning as she was having breakfast on the terrace with Brenda and Mel. It was the earliest Angel had ever been up.

"Good morning, all," she said breezily as she helped herself to some coffee.

The others were dumbfounded. She was her usual self, full of the joys of spring.

"Well, it is a surprise to see you out and about so early," Lexi observed. "How are you feeling?"

"Much better, honey. I guess I must have eaten a dodgy shrimp the other night."

The three women looked at each other in amazement. Angel was obviously going to blame the crustacean for her disposition of the day before.

"Well, what's on the agenda today?" she enquired, smiling at them.

"Troy has invited us out on his yacht this morning and we'll have lunch on board. Will you be up to it, do you think?" Lexi asked.

"But of course. I wouldn't miss it for the world. Troy is a fabulous guy and I quite fancy him. I have big plans for him." She winked at them. "I'm really looking forward to seeing this yacht of his."

Mel shook her head and threw a disgusted look at Brenda. Angel was behaving as though everything was normal. There was no way they could have any kind of discussion with her about her drinking as long as she was in denial about her problem.

"By the way, Kenny has been calling wanting to talk to you."

"Kenny?" Angel asked, her face blank. She screwed up her eyes as she tried to remember who he was. "Oh yes, Kenny," she said. "He's a bit old for me, isn't he?"

Mel shook her head in disgust.

"Anyway, what time are we meeting up with Troy this morning?" Angel wanted to know.

"Nine fifteen in the marina. We leave here at nine."

Angel looked at her watch. "Gosh, I'd better go and get ready." She knocked back her coffee and jumped up.

"Won't you have some breakfast?" Lexi asked her.

"The coffee was my breakfast," Angel replied, blowing her a kiss before skipping away in through the French doors and up the stairs.

Lexi looked at the other two helplessly. "I don't know how she can survive. She didn't eat a thing all day yesterday. She has to eat."

"Yeah, well, people who survive on alcohol and drugs rarely bother eating."

"Drugs!" Brenda and Lexi exclaimed together.

"You're not saying she's on drugs?" Brenda asked anxiously.

"Well, I noticed Ambien on her bedside table last night and

I also saw some Prozac. That combination along with alcohol is lethal. It's no wonder she was so out of it the other night."

"My God, if that's the case it's worse than I thought," Lexi said in an anguished voice.

"Maybe we'll get a chance to talk to her today," Brenda suggested.

"Maybe, but I doubt she'll listen," Mel said resignedly.

* * *

Lexi, Mel and Brenda were all gathered in the foyer before nine but there was no sign of Angel even when the hour passed. She eventually made her entrance five minutes later looking as if she was on her way to a photo-shoot for the cover of the swimsuit edition of *Sports Illustrated*. She was wearing a tiny white bikini top which barely covered her ample assets and a white and gold chiffon wrap skirt which no doubt was covering an equally skimpy bikini bottom. She was wearing full make-up and her gold and crystal bead necklaces and bracelets all jangled as she walked. She was perched on a pair of gold platform sandals and sported a Michael Kors gold tote bag, huge Prada sunglasses and a big floppy white hat.

The other three gaped at her in silence before Mel finally burst out laughing.

"Where in the name of God do you think you're going in that get-up?" she asked Angel. Mel herself was dressed in a pair of cut-off denim shorts, an oversized check shirt and flip-flops.

"Don't look at me like that," Angel replied in a hurt voice. "One has to dress appropriately on yachts."

"It's not the *Christina* or *Britannia* you're sailing on, it's just a normal yacht. I doubt Troy and Marvin will be dressed as appropriately as you expect," Lexi remarked. "Come on, we're late. Let's get a move-on."

As Angel minced out to the car, Mel threw her eyes to heaven causing Brenda to giggle. This was going to be some day!

* * *

Angel had the same effect on the two men as she'd had on her three friends. They stared at her disbelievingly, their mouths open. Troy was in shorts and had no top on while Marvin was in jeans and a T-shirt. Both men were wearing flip-flops.

"I'm afraid this is not the *Eclipse*, Angel," Troy said as he helped her aboard the *Aurore*. "I'm not quite as wealthy as Roman Abramovich."

"Nonsense," she giggled, "this is a lovely yacht. It's bigger than Lexi led me to expect." In truth she was so busy eyeing Troy's toned body that she hadn't paid much attention to the seventy-five-foot boat. Looking around now she noted that it was quite luxurious despite Troy's casual dress. It would have been nice if he'd been dressed in a navy blazer and white trousers with deck shoes but then she'd have missed those glorious pecs. She guessed he must work out every day.

Brenda's eyes were out on sticks as she gazed at the beautiful yacht. She'd never seen anything like it. There was certainly nothing in Dun Laoghaire harbour to match it. As Troy helped her aboard she avoided his eyes but couldn't help blushing. He squeezed her hand and she felt her heart race but refused to catch his eye. She hoped this wasn't going to be awkward but she was determined to keep him at arm's length. However, she couldn't help but notice his tanned athletic body and admire his taut muscular physique. For a brief second she wondered what it would be like to lie against that smooth skin but immediately pushed that thought to the back of her mind. This was dangerous territory.

Mel was equally impressed as he showed them around his yacht. It was all maple wood and white leather and when he showed them the master stateroom with its king-size bed and marble en-suite bathroom they gasped with awe.

"I bet that bed has seen some action," Angel said in a seductive voice.

"I'm afraid not," Troy replied. "I only have this boat about a year and my last relationship ended two years ago."

"Well, I wouldn't mind spending a night in this gorgeous bed," Angel purred, rubbing his arm and leaving him in no doubt as to what she meant.

Troy looked discomfited but said nothing. Mel threw her eyes to heaven as she glanced at Brenda. Neither of them could believe Angel's brazenness.

Before they set out Troy opened a bottle of champagne, adding fresh orange juice to their glasses, and they toasted the *Aurore* before heading out of the marina. They were all in high spirits and looking forward to the trip.

"I could get used to this life," Mel said as they sipped the lovely Buck's Fizz.

"I never could, I'm afraid," Brenda confessed. "It's so different to my lifestyle that it would always feel decadent."

"I must say it's very impressive," Angel said as she ran her hand over the polished rail. "This boat must have cost you a fortune, Troy."

"Well, I was lucky. As I'm in the business I snapped it up for a mil before anyone else had a chance to see it." He laughed as he threw back the last of his champagne. "Well, ladies, if you'll excuse me, I have a boat to run."

He and Marvin went afore to manoeuvre the boat out of the marina.

"Did he mean a million dollars?" Brenda asked in a low voice.

"He did indeed," Mel replied.

"And it was a steal," Lexi laughed, seeing Brenda's gobsmacked look.

"Wow!" was her flabbergasted response.

* * *

Finally they were out in the gulf and it was glorious sailing along with the soft wind in their faces. Marvin had come back to join them and the girls leaned over the rail as Marvin pointed out the sights of the Florida coastline. Brenda was relieved that Troy was at the wheel so she could avoid him if necessary. She didn't trust her own feelings when she was around him.

Marvin opened another bottle of champagne but Angel was the only taker.

"I don't want to get drunk and miss this wonderful experience," Brenda declared.

As they moved south towards St Petersburg the girls stripped off their shorts and tops down to their bikinis. As expected, Angel's bikini bottom was no more than a miniscule slip of material. There was no doubt about it, she had a sensational body.

"I can't sit in the sun," Angel announced, wrinkling up her pert nose. "I'm going up front to sit under the awning. I'm sure Troy will be happy with the company," she added as she sashayed barefoot up the deck. Troy had insisted she take off those ridiculous stilettos.

"I'm sure he will," Mel replied sarcastically.

Brenda felt a pang of jealousy. She feared Troy couldn't but be attracted to Angel's obvious charms and take her up on her previous offer. It was obvious she'd set her cap at him.

"You have to hand it to her," Mel remarked, "that girl has chutzpah by the bucketful."

Angel was back a moment later and grabbed the bottle of champagne. "If you gals want another glass just holler." She returned to the front of the boat clutching the bottle of champagne.

The other three exchanged worried glances.

"I hope it's not going to be a repeat of the birthday party," Mel commented.

"Oh dear," Lexi sighed. "I had really hoped to have a chat with her today."

"Don't bet on it," Mel said harshly.

She and Brenda climbed up to the upper deck where they found leather sunbeds with beach towels laid out on them.

"How thoughtful of Troy to provide towels as well," Brenda observed.

"He really is a terrific guy," Mel agreed. "I'm sure he has women throwing themselves at him all the time just like Angel back there."

Brenda felt that jealous pang again and busied herself applying sun cream. They lay on the sunbeds, enjoying the heat of the sun on their bodies. Lexi and Marvin stayed down on the lower deck, chatting quietly.

"I'm rather glad Jack is not here today," Mel said as she turned her face to the sun. "I guess even the saintliest saint, whoever he may be, could not resist Angel in that bikini."

This made Brenda feel more jealous still. She wondered what was going on up front between Troy and Angel. "I'm dying to hear all about yesterday. Was it fabulous?" she asked Mel.

Mel sat up on one elbow, her eyes glowing. "You have no idea, Brenda. Jack is wonderful. He's simply fascinating and so exciting."

"And the sex?"

"Unbelievable! We can't get enough of each other. I've

never felt like that about anyone before. Never!"

"Gosh, Mel, that's great but what happens when you leave?"

"I don't know. I'm afraid to think about it."

Her voice was so forlorn that Brenda sat up and turned to her. "You've really fallen hard for him, haven't you?"

"I afraid so. I'm hoping that he might come to New York." Mel's voice was quiet yet hopeful and Brenda's heart went out to her.

"I'm not sure that's in his plans, Mel. Have you talked to him about it?"

"No," Mel whispered, "I'm afraid of what he might say."

"You poor baby," Brenda said, reaching for Mel's hand as she would have done to her own daughters. "Life is a bitch," she sighed, "especially where love is concerned."

Mel heard the dejection in Brenda's voice and looked at her quizzically. "Don't tell me you're having problems," she cried. "I thought you had the perfect marriage."

"I'm afraid not. It's very rocky at the moment."

She went on to tell Mel what she'd already told Lexi about her life with Bob. "I've been afraid to face it but once I voiced it aloud to Lexi, I realised it was time to confront the problem head on. I don't know what's going on with Bob. I've been trying to contact him but he won't answer the phone. He's annoyed with me for coming here."

"I'm so sorry to hear that," Mel said gently. "What can you do about it?"

"I don't know. I honestly don't. I have to try to get through to him and break down this barrier between us, I suppose. Otherwise it's curtains."

At that moment Marvin called them to come to the front of the boat to show them Caladesi Island where they would dock after lunch. It was an idyllic island with miles of almost deserted, pristine-white beach framed by palm trees.

"It's beautiful," Brenda said with awe.

"Would you like to take the wheel?" Troy asked her.

"Could I?"

"Of course. Come here, it's easy."

She moved in to the wheel and Troy put his arms around her from behind, placing her hands on the wheel. She was aware of his closeness and exhilarated as she felt the boat surge beneath her hands. For a brief moment she felt like Kate Winslet in *Titanic* and she leaned back into Troy's body.

"It's a good feeling, isn't it?" he asked and she wondered if he knew what she was thinking. She could have stayed there forever.

It was Angel who broke the spell. "Can I have a go too?" she squealed as she jumped up and down, her big boobs bouncing and threatening to escape her bikini top. The champagne was obviously kicking in.

Reluctantly Troy agreed and let go of Brenda. Angel moved in to the wheel, smiling seductively at him as she pressed her body to his. Brenda felt a flash of jealousy as she saw Troy put his arms around Angel, then relief when after a few moments he released her.

He smiled across at Brenda and winked at her.

"Just look, she has practically finished that bottle of champagne," Mel whispered to Brenda, pointing to the almost-empty bottle.

"My God! And it's not even noon yet."

"I guess we're in for a long day," Mel muttered.

* * *

They headed south, admiring the beaches and islands they passed along the way. At around midday Troy dropped anchor and they gathered under the awning at the rear of the boat where Marvin had prepared a large jug of margaritas. It was a happy group that finally sat down to lunch which was served below in the lovely air-conditioned dining room. Brenda was amazed to see silver cutlery and crystal glasses on the pristine white tablecloth. This was a world away from her real life and she didn't know how she would ever come down from it. She wondered what it would be like to live like this all the time. As always, Angel ate very little but drank copiously of the wine on offer as she flirted with Troy. He didn't respond to her advances which puzzled her. She wasn't used to men ignoring her.

After an extended lunch, they set off back towards Caladesi Island. There Troy berthed the boat in the marina and they made their way to the glorious beach.

"This is like something from a travel brochure," Brenda observed as she stopped to admire the view. It reminded her of photos she'd seen of the Maldives or Seychelles.

"It really is beautiful," Lexi agreed. "It was voted the number one beach in America in 2008."

"I'm not surprised," Brenda said as she felt the soft white sand beneath her feet.

Troy fell into step beside her as they walked to the hut to rent sunbeds.

"I've a feeling you've been avoiding me. I'm sorry if I offended you last night," he said in a low voice. "I was out of order. I promise it won't happen again. Am I forgiven?"

"Of course," she smiled. It was impossible to resist his charm but she would be careful not to be alone with him. It wasn't that she didn't trust him – she didn't trust herself.

* * *

Angel slept on a sunbed in the shade of a palm tree while the

132

others swam in the crystal blue sea. It was glorious and afterwards they played a game of frisbee. Lexi opted out and went to sit under the shade beside Angel, who had just woken up.

"Angel, we have to have a talk."

"What about?" Angel asked, her voice wary.

"About your drinking. You are drinking far too much and –"

"No, I will not discuss it," Angel cried, putting her hands over her ears as she'd always done as a child when she didn't want to talk about something.

"Angel . . ." Lexi continued, pulling her hands down, "we have to talk about it. I only want to help. We're worried about you."

"Well, you needn't be. I'm fine. Leave me alone." She jumped up and stalked off down the beach. Lexi looked after her helplessly. How could she get through to her? It was obvious Angel needed professional help.

* * *

They arrived back in Clearwater just before sunset. Angel was sullen and refused to join in the conversation despite Lexi's best attempts to include her. Troy dropped anchor off the coast and they stood at the rail, sipping margaritas as they watched the huge orange ball of the sun dip into the ocean. It was very romantic and Mel wished Jack was there with her to share it. Marvin had his arm around Lexi's shoulders as they enjoyed the moment and when Troy slipped his arm around Brenda's shoulder she didn't pull it away.

Angel saw this and it angered her. No wonder Troy hadn't responded to her advances. He had the hots for Brenda who already had a husband. It was so unfair and made her more depressed than ever.

Chapter 17

It was just past seven when they got home and Brenda went up to her room to call Bob. He would surely be there now as it was midnight in Ireland. She was relieved when he answered the phone.

"Bob, I got you at last," she said, trying to keep her voice light and not sound accusing. "I've been trying to call you for days but you haven't been answering my calls."

"I've been busy. You don't expect me to sit in waiting for you to ring me?"

She was taken aback by his curt tone. "Of course not. I was just worried about you."

"I'm sure!"

Brenda heard what she thought was a voice in the background. "Is there someone there with you?"

"No. It's . . . erm . . . the television. Hang on a second."

She heard a door closing and he resumed talking. It was all very strange. "Well, I take it you're having a good time," he said.

"Yes, it has been great. We went out on a yacht today with

Lexi's friends. It was wonderful. How about you? What have you been doing?"

"Not swanning around on a yacht, that's for sure! Friends have had me for dinner most evenings. They're feeling sorry for me."

Brenda wondered who he was talking about. "What friends?"

"Oh, you know," he replied vaguely.

"But Bob, I've left enough dinners for you in the freezer."

"It's not much fun eating alone, is it?"

Brenda heard the bitterness in his voice. So he was still resentful of her having this holiday. She was about to chastise him for not ringing to wish her a happy birthday when she thought she heard a door open at his end.

"Sorry, I have to go, Brenda. Goodnight."

She sat staring at the phone not believing that he had hung up on her. She was convinced that there was someone else in the house with him. She hoped to God he hadn't started playing poker again.

Bob had been an inveterate gambler many years ago which had brought them to the brink of bankruptcy but after a spell with Gamblers Anonymous, he had quit and promised never to play again. So far he'd kept his word but now she was worried that because of her trip here he had started playing again. She hoped this was not the case. She couldn't go through all that again. She felt helpless but there was nothing she could do about it from the other side of the Atlantic.

Was this his revenge for her trip to Florida? She hoped not. She took a quick shower and slipped on some shorts and a T-shirt before going downstairs to have a light supper with the girls.

"Where's Angel?" she asked, as they sat down to supper.

"Gone to bed," Lexi replied.

"Drunk of course," Mel said cattily.

"I tried to talk to her about it today but she stalked off and wouldn't discuss it," Lexi said, a worried frown on her face. "I don't know how we can get through to her."

"Maybe if Brenda had a word with her?" Mel suggested.

"If Lexi can't get through to her then I doubt I could."

"How about if we all tackle her together then?" Mel said.

"It's worth a try, I suppose," Lexi said thoughtfully. "Better leave it till Friday. We don't want to spoil Thanksgiving tomorrow."

"Agreed!" Mel and Brenda chorused together.

* * *

Thanksgiving dawned bright and sunny. Mel and Brenda joined Lexi in the pool that morning.

"Happy Thanksgiving!" Lexi called out to them as they entered the water. Brenda had never celebrated this holiday before but thought it was a lovely tradition. To give thanks for all the good things in your life was a lovely idea. People travelled from far and wide to spend it with their families. Thanksgiving dinner was seemingly like the Irish Christmas dinner with turkey and cranberry sauce and lots of side dishes. The only difference was that it was followed by pumpkin pie instead of Christmas pudding. She was really looking forward to it.

After their swim, they showered and dressed and Lexi got busy cooking up a real Irish breakfast with the goodies Brenda had brought with her from Ireland.

"Mmmm . . . that smells divine," Mel cried, coming into the kitchen. "Makes me feel quite homesick for Ireland."

They helped Lexi carry the dishes of eggs, Denny's bacon and sausages, Clonakilty pudding and potato cakes to the table. Lexi had given Maria and Pablo the day off so they could spend it with their family.

"What about Angel?" Brenda asked. "Shouldn't we wait for her?"

"We'd have to wait till lunchtime," Mel commented.

"I'd put some by for her but I don't think she'd eat it," said Lexi. "She never eats breakfast. In fact, she never eats at all."

"I don't know how she can sleep so long," Brenda observed. "How does she do it?"

"With a lot of chemical help, I imagine," Mel replied. "Mmmm . . . these sausages are to die for. Are you not having any, Brenda?"

"I'd feel guilty taking them when I can have them every day at home. I'll leave them for you guys."

"Don't be silly – have some, there's plenty," Lexi insisted. "It's Thanksgiving after all."

"I'll take one so," Brenda succumbed, putting the smallest one on her plate.

"Great, I'll have your other ones in a sambo for lunch," Mel said, licking her lips at the thought.

* * *

The three of them spent the morning in the kitchen preparing the food for the dinner that evening. It was after one o'clock and they had stopped to have some lunch when Angel put in an appearance.

"Mmmm . . . something smells good here," she declared as she came into the kitchen.

"The turkey has just gone in the oven," Lexi said.

"Oh I forgot, it's Thanksgiving, isn't it?" Angel sighed.

"Yes, you missed a great Irish breakfast this morning," Mel informed her.

"I can cook some for you now if you like?" Lexi offered.

"Or why don't you have a sausage sandwich? Mel is heating some up now."

"Okay, maybe I'll have a sausage sandwich," Angel consented, much to Mel's disappointment.

"And I have something special, seeing as how it's Thanksgiving," Lexi announced.

They looked at her curious to know what it was. "Ta-da!" she cried producing the packets of Tayto Brenda had brought with her.

"Oh my God, Tayto!" Mel and Angel squealed, grabbing a packet each.

Even Angel wolfed hers down in jig-time.

"So who's coming to dinner tonight?" Angel asked as she rummaged in the bag to make sure she had not left a single crumb of crisp behind.

"Well, there'll be the four of us, Marvin and Troy, Jack and Kenny." Lexi told her. "Just the eight of us."

"How cosy! I take it Kenny is there for me? To even up the numbers." She was still disconcerted that Troy had been immune to her charms and preferred Brenda to her. She was worried that she was losing her touch.

"No, actually, I've invited him because he has no family here and he's a good friend."

Angel heard the rebuke in Lexi's voice and stayed quiet.

"You know, Angel, he's a terrific guy and he's very taken with you," Lexi said. "You could at least give him a chance."

Angel pulled a face on hearing this. "He's not my type," she replied.

That afternoon while Mel and Brenda were busy helping Lexi, Angel sat in the shade on the terrace playing with her iPad.

"God, she makes me sick!" Mel spoke vehemently after Angel had breezed in and helped herself to a glass of wine from the fridge. "You'd think she'd offer to help."

"Too many cooks spoil the broth," Lexi said, hoping to calm her down, "and I think three cooks in the kitchen is enough, don't you?"

"I don't think Angel is big into cooking," Brenda joined in.

"Probably not but she could offer," Mel said, still disgruntled.

By five o'clock all was ready and they collapsed on the sofa and sipped the glasses of wine Lexi had poured for them. They then went up to shower and change before the guests arrived. Brenda had ditched the bath now in favour of the shower. There was so much to do here that she rarely had the time to take a bath any more. She changed into the red Ralph Lauren silk jersey dress that she'd worn the first night she'd met Troy. Her tan was deeper now and her hair more blonde so the dress looked even more stunning than before.

She was putting the finishing touches to her make-up when she heard a knock on her door. It was Angel.

"Hi, sweetie, I've mislaid my brown eye-shadow. Would you happen to have . . ." She stopped in her tracks as she looked at Brenda. "Wow! You look fabulous in that dress but the shoes are wrong. You need red shoes to go with it. I think we're about the same size, if I remember. You're a four-and-a-half Irish, aren't you? That's a seven American. Let me go and get my red shoes."

"No, honestly, these black ones will do."

"They will not do! My red ones will look so much better."

She hurried away and was back two minutes later with the gorgeous red shoes she'd worn the night of the party.

"They're beautiful," Brenda murmured as she stroked the wide jewelled ankle strap.

"Come on, try them on," Angel insisted, pushing Brenda down on the chair and putting the shoes on her.

"Look!" she said with a flourish. "They're perfect!"

Brenda had to agree with her. They were indeed perfect. She twirled in front of the mirror. "Oh God, Angel, they're divine. Are you sure?"

"Of course I'm sure. I've got tired of them anyway. You can keep them. They look great with that dress."

"Oh, I couldn't possibly –"

"Look, just give me some brown eye-shadow and we'll call it quits."

Brenda handed over her eye-shadow thinking that she'd definitely got the best out of this deal. Angel had always been very generous and that obviously hadn't changed. Brenda was in love with these shoes with the red soles. They were the most beautiful things she'd ever seen and made her feel extremely sexy. As she came down the stairs to celebrate her first Thanksgiving she was walking on air.

Everyone had dressed up for the occasion and it was a very smart group who toasted each other with champagne and sampled the delicious hors d'oeuvres the girls had prepared that afternoon. Even Jack had made an effort and was wearing a white linen suit with a navy shirt. He had drawn a line at wearing a tie.

Mel thought he looked more handsome than ever and was holding on to his arm as they chatted to the others. Angel was, as always, wearing a figure-hugging dress with a low neckline and Kenny couldn't keep his eyes off her. He was obviously smitten with her but she was much more interested in Jack, much to Kenny and Mel's chagrin. Mel wished that Jack would have ignored Angel's flirting but he seemed to be enjoying it. She even caught him gazing at Angel's cleavage as he laughed at something she'd said.

It was time to go to the table and Lexi had really outdone herself. The dining-room was candlelit and she had brought out the Waterford crystal and Irish silver. It was very romantic. Mel was not happy to see that Angel was sitting on the other side of Jack but there was nothing she could do about it. Before dinner they all held hands and each one had to give thanks for the good things in their life. It was a lovely tradition and Brenda decided she would instigate it in her own home this Christmas. There was a lot of love around the table and each one of them acknowledged how grateful they were for their friends.

The dinner was fabulous and there was a lot of laughter. Angel was in top form and kept everyone amused with her stories. She had a natural gift as a raconteur and Mel was perturbed to see that she continued flirting with Jack who didn't appear to discourage her. Mel was soon feeling miserable and very insecure knowing she couldn't hope to compete with Angel. She was relieved when the main course was over and she could get Jack alone.

"Why didn't you tell Angel to go take a jump?" she asked him as they went outside for a cigarette.

"Why should I?" He laughed. "She's very amusing."

"Well, it was disgusting the way she was flirting with you. I think you could have discouraged her." She knew she sounded petulant.

"Don't be silly! She flirts with every man. Actually, she's good company when she's not drunk."

"Which is hardly ever," Mel replied bitterly.

"Hey, isn't she meant to be your friend?"

"Yes, but friends don't behave like that."

"Don't tell me you're jealous, Mel," he said, looking at her warily. "I didn't take you for the possessive type."

"It's just that I love you so much," she replied, tears coming to her eyes.

Jack looked thoughtful and didn't reply.

He had never met a girl like Mel before. He'd had lots of flings but no girl had ever got under his skin like she had. That worried him and he knew now that he should have split sooner and not let her get too involved with him. Now she was saying that she loved him. Christ! What was he going to do? He wasn't ready to settle down. He still had places he wanted to see. He was perplexed and wondered how he could extricate himself from this situation. He dragged deeply on his cigarette as he considered it.

Mel waited for him to say he loved her too but he was silent.

"Let's go back inside," was all he said as he stubbed out his cigarette.

She was upset with his reaction. He hadn't even tried to assuage her fears. Jack was very quiet for the rest of the meal and when it was over he thanked Lexi graciously and said he was sorry but he'd have to leave.

Mel went into the garden with him, expecting him to ask her to go back and stay the night with him.

Instead he said, "Look, Mel, I have an early start in the morning. I need to get going now. I really enjoyed the evening."

He kissed her briefly and she stared at him panic-stricken.

"What's happened? What did I do wrong?" she asked. "It's Angel, isn't it? It's all her fault."

"Don't be ridiculous, of course it isn't. Lighten up, Mel. I have to go. Goodnight." He turned from her and walked away.

She longed to run after him but she knew it would do no good. He'd had a steely look in his eyes that she hadn't seen before and it scared her. She went down to the beach and sat hugging her knees as she sobbed her heart out.

When she got back inside the other guests had gone and Lexi, Brenda and Angel were curled up on the sofas in the lounge.

"What's wrong?" Lexi asked, seeing Mel's tear-streaked cheeks.

"She's what's wrong," Mel cried, pointing a finger at Angel.

"What do you mean?" Angel asked, her words slurring slightly.

"I mean, you bitch, that you've done it again! You have to steal every man I love away from me, don't you?"

Lexi and Brenda sat open-mouthed, shocked at this exchange.

"Now, girls –" Lexi started to say but Mel cut her short.

"You have no idea what she's really like, Lexi," she cried, her voice bitter. "You remember that time she came to stay with me in New York? I was living with Simon and we were planning to get married. Well, guess who I found in bed with him one day when I came home early? Yes, that bitch!" she yelled pointing at Angel. "She was supposed to be my best friend but what best friend behaves like that? Simon and I split up naturally, and all over that trollop."

Tears were streaming down Mel's face now.

Lexi looked shocked as did Brenda.

"Is that true, Angel?" Lexi asked.

"He was a waster. He would have made a lousy husband," Angel replied. "I had to make her see that."

Lexi couldn't believe what she was hearing. "Surely there was another way to show her that besides sleeping with him?"

Angel looked away, embarrassed.

"Of course there was but don't you know that's Angel's way of doing things?" Mel cried.

"That's despicable, Angel."

"She can't bear any of us to be happy," Mel cried, verging on hysteria. "She has to prove that she can take our men and she tried it again tonight with Jack. Well, congratulations, Angel! It worked."

"He was never seriously interested in you," Angel screeched, upset that Mel was denigrating her in Brenda and Lexi's eyes.

"What would you know? You're a fucking alcoholic!"

"How dare you call me that!"

You could have heard a pin drop in the room. Brenda and Lexi looked distraught.

"We all know you are. We've been discussing how to tackle you about it all week. You need help, lady."

"Is that true?" Angel asked Lexi. She saw by Lexi's face that it was.

"Thank you, girls. I'm outta here," Angel said, walking as steadily as she could from the room.

"My God! How did all that happen?" Brenda asked when she'd left.

Lexi had gone pale. "I'd better go after her," she said shakily, getting up. "Oh lord, what a mess!"

She knocked and knocked on Angel's door but the only response she got was "Go away and leave me alone!" Eventually she gave up and went back downstairs, deeply worried.

Brenda was sitting with her arms around Mel who was still crying.

"What happened with Jack?" Lexi asked.

"He told me that I was jealous of Angel and that I was too possessive." She wiped her eyes with the Kleenex Brenda had handed her. "I'm not, am I?" she pleaded. "It's just that she ruined my relationship with Simon. I forgave her eventually for that but now she's trying to take Jack away too." She started crying again.

"Look, things will look different in the morning," Lexi said. "We've all had a lot to drink. Why don't we all go to bed now and we can discuss it tomorrow, together with Angel?"

"Don't you want us to clear up?" Brenda asked.

"No, Maria and I will do it in the morning. Why don't you take Mel up and I'll just put the leftover food in the fridge."

Brenda helped a distraught Mel up the stairs, not knowing how to comfort her. She listened to Mel haltingly tell her what had transpired with Jack and quickly came to the conclusion that Jack had run scared. They'd all known that Jack was a traveller and now it transpired that he was not as involved with Mel as she was with him. Poor Mel, what bad luck to fall for a rover like Jack! Eventually Mel got into bed and was dozing gently as Brenda left her room. She knocked gently on Angel's door but, getting no reply, left and went to bed. What a disastrous evening it had turned out to be! She hoped they could sort things out between them tomorrow. Her last thought as her head hit the pillow was how bloody complicated life had become.

Chapter 18

Lexi was distraught as she tossed and turned in bed, unable to sleep. How on earth could she sort out this latest catastrophe? She hoped that by morning common sense would prevail after the effects of the alcohol had worn off but she was filled with apprehension about what lay ahead. Eventually she dozed off but her dreams were peopled by monsters and she woke at five thirty, relieved to find they weren't real. She decided to get up for fear that she might fall back into the nightmare and came downstairs to make herself some hot milk.

The first thing she saw was the note addressed to her, propped up on the kitchen island counter. Recognising Angel's writing she opened it with dread.

Dear Lexi,
By the time you get this I will be well on my way to Los Angeles. Please forgive me for spoiling your birthday week but I just can't take any more. You are my dearest friends and to think that you all think so badly of me fills me with despair. I did not mean any harm to Mel although I have, as she said,

146

hurt her in the past. I thought she had forgiven me for that but it seems that's not the case.

I could not bear to face you all tomorrow and perhaps lose your friendship forever so I am leaving for home now.

Please forgive me and don't think too badly of me. Hugs to Brenda and tell her I'm sorry for spoiling her holiday.

With tears,

Angel xx

Lexi clutched her throat as she read. She ran up the stairs and into Angel's room and sure enough all her stuff was gone. How had she managed to leave the house without any of us hearing her, Lexi wondered. She came slowly down the stairs and made some coffee, then wrapping a shawl around herself went out on to the terrace. She curled her knees up into her chest as she watched the waves break on the shore.

She felt desolate. How had it come to this? They had been best friends for thirty-five years. Was it all going to end like this? She tried Angel's cellphone but it was turned off. She felt the need to reach out to her but that would not be possible until Angel touched down in LA. Devastated, Lexi felt the tears flow as she contemplated what she could do to make things right again. She prayed that their friendship would survive and that they could overcome this but she had no idea how to bring that about.

* * *

As Lexi sat worrying about her, Angel was winging her way to LA. She had been upset by Mel's tirade the previous evening but it was the look in Lexi's eyes that had cut her to the core. Lexi, who had always supported her and whom she idolised, had looked disgusted at Mel's revelations and had obviously been discussing her with the others, behind her back. Angel was feeling far too fragile to face her three friends the following morning.

So when she was sure they were all asleep she had packed, called a taxi and quietly made her way down the stairs and outside which was a major undertaking, given the amount of luggage she had. But she'd made it. Before leaving she'd written a note for Lexi in the hope that she would understand.

Arriving at the airport Angel discovered that there was a flight leaving at six fifteen which would have her home just after eleven Pacific time. She purchased a First Class ticket which meant she would have a bed and could get a few hours' sleep en route. She went to the first-class lounge to await her flight and availed of the free champagne on offer there. Ignoring the strange looks she was getting from the businessmen and airline staff on duty, she polished off the best part of a bottle, popping an Ambien with the last glass. By the time she boarded her flight she was feeling quite numb and ready to sleep.

*　*　*

Mel woke early and when she came downstairs was surprised to find Lexi sitting huddled on the terrace.

"Are you okay?" she asked, her voice full of concern. She was feeling rather guilty about the way she'd behaved last night.

"Angel's gone."

"Gone? Gone where?"

"Back to LA," Lexi said, her voice sombre.

"Oh no!" Mel cried, plonking down on the chair beside Lexi and covering her eyes. "When did she leave?"

"In the early hours of the morning. I can't believe I didn't hear her."

"I didn't hear a thing. Are you sure she's not just walking on the beach?"

"No, she left me this note." She handed it to Mel.

Mel's hands shook as she read it. "How awful! I'm so sorry, Lexi. I shouldn't have exploded the way I did. I shouldn't have said that we'd been discussing her drinking amongst ourselves. It's all my fault."

"It's nobody's fault really. You were upset, and understandably so, that she'd been flirting with Jack especially after what you revealed about her and Simon. I do wish you'd shared that with me before. It explains why you didn't trust her and were angry about her behaviour towards Jack."

"Yeah, but I probably overreacted. Jack was as much to blame as Angel – like Simon before him. I was just very upset about it."

"And what's happening now with Jack?"

"I've no idea." Mel sighed. "And what about Angel? I hope she's okay."

"I can't contact her until she gets to LA which will be sometime this afternoon I expect."

"Can I get you a coffee?"

"No, thanks. I think I'll go for a swim first and then we'll have breakfast together."

"Okay. I don't feel like swimming this morning. Think I'll grab a coffee and then go for a walk on the beach and try and clear my head."

* * *

They were sitting having breakfast when Brenda appeared. She was looking anxious. "I looked in on Angel and her room is empty," she told them, a worried frown creasing her face.

"I'm afraid she's gone back to LA," Lexi said sadly.

149

"Oh dear! I was hoping we could clear things up this morning."

"Not to be, I'm afraid." She handed Brenda the note from Angel.

"Poor Angel," she said when she'd read it. "I do hope she's okay."

"Well, I'll try calling her later once she gets home."

Mel said nothing but sat there looking downcast. She felt responsible for the whole problem. She excused herself shortly afterwards and went up to her bedroom to call Jack, hoping to salvage something from this mess. Her call went to voicemail and she left a message asking him to call her. Shortly afterwards she received a text from him.

Mel, I'm really sorry if I misled you at any stage. I'm very, very fond of you but love is not on my agenda till I complete my travels (which may be never). I have really enjoyed our time together and will always remember the good times we shared. However, it's over now and I am leaving Florida today to complete my 50 states. I wish only the best for you. You will always be very special to me. Jack xx

Mel sat staring at the message reading and re-reading it. Finally it sank in. Jack was gone. She'd been a fool to think it could have been anything more than a fling. He'd warned her that he wasn't ready to settle down. It had been so wonderful between them that she'd hoped he would change his mind but she'd been living in fantasyland. She still loved him and would never forget him. She was heartbroken but accepted that it had been too good to be true and she realised that it was time to get back to real life. She knew what she had to do. She started to pack.

* * *

Lexi and Brenda looked up in surprise as Mel came out on to the terrace dressed in her New York clothes.

"Mel, what's up?"

"I have to go, Lexi. I've made a mess of everything. Angel's gone and now Jack has left Florida too." Her voice wobbled as she spoke. "Looks like I'm good at getting rid of people."

"Ah Mel, are you sure you have to go? You know we'd love you to stay. It's better to be with friends at a time like this."

"No, I'd have to go tomorrow anyway. Right now I need to get back working so I can immerse myself for a few days but you and Brenda will still come to New York next Wednesday, won't you?"

"Of course, if you still want us."

"Are you sure you'll be okay?" Brenda asked anxiously.

"I'll be fine, I'm a big girl," Mel smiled at her. "And I have your visit to look forward to next week. Better go now. My taxi is due any minute."

"Don't be silly, Mel. I'll drive you to the airport," said Lexi.

"No, I've already called a taxi. I'd prefer to say goodbye here. I hate goodbyes at airports."

"Mel, honey, I really hate you going like this," Lexi said, putting her arms around her.

"You take care," Brenda instructed, hugging her tightly.

"See you in the Big Apple," Mel replied, tears in her eyes. And then she was gone.

Lexi and Brenda sat glumly together after she'd gone.

"And then there were two," Lexi remarked, but neither of them smiled. It was a sad end to what had promised to be a wonderful week.

"Well, there's not a lot we can do about the situation," Lexi grimaced as she finished her breakfast. "I'm going to help Maria clear up and then we can indulge in some retail therapy. It is Black Friday after all and I did promise to take you to experience it. There will be lots of bargains out there and hopefully it will take our minds off things for a while."

"Good idea. I think we need to keep busy," Brenda agreed. "Let me help you clear away."

"No, no. Maria and I can manage. Here, have a look through the paper. There are discount coupons there for many of the stores." She handed Brenda the *Tampa Bay Times* which was the size of ten *Sunday Times* back home.

"My God," Brenda exclaimed buckling under the unexpected weight of the newspaper. "What on earth is in here?"

"About twenty pages of news and five hundred brochures and leaflets of advertisements and coupons," Lexi said, laughing.

Sitting down, Brenda sifted through the bundle. Lexi hadn't been joking! An hour later she was still reading when Lexi came out with two coffees.

"Well, did you find anything you like?" she asked, sitting down.

"Oh my, just about everything. It's fabulous. I would like to go to JC Penney for some stuff for the girls."

"Okay, we'll head there first but it may be just too busy. I've been thinking that we might go down to Ellenton and stay the night on Anna Maria Island. It'd beautiful there and you can shop this afternoon and again tomorrow if you wish."

"I'd love that. It might lift our spirits to get away."

"That's what I was thinking too."

As they prepared to leave the telephone rang. It was Kenny.

"Hi, Lexi. Great night last night. I've been trying to call Angel but her cellphone is off. Could I have a word with her?"

"I'm afraid she left for LA early this morning?"

"She what?" He sounded distressed. "But she agreed to come to lunch on my yacht today."

"I'm sorry, Kenny, but she had to leave." She made a face at Brenda as if to ask 'what can I say?'.

"I am very upset to hear that. She's quite a gal. I'll try her again later. Thanks, Lexi."

* * *

The stewardess woke Angel to tell her that they were about to make their descent into Los Angeles airport. She groggily came to, wondering what she was doing there, and then it all came back to her. She popped a Prozac into her mouth as they came in to land. She felt absolutely dreadful and couldn't wait to get home and into bed, after a whisky or two of course.

She hadn't called Will to tell him she was home and guessed he would be still be sleeping as it wasn't yet noon. She would surprise him and sneak in beside him in the bed where doubtless he would be as horny for her as she was for him. After all, it had been a whole week since they'd had sex and she had missed it.

* * *

Angel paid the taxi driver and let herself into the house then stopped dead, appalled at the scene before her. The place was a dreadful mess. There were empty beer and wine bottles side by side with overflowing ashtrays on every surface. Half-eaten pizzas littered the coffee table and various items of clothing were strewn on the floor. She went into the kitchen to find Consuela, her housekeeper, to demand the reason for this mess but she was nowhere to be found. How strange!

Getting more angry by the minute she climbed the stairs to confront Will. She opened the door to her bedroom and gasped in shock at the sight that greeted her. Will's naked buttocks were in the air, moving rhythmically up and down, a pair of slim tanned legs wrapped around his waist.

Angel screamed.

Will leapt up, his obvious erection deflating before her eyes as the young girl beneath him tried to cover herself with the sheet.

"I can explain, Angel," he muttered, grabbing a towel to cover his nakedness.

Just then a very pretty teenage girl sauntered out of Angel's bathroom. "My God, that must have been some orgasm," she sniggered before she caught sight of Angel. "Holy Cow!" she cried, rushing back into the bathroom.

"Just what do you think you're doing in my bed?" Angel yelled, barely able to believe what she was witnessing.

"Well, it's a long story . . ." Will began, but Angel stopped him.

"Save it!" she snarled. "If you're not out of here, all of you, in three minutes, I'm calling the sheriff and you can explain to him what you're doing having sex with two underage girls."

"Please, Angel, I'm so sorry . . ." Will stammered.

"Get out . . . now!" She grabbed his keys off the dressing table. "Leave the car and don't dare show your face around here again." She looked at her watch and picked up the phone. "Your three minutes start . . . now!"

It gave her some satisfaction to see how quickly the three of them managed to vacate her house. They were gone in under two and a half minutes, all of them partially dressed. She locked the door after them and sank down on the sofa. She then called Consuela.

"Consuela, where are you? Why aren't you here?"

"Ah, Miss Angel. You back? Mr Will say you not be back till tomorrow. He tell me you say for me go stay with my daughter this week and to come back tomorrow morning."

"No, Consuela, I didn't say any such thing. I need you to come in immediately. The place is in a terrible state," Angel said, suddenly drained.

She poured herself a large whisky and knocked it back. Then went up to the guest bedroom where she stripped off and took a long shower in the en-suite bathroom there. She couldn't face her own bedroom again until Consuela had cleaned and disinfected it and dumped the bedclothes. God knows how many sluts Will had entertained in there while she'd been gone.

Putting on her bathrobe she came downstairs and poured another very large whisky then sat rocking back and forth in the rocking chair.

"Oh, Miss Angel, what happen here?" her housekeeper asked when she came in and saw the mess.

"Don't ask, Consuela," Angel replied tiredly. "Can you just clean it up as quickly as possible, please?"

"Sure thing, Miss Angel. Mr Will do this?"

"Who else?"

"You feel okay?" Consuela looked with concern at her mistress.

"I'm okay and please don't let Mr Will back in here for any reason. He's finished, kaput!" She made a slashing gesture to her throat.

Consuela understood. "I make you something to eat, Miss Angel?"

"No, thanks, Consuela. I'm going to bed in the guest room now. If anybody calls, I'm unavailable. Understood?"

"Yes, Ma'am," Consuela nodded and set about cleaning up the mess.

Upstairs Angel washed down a sleeping pill with the whisky. Feeling very sorry for herself, she slipped between the

155

fresh sheets and curled up in the foetal position. She had no friends left and now no boyfriend either. As she drifted off to sleep she wished with all her heart that her father were still alive. He would have taken care of her and let no one hurt her. He was the only one who had ever truly loved her. She missed him so much. How could she ever go on?

Chapter 19

Lexi and Brenda arrived at the Countryside Mall and circled around and around looking for a parking space. Eventually, after fifteen minutes they were lucky enough to find someone pulling out and Lexi speedily pulled into his place.

"My God, this is crazy," Brenda exclaimed as she looked at the thousands of cars in the huge parking lot.

"Welcome to Black Friday," Lexi grinned.

They walked into the mall which was crowded with people of all ages battling their way through the throng. There was a skating rink in the centre with cute kids whizzing around attempting turns and jumps as their proud mamas looked on.

Walking down the mall Brenda was bumped and jostled by numerous people carrying huge bags and boxes. There was a line of about twenty people queuing outside the Disney shop, waiting to be admitted as the shop was overcrowded. It was incredible.

They made their way into JC Penney and gasped when they saw the length of the lines at the cashier desks. They looked at each other in horror.

"I'm feeling quite claustrophobic," Brenda admitted.

"Me too, let's get out of here. We'll come back on Monday when there will still be things reduced. Nothing is worth this."

Relieved, they exited the mall and as they pulled out two cars almost collided in an effort to get into Lexi's vacated parking space.

"And I thought Dublin was bad!" Brenda laughed.

"We do everything bigger and better in the US of A!" Lexi said with an American twang. "Ellenton will be much less frantic as the shops are more boutique-like but it will still be busy. But I know you'll find great stuff for the girls there."

They headed south and Brenda was fascinated as they crossed over the Sunshine Skyway Bridge to see a cruise ship about to sail under it on its way into Tampa.

"Wow!"

"Impressive, isn't it?" Lexi asked as they reached the top of the bridge.

"I'll say. You sure do everythin' bigger and better in the US of A," Brenda agreed with her, attempting an American twang.

"Your accent is atrocious," Lexi exclaimed laughing as they made their descent down the four-mile bridge.

* * *

Brenda loved Ellenton. It was all so compact, in the same style as Kildare Village but much, much larger of course. They got a plan of the centre and Brenda marked off the shops she wanted to hit first. Armed with a list of her kids' sizes and their favourite designer brands, she went into battle. Two hours later the two women, laden down with bags from the Levi store, Nike, Tommy Hilfiger and Calvin Klein, struggled back to deposit them in the car.

"Lordy me, I just can't believe how cheap everything is

here. It's unbelievable," Brenda exclaimed.

"I did warn you. How about some lunch?"

They made their way to the Food Court where Brenda discovered that the shopping had made her ravenous. When they'd finished eating Brenda pored over her plan again.

"I hope you don't mind, honey, but I'm tired so I'm going to let you off on your own now. You'll be quicker without me. I'll just sit and rest here for a while and then I want to have a look in the kitchen shop. I'll give you the key so you can put your purchases in the car and we'll meet back here at say . . ." she looked at her watch, "four thirty. Is that okay?"

"Are you sure, Lexi? Would you rather go now?"

"Not at all. You go off and enjoy yourself. See you at four thirty."

Brenda went crazy over the next two hours and arrived back to meet Lexi, laden down with bags again.

"I hope you got something for yourself and not just for the kids," Lexi asked her.

"No, I didn't," Brenda admitted. "I'm a bit worried about my baggage allowance."

"Don't worry about it. You came with an empty case and you're allowed two bags in business class so you needn't worry. We'll drop in here tomorrow before we leave for home. You have to think of yourself too, honey. Now I suggest we head to Anna Maria Island and find somewhere to stay for the night."

They left Ellenton and drove the short distance to the island which Brenda saw was picture-postcard pretty.

Lexi tried to call Angel after they had checked in to a lovely little hotel that was right on the beach. Consuela answered and said that Angel was sleeping and had left orders that she did not want to be disturbed.

"Poor dear. I do hope she's okay," Brenda said, biting her lip.

"A good sleep will work wonders. I'll try her again later."

* * *

Lexi tried again later that evening but the response from Consuela was the same. "She very tired, Miss Lexi. Maybe you call tomorrow."

"I will, Consuela. When she wakes could you please tell her I called and that Brenda and I are thinking of her and we love her."

"Sure will, Miss Lexi."

There was nothing else they could do.

They went for a swim in the sea and then walked along the beach to a small restaurant where they enjoyed some delicious fish. Afterwards Lexi declared that she was dog-tired and headed for bed.

Brenda was more worried than ever at how easily Lexi became tired though she supposed all the drama surrounding Angel and Mel had taken its toll.

* * *

Mel couldn't sleep on the flight home but was glad to be back at last in her familiar apartment where she could quietly relive every minute of the days and nights she'd spent with Jack. She was heartbroken but she wouldn't trade a single moment of that time for all the tea in China. For that brief time she'd come alive and she would always be grateful to him for that. She knew she would never see him again so there was nothing for it but to throw herself straight back into her work.

She felt guilty about the scene with Angel and how she'd spoiled the party by leaving but after Jack's text she'd needed to get away and be on her own. Lexi and Brenda would be coming to New York the following week and she vowed she would make it up to them then. She called Lexi to say she'd arrived home safely and that she was looking forward to their visit.

She also called Angel to apologise but had got the same response as Lexi had got from Consuela. She left a message saying she was sorry.

* * *

The following day the two girls made their way back to the Ellenton Outlet where Lexi insisted that Brenda buy something for herself. Under Lexi's eagle eye she succumbed and bought a pair of tan leather boots and a beautiful camel cashmere coat that would be very welcome when she returned to the freezing Irish winter. Filled with the euphoria that comes from getting a great bargain Brenda settled back to enjoy the rest of the day.

They were stopping off in St Petersburg on the way home to visit the Dalí Museum. Lexi was so excited about it that Brenda hoped she wouldn't disappoint her by not liking it. She wasn't an art-gallery type of girl and hadn't been to one since her schooldays but she needn't have worried. This was nothing like the fuddy-duddy museum she'd expected. For starters, it was an amazing building right on the waterfront which had been built specially to house the collection. But it was the paintings by Dalí which enchanted her and had her enthralled.

"He was a genius, you know," Lexi explained as they wandered around the bright airy rooms. Being an artist herself she was able to explain things better than any guide. Brenda was fascinated. She loved the quirkiness and the way Dalí had looked at things. She now understood what the word *surreal* meant. His work was magical and the hours flew by as she soaked it all in. They broke for a snack mid-afternoon in the terrific Spanish tapas restaurant on the ground floor. It was delicious. Replenished, they continued with their tour.

Too soon it was time to leave. They drove back in silence, both of them uplifted, their minds still immersed in the Dalí paintings and they stopped off at the Bon Appetit in Dunedin to catch the sunset. It was a fitting end to a lovely day.

The only fly in the ointment was Angel who was still refusing to take their calls. Consuela was no longer picking up and it was going straight to voicemail. Both Lexi and Brenda left a message but Angel didn't call back. They figured she was still annoyed with them. Well, sooner or later she'd have to speak with them.

* * *

Angel had slept almost around the clock. She awoke feeling groggy, not knowing where she was. Slowly it dawned on her that she was in her own guest room and the memories came flooding back. She remembered the terrible scene with Mel, flying home and then finding Will having sex with that bimbo. Burrowing deep under the covers she considered taking more sleeping pills but she hadn't eaten since Thursday evening and she knew she needed to eat something. She was also desperately thirsty.

Crawling out of bed she flung on a bathrobe and went downstairs. Relieved to see the living room was back to normal she searched in her bag for a Prozac and made her way to the kitchen.

"Miss Angel, *buenos días*. You feel better?"

Angel murmured what she hoped sounded like 'good morning' back. Her mouth was dry and she felt her tongue was swollen. She also had a dreadful headache. She popped the Prozac in her mouth and drank a glass of water.

"Any coffee there?" she asked, hoisting herself up on a stool.

"Sure thing."

Sipping the coffee Consuela poured for her she began to feel a little better.

"Now I make you nice breakfast. Some eggs maybe?"

"No, no, just some toast is all I need."

Her housekeeper tut-tutted and muttered something under her breath that Angel did not understand. Consuela, who was small and very round, was constantly berating her for not eating.

Placing the toast in front of Angel she informed her, "That nice Miss Lexi, she call many times and also Miss Mel and Miss . . ." she consulted a notepad, "Miss Bren – da. They nice ladies."

Angel groaned. "Did they leave any message?"

"They say they love you and Miss Mel, she say she sorry."

Angel buried her head in her hands. She couldn't possibly talk to them any time soon. She was far too fragile.

"And Mr Will he call many times but I tell him he finished, like you said." She drew her hand across her throat as she'd seen Angel do.

"Thank you, Consuela. I don't know what I'd do without you."

Consuela beamed with pleasure. "And bedroom all clean for you, like you ask."

"You're a pet," Angel said as she went into the living room and poured herself a whisky. To hell with them all, she thought as she downed it, they don't understand how difficult my life is. She was still smarting from Mel's accusations. Pouring another drink she took it and the bottle into the den and turned on the TV. She watched some mindless programmes as she drank steadily and when later Consuela came in with some food she ate it just to please her.

Consuela normally had weekends off when she babysat her grandchildren and Angel insisted that she leave on Saturday afternoon, as she always did. Consuela was reluctant to do so and offered to stay as she was worried about her mistress but Angel wouldn't hear of it.

The day passed in a haze as Angel heard the phone ring and go to voicemail but she didn't answer it or listen to the messages. Eventually she passed out on the sofa and when she woke, it was dark. She took two more sleeping pills and headed up the stairs to her own bed and collapsed into it.

*   *   *

Meanwhile, Lexi was determined to make sure that Brenda would enjoy the remainder of her holiday. On Sunday morning they went to church and afterwards went to the Wagon Wheel which was a big flea market about twenty minutes away. Brenda loved it and the fun atmosphere there. She found a fake Michael Kors bag in the exact tan as her new boots which she snapped up along with some cheap T-shirts. She would have bought more if it was not for the problem of fitting all she'd bought in the two bags she was allowed flying home. She saw some fake Pandoro bracelets, filled with charms, that looked so realistic she bought one each for her three girls and her two sisters.

As in Ellenton, Lexi got tired very quickly and they made their way to the outdoor bar where there was a live group playing. She insisted that Brenda head off on her own and meet her back there when she'd finished. When Brenda came back they sat listening to the group who were really good.

When they got home they went for a swim and then Marvin and Troy came over for a barbeque.

Lexi and Brenda sat back sipping margaritas while the two

guys busied themselves over the grill.

"That's the great thing about barbeques," Lexi whispered to her. "Men think they're the only ones who can do it so we leave them to it."

Brenda had now given herself up to enjoying Troy's company. He understood that there was a line that couldn't be crossed and although there was still great chemistry between them she knew that they would do nothing about it.

They had another great evening and somehow the absence of Angel and Mel receded. Neither girl mentioned anything about the fiasco on Thanksgiving night to either of the men.

Brenda saw the wonderful relationship between Lexi and Marvin and envied them. They were almost on the same wavelength and often finished each other's sentences. They had so much in common, much more than she had with Bob right now and Brenda realised that that really was the secret of a great relationship.

When Troy heard that they were going to Busch Gardens, the well-known amusement park, the following day he asked if he might come along too.

"I've never been, would you believe?"

"Why didn't you tell me?" Marvin exclaimed, shocked. "It's our biggest tourist attraction. You absolutely have to go. Why don't we all go together tomorrow?" he suggested. "It's years since I've been there."

"You're on," Lexi replied laughing. "Busch Gardens it is!"

* * *

Sunday was pretty much a re-run of the day before for Angel and when Consuela arrived for work on Monday morning Angel was still sleeping. Consuela thought about contacting Miss Lexi to tell her how worried she was about her mistress but she was too afraid of Angel's anger if she did that. So she did nothing. She figured Miss Angel was just upset about Mr Will and would come around soon. She certainly hoped so.

* * *

They left early the following morning for the visit to Busch Gardens. Marvin had bought the tickets online. As a Florida resident he had got them at a discount. Brenda offered to pay for her and Lexi's tickets but he wouldn't hear of it.

She had heard how wonderful Disney World in Orlando was but when she saw how beautiful Busch Gardens was she found it hard to believe that there could be something even better. Luckily it was a Monday and not the holiday season so there were no queues. They tried most of the rides but Brenda drew a line at the crazily high Kumba and Montu rides. She'd been pretty terrified on the SheiKra ride even though she'd kept her eyes closed and Troy had held her, but these other two were just too scary for her.

Lexi had opted out but had sat laughing as Brenda screamed with the thrill of it all. Marvin and Troy insisted on riding all the rides but the girls were convinced it was just bravado as they both looked quite green coming off the Kumba. The water rides were more enjoyable and less frightening although they were all soaked after them but they dried up quickly in the warm sun.

They broke for lunch at the Zambia smokehouse where Brenda tasted baby back ribs for the first time. She wondered how they managed to get such flavour and tenderness in the meat. She savoured it, closing her eyes, knowing that it would probably be many years before she'd have them again.

After lunch they headed for the animal park and as they passed through Serengeti Park Brenda was amazed to hear that Troy had actually seen the migration of the Serengeti in Tanzania a couple of years before.

He then spoke of his time in Africa and she marvelled at what an exciting life he'd had. She was beginning to see how important it was to travel and visit other countries and see other cultures. She'd missed out on that but she was happy to know her children were now getting that chance.

Chapter 20

Tomorrow would be Brenda's last day in Florida and she had loved it so much that she would be sorry to leave. Although excited about going to New York it also signalled the end of a magical time. The thought of going back to Ireland to face the problems in her marriage was depressing but she tried to put it out of her mind and make the most of the rest of the holiday.

She called Bob as soon as they got back from Busch Gardens as it was after midnight in Ireland and he should be in. She had told him, the last time they'd spoken, that he could call her anytime but he hadn't bothered to contact her. She wondered if he was still sulking. She had yet to break the news to him that she would be visiting New York on the way home and she was apprehensive about it.

She was relieved to find him in. He sounded strange and ill at ease. He took the news of New York calmly which astonished her.

Then she heard a voice in the background.

"Do you have people in?" she asked him, surprised he had not mentioned it.

"No, no. It's just the television," he replied. "I'll go and turn it off."

Brenda was perplexed, wondering what he could possibly be watching at this hour. It was after midnight in Ireland and Bob started work at six thirty every morning. She waited for a full two minutes before he returned.

"Sorry about that," he said and for the first time she realised that he'd been drinking.

"Bob, is everything okay? You're not having a poker game, are you?"

"Of course not," he replied angrily. "And so what if I was?"

Brenda sighed. She knew from experience that there was no point in continuing this conversation when he'd been drinking.

"Look, I'll call you from New York and let you know what time I'll be in on the Tuesday."

"Okay," he said gruffly, hanging up.

She let out another huge sigh as she replaced the receiver. She didn't know what was going on with him but she suspected now that he was far more resentful of her trip to Florida than he'd let on. She went downstairs with a heavy heart, her previous high spirits evaporated. Maria had prepared a light supper for them and they were having a drink before it.

"What would you like, Brenda?" Marvin who was acting barman asked her.

"A large vodka and orange juice would do the trick."

Troy and Lexi raised their eyebrows in surprise.

"Is everything alright?" Lexi asked, concerned.

"Yeah, fine," Brenda replied without much enthusiasm.

Lexi didn't pursue it.

Brenda drank the vodka in double-quick time and Marvin

refilled her glass. By the time they sat down to the seafood salad she was quite tiddly.

"Are you okay?" Troy murmured while rubbing his hand on her back gently.

She nodded and closed her eyes wishing that they could stay like this forever.

"If you want to talk, I'm here," he said softly and the kindness in his eyes brought a lump to her throat.

"I'm fine, honestly," she told him, smiling brightly.

"Well, remember what I said."

* * *

The following day was her last in this beautiful place and Troy took them out on the boat again. This time there was no Angel jigging around trying to attract his attention and it was a simply magical day. She went up front with him and he let her take the wheel and like the last time he wrapped his arms around her. This time he kept them there and the closeness of his body excited her. When he kissed the nape of her neck she thought she would melt with pleasure. She could feel his hardness against her and the temptation to turn and feel his kisses on her mouth was overwhelming but somehow she resisted.

"You're very beautiful," he said, pressing his face into her hair. "I wish with all my heart that you were my wife."

At the mention of the word 'wife' she came down to earth with a bang. She was a wife, Bob's wife, and no matter how he was behaving, this was wrong. Swiftly she let go of the wheel and slipped out from under Troy's arms.

"I'm sorry, I can't do this," she said with a sad smile. Deep down she wished it could be otherwise but that wasn't possible.

"I understand," he replied softly as she left to go and join

Lexi and Marvin at the stern.

Despite all this she had an achingly lovely day. They sat and watched another magnificent sunset and when Troy took her hand she didn't pull it away. Tomorrow she would be gone. Why not have this last small pleasure?

They had dinner at the Beachcomber but Brenda could hardly eat. With a heavy heart she said goodbye to Troy for the last time.

"Thank you for everything. You have no idea how much I appreciate having met you."

"And you have no idea what you have done to my heart," he whispered softly. Then he kissed her gently on the lips and left.

Feeling very lonely, Brenda went up to pack. It took her ages to take off all the labels and price tags from the stuff she'd bought but eventually she was done. She'd had to buy a lightweight bag in Ross as her case couldn't hold all she'd bought. It was lucky she was travelling home business class and was allowed two bags or she would have had to leave some stuff behind.

She was sad to be leaving Florida. She'd had the time of her life there and had found herself again. She felt attractive and worthwhile and much of that was due to Troy. She would miss him.

* * *

Mel was buzzing around making sure that all was in place for the girls' visit. She had gone shopping and her fridge and larder were more full than they'd ever been before. Strangely, since she'd come back from Florida she found herself hungry all the time. She guessed that the week there eating all that lovely food had reawakened her appetite. She was now eating decent meals and even taking a lunch break for food – as opposed to Botox sessions and manicures.

The other thing that she couldn't understand was that her work was not absorbing her in the way it used to. She was doing her work as required of course, but it wasn't her whole life any more. The CEO was more than surprised when she told him that she was taking the next three days off because her friends were coming to town.

"That's most unlike you," he remarked. "As far as I'm aware you haven't taken time off in two years and now two weeks in a row. And you look different," he observed, cocking his head to one side as he surveyed her. "Is it possible that something happened in Florida that has changed you?"

Mel blushed which convinced him he'd hit the nail on the head. He surmised it must be a man.

"Well, my dear, I'm happy that you have seen sense and are making time for yourself," he beamed at her. "And take as long as you need. We'll manage here." He winked at her as she got up to leave, making her blush even more.

*   *   *

Meanwhile one day was running into another for Angel and she was drunk most of the time and knocked out on sleeping pills at night. Sometimes she couldn't tell whether it was day or night.

By Wednesday morning Consuela decided she had to intervene and bustled into Angel's bedroom, full of purpose.

"Okay, Miss Angel, it time you stop this now," she said sternly.

Angel woke and put her hands over her eyes. "Close those curtains, Consuela, please. The light is hurting my eyes."

She pulled them half over but left them so that there was still light coming in.

"C'mon now, Miss Angel. I bring you a nice cuppa coffee."

"No, no, I want to go back to sleep," Angel cried, snuggling down under the covers.

Consuela whipped the covers off her as Angel stared at her in shock.

"I no stand by and see you kill yourself, Miss Angel. No man worth that. Now c'mon and drink this here coffee."

Angel started to cry and Consuela wrapped her motherly arms around her and rocked her back and forth as she sobbed.

"C'mon, honey, everythin' be okay."

"Oh Consuela, it's not just Will, it's everything. I've lost my friends too." Angel managed to splutter in between her sobs.

"What you mean? You not lose your friends. They call and say they love you, *siempre*."

Angel was silent as her sobs receded and she sipped the coffee Consuela handed her.

"You special lady and great actress. You no need pills and whisky. The friends and many people, they love you, but maybe you not love yourself."

Angel looked at her, her big blue eyes full of tears. "What can I do, Consuela?"

"I make you nice bath then you put on nice clothes and I cook good breakfast for you. Then maybe you go hairdresser and she make your hair pretty cause it no look good now."

As she went into the bathroom to take her bath Angel looked in the mirror and saw with a shock that she looked a mess. She allowed Consuela to help her into the bath and felt a little better as she sank beneath the bubbles. Thirty minutes later Consuela came to help her out and get dressed.

The smell of fried bacon assailed Angel as she came down the stairs and she suddenly realised that she was starving. She guessed it must be five days since she'd eaten – she couldn't really remember. She devoured the delicious breakfast, leaving not a morsel on the plate. Two more cups of coffee and she felt much better.

"You're so good to me, Consuela. I don't know what I'd do without you."

"*Gracias*," Consuela replied, beaming with pride. She was happy to see Miss Angel get back to her old self.

Angel decided to take a Prozac to help her get through the day but was shocked to find that the box was empty. She felt a wave of panic sweep over her and she knew she'd never get through the day without it. Checking her supply of Ambien she saw that it was almost gone too. Goodness! How had that happened? Had she taken all of them in such a short time?

She immediately rang the doctor, out of earshot of Consuela, and made an appointment for that afternoon. She hoped she'd last that long.

On her way to the hairdresser's it felt strange being out and about again and she drove very slowly, ignoring the angry honking of other drivers, because she still felt a bit groggy.

She consumed numerous cups of coffee as Zach styled her hair. She tried not to look at her reflection in the mirror and refused to take off her sunglasses when he asked her. He shook his head and threw his eyes to heaven, understanding why Angel looked so crappy today. He was used to the substance abuse of his many celebrity clients. This was Beverly Hills, after all.

Crystal, the manicurist, also noticed how off-form Angel was and didn't chatter as she filled Angel's gel nails and painted them a bright red.

Angel was relieved to get out of there and was sitting in the doctor's waiting room fifteen minutes before her appointed time. The receptionist was surprised to see her so early as she normally turned up late. To Angel's relief the doctor took her straight away and the moment she left him she went into the restroom and popped a Prozac. Five minutes later she began to feel its effect. Happier now, she drove down Rodeo Drive where she treated herself to a Dolce and Gabbana dress and a gorgeous pair of Valentino shoes. She considered going into the Beverly Wiltshire for a quick drink but decided not to as she would surely bump into people she knew and have to make small-talk. There was also the danger that the paparazzi who constantly prowled outside would snap her which was the last thing she wanted at this moment.

Instead she drove to an off licence and bought a case of whisky which she put in the trunk of the car. She would sneak it into the house after Consuela left. Pleased with herself she drove home.

"Now you very pretty," Consuela exclaimed when she saw her. "Very beautiful."

"I wouldn't quite say that," Angel murmured under her breath as she made for her bedroom, one of the bottles of whisky secreted in her Jessica Simpson hobo bag. Once there she downed a glass in one go. As she felt the heat of the liquid spread through her she felt a sense of euphoria take over. She would need to be very careful not to arouse Consuela's suspicions but she knew she could achieve that. She was an actress after all and a damn good one at that!

Chapter 21

Brenda settled back in business class on the flight to New York.

"I could get fond of this," she grinned at Lexi. "I don't know how I'll ever be able to fly Ryanair again."

"Is it so bad?"

"Well, let me put it this way, if people could afford to travel any other way, they would. But it is a cheap way to fly."

The stewardess offered them a glass of champagne which they happily accepted.

"To New York!" Lexi toasted, raising her glass to Brenda.

"To The Big Apple!" Brenda grinned, clinking her glass.

"I hope Mel is okay and not too upset over Jack," Lexi said as she sipped her drink.

"She fell really hard for him, didn't she?"

"She sure did. I don't understand how she could fall in love in such a short time. I'm actually more worried about Angel," Lexi confessed, biting her lip. "Mel is a tough old bird but Angel is terribly fragile."

"I'm surprised to hear you say that. Angel has everything going for her. She's beautiful and famous and all her life she's been adored and petted. Men idolise her and she appears to be full of confidence."

"But she's not, you know. She's terribly insecure. Deep down she feels worthless because her mother never loved her."

"What?" Brenda exclaimed, spilling some of her champagne as she turned to Lexi. "You're not serious?"

"I'm afraid so. Angel's father was so thrilled with his 'little princess' as he called her that her mother became insanely jealous of her pretty little daughter. She was extremely cruel to Angel as she was growing up but Angel never told anyone. Her mother threatened to kill her if she breathed a word, especially to her father, so Angel suffered in silence."

"How do you know this?"

"Because she came to my house once in a terrible state. Her mother had given her a beating and left welts on her back. She made me promise not to tell my parents and I didn't. I regretted making that promise. Then when she was down visiting me in Florida another time she unburdened her heart to me one night after a few drinks. She revealed that her mother had been physically and verbally abusive. I couldn't believe the things her mother used to say to her. She totally demolished Angel's self-esteem. She was a vicious woman."

"I remember her as being cold and aloof."

"She was. Then when Angel's father was dying her mother never informed her and he was dead and buried before Angel even found out. She was in America then of course. She never forgave her mother and hasn't spoken to her since."

"Is she still alive?"

"I don't know. I presume so. I know she moved to the south of France after her husband's death. Angel never mentions her but she still bears the scars."

"Poor thing! No wonder she's so messed up. Does Mel know any of this?"

"No. I never discussed it with her and I doubt Angel did."

"Maybe you should tell her. It might help Mel understand her better."

"Yes, I've been debating that since the blow-up they had. Maybe I will talk to her. We'll see."

The stewardess arrived with their lunch which was as good as anything served in the best restaurants.

After the meal Lexi dozed off and as Brenda looked out the window at the beautiful clouds her thoughts turned to Troy. She missed him. He'd made her feel attractive and desirable and she understood how Mel had fallen in love with Jack in such a short time. It had almost happened to her with Troy but luckily she'd been able to stop and nip it in the bud. She was trying not to dwell on her feelings for him. She couldn't afford that luxury. That was dangerous territory.

Lexi slept for the rest of the flight and Brenda's worries about her surfaced once more. When she woke up Brenda broached the subject with her.

"Lexi, I can't help notice how easily you tire lately. Don't you think you should see a doctor about it?"

"Don't you start! Marvin is forever on at me about it but you know I hate going to doctors. It's probably just that I'm run down. I'll start a tonic when I get back home, okay?"

"But Lexi –"

"Subject closed," Lexi stated firmly and Brenda stayed quiet.

* * *

Once again Brenda saw the skyline of Manhattan loom into sight but this time she'd get to see it from the ground too. She was really excited about seeing New York as she'd heard how fabulous it was.

Mel was there to greet them and seemed in great form as she hugged them.

"How are you?" Lexi asked her anxiously.

"I'm surviving," Mel smiled. "A little heartbroken but you know if I had to do it all again I would. Jack opened my eyes to so many things."

Brenda squeezed her arm. "I'm happy you're not hurting too much."

"Well, you know what they say: better to have loved and lost than never to have loved at all."

"You're taking it very well I must say," Brenda observed.

After they had collected Brenda's luggage, Mel led them to a waiting limousine.

"Wow!" Brenda exclaimed. She'd never been in a limo with a chauffeur before. "Don't you drive?" she asked Mel as she got in.

"Of course not! Nobody with any sense drives in New York except for cab drivers."

"And how do you get around?"

"Well, the company provides me with this limo complete with the lovely Franco here but if I'm starting very early or working late I generally take a cab to and from work."

"Which is nearly every day," Lexi couldn't resist commenting.

Mel threw her eyes to heaven at this remark but she was smiling.

"Wow!" Brenda whistled. "Have your parents been here? They must be proud of you when they see this." She waved her hand, indicating the limo.

"They came for a visit once but didn't seem overly impressed by my achievements," Mel grimaced. "They didn't like New York."

"Well, I'm very impressed," Brenda assured her.

"And we're very proud of you," Lexi said, patting her

hand. It hurt her always to hear how Mel's parents continued to denigrate her.

"Now tell me, is there anything special you want to see while you're here?" Mel asked.

"Everything!" Brenda cried as the others laughed at her enthusiasm.

"I've taken the next three days off to show you around," Mel announced.

Lexi looked at her in surprise. Mel had never taken a day off as far back as she could remember. "That's very kind of you," she said, looking at Mel intently. Mel looked different. She was softer, gentler somehow. That hard edge had disappeared. Thank God something good has come from all this, Lexi thought as they arrived at Mel's apartment which overlooked Central Park.

* * *

When they'd dumped their luggage and freshened up they set off in the limo again. Brenda was beside herself with excitement as they drove down Columbus Avenue past the Lincoln Centre on their way downtown. Mel told them they had the limo for the afternoon and suggested that they do a full tour to show Brenda the sights and give her a feel for the city.

"We'll make a plan tonight," she said as she pointed out the Plaza Hotel. "Then tomorrow we'll visit the sights individually by cab and on foot. What do you think?"

"Sounds great to me," Brenda nodded enthusiastically as they turned onto 5th Avenue.

Her eyes were out on sticks as they passed the famed Bergdorf Goodman and Saks Department Stores. Mel was giving a running commentary and pointed out St Patrick's

Cathedral and across from it the Rockefeller Centre with its skating rink and massive Christmas tree. She also pointed to a very elegant building which was where she worked. Brenda's head was swivelling left and right as she took it all in and then suddenly they turned a corner and ahead of them lay Times Square. She squealed with excitement as she saw the famous place that she was so familiar with from television.

Lexi and Mel laughed at her, enjoying her enthusiasm.

"You'll see it all better tomorrow," Mel informed her as they left the crowded Square and made their way down Broadway. Mel was better than any guide and, as they passed through the Garment District, explained all about the different districts of Manhattan. It was fascinating.

"That's Macy's," Mel pointed out as Franco turned on 35th Street and drove the length of the famous department store that seemed to go on and on.

"It's e-normous!" Brenda shrieked as she took it in.

He drove around it and then back across Broadway where the impossibly high Empire State building rose up before them. Brenda gazed up at it, wondering if she would have the nerve to go to the top.

Driving south on Broadway again they passed the Flatiron Building while Mel relayed the history of New York. A short while later she stopped talking all of a sudden and Lexi whispered that it was because they were passing close to Ground Zero. They were all silent and Brenda felt immeasurably sad as she thought of the horror that had occurred there.

Finally the most famous landmark of all came into sight – the Statue of Liberty. Mel ordered the chauffeur to pull over at Battery Park and they made their way to the bay.

As they stood at the railings and saw Lady Liberty in all her glory Brenda felt overcome by the magic of this wonderful city. She threw her hands in the air and cried out: "New York, I love you!"

Lexi and Mel roared with laughter.

"Uh-oh, she's been bitten by the bug already," Lexi declared.

"I can't believe I'm here," Brenda cried. "All these famous places that I've seen on TV and in photos and now I'm actually here! And it's even more thrilling than I expected. This is the most exciting time I've ever had in my whole life. Thanks a million for making it happen, girls." She reached over and hugged them both.

"Our pleasure!"

"Most definitely!" Lexi and Mel grinned happily at their enthusiastic friend.

Brenda felt a lump in her throat when Mel pointed out Ellis Island. The three women stood silent, staring at the place where so many Irish emigrants had arrived in America.

"It never ceases to move me," Lexi said quietly, "to think of how terrified they must have been, landing in this strange place with nothing but the clothes on their backs."

"Yes, having left everything behind knowing that they'd never see Ireland or their loved ones again," Mel added.

"It must have been heartbreaking," Brenda agreed, tears coming to her eyes.

They quietly made their way back to the limo and went back uptown, passing through Chinatown, Little Italy and Greenwich Village.

"It's hard to believe that we're still in New York," Brenda said as they drove by small narrow streets with brownstone houses. "It's such a contrast to 5th Avenue."

"That's what's so exciting about it," Mel explained. "It's very eclectic as are its inhabitants."

"I love it," Brenda declared.

"Me too," Mel and Lexi chorused together.

* * *

"How is Angel?" Mel asked, as they sat having a glass of wine before dinner.

"I don't know. She won't take my calls," Lexi replied.

"Oh, I thought it was just me she wouldn't talk to," Mel said, relieved slightly.

Brenda threw Lexi a glance which said 'Why not tell her?'. Lexi took the hint and disclosed to Mel what she'd told Brenda earlier of Angel's relationship with her mother.

"I never knew any of that," Mel exclaimed, her face growing pale. "Why did she never say?"

"I think she was ashamed. She somehow thought it was her fault that she was unlovable."

"But everyone loves Angel!"

"True, but I suppose she needed her mother's love more than anything else."

"That more or less explains why she behaves like she does," Brenda said.

"I guess it's why she craves love and attention all the time," Lexi agreed.

"God, I feel bad now." Mel was visibly upset. "Could we try calling her now?"

Lexi looked at her watch. "California is three hours behind us. I guess it's worth a try."

She dialled Angel's number and as usual it went to voicemail. "Are you there, Angel? If so, please pick up. It's Lexi, and Mel and Brenda would really love to talk to you too. Please, Angel, pick up!"

To her surprise Angel answered. Lexi put on the speaker so that the others could hear too.

"Hi, Lexi." Her voice was slurred and it was obvious that she'd been drinking. The three girls looked at each other in dismay.

"Thank God we got you. Are you all right? We're all desperately worried about you."

"Hi, Angel. I'm glad to hear you're okay," Mel said. "I'm sorry for losing my cool with you in Florida but I was pretty upset that night."

"S'okay, Mel, s'okay."

Mel looked relieved. "You take care now."

"Yesh, I will."

"Hi, Angel. It's Brenda here. How are you doing?"

"Fine. Howsh New York?"

"Wonderful! I love it like crazy."

"We just wish you were here, honey," Lexi added.

"Me too," Angel replied. "Gotta go now. Byeee."

Lexi hung up, her concern showing on her face. "I hope she's gonna be okay," she said to the others.

"She doesn't sound great," Brenda commented.

"No, but at least she's talking to us," Lexi replied hopefully.

"You know, I've been thinking about it," Mel said. "I was so angry with her but she was right about Simon. He was a bastard. I can't only blame Angel for his betrayal. He could have said no to her. He obviously didn't love me and now, thanks to Jack, I'm beginning to see that I didn't really love him either so our marriage would have been a disaster."

"Well, it's good that something good has come out of all this," Lexi said softly.

* * *

The next three days were a whirlwind of activity as the girls criss-crossed the city, visiting all the places that had so excited Brenda on the drive they'd taken on the first day. There weren't enough hours in the day for all she wanted to see but they did their best.

They went for breakfast every morning to a different restaurant and Brenda was overwhelmed by the delicious food in all of them but the buffet breakfast at the Waldorf Astoria was hands-down the absolute best.

The highlight of their first day was the visit to Ground Zero which brought the horror of 9/11 alive again for all three women. Brenda couldn't hold back the tears as she looked up at the lasers representing the twin towers and recalled the horrific events of that day. The others also shed tears as they toured the museum that had been newly opened on the site. Then they visited the small St Paul's Church nearby which had been a haven for the rescue teams at the time and was now a memorial to those brave men and women, many of whom had died as they tried to save others.

After a quick lunch they took the ferry across to Ellis Island. Brenda was shocked to hear that neither Lexi nor Mel had ever visited there before. It was very moving and impossible to believe that these poor immigrants were the ancestors of so many successful Irish Americans, one of them even becoming President of the United States.

They planned to go to the Statue of Liberty next but Brenda and Mel could see that Lexi was exhausted and offered to go home with her.

"No, no, you two go on," Lexi insisted. I've been there before and I don't want to spoil your fun. I'll take a cab back to the apartment for a nap so I'll be ready to party this evening."

Reluctantly, the girls agreed and did as she asked and took the ferry over to the Statue which was enormous close up. It was so symbolic of New York that it was a thrill for Brenda to climb to the top of this famous landmark.

"I'm awfully worried about Lexi," Brenda confided to Mel as they sipped a hot chocolate to warm themselves after the climb. "She tires so easily."

"Have you said anything to her about seeing a doctor?"

"Yes. I suggested it to her on the flight here but she absolutely refuses to talk about it."

"You know Lexi – she's as stubborn as a mule."

"I know but she mentioned that Marvin is seemingly on at her too about it."

"Maybe he'll have more luck persuading her than we've had," Mel said hopefully.

"I don't know. He hasn't so far," Brenda replied unhappily.

* * *

This became the pattern for the rest of their stay. At about three o'clock Lexi would return home and the two girls would continue exploring New York.

Mel took Brenda skating at the Rockefeller Center which was great fun and also up to the top of the Empire State Building. They took the ferry across to Staten Island which was still recovering from the awful devastation of Hurricane Sandy. They took photos with the naked cowboy on Times Square and generally did all the tourist things that people did in the Big Apple.

The evenings were equally thrilling and Lexi joined in these with gusto. Mel knew all the best restaurants and as she often entertained clients there, the maître d's were effusive in their welcome making them feel like important guests. They ate in Little Italy one night which was great fun and on the Friday Mel sprang a surprise on them. She had managed to get tickets to the Broadway show, *The Lion King*, which was a fantastic experience for Brenda. Afterwards they had eaten in Joe

186

Allen's and were thrilled to meet some of the cast there.

"You can't leave New York without seeing some of the fabulous stores here," Mel insisted and took them into Bloomingdales and Saks and Bergdorf Goodman.

After one look at the prices Brenda cried, "I couldn't possibly afford anything here!"

"Don't worry, I don't buy anything here either," Lexi confessed.

"Me neither, even though I could afford it," Mel confided, "but I couldn't let you leave New York without visiting these famous stores. Never mind, tomorrow I'll take you to Century 21. The prices are much more reasonable there."

Chapter 22

Meanwhile in LA, Angel was very pleased with the way she'd managed to hold it together in front of Consuela on the Thursday and Friday. At times the craving for a drink became so unbearable that she would creep up to her room and take a drink straight from the whisky bottle. She would then wash her teeth, use mouthwash and then suck a mint, all in an effort to pull the wool over her housekeeper's eyes. She was taking more Prozac than usual but she had to do something to curb her depression.

The call from Lexi had helped and she was happy that Mel had apologised, but hearing them all having a ball together in New York without her made her more depressed than ever. But she was not an actress for nothing and she put on a great show of normality in front of Consuela. By Saturday morning she was beginning to crack so she devised a plan. Getting dressed and putting on her make-up, she descended the stairs smiling brightly.

"Good morning, Consuela," she said pouring herself a coffee.

"You look pretty, Miss Angel. Is good," Consuela declared

beaming, happy to see her mistress all dressed up.

"I'm meeting friends for lunch and then going on to a gallery opening with them so there's no need for you to stay here today, Consuela. Why don't I drop you home on my way?"

"You sure? You no need me?"

"I probably won't be home till late tonight. No, you go off and enjoy the weekend with your grandchildren."

Consuela looked uncertain but was pleased with this suggestion.

"Well, if you sure, Miss Angel."

"I'm sure," Angel nodded, smiling confidently at her. "Now run along and grab your coat and bag. I need to leave now." She went and switched on the answering machine.

Consuela did as she was told.

"I hope you have nice day," she said to Angel as she was dropped off.

"You have a nice weekend too."

Angel drove off and when she'd turned the corner she headed back for home. Going inside she went upstairs for her secret stash and poured a large glass of whisky. She sighed with pleasure as the warm liquid made its way down her throat. Relief flooded through her as she felt its effect. It was the most heavenly feeling in the world.

Kicking off her shoes and getting into her bathrobe she made her way downstairs and, after double-locking the door, curled up on the sofa the bottle of whisky close to hand. Soon she would forget everything as the whisky did its job.

* * *

The following day was Brenda's last in New York and Mel suggested that they take the subway to Century 21, the huge cut-price store that was close to Ground Zero.

"You absolutely have to travel at least once on the subway," Mel insisted as she led them down to the underground.

"It's an experience," Lexi said, rolling her eyes to heaven. "All human life is there, rushing past you, almost knocking you down, as only New Yorkers can."

"Ah, it's not too bad if it's not rush-hour," Mel replied.

"How often do you travel by subway?" Lexi asked her.

"Only when I want to treat a visitor to the experience," Mel grinned sheepishly.

"As I thought," Lexi nodded and they all laughed.

"You wouldn't believe the musicians that busk there at all hours," Mel confided.

"That reminds me," Lexi said, "about the famous violinist, Joshua Bell, who sold out a Boston theatre and two days later took his $3.5 million-dollar violin and played Bach for forty-five minutes in a Washington DC subway. Most people ignored him except for six people who stopped to listen. Believe me, if it had been the New York subway, nobody would have stopped."

"Heavens, that's incredible," Brenda remarked.

"Isn't it just?" Lexi agreed.

Brenda was glad that Lexi had encouraged her to buy the cashmere coat and boots in Ellenton as it was freezing cold in New York and she'd have been lost without them. She was pleased to see that the prices in Century 21 were really low and bought a few last-minute presents.

Mel took them to lunch in a lovely Belgian restaurant, Les Halles, just across Broadway and then they took a stroll down Wall Street which was surprisingly narrow.

"You'll have a permanent crick in your neck from looking up at all these tall buildings," Lexi teased Brenda who was staring skywards yet again.

"I just can't believe how high they all are."

"The Twin Towers dwarfed them all," Lexi said, her voice sad.

They were silent for a while and then Mel announced: "And now, another surprise. We are now going on the *Sex and the City* tour."

Brenda squealed with delight and clapped her hands.

"Are you serious?" Lexi asked.

"Deadly," Mel grinned.

"In that case I'll forego my rest this afternoon. After all, I'll be sitting on a bus, won't I?"

"Yes, and you can doze off if you want to."

"Not on your life," Lexi nudged her playfully. "I wouldn't miss this for anything."

All of them were huge fans of the late-nineties TV series. They'd often compared themselves to the four women on the show although none of them would admit to being like Samantha. However Mel, Lexi and Brenda were in no doubt but that Angel had that one in the bag!

The tour was great fun as they visited places featured in the series and took photos of each other sitting on the steps of Carrie's apartment.

"Isn't it a shame Angel isn't here?" Lexi remarked.

"Well, I did invite her," Mel said.

"She would have loved this," Brenda observed wistfully as they ate cupcakes in the same Magnolia bakery where Miranda had been seen stuffing her face in one episode of the TV show.

However, they all agreed that though they missed her entertaining way they didn't miss the drama that inevitably followed whenever she was around. Things were much calmer without Angel, that was for sure. The three of them were easy and relaxed together just like old times. Although Angel had always been the fun one of the group, sadly she had lately been causing more disharmony than fun.

They had a hilarious afternoon and after a wonderful farewell dinner in the revolving rooftop restaurant of the Marriott Hotel in Times Square, it was back home to pack.

Brenda had called Bob earlier and as usual it had gone to voicemail. She tried his mobile but it was turned off so she rang home again and left a message telling him of her arrival time Tuesday morning. He certainly seemed to have been occupied while she'd been away.

* * *

Franco called to collect Brenda and Lexi at one thirty the following afternoon to take them to the airport. Mel had opted out of accompanying them.

"I hate goodbyes at airports," she explained, "and, besides, I suppose I had better show my face in the office."

"Thank you so much, Mel. I've had a truly wonderful time. I don't know how I can ever repay you," Brenda said, as she hugged Mel tightly.

"I've really enjoyed having you," Mel replied, "and I do hope you'll come more often. It's been great fun."

"Goodbye, honey, and you take care. I've had a wonderful time too," Lexi concurred.

"I'm happy. And I'll be fine, honestly. Don't worry about me. It's been great having you both here. Now go before I start crying." She ushered them into the limo, waving as they drove off.

* * *

After Brenda had put her bags through, she and Lexi went for a last coffee. Lexi's flight was from another terminal so unfortunately she couldn't go through to the business-class lounge with Brenda. They were both sad when the time came to say goodbye.

"I'm going to miss you so much," Lexi said. "It's been wonderful to have this time together."

"I'll never be able to thank you enough," Brenda replied, tears coming to her eyes. "I'll miss you too, more than you'll ever know. Thank you so much for this, Lexi. I've had a fantastic time, the best time of my life."

Lexi held her tight and then quickly broke away, afraid she might cry. Her last sight of Brenda was as she was going through security and she could see Brenda was crying. With tears in her eyes Lexi turned away and made her way to Terminal 3.

* * *

As Lexi entered the terminal her phone rang.

"Hello, Miss Lexi?"

Lexi recognised Angel's housekeeper's voice and heard the anguish in it. Fear gripped her heart. "What is it, Consuela? Is there something wrong with Angel?"

"Yes, Miss Lexi," Consuela sobbed. "She in hospital. We go in ambulance."

Lexi gasped and clutched at her chest. She sank down on a nearby chair, afraid that her legs might give way.

"What happened? Talk slowly, Consuela."

"Miss Angel, she no wake up when I come in today." The poor woman was obviously distraught as she lapsed into Spanish.

"Consuela, listen to me. Are you at the hospital? Can you put a nurse on the phone to me?"

She heard Consuela crying as she handed over the phone.

"Hello, who am I speaking to?" asked an unknown voice.

"Lexi Moretti. I'm Angel Flannery's next of kin. Can you tell me what's happened?"

The nurse could hear the anxiety in Lexi's voice. "Well, she's unconscious and in intensive care at the moment," she informed her. "I'm afraid it looks like she has overdosed."

Lexi gasped. "Oh my God!" she cried. "What hospital?"

The nurse gave her the name and address.

"I'm at JFK at the moment," Lexi told her. "I was on my way to Tampa but I'll catch the next available flight to LA."

"Very good, Miss Moretti. I'll leave your name at the desk so just come straight to intensive care when you get here."

"Thank you," Lexi said. She was already making her way to the ticket counter. She was in luck. There was a flight leaving in thirty minutes and if she ran they said she might make it.

She made it – just! Luckily she had only a pull-along bag with her. Sinking in to her seat she prayed like she'd never prayed before.

Waiting for take-off she called Marvin to tell him she would not be home tonight and briefly explained why not. Then she quickly dialled Mel's number. As usual it went to voicemail.

"Mel, something has happened to Angel. She's unconscious and in intensive care. I'm on a flight to LA. I'll call you when I get there."

"Sorry, madam, but you have to switch off immediately for take-off," the cabin steward informed her.

"Have to go," Lexi whispered. "We're taking off."

She was glad she had no time to call Brenda. No point in upsetting her before her long flight back to Ireland. Besides there was nothing any of them could do except hope and pray.

* * *

It took Lexi over five hours to get from JFK to LAX but it felt like twenty-five. Her phone rang as she was walking through the arrivals hall in LA. It was Mel.

"What's happened? Has she been in an accident? I've been sick with worry. Do you want me to take the red-eye tonight?"

"No, Mel. Wait until I get to the hospital and find out more. It appears she's overdosed. Consuela said she came in this morning and couldn't wake Angel. I spoke to a nurse who said that she was unconscious and in intensive care but of course it may have changed since then. Look, I'll call you the moment I find out."

"Does Brenda know?"

"No, I had left her when I got the call from Consuela. I thought it better not to call her until we know more. Brenda's still in the air now. In any case, time enough to let her know when I find out more. Better go. I'll call you as soon as I can."

"Hope she's okay, Lex. I'm glad you can be with her."

* * *

It took almost an hour to get to the Cedars-Sinai Hospital and Lexi ran to the intensive care unit where they told her there was no change in Angel's condition. She put on the gown and mask they gave her and was shown into the room where Angel lay like a rag doll surrounded by tubes. She was on a ventilator and the only sound in the room was the bleep of the heart monitor over her bed. She looked so pale and fragile that Lexi feared the worse. She took the tiny lifeless hand in hers and stroked it as she spoke to Angel.

"It's Lexi, honey. I'm here. Can you hear me, Angel? You're going to pull through this. Can you open your eyes for me? C'mon, Angel, wake up."

There was no response and Lexi looked at the nurse, tears in her eyes.

"Keep talking to her," said the nurse. "It may bring her round."

Trying hard not to cry Lexi kept talking but Angel lay lifeless and still as Lexi told her about their trip to New York. Still no response.

She kept talking about everything and anything that came into her head, even reminiscing about their schooldays. She had to leave the room shortly afterwards when two doctors came in to check on Angel.

Lexi took the opportunity to call Mel although it was very late in New York. Mel answered on the first ring.

"Oh God, no!" she cried as Lexi described Angel's condition. "It's all my fault for saying those awful things to her in Florida."

"Don't be silly, Mel. This is no one's fault. I'll be in the hospital all night. I'll let you know if there's any change."

"Are you sure you don't want me to come out?"

"No, there's no need. There's nothing you can do here. I'll keep you informed."

* * *

"It's touch and go with her," the doctor informed Lexi after he had examined Angel. "We pumped out her stomach but she must have been taking barbiturates for quite some time. On top of that she had enough alcohol in her blood to kill someone so slight. She's had a lucky escape."

Lexi looked at him numbly. "Is there nothing you can do?" she asked, unable to conceal her anguish.

"It's up to her now," a younger lady doctor said gently. "It's good if you can keep talking to her. It may help to get through to her."

So Lexi stayed the night, sitting in an armchair beside the bed, all the while talking to Angel, willing her to wake up. Barely able to keep her eyes open, she nodded off from time to time but thanks to the lovely nurse who kept her supplied with coffee throughout the night she managed to stay awake most of the time. It was around seven the following morning when she felt Angel squeeze her hand. At first she thought it was her imagination but then she felt it again.

"Oh Angel, honey, it's okay. Wake up, darling. Lexi's here," she cried. She stood up and stroked Angel's hair and face and her heart leapt as she saw Angel's eyes flutter.

She rang for the nurse as she'd been told to do and within seconds she was in the room talking to Angel and rubbing her hands.

"C'mon, Angel, wake up. C'mon, girl. Lexi's here," the nurse was saying loudly.

At last Angel opened her eyes. She smiled wanly at Lexi and tried to say something but couldn't with the mask over her mouth.

"It's okay, Angel, it's okay," Lexi cried, smiling through her tears. "Everything's going to be all right."

Two other nurses hurried in and bustled around, administering to Angel.

"Do you want me to leave?" Lexi asked, standing up and moving out of their way.

"No, you're fine there. Keep talking to her. It's good for her to hear you and know you're here."

When they had finished Angel looked wanly at Lexi and reached for her hand.

"You're going to be okay now," Lexi assured her, taking the frail hand and squeezing it.

Angel smiled at her then closed her eyes and fell asleep.

"She'll be okay now," the nurse assured Lexi. "She'll sleep

now for hours. Why don't you go and get some sleep yourself?"

"I suppose I should. I could certainly do with a shower but I don't like to leave her. Look, I'm staying in the Four Seasons. Could you call me if she wakes? I could get here in ten minutes. Here's my number." She handed her card to the nurse.

"Angel's a lucky girl to have such a friend," the nurse replied, putting the card in her pocket. "We almost lost her, you know."

"I know," Lexi said sombrely.

Chapter 23

Brenda was having a wonderful flight, oblivious to all the drama. She enjoyed the complimentary champagne and delicious meal with wine as she thought about her holiday. She'd had a wonderful time and felt rejuvenated but now she had to face reality again. She would have to forget about Troy and how he'd made her feel if she was to settle back into her normal life.

Having finally acknowledged the problems in her marriage she knew she would now have to do something about it, if it was to be saved. The first step would be to sit down and talk with Bob and she resolved to do that as soon as possible. Happy with her decision, she watched a movie and feeling sleepy, activated the lie-flat bed and slept for the rest of the flight. She would be eternally grateful to Lexi for booking her business class.

Feeling refreshed, she came through the arrivals at Dublin Airport to find no sign of Bob. She looked around, wondering where he might be and after ten minutes called his mobile.

"Where are you?" she asked.

"I'm on my way. Go and have a coffee," he said gruffly. "I'll be at departures in about fifteen or twenty minutes."

"I can see you're obviously delighted to have me home," she muttered as she heard him hang up.

Fifteen minutes later she was standing in the freezing cold at the departures entrance but there was still no sign of Bob. Ten minutes later, her toes and fingers numb, she saw his taxi pull up.

He got out and kissed her perfunctorily on the cheek as he put her suitcases in the boot.

"God, it's freezing," she exclaimed as she sat into the car.

"Welcome to the real world. You're not in Florida any more."

She detected the sarcastic note in his voice and stayed silent as he manoeuvred the car into the early morning traffic.

"You couldn't have come in at a worst possible time," he grumbled as they were caught up in the commuter traffic on the M50.

She was tempted to reply that she wasn't responsible for the Aer Lingus schedule but she bit her tongue and stayed mum. The last thing they needed now was an argument. She had hoped that he would be pleased to have her home and that they could start afresh but that was obviously not the case. He uttered not a single word as he drove her home except to mutter about the "bloody traffic".

"Any news or scandal since I left?" she asked, hoping to thaw him out.

"None," he replied, lapsing into silence again. He never asked her once what she'd done or even how she'd liked New York. She'd hoped he might have told her she was looking well or that he liked her coat but he didn't even seem to notice. It was obvious he was still resentful of her trip so she didn't dare say anything about it. She was hurt and turned to look out the window so that he wouldn't see the tears in her eyes as she tried desperately to stop them falling.

When they arrived home he took her cases out of the car and left them on the front doorstep. He opened the front door and then turned back, heading to the car.

"See you later," he said as he got into it.

"Aren't you coming in?" she asked, shocked.

"No, somebody in this house has to earn money rather than spend it," he said spitefully, and then he was gone.

Brenda hoisted the heavy case and bag inside, feeling angry and hurt. How could they possibly solve their problems if he wouldn't even talk to her? Bob had built a wall around himself which excluded her and she had no idea how she could get through it. She made herself some tea then sat down at the kitchen table and wept. Then she went upstairs and climbed into bed. She slept until midday and when she'd showered and dressed in warm clothes she tried calling Lexi to say she was home, safe and sound. There was no reply from her home phone and Brenda left a message. She then tried Lexi's mobile but it was turned off.

She felt deflated as she roamed around the empty house which suddenly seemed small and poky after Lexi's mansion. The grey wet weather didn't help nor the fact that she couldn't get warm. She thought back to the constantly warm sunny days in Florida and felt a pang of regret that she couldn't be back there. Adding to her depression was Bob's behaviour that morning which had disturbed her greatly.

She knew he'd been resentful of her trip but now it had gone far enough. She couldn't believe he was being so childish. She Skyped Alex and was delighted to find her online. She smiled brightly, trying not to let her daughter see how despondent she was, as she told her all about the trip.

Her sister Jean arrived just as she'd finished.

"I am simply dying to hear all about it," she cried as they hugged.

Brenda put on the kettle and made some sandwiches as she started to describe the fabulous time she'd had.

"I'm green with envy," Jean exclaimed. "It sounds like heaven."

"It was. It was the trip of a lifetime but I'm having withdrawal symptoms," Brenda smiled ruefully. She omitted any mention of Troy although she was tempted to tell Jean about him. She finally told her about Angel and her drink problem.

"That's so sad. I remember how I envied her when we were at school. She was so beautifully dressed and I wanted to look like her more than anything," Jean said. "Just goes to show, beauty doesn't buy happiness."

"No. She's still beautiful but very unhappy. It's a pity because it caused a rift between us in the end. She and Mel had a dreadful row and she rushed off back to LA in the middle of the night."

"Oh, no! That must have been awful. You four were always so tight-knit. I envied that too." Jean sighed.

Brenda then went on to tell Jean about Bob's welcome that morning. "I don't know what the hell is wrong with him and he won't talk to me about it."

"Well, he was acting very strangely while you were away. I invited him over numerous evenings for dinner but he replied that he was busy every evening. I even invited him to lunch the three Sundays you were away but he didn't come." Jean frowned. "I don't know what's bugging him, sis, but something is." She hesitated, "I don't know if I should mention this but I did see him in Ryan's pub with that young one who works in the taxi office. You know the one I mean – tits hanging out, skirt up to her arse."

"I know who you mean. Bob often goes out for a jar with the other drivers after work. She probably tagged along. I wouldn't worry about that."

"Maybe, but what was he so busy doing every evening if he couldn't come for dinner even once?"

Brenda got up and paced around the kitchen. "I don't know. I wonder where he was eating? I left a freezer full of cooked meals for him but they've hardly been touched."

"I think you should ask him what's going on," Jean suggested matter of factly. "Sounds fishy to me." She looked at her watch. "God, I better run. Mrs Brady is coming in for her colour at two and you know what an old biddy she is. She'll hit the roof if I'm not there."

"I've brought you a present from New York but I haven't unpacked yet."

"Oooooh, lovely. Don't worry, I'll get it next time. Call and let me know how your talk with Bob goes."

"I will. See you tomorrow, sweetie."

"Three weeks in the States and you're talking like one of them already, sweetie," Jean laughed as she ran out the door.

* * *

When Lexi got to the hotel she rang Mel and told her what the doctors had said. "It was an overdose but they're not sure if it was intentional or an accident. They say she must have been abusing drugs for quite some time."

"She was. I feel so guilty. I knew it and I should have done something about it."

"Mel, stop it!" Lexi said harshly. "This is not your fault. She wouldn't listen when we tried to talk to her. There was nothing you could have done. She has to take some responsibility for her own actions."

"What's going to happen now?"

"I don't know. I'll meet with the doctors later. I suppose she'll have to go into rehab."

"Will she agree?"

"I guess after this scare she won't have any choice."

Lexi rang Consuela to give her the good news that Angel was now conscious and sleeping.

"*Gracias a Díos*," she cried, her relief obvious. "I come see her now?"

"No need to come in until this afternoon, Consuela, as the nurse told me she'd be sleeping till then."

"I very happy, Miss Lexi. I come visit then."

Lexi also called Marvin to tell him what had transpired and it gave her great comfort to hear his voice.

"It's very lonely here without you," he said. "When do you think you'll be home?"

She felt warmed by his words. "I really can't say. It depends on Angel's recovery."

"I miss you."

"I miss you too, Marvin."

When they'd hung up Lexi, counting forward eight hours, saw that it was mid-afternoon in Ireland. She called Brenda who was unpacking at the time and was delighted to hear Lexi's voice.

"I left a message on your home number to let you know I'd arrived home safely," Brenda said.

"I'm not in Florida, I'm in LA."

"You're where?" Brenda gasped. "What are you doing there? When I left you were making your way to Tampa."

"It's a long story," Lexi said, exhaustion almost overwhelming her. She explained about Angel to Brenda who was shocked and upset at the news.

"Will she really be all right?" Brenda asked worriedly.

"Yes, it was touch-and-go for a while but they've assured me she'll be fine. She'll have to go into rehab for quite some time but hopefully after that treatment she'll be back to her old self."

"Oh, I do hope so. Poor Angel! Give her my love when she wakes up."

"I will of course. You got home okay?"

"Yes, I had a lovely trip."

Lexi then took a very welcome shower and crawled into the comfortable bed, exhausted. She set the alarm for noon and seconds later was fast asleep.

* * *

Angel was still sleeping when Lexi got back to the hospital but her breathing was now stable and the colour was back in her cheeks. The doctor arrived to check on her and proclaimed himself satisfied that she was out of danger and that she could come off the ventilator. He spoke gravely to Lexi and said that Angel would have to go to rehab and be weaned off her addiction to alcohol and prescription drugs.

"She's very lucky, you know. If her housekeeper hadn't found her when she did, she would not have survived."

Consuela arrived shortly after and when Lexi assured her that Angel would be okay she burst into tears. She admitted that Angel had been drinking heavily, saying that she'd found a hoard of empty whisky bottles in her bedroom. She'd also found her greatly depleted stash of Prozac and Ambien.

"I think she die," Consuela said tearfully, "but I pray all night and *Díos*, he listen."

Lexi put her arms around the shaking woman. "Thanks to you, Consuela, she's going to be okay but she might have to go away for a long time, to get better."

Consuela nodded. She understood. She went in and sat with Angel while Lexi went for something to eat. When she came back the two women sat quietly, watching Angel sleep.

* * *

It was mid-afternoon when Angel opened her eyes. She looked very much better than she had earlier and when she saw Lexi and Consuela by her bedside, she started to cry. She became very emotional when they told her that she had almost died.

"I'm sorry, I'm so sorry," she whispered, tears rolling down her cheeks.

"Did you mean to do it, Angel? Did you want to take your own life?"

"No, no," Angel cried, struggling to sit up.

"Thank God for that!"

The nurse, who had come in, gently pushed her back down on the pillow.

"You must take it easy now, Angel. No upset." She looked at Lexi disapprovingly. "There'll be plenty of time to talk in the next few days. Now you must get better."

"Sorry," Lexi said, slightly ashamed. "I didn't mean to upset her."

"That's okay," the nurse said. "The doctor would like to see her now, if you don't mind?"

"Of course," Lexi replied, blowing a kiss at Angel as she and Consuela exited. She took the opportunity to text Mel and Brenda to assure them that Angel was awake and recovering well.

* * *

Brenda was relieved when Lexi texted to say that Angel was awake and had pulled through. She couldn't imagine what they would have done if she hadn't. That was one positive thing in the day, she thought, as she wondered where Bob was. He usually finished at five o'clock and she'd been expecting him home shortly after. It was now six thirty and there was still no sign of him. It hurt her to think that he was obviously avoiding her.

She had taken out two of the chicken curries she'd left for him in the freezer and had reheated them and boiled the rice to go with them. Eventually, she ate her own. No point in having two spoilt dinners!

She was sitting reading when she heard his key in the door.

"Hi, what's for dinner?" he asked, poking his head in the living-room door.

"Good evening to you too," she replied icily. "Your dinner has been in the oven since five thirty."

She heard him washing his hands and going into the kitchen. She started to get angry and by time he'd finished eating and reappeared, with a beer in his hand, she was ready to confront him.

"Okay, enough!" she said, looking at him directly. "I want to know what's going on."

"What do you mean?" he asked, avoiding her eyes and turning on the TV before slumping in his armchair.

"You know bloody well what I mean! You were never here when I called. You didn't call me on my birthday and now you're acting like the wronged party." She glared at him but he continued to look at the TV screen.

"Look at me!" Brenda cried, turning off the TV. "We need to talk. Why didn't you eat any of the meals I left for you to have while I was away? Where did you eat every evening? I'm curious. Tell me the truth."

"Well, I went out with the guys to Ryan's most evenings and it was easier to eat there."

"Yes, Jean said she'd seen you there."

"She did?" he asked warily.

"Yeah."

He looked startled. "Did she say anything else?"

"Like what?" Brenda looked at him strangely.

"Well, you know . . . anything else?"

"Well, she said she invited you for dinner but you said you were busy every evening."

Brenda saw the way his eyes shied away from hers and knew something was up. "Bob, what's going on? Tell me the truth."

He looked at her for a long moment and then his face appeared to crumple. He took a deep breath.

"I don't know how to tell you this, Brenda, but there's someone else." His voice was so low that she'd thought she'd misheard him.

"What did you say?"

"I said, there's someone else," he repeated, louder this time.

She felt her heart stop. "What do you mean 'there's someone else'?"

"Well you know, I felt abandoned when you went off to Florida and this other girl was there for me."

She looked at him, trying to take in what he was saying, thinking it must be a joke. "I didn't abandon you, Bob. I was just on holiday with my friends," she said.

"Well, I felt abandoned," he replied pettishly.

"Who is this woman? Do I know her?"

"It's Crystal, the receptionist in the office." He was standing now, taking a swig of beer.

"Crystal?" Brenda repeated, shocked. Although Jean had said he'd been with the busty blonde in Ryan's, she'd never imagined there could be anything between them. Crystal couldn't be more than twenty-five. "But she's not much older than Alex and, besides, she's a tart."

"Don't call her that," Bob said spiritedly. "She's a great girl."

"Isn't she married?"

"Her marriage has broken up and she's upset about it. I was alone too. You know how it is."

"No, I don't know how it is. I was gone less than three weeks, Bob. How could you do this?"

She sank onto the sofa, her head in her hands. After a few moments she looked up at him. "Is it just sex or do you have feelings for her?"

He nodded his head, looking at the ground. "I love her," he mumbled.

Brenda groaned. "Does she love you?"

"Of course. That's why she left her husband." He sounded almost proud of this announcement.

And then the penny dropped and Brenda understood. "How long has this been going on, Bob? Please tell me the truth." Her voice was a whisper.

He shifted from foot to foot as he muttered, "About six months."

"I should have known," Brenda said bitterly. "My going to Florida had nothing to do with your behaviour, did it? But you let me think it did. You're despicable."

"Let's face it, Bren, our marriage wasn't great anyway."

"No, it wasn't, because you put up a huge barrier between us. You didn't want to make love to me any more which left me frustrated and made me think I was unattractive and undesirable."

"You've changed. All this talk of studying and wanting to better yourself. I blame those la-di-dah bitches of girlfriends you have. Putting notions in your head that you can better yourself."

"How can you say that, Bob? That's so unfair! They've been my best friends since I was four. And of course I've changed. You've changed too. We've been together for twenty-five years, Bob. Is our marriage not worth saving? Are you going to throw it all away on some floosie?"

"Don't talk about her like that!" he said indignantly. "She understands me and thinks I'm wonderful."

"Well, go to her then, right this minute," Brenda cried, flinging a cushion at him. "Out, get out! This minute!"

She advanced towards him, fists flailing. He was shocked. He'd never seen Brenda so angry. "Go to your mistress and good riddance!"

"Hang on a minute, Bren!"

"Get out!" she shrieked.

Bob skedaddled out as quickly as he could, afraid of what she might do to him. He knew hell hath no fury . . . and he wasn't about to hang around to find out.

Brenda sat shaking for a long time afterwards, hardly able to believe what had just taken place. How had she been so blind? Six months! She couldn't cry – she was too shocked and hurt. No doubt the tears would come soon enough. She rang Jean.

"Well, did you have that chat with Bob?" her sister asked.

"I sure did and I found out what's been bugging him," Brenda's voice broke as she spoke.

"What is it, Brenda? What's wrong?"

"He has someone else. He's leaving me."

"He what?" Jean shrieked. She couldn't believe what she was hearing. "Where is he now?"

"He's gone. To his lover, I presume. I threw him out!"

"Oh my God, Brenda, I can't believe it. I'll be there in five minutes."

* * *

When Brenda saw Jean standing on the doorstep, she broke down. Jean hugged her and led her into the living-room as she sobbed her heart out. Pouring two glasses of whisky from the bottle she'd thought to bring with her, she handed one to Brenda. Sitting on the sofa beside her, she took Brenda's hand and waited patiently until her sobs had subsided. Sipping the whisky slowly, Brenda told her what had transpired with Bob earlier.

"The bastard!" Jean exclaimed indignantly. "And what an idiot falling for that Crystal one. I know her, she's a client of mine and a right slapper. It won't last, trust me."

"I don't care whether it does or not. They're welcome to each other." Brenda's voice was bitter.

"It's probably just sex. Wait till you see – within six months he'll come crawling back, begging your forgiveness."

"Well, he'll be wasting his time. I'm done with him. I'll never take him back."

"Oh, Brenda, he's a fool." Jean hugged her older sister who had always been her rock. She was glad she could be here for her now. "I know you were having problems in bed but I never imagined he'd do anything like this."

"Me neither. Even though things have not been great, I did think we could work it out. I came home with the express intention of making him talk. And now this! I certainly never expected it to end like this." She drained her glass and Jean got up to pour her another one.

"What happens now?" Jean asked, handing her the tumbler.

"I have no idea. I need time to think about it. By the way, I had bad news from Lexi today."

She then related what Lexi had told her about Angel.

"Oh my God, that's awful! You've certainly had a day of bad news."

"At least Angel has pulled through and will recover. I can't say the same for my marriage." She grimaced.

"You'll be fine. You're strong and you're still young. You have a whole life ahead of you."

Brenda sighed. Suddenly the jet-lag hit her and she was overcome with tiredness. She yawned.

"Do you mind if I hit the sack? I'm shattered."

"Course not. I've brought you a sleeping pill. You could do with a good night's sleep after today's drama." She handed Brenda the tablet.

"Oh, I don't think I need –"

"Take it, it's very mild, and I'm also staying the night with you," Jean insisted.

"Yes, boss," Brenda giggled, swallowing the pill. The whisky was already taking effect.

She made her way up to bed and decided to sleep in Carly's room, thinking that Bob had probably had sex with the slapper in their bed. Thankfully the sleeping pill did its work and within seconds she was fast asleep.

Chapter 24

Angel was deemed well enough to be moved out of intensive care that evening. She was also well enough to demand that she be given an executive suite on the VIP floor.

"Of course, Miss Flannery. That will not be a problem," the nurse smiled sweetly.

Angel was coming back to her old self. She ordered Consuela to take a cab back to the house and pack up some things she would need. She got Lexi to write the list as she dictated what she wanted. Besides all the cosmetics and clothes that she requested she also asked Consuela to bring the medication on her night table. "And maybe you could bring in a bottle of whisky. After all, if I'm going into rehab soon . . ."

"Uh-oh, Angel, I don't think that will be allowed," said Lexi.

Angel started to protest but unfortunately for her the nurse had come into her room and heard these last requests.

"Now, now, Miss Flannery, you are not allowed to bring your own medication in here and definitely no alcohol," she reprimanded, her voice stiff with disapproval.

"But I won't be able to sleep," Angel objected, not giving up without a fight.

"Don't you worry about that. We'll give you something to help you sleep."

Angel made a face behind her back.

"Okay, Consuela, off you go," Lexi said, handing over the list.

"Is okay, Miss Angel?" Consuela appealed to her mistress.

Angel dismissed her with a wave of her hand. "Yes, just do as they say," she said irritably.

When she was gone, Lexi took Angel's hand in hers. "Angel, things have to change. You almost died, you know. Next time you might not be so lucky."

Angel started to cry softly. "I know but I don't have anything to live for, do I?"

"How can you say that?" Lexi exclaimed angrily. "Do you know how many people, right in this hospital, are fighting for their lives at this moment? People with cancer and other serious illnesses who would give anything to be in your shoes right now? How can you be so selfish?"

Angel stopped crying, shocked and frightened by this outburst. "I'm sorry, Lexi, but life just looks so bleak. I don't know how I can go on."

"You can go on, honey, I know you can. You can beat this. There are wonderful people in these rehab centres who can help you. You've got to get your life back on track. It's your only hope."

"I don't know if I could hack that," Angel said, starting to cry once more.

"If you don't then I'm out of here and you'll never see me again," Lexi said resolutely, hoping to shock her into compliance.

Angel looked at her aghast. She knew by the stubborn jut of Lexi's chin that she meant every word she'd said. She covered her face with her hands. If Lexi left her she would be finished. Lexi was her rock.

"Okay," she whispered. "I'll go into rehab if that's what you want."

"It's not just what I want, sweetie, it's what the doctors want and what you must do if you're to survive."

"All right," Angel gulped, crying softly.

Lexi had to steel herself to stand firm when she saw how distressed Angel was but just then the nursing aides came to move her to her new room, so the moment passed. Lexi took the opportunity to call Mel at that stage and give her an update.

Lexi found that Angel's new room was even nicer than her own room in the Four Seasons and when Consuela arrived back with a case full of her stuff, Angel perked up. Finally, the nurse came in to say they had to leave and, seeing Consuela into a cab, Lexi took another one back to her hotel. Utterly exhausted, she fell into bed and into a deep sleep.

* * *

Mel was relieved that Angel had pulled through. She would have felt personally responsible if anything had happened to her. She realised now that with all the prescription drugs Angel had been taking, coupled with the amount of alcohol she had been downing, she had probably been out of it the night of the row.

She felt guilty at the way she'd attacked Angel. They went back a long way and Mel determined that no man would come between them in the future. She planned to fly to LA at the weekend to visit Angel.

Lexi as always was being a rock, staying by Angel's side throughout, at the expense of her own life. Not for the first time she wondered what any of them would do without her.

Mel was feeling down since the girls had left. She'd enjoyed showing them her city and they'd had a lot of fun. She missed them both. She was thinking a lot about Jack too and the good times they'd had. In those few days with him he had shown her an alternative way of living that made her own life seem rather pointless. She felt that her career was of little consequence and she was finding it difficult to immerse herself in it the way she once did.

Angel's near-brush with death had also made her question her own raison d'être. She felt lethargic and down and hoped this ennui would leave her soon.

* * *

Lexi was still feeling exhausted when the alarm went off the following morning. All this drama was sapping her energy. She longed to be back at her easel, doing what she did best. She was also longing to be back in Marvin's arms but she put that thought right out of her head. Angel needed her now, so here she would stay. She would not leave until she had Angel safely installed in a good rehabilitation facility. She dragged herself out of bed and felt a little better after her shower. She was having breakfast when Brenda rang.

"Hi, sweetie, how's the jet-lag?"

"Oh Lexi, I'm afraid I've more than jet-lag to worry about now. Bob has left me."

"What?" Lexi gasped, thinking she'd misheard.

"He says he's met another woman – well, girl, actually – she's not much older than Alex."

Lexi was speechless.

"Are you there, Lexi?"

"Yes, yes, I'm here. I just can hardly believe what you're saying."

"I know. I'm having a problem believing it too, but it's true. He's been having an affair for the past six months with this twenty-five-year-old. He says he loves her and she's left her husband for him." Brenda attempted a laugh but it came out like a croak.

"Oh, honey, this is terrible news. I know you told me things were not good between you but I never would have suspected this."

"Me neither, Lexi. I'm very hurt and shocked and I feel betrayed even though I haven't been happy for some time now. And obviously Bob hasn't either, at least not with me."

Lexi heard the anguish in her voice and her heart hurt for her friend.

She spoke very gently, choosing her words carefully. "You know, Brenda, you got married very young and, although Bob was the right person for you back then, maybe he's not the right person for you now. And life is too short to spend it with the wrong person."

"It's funny you should say that. That's what Troy said to me the first night I met him."

"Well, I think he's right, don't you?"

"I don't know," Brenda replied, a wobble in her voice. "I feel like it's my fault and that I've failed."

"You haven't failed. You've been a great wife to Bob and a fantastic mother. Maybe it's just time to move on."

"Maybe," Brenda sighed, unconvincingly. Move on to where? "Now tell me, how is Angel?"

"Good news. She's been moved into a fabulous suite on the VIP floor which is more her style. We're meeting with her doctor and therapist later this morning. They say she's got to go into rehab and I think I've convinced her she has to go."

"Oh God! I wish I was there to help."

"You've enough on your plate and Mel is flying in on

Friday. Sorry, I have to rush Brenda. You take care and I'll keep you informed."

"Thanks, Lex, you're a rock."

"I feel like one built on quicksand right now," Lexi said ruefully. It was true. Everything seemed to be coming apart at the seams at the moment. She wondered what was next.

* * *

Things moved with lightning speed after that. Lexi sat with Angel as the doctor and therapist tried to impress on her just how close to death she had come. After copious tears, Angel finally agreed to go into rehab right away.

"Could she check into a facility in Tampa so that I could visit her regularly?" Lexi asked.

"I'm afraid she won't be allowed any visitors for at least six weeks, whatever rehab she goes into. It's part of the programme."

"What?" Angel stopped her crying in order to shriek.

"I'm afraid total immersion in the programme is essential which means isolation."

Lexi was afraid to look at Angel to see how she was taking this. When she did she saw the panic in her eyes. Taking her hand, Lexi said, "You must do as they say, Angel. You won't feel six weeks pass."

Angel seemed to shrink into the bed. "When do I have to go?" she asked the doctor dully.

"We can move you there this afternoon. It's a luxury facility, the best in the area. You'll be very happy there, I'm sure."

"This afternoon?" Angel sounded shocked but didn't protest. "Can Lexi come with me?" she asked in a small voice.

"Of course."

* * *

218

By three o'clock they were on their way and both of them were pleasantly surprised by the opulence of the La Vista Rehabilitation Centre which was more like a luxury spa. The director welcomed them and showed them around. When Angel saw the luxurious beauty and nail salon, she became less anxious and smiled for the first time that day. Lexi breathed a sigh of relief.

While Angel was settling in, Lexi took the opportunity to text Brenda and Mel and give them the good news. She promised to Skype them both the following day with all the details.

When it came time to leave Angel, she did so with a lighter heart. It was still not easy leaving her there. She looked so fragile, like a little-girl-lost.

"Oh, Lexi, I'm so scared. I don't know if I can do this."

"You'll come through this, honey. I know you will. I believe in you."

"I'll try not to let you down, I promise."

*　*　*

Lexi sank back into the first class seat on the Southwest Airways flight to Tampa. She was utterly exhausted, physically and mentally, and longed to get home. What a week it had been!

She slept all the way and Marvin met her at the airport, enveloping her in a great bear hug. It felt good.

"C'mon home, darling, and let me take care of you now. You need some TLC after all you've been dishing out."

Lexi smiled up at him. He was so right. She was tired of being the 'rock'.

As she lay wrapped in his arms that night she felt safe and cared for. Perhaps he was right. Perhaps it was time to make this permanent. She vowed to give it some serious thought.

* * *

Brenda had tried to keep herself as busy as possible since Bob's defection. However, she found herself crying at the least thing – a song on the radio, a photo of them in happier times – it was a sad thing, she'd found out, ending a marriage. She still hadn't had the courage to tell the children. She couldn't deliver this news over the phone, she'd rather tell them face to face. She would tell the boys and Carly when they came home for the Christmas holidays, which would be in a little over two weeks, and she would Skype Alex and Megan just before that. It was not a task she was looking forward to. She knew the children would be furious with Bob and she hoped it wouldn't cause a rift between them but he had brought it upon himself. She heard from Jean that he had moved in with the slapper and she did not think that the kids would take too kindly to his new paramour. Brenda couldn't bring herself to say her name. She even doubted it was her real name. Who, besides Hollywood celebrities, called a child Crystal?

Jean had been her rock and her saviour as she tried to come to terms with it.

On the second day after Bob left, Jean rang her bubbling with excitement. Her receptionist, who was pregnant, had been rushed into hospital, and she asked Brenda if she would stand in for her in the salon.

"Oh, I don't know. I'm such a misery-boots at the moment that I'm liable to burst into tears at any time."

"Nonsense, you'll be far too busy to have time to cry. Besides, I'm desperate. Please Brenda?"

Brenda agreed and to her surprise, loved it. There was never a dull moment in the salon and she fell into bed every night exhausted, her feet sore and her voice almost gone from all the talking. Jean had been right, she didn't have time to cry or feel sorry for herself. An added bonus was that she had a captive audience for her Avon products and Jean encouraged her to sell to the clients. As a result her sales soared and she was earning good money which was always welcome.

Her family also rallied round and one or other of them invited her for dinner every evening or for Sunday lunch. They were happy to be able to repay their sister for all she'd done for them over the years. She laughed now to think how she used to envy Lexi and Angel, having no brothers and sisters. At times like this it was a blessing to be from a large family and to have their support.

She had only seen Bob once when he had called to collect his things. He rang to tell her what time he'd be there and Jean made sure to be there too. He slunk in, avoiding Jean's icy stare. She had wanted to bawl him out but Brenda had begged her not to say anything. He collected his clothes and his few meagre possessions and slunk out again. He was so afraid of his sister-in-law that he decided not to risk her wrath by taking anything from the house, not even his tools. He wanted out of there as quickly as possible. Jean insisted that Brenda get the locks changed the next day, which she did.

Mel and Lexi Skyped her often, both of them very concerned about her. Angel knew nothing about her situation which was just as well. She had enough on her plate as it was.

* * *

Lexi regularly called Dr Kirk, the director of La Vista, who told her that Angel was having a problem settling and not adapting too well to the programme. She arranged for Lexi to call her once a week for a progress report on Angel. The woman sounded positive, however, and Lexi was happy that Angel was in the right place and in good hands. She prayed it would be a success and that Angel would get back to her old self.

Chapter 25

Lexi started painting again but found it difficult to work like she used to. For starters she was tired all the time. The week with the girls here in Florida, then the New York trip and not least the trip to California had all left her exhausted. It was as if they had sapped all her energy. The worry over Angel, and now Brenda, had taken their toll. No matter how much she rested or slept she couldn't shake the bone-tiredness she was feeling.

Marvin was worried about her, she knew, and pestered her to go to the doctor but she resisted. She disliked doctors and had little faith in them. All they did was dole out prescriptions for chemicals which couldn't be good for your body. Lexi preferred homeopathic and natural remedies.

The other thing that worried her was the way her latest painting was coming along. She was famous for her bright vivid colours but they had deserted her and this newest one was increasingly melancholy and dark. She wondered whether it might be her state of mind or physical tiredness that was the cause.

The good news was that Brenda had started working and seemed to be enjoying her new job. She was lucky she had her family to support her and her kids would be home for Christmas which would be a big help. Every day Lexi thanked God for Skype. It was wonderful to be able to talk to her regularly and see her at the same time.

Although Mel had had no catastrophe in her life – though finding and then losing Jack could probably be counted as one – she too seemed to have changed since that fateful Thanksgiving night. She was more apathetic towards her job which was most unusual and was obviously not working the long hours she had worked previously. She also complained of feeling tired, making Lexi wonder whether the whole drama had sucked all their energies. Intense relationships could do that she'd read somewhere.

She would like to have been able to Skype Angel too but that was forbidden, of course.

Lexi called Dr Kirk the following week only to be told that Angel was not co-operating with them.

"I have you down as next of kin," the director said. "But I understand now that Angel's mother is alive and living in the South of France."

"Yes, but they're estranged. They haven't spoken in years," Lexi explained. "She has no other relatives and when her father died she asked me if I would act as her next-of-kin. Naturally, I agreed."

"Ah, I see," Dr Kirk, replied. "How unfortunate. That explains a lot of Angel's problems, I think. Thank you, Mrs Moretti."

Lexi was very impressed with Dr Kirk and her team and prayed that they would get Angel back on track.

Meanwhile, Marvin was turning into her rock and they were growing closer every day. He was staying over almost every night now and Lexi found it comforting. She was considering asking him to move in permanently in the New Year.

Troy was spending Christmas back in New York with friends, and Lexi was looking forward to a nice quiet time with Marvin. She'd had enough drama since Thanksgiving to last her a whole year!

* * *

Brenda was very apprehensive in the run-up to Christmas. The kids were due home on Friday and she dreaded having to tell them about the split. She planned to Skype Alex on Thursday to break the news. She wasn't sure when she would talk to Megan who was in Nepal last time they talked but Megan would certainly be in touch over Christmas.

The receptionist she was replacing in the salon had been diagnosed with toxaemia and ordered bed-rest for the remaining three months of her pregnancy so Brenda had agreed to fill in for her until she'd had her baby. Secretly she was delighted as she simply loved the job and it was great to be earning her own money.

At Jean's insistence she had been in touch with a solicitor about filing for a legal separation and had made an appointment to see her after Christmas. When she contacted Bob to tell him, he was horrified.

"What's the hurry?" he asked. "You can stay in the house as long as you like and I'll continue to support you and the kids financially."

"Yes, but don't you think we should make it legal?"

"No. Why make the lawyers rich?"

"Well, maybe you'll want to get married again to . . ." Brenda couldn't bring herself say her name and certainly couldn't call her 'the slapper' . . . "to your girlfriend."

She heard his hesitation. "Er . . . I don't think that's an issue," he said tersely.

When Brenda recounted this conversation to Jean, her sister squealed with delight. "I told you. He's regretting it already!"

"Don't be silly."

"Trust me. If he loved her he'd be panting for a divorce so that he could marry her."

"You think so?" Brenda looked dubious.

Jean let out a whoop. "Take my word for it. Before you know it he'll come crawling back with his tail between his legs."

"I doubt that very much."

"For sure. And he probably misses your cooking too. I can imagine he's having to eat McDonald's every night."

Brenda laughed. Jean could be so funny sometimes. She sure hoped Bob and the slapper would never cross paths with her sister. If they did, she felt sure Jean would not come out the loser.

Brenda was delighted to have no Christmas shopping to do as she had done it all in Florida and New York. She wrapped a few of the kids' presents each night so she wouldn't have to do them all at the same time. Ryan and Dylan would put up the tree at the weekend and she and Carly would decorate it. She was really looking forward to having them home for Christmas although she was dreading their reaction to the news that their father had left.

* * *

On Friday evening Brenda waited, excitement mixed with apprehension, for the kids to arrive. Ryan and Dylan were due in first and she'd prepared their favourite dinner of shepherd's pie for them the evening before. All she had to do was reheat it when they got in. She had told them that Bob couldn't meet them and to get the Luas from Connolly station. They burst through the door in their usual high spirits, flinging their bags down in the hall as Ryan swung her off her feet and twirled her around.

"Happy Christmas, Mum," he cried. "It's great to be home."

"Happy Christmas," Dylan said, hugging her. "Gosh, Mum, you look wonderful. What did you do to your hair?"

"Do you like it?" she laughed, pleased he'd noticed it and delighted to have them home again.

"And you've lost weight. Everyone will think you're our sister now," Ryan cried. "Won't they, Dyl?"

"Get out of it!" Brenda swatted him jokingly. "You're as full of blarney as ever."

Dylan smiled, seeing that Brenda was enjoying the compliments. "You are looking great, Mum, seriously."

"Thank you, love," she said.

"Where's Dad?" Ryan asked. "Why didn't he meet us, as usual?"

Here came the moment she dreaded. "I just want to put the dinner in the oven. Why don't you take off your coats and grab a beer? I have a big fire going in the living room. I guess you must be freezing."

Ryan threw off his coat and grabbed the beers but Dylan looked at her earnestly. He'd heard the tension in her voice. "Is everything okay, Mum?" he asked worriedly.

"Pour me a glass of white wine, love – it's in the fridge, and I'll tell you everything."

He did as she told him and when they were seated in the comfy warm room she broke the news to them that their father had left her.

"The bastard!" Ryan yelled, jumping up and making a fist.

"I'll fucking kill him!"

"Calm down, Ryan. These things happen."

"Not to my mother, they don't," he shouted.

"Sit down, Ryan," Dylan said quietly and Ryan did as he was told. "What happened, Mum?" he asked in a gentle voice.

Brenda took a sip of her wine and told them as honestly as she could.

"I don't believe it! Has he lost his senses?" Ryan cried.

Dylan quelled him with a look. "How do you feel about it, Mum?"

"Well, naturally I was shocked but, to be honest, things have not been good between us for some time. I was so busy with the five of you over the years that I didn't notice how your dad and I were growing apart but once you'd all left home it became very obvious to me."

"What will you do now?"

"What can I do? I love working in Jean's salon so hopefully I can keep doing that, part-time at least, and then who knows? It's not as if I'm over the hill." She laughed.

"Of course not," Dylan squeezed her hand. "You have plenty of opportunities ahead of you. I'll speak to Dad. I'm sure it was just a stupid mistake and he's regretting it now."

"I don't think so. He's living with her now, isn't he?"

"The bastard!" Ryan yelled again, jumping up. "Where does this slapper live? I'll make sure he comes right back here tonight!"

Brenda couldn't help but smile at his use of the word 'slapper'. "Sit down, Ryan. I don't think I could take him back after what he's done. I'm afraid I'm no Robert Pattinson who can forgive and forget."

"Are you sure, Mum?"

"Yes, I think so," she replied, smiling at them. She hoped this was true. She wanted to move on with her life. Bob was gone. She had to accept it. "Sometimes these things are meant to happen," she said sadly.

"Do the girls know?" Dylan wanted to know.

"Just Alex. We spoke on Skype yesterday. She was good about it. She wants what's best for me."

"So do we, Mum, so do we," Dylan assured her, squeezing her hand.

"What about the others?" Ryan wanted to know.

"Well, I'll tell Megan when I speak to her, which will probably be Christmas Eve, and Carly should be home any minute."

No sooner had she spoken than they heard Carly's key in the door. She'd got a lift from Limerick with a friend's brother.

"Hiyee!" Brenda's youngest daughter erupted into the room, in her athletic exuberant way.

"Hi, Mum, hi, guys." She hugged Brenda and then Ryan and Dylan in turn.

"Hey, what's wrong?" she asked, sensing the sombre mood. "Aren't you pleased to see me?"

"Of course we are, chicken," said Brenda. "Come on, take off your coat and sit down. What would you like to drink?"

Carly saw her mother was drinking white wine. "Could I have a glass of wine?"

"Of course. Dylan, will you get it for your sister?"

Dylan smiled and went to pour the wine. Ryan was sitting down again, looking tense.

"You look terrific, Mum," said Carly. "Was America fabulous?"

"It was simply wonderful. Honestly, it was a dream holiday. I'll tell you all about it later."

"And how are things in Derry?" she asked, turning to Ryan.

"Fine," he answered tersely.

"What's wrong? There's something wrong, isn't there?" she asked fearfully.

Dylan handed her the wine. "Mum has something to tell you, Carly."

Carly looked at her mother, panic-stricken. "You're not sick, Mum, are you?"

"Not at all," Brenda laughed. "I'm as healthy as an ox."

"Dad has left her!" Ryan spat out bitterly.

"What?" Carly's eyes were like saucers. "You're not serious?" She looked at Ryan, thinking it was a joke.

"Deadly serious! He's moved in with a twenty-five-year-old tart."

Carly saw from her mother's face that it was true.

She burst into tears and Brenda took her in her arms. "It's okay, honey. Honestly, I'm fine with it now. I even think it might be for the best."

"How can you say that? Who is she?"

"The slutty receptionist who works for the taxi company."

"Oh no, not that Crystal one?" Carly looked horrified. "That can't be. Alex, Megan and I met her a couple of times when we were waiting for Dad to give us a lift home. She's awful, really common."

"That's her all right," Ryan confirmed. "I told you, a tart."

"How could he do such a thing?" Carly cried, a stricken look on her face.

"These things happen, chicken," Brenda said sadly. "Marriages sometimes fall apart and it's no one's fault."

"This was Dad's fault," Ryan interjected fiercely.

"Well, there are always two sides to every story. We had grown apart. If our marriage had been strong enough then this wouldn't have happened."

"Oh, Mum, I'm so sorry," Carly sniffed.

"Don't be. I'll be fine. Now, come on, you guys. Shepherd's pie's up."

Despite the bombshell she'd dropped they had a fun

evening, exchanging news. Brenda told them all about her trip and kept them enthralled with the lifestyle she'd enjoyed there.

"It sounds fabulous. There's a summer camp for kids somewhere near Tampa that have advertised for counsellors for next summer," Carly said. "My friend Sarah and I were thinking about applying for it. We couldn't decide between that one and one in Colorado."

"No contest! Take Florida," Ryan advised.

"Ryan is right and you'd be close to Lexi there if anything went wrong," Brenda added.

"I'd like to work in New York for the summer," Ryan said. "I was hoping Aunt Mel would be able to help me. I could do with some experience, not to mention money." Ryan was very ambitious and keen to make money. He worked as a barman in Derry during college term and even in Dublin city during the holidays.

"I'm sure she would. She's very high up in the firm and has lots of contacts. I'll certainly ask her. She gave us a wonderful time in New York. She's a great hostess."

"What about you, Dyl?" Carly asked. "Where do you want to go for the summer?"

"Haven't really thought about it. I'll probably stay here in Dublin."

"Of course you won't. If I go to New York, you're coming too." Ryan said confidently.

Dylan shrugged his shoulders. Brenda smiled, knowing that wherever Ryan went, Dylan would follow.

* * *

Despite the luxury Angel felt she didn't belong in La Vista. She cried constantly and couldn't face the other clients – she'd called them inmates the first day and been sharply reprimanded by Dr Kirk. She'd had to go cold turkey that first week and it was hell. Her craving for alcohol was eating her up and she knew she'd never stick it. She was sullen and uncommunicative when she had to go to group sessions and the other patients avoided her. People with her attitude did not help their recovery.

She did make one friend in her second week there, if you could call him that. Alan was also an actor, quite a famous one, and he was being treated for sex addiction. He had caused a major scandal and both his wife and his agent had given him an ultimatum, insisting he go for treatment or they would jump ship. He didn't want to give up his philandering, he loved women too much, and only agreed to enter La Vista to get them off his back. Although ten years her junior he was instantly attracted to Angel.

He pursued Angel relentlessly, but she was in such a dark place that she refused his advances. Eventually, he found a way into her bed. He got a friend to smuggle in a bottle of whisky and came to her room one night.

"Go away," she said, feeling maniacally depressed.

"I have something for you," he whispered through the crack in the door, showing her the whisky.

Like a flash she let him in. Pouring a large one into her bathroom tumbler she downed it in one. It felt so good. The feel of the warm liquid making its way down to her stomach was like heaven. She smiled at Alan, who poured another for her. Ten minutes later they were in bed. It seemed like a good exchange to Angel – sex for whisky – that way they both got what they wanted.

Angel covered it up well for about a week but when she refused to go for any more therapy, Dr Kirk guessed that she was drinking again. When she questioned her about it Angel at first denied it but eventually confessed that she'd been drinking for the past week. The director didn't know where Angel was getting it from. It didn't really matter. They could do nothing for her if she didn't want to be helped.

Dr Kirk gave her an ultimatum, either she stop drinking or leave.

Angel left. She'd spent less than three weeks in the clinic. Alan left with her which told the director where she'd been getting the alcohol.

Dr Kirk was upset about it. Two failures in the one week.

They took a cab to Angel's house and spent the day drinking and having sex until their party was cut short by the arrival of Alan's wife. It hadn't been difficult to locate him. Dr Kirk had shown the way. She dragged him out and took him home, terrified that word would get back to the media. It was the day before Christmas Eve and Angel was on her own again with just her whisky bottle for comfort.

Chapter 26

Donna was a bright ambitious young woman who had joined Mel's company three years previously. Mel, recognising her talents, snapped her up and brought her to work in her office as her right-hand woman. Donna admired Mel greatly and modelled herself on her mentor, ambitious to become a senior partner one day, just like her boss. They had a great working relationship and Mel lauded the younger girl's drive guessing that Donna would certainly succeed in her goal.

Although they worked closely together, their relationship was strictly business and never ventured outside of the office.

Donna, very receptive to her boss's mood, knew instantly that something had happened to change Mel while in Florida. No longer at her desk before seven every morning nor staying on till nine or ten at night, Donna wondered what it could have been. She often came into Mel's office to find her staring out the large glass window, gazing out over the buildings of Manhattan as if in a daydream. Could Mel have fallen in love? Donna doubted it as she knew Mel was like herself, a hard-bitten career woman who had no time for such fripperies as love. Still, there was a new softness to Mel which was unnerving.

It revealed itself the night of the Christmas party. Mel was in high spirits and Donna was surprised to see her drinking champagne. She'd never drunk alcohol in previous years.

"Well, another year done," Mel declared, smiling at Donna as they sat together.

"You and I are working tomorrow, aren't we?" Donna asked. Most of the staff had finished for the holiday but Mel had asked Donna to come in to tie up some loose ends.

"Yes, but we'll be finished by noon. How would you like to come out for a Christmas lunch with me then?"

Donna almost fell off her chair. Mel had never, ever, mixed business with pleasure before. Donna knew nothing about her boss's life outside the office, nor did Mel know anything about hers.

"That would be lovely," Donna replied when she'd recovered from the shock.

* * *

The following day, Christmas Eve, they went for lunch in the Plaza. After they'd given their order to the maître d', Mel ordered two glasses of champagne.

"After all, we're not driving, are we?" she laughed. "Tell me about yourself, Donna. Where do you live?"

Surprised by this new friendly Mel, Donna told her that she lived in Queens with her large family, who were Italian.

"I'd really like to have my own place as our house is always full of various relations, but Mama wouldn't hear of it."

"They must be very proud of you."

"Well, yes, they are. I studied very hard and am the first one of my family to go to university," Donna blushed. "There

234

are eight of us children and Papa is a cook in a restaurant in Little Italy. He's a great cook and so is Mama," she stated proudly.

"It must be great to be from a large family," Mel said wistfully. "I only have one brother and he left home when I was fourteen. My parents were very strict, both teachers. I've had a lonely life."

Donna listened, feeling sorry for Mel who seemed to have everything and yet was lonely.

As they were waiting for their starters to be served, Mel reached into her bag and took out a package.

"I'd better give you this before I forget," she said, handing the present to Donna.

Surprised, Donna opened it to find a beautiful necklace of many-coloured stones. "Oh, it's beautiful," she exclaimed, admiring the design and fingering the semi-precious stones. "I love it. Thank you so much."

"I'm glad. I saw it in Florida and the vibrant colours reminded me of you."

Donna was moved by the compliment from her idol. "Thank you, Mel. I'll treasure it forever," she smiled, putting the necklace on over her white business shirt.

"You remind me of myself ten years ago," Mel remarked as the waiter brought their starter and two glasses of chardonnay. "I was as ambitious as you are but I hope you don't make the same mistakes I did."

"What do you mean?"

"Well, I was so determined to be a success that I made my career my sole focus, thinking that was the most important thing in the world. Now I realise that I was wrong. People and love are much more important. It's too late for me now but not for you. Please don't sacrifice everything for your career, Donna, because it isn't worth it."

The younger girl looked at Mel and saw the bleakness in her eyes. Unthinkingly, she reached out and took Mel's hand. Mel didn't pull away.

"Your family are all in Ireland, aren't they?" Donna asked.

"Yes."

"And where will you spend Christmas Day?"

"In my apartment, with a Chinese take-away. See what I mean? Your career doesn't keep you company on Christmas Day."

Donna was moved by her admission and honesty. "In that case you'll have to come and spend it with us. You'll be very welcome."

"Oh, no, I couldn't possibly –"

"Nonsense," Donna replied adamantly, showing the determination that she often showed at work. "I insist! Nobody should be alone on Christmas Day."

"Thanks, but honestly I'll be fine. I couldn't possibly intrude."

"You won't be intruding and my family would never forgive me if I took no for an answer. I better warn you though, they're a noisy bunch and you might be sorry you agreed," Donna laughed and Mel joined in.

She felt it would be churlish to refuse, so she agreed to go.

They had a wonderful time after that as Mel ordered two more glasses of wine with their main course.

"You must let me share the check," Donna said as the waiter brought it.

"Are you mad? It's on expenses."

Both girls laughed as Mel decided they'd crown the meal with two expensive cognacs. It looked like it was going to be a good Christmas after all.

* * *

The hair salon was crazily busy on Christmas Eve and Brenda was run off her feet. There was a party atmosphere in the place and everyone was happy and looking forward to the days ahead. Carly, who since she was fourteen had helped out in the salon during the school holidays, was busy handing out mince pies and mulled wine to the clients.

Luckily Carly was busy making more mulled wine in the back kitchen when Brenda heard the rough Dublin accent. "Is there no fuckin' receptionist here? I'm in a hurry."

Brenda had left the desk for a minute to take an Avon order from a client but recognised the voice. She turned slowly and there, standing in front of her was her husband's lover. She quickly took in the big blonde hair, heavy make-up, tits hanging out, the mini-skirt and the six-inch-heels and unconsciously wrinkled her nose in disgust. Glancing at the kitchen door furtively Brenda prayed that Carly would not come out and have to encounter her father's mistress.

Struggling to keep her composure, she spoke coolly. "Can I help you?"

She saw the look of surprise on the slapper's face and felt a moment of triumph.

"Oh, it's you. I didn't expect to see you here," the other girl said, flustered.

Brenda knew she was looking good and it gave her confidence. She was not going to pretend to recognise this tramp. "What can I do for you, Miss . . ."

"Kearns," the slapper replied, looking put out. "I have an appointment with Jade."

Quaking inside, Brenda pretended to look at the diary although she couldn't focus on it. Luckily, Jean had spotted Crystal and, dropping her scissors with a clatter, left her astonished client and flew to the reception desk.

"What are you doing here?" she hissed.

"I have an appointment with Jade," the slapper replied, unnerved by the venom in Jean's eyes.

"Well, you're not welcome here, not today, not ever."

"But . . ." the slapper started to protest.

"Out!" Jean cried as everyone turned to look at this commotion.

The slapper turned to Brenda and reaching over the desk so that her breasts practically plopped out onto it, hissed, "This is all your fault. I'm glad I stole your husband, you posh bitch! You and your blonde stuck-up daughters who think they're so high and mighty!"

Brenda stood transfixed. How had Bob ever got entangled with such a piece of shit? Was he out of his mind? Nervously, she looked around to make sure Carly had not seen or heard what was happening. Thank God she hadn't.

"Well, I never," Jean said grinning. "Didn't know I had a 'posh' sister."

She laughed and Brenda joined in, more with relief than anything else, as Crystal stormed out. They knew the slapper would never get an appointment anywhere else today.

"Poor thing! Imagine having to spend Christmas Day with that mess of hair," Jean said bitchily as they both returned to work.

* * *

Bob had rung twice, hoping to speak to the kids but each time it was Ryan who answered and after a few expletives banged the phone down on him. Dylan said he would have talked to his father but one look from Ryan and he backed down. Carly said she had no intention of meeting his tart either, so Bob was left without seeing any of his children over the Christmas.

Brenda knew they were just shocked and being loyal to her and felt that with time they would come around. Well, Dylan and Carly anyway. She couldn't be sure about Ryan. He was absolutely furious with Bob.

* * *

On Christmas morning Brenda made a big Irish breakfast as she'd always done. She knew the smell would eventually entice the lazy teenagers out of their beds. She remembered all the Christmases past when she and Bob were often wakened in the early hours of the morning as five excited children dashed downstairs to see what Santa had brought. They'd been so happy then. What had happened?

This was the first Christmas that all seven of them would not be together. Even if Bob had been there, Alex and Megan would not. Such was life, things changed all the time. Megan had rung the night before and had taken the news of Bob's leaving with equilibrium.

"Frankly, Mum, you'll be much better off without him."

Brenda wondered at her two eldest daughters' take on life. They had old heads on young shoulders and she had no fears for them or their future. The boys were another story, not nearly as mature as the girls.

One by one they came down to breakfast, suffering hangovers she suspected, as they had met up with their old school friends the night before. It was the same all over the country, Brenda guessed, as old school friends returned from colleges to their home towns and reunited.

After breakfast they opened their presents and she was happy with the reception the clothes from the States received. With the money she was earning in the salon, she had bought them each a new iPhone. There were hoots and hollers of appreciation at these. Like all the younger generation they spent hours texting their friends every day.

Alex Skyped them just then and Brenda held up her Christmas presents for her to see.

"Oooh, Earl jeans, I love them!" Alex cried. "And a Jessica Simpson bag. Gosh, Mum, they're gorgeous. Thanks a million."

"They'll be waiting here for you when you come home – unless you'd like me to send them on."

"Good heavens, no. I'd have no use for them here. I'll have them to look forward to on my next trip home," Alex said happily.

Brenda was delighted that she liked them. Alex then had a long chat with Carly, Ryan and Dylan as they exchanged news of what they'd been doing. Alex didn't mention Bob and Brenda was glad. It would have spoiled the happy Christmassy atmosphere.

When she'd rung off, the kids changed into their new gear and they all set off for Jean's where they would spend the day. Another exchange of presents took place there before Roy, Jean's husband, opened a bottle of champagne and got the festivities under way.

They had a wonderful day and after a delicious turkey dinner, they played charades, which they did every year. Jean was pleased to see Brenda happy and smiling and having fun. Jean's two kids were younger and adored their older cousins. From time to time a dark cloud passed over Brenda's face and Jean knew that she was thinking of Bob. She was wondering where he was and whether he was happy.

* * *

Bob was anything but happy. Crystal had been giving him grief ever since she'd come home from the hair salon the day before.

"How could you have stayed married to that posh bitch

240

for all those years?" she'd ranted.

He'd never considered Brenda posh, nor a bitch for that matter. He had accused her of trying to better herself but he could never accuse her of putting on airs and graces. He supposed, in comparison to her rough family, Crystal would consider his wife posh. Lord knows what she would think of Brenda's wealthy friends. Posh didn't go half far enough to describe Lexi, Mel and Angel.

He was already beginning to realise that there were a lot of things he hadn't known about Crystal before he'd moved in with her. She was incredibly messy and the small apartment was like a kip. She couldn't cook for nuts and though he didn't want to make comparisons between her and his wife it was hard not to. Brenda was a great housekeeper and very organised and their house had always been a haven to come home to. She was also a wonderful cook, something he missed badly. Coupled with that was the fact that Crystal wanted to party and go clubbing every night which might be fine for twenty-five-year-olds but not for old codgers like him in their forties. Besides which, he couldn't afford the exotic drinks she favoured.

While the sex was great, he was beginning to tire of her constant and frequent demands for it. The kinkier the better, was Crystal's motto. He was forty-two years old, for God's sake! After nights of being handcuffed to the bed and role-playing he began to tire of it and he thought ruefully of Brenda's accusation that Crystal was a tart. Maybe she hadn't been too far off the mark. He wondered where she had learnt all this kinky stuff. It was worrying. He was starting to have regrets and beginning to think that he'd made a dreadful mistake. The old saying 'If you want to know me, come and live with me' ran through his mind frequently.

He was also very upset that the kids wouldn't speak to

him. He knew they would despise Crystal anyway. On Christmas night, while all her loud family were drunk and fighting, he longed to be back with his own family, playing charades and having good, simple fun. He presumed they'd be in Jean's as they alternated every year and her family had been with them the year before. Feeling sorry for himself he left and went for a walk and found himself walking down Jean's road. The curtains were drawn but there was a window open and he could hear laughter from inside. He felt an overwhelming urge to walk in there but knew he wouldn't be welcome. Dragging his heels he went back to Crystal's parents' house. She was so drunk, she hadn't even missed him!

* * *

Lexi passed a lovely quiet day. She and Marvin slept in a little and then went for a swim before breakfast, a real Irish one with the remainder of the Denny's sausages and Clonakilty pudding that Brenda had brought. Marvin opened a bottle of champagne and they had mimosas as Lexi cooked the breakfast. Then they went for a long walk on the beach.

That afternoon they went for lunch to the Beachcomber restaurant which was crowded with families enjoying the festivities. The food was as wonderful as ever and Lexi said she couldn't possibly have anything else but the Irish Christmas dinner of turkey and ham which she'd had every Christmas of her life. Marvin teased her about it but ordered turkey and ham too.

"If you can't beat them, join them," he said laughing.

Lexi touched his hand as she laughed with him, thinking how much she enjoyed being with him.

They got home at around five thirty, just in time to catch the sunset. Marvin carried two folding chairs and Lexi two glasses of champagne down to the beach and they sat and watched as the sky turned a glorious orange and the big golden sun dipped in the sky. As it did, Marvin turned to Lexi and took her hand and kissed it.

"You know I love you, Lexi, and I want to spend the rest of my life with you."

She looked at him and in that moment knew she wanted that too.

"Are you asking me what I think you are?"

"Yes, I sure am," he smiled.

"Well, in that case, as I'm such an old-fashioned girl, I think you should do so in the old-fashioned way."

He threw back his head and laughed then went down on one knee in the sand. "Will you, Alexandra Moretti, do me the honour of becoming my wife?"

"Oh, Marvin," she said, stroking his cheek lovingly, "I would like that very much."

"You've just made me the happiest man in the world," he declared.

To her surprise he then took a small velvet box out of his pocket and opened it displaying the most beautiful ring she'd ever seen. It had an antique gold setting with a lustrous pearl in the centre, surrounded by smaller pearls interspersed with diamonds, in the shape of a flower.

"It's exquisite," she whispered, awed by its beauty.

He slipped it on her finger. "They are natural pearls and it belonged to my great-grandmother. It was the only jewellery that my grandmother smuggled out of Russia after the revolution. She risked death doing so but couldn't bear to leave it behind." His voice was emotional as he spoke. "My grandmother passed it on to my mother who left it to me – with strict instructions how to care for it, I have to say." He laughed.

"It's beautiful and I am honoured to wear it," Lexi replied, moved to tears by its history.

"And now, if you don't mind, I'd like to get up off my knee."

They both laughed as he got up, the sand staining the knee of his elegant grey linen suit.

"I'm sorry," Lexi said. "I shouldn't have made you kneel."

"It was worth it," he replied, kissing her. "I guess I'd better go in and get a bottle of champagne to celebrate."

"Of course!" she hesitated. "And Marvin," she said softly as he moved away, "I love you very much."

He smiled happily at her and blew a kiss as he left.

Chapter 27

Mel looked out the cab window as they passed over the Queensboro Bridge and wondered if she was crazy, leaving Manhattan to spend Christmas with people she didn't even know. What had possessed her to say she'd come? She was tempted to turn back but couldn't very well as she'd promised Donna she'd be there.

Like all Manhattanites, she considered anywhere over the East River to be alien country. She'd only crossed it once before to visit friends of Simon's in Brooklyn and had vowed to stay on terra firma after that experience. She totally understood Miranda's shock – and that of the other girls too – in *Sex and the City*, when Steve suggested that they look for a house in Brooklyn. For them, and Mel, New York was that piece of land from Battery Park up to mid-Central Park, full-stop! Yet here she was on her way into that other world and feeling very apprehensive about it.

She was surprised when the cab stopped outside a detached house with a small garden in the Forest Hills area. It even had a garage. This was not what she'd expected, so with a lighter heart she paid the driver and made her way up to the front door. She could hear laughter and noise coming from within and had to ring twice before it was answered by a large handsome man with black curly hair and twinkling brown eyes.

"Ah, you must be Mel," he cried in a very Italian accent, before pulling her into the hallway and enveloping her in a big bear-hug. "*Benvenuto e Buon Natale*!"

"Hello, Mr . . ."

"Call me Papa. Everyone calls me Papa. Donna, Mam!" he yelled and Donna came running out, flushed and excited, followed by a beautiful dark-skinned woman.

"Mel, I'm so glad you came," Donna exclaimed. "Happy Christmas! I see you've met Papa."

"Yes," Mel smiled, still a little shell-shocked from Papa's welcome.

"And this is Mama," Donna said, introducing the woman. Mel couldn't believe she was Donna's mother. She couldn't possibly have a daughter as old as that. She didn't look a day over forty.

"*Benvenuto*," the mother said shyly. "Donna tell me a lot about you."

"Come in, come in. Let me take your coat," Papa said, helping her off with it.

"Thank you. This is for you," Mel said to Mama as she handed her the gift basket she'd picked up in Balducci's after leaving Donna the day before.

"*Oh, Mama mia! Grazie, grazie*," Donna's mother exclaimed, beaming as she took it.

"You shouldn't have," Donna admonished her, leading her into the big living-room which was packed with people of all ages. She led her over to introduce her to her grandparents – all four of them – and her three great-grandmothers.

Luckily Mel was told to call them Nonna and Bisnonna as she would never have remembered all their names. She looked around at all the smiling faces as uncles, aunts and cousins came to say hello and Donna also introduced her brothers and sisters. Mel had heard of big Italian families but this was ridiculous.

Papa handed her a glass of Prosecco as she wished everyone a Happy Christmas and so began the happiest Christmas Day that Mel had ever spent. The warmth and love in the room made Mel wish that she was a part of this family. She envied Donna and knew that if she'd been surrounded with this love growing up she would have turned out a different person. They were such fun and one by one she met with them and heard their fascinating stories.

While Mel was enjoying the chat, Mama and the grandmothers were busy in the kitchen.

"Today I don't cook," Papa said grinning. "Today is my day off."

Finally they sat down to dinner at two long tables set up in the very large dining room. It was obvious that these large family gatherings were a regular occurrence.

"In summer, we eat al fresco in the garden," Donna explained when Mel commented on the number sitting down to eat. "Then we can have as many as forty at a meal."

"Amazing!"

Mama had cooked not one but two turkeys, one stuffed with chestnuts, the other with a sage stuffing. Before this there was minestrone soup and two huge bowls of meatballs and ravioli as well as other pastas. Dessert was panettone, tiramisu and torrone, a delicious nougat. Mel had never tasted anything so good. It was the best meal she had ever had.

The party went on late into the evening. Some of the uncles played music and everyone danced, Mel being very much in demand. She had a wonderful time.

"I wish your parents would adopt me," she said to Donna as she took her leave.

"Oh, they already have," Donna laughed.

"It's been the best Christmas I've ever had," Mel said. "Thank you so very much for inviting me."

"We all loved having you. You'll be welcome here anytime."

Mel knew it was true. Tired but happy she made her way back across the East River as midnight approached. Maybe she needed to broaden her horizons, she thought sleepily. Manhattan wasn't the only place in the world!

* * *

Lexi rang Brenda the following day with the news of her engagement.

"That's wonderful, congratulations! When is the big day?" Brenda asked, although she knew there was no way on earth she would be able to attend.

"We haven't discussed that," Lexi replied. "For now I'm happy just being engaged. Marvin is moving in permanently this week and we'll take it from there. Troy is going to stay on in Marvin's house for the moment as he hasn't found one he likes yet. It will be great having him next door."

"How is he?" Brenda asked.

"He's great. He asked me only yesterday how you were doing. I haven't told him that you and Bob have split up. Do you want me to tell him?"

"No. What's the point?"

"There's no chance you and Bob will get back together?"

"I don't think so. I've been too hurt. I'm applying for a separation this week."

"Ah, of course, divorce Irish style. You have to be separated for something like four years, isn't it, before you can even apply for a divorce?"

"Something like that. I'll know more after I speak with the solicitor."

* * *

Lexi then rang Mel next to share the good news of her engagement.

"Wow, that is a surprise but I'm delighted to hear it. You two were meant for each other," Mel said happily, congratulating her.

"How was your Christmas day?"

"Great, but not as good as yours." Mel laughed. "I guess I ate too much yesterday because I'm feeling really ill today."

She then told Lexi about the wonderful day she'd had with Donna's family.

Lexi was pleased to hear it. She hoped it meant that Mel had taken her advice to enjoy life and not focus solely on her work. There was no doubt about it, she had changed a lot since her visit to Florida. She supposed she had Jack to thank for that!

"I was thinking of coming down to you for a long weekend in February," Mel said.

"That would be great. Wonders will never cease!" Lexi laughed. "Twice in three months! That's something of a record."

* * *

After speaking with Mel, Lexi rang the clinic to ask Dr Kirk to pass on her good news to Angel.

"I'm sorry, Ms Moretti, but Angel left here two days before Christmas."

"She what?" Lexi cried, shocked.

"Yes, I'm afraid we were not able to help her. I assumed she would have contacted you."

"No," Lexi replied. She was shaking so much that she had to sit down and Marvin looked at her worriedly.

"Yes, she found someone, another client, who secured alcohol for her and refused to continue with her therapy. There was no point in her staying on here so I suggested she leave."

"Oh my God! What can I do now?"

"There is nothing you can do, Ms Moretti. Until Angel wants to do it for herself, there's nothing anyone can do. She's an addict."

"Oh Lord, I had hoped this would work."

"I'm sorry, but until she hits rock bottom, she'll probably continue on this self-destructive course."

When Lexi had hung up, Marvin came and knelt beside her. "What is it, honey?"

"Angel started drinking in the clinic and she walked out before Christmas."

"Christ! What is wrong with that girl? After all you've done for her!" He was angry and concerned about Lexi. She'd gone out of her way to help Angel, and for what?

"I don't know what I can do for her now."

"You've done enough. She has to start taking responsibility for herself sometime."

Lexi rang Angel's number and as she expected it went to voicemail. Then she rang Consuela's number to find out if she'd seen Angel.

"Miss Lexi, is good to hear you. How Miss Angel doing?"

"I'm afraid she's drinking again, Consuela. She walked out of the clinic just before Christmas. You haven't seen her, have you?"

Lexi had wondered if Angel's housekeeper was covering up for her but from her reaction, she realised that Consuela knew nothing.

"*Díos mío*, Miss Lexi, that terrible. I think she happy in there. This bad news."

Lexi heard the sadness in Consuela's voice. "I think she get bad fright last time."

"Me too, Consuela. Maybe you can go check on her soon, could you?"

"I go now. I hope she okay."

"Could you call me back and let me know how she is."

"*Sí*, Miss Lexi."

* * *

Consuela rang back two hours later. "She like before, Miss Lexi. She drunk."

Lexi heard the hopelessness in the housekeeper's voice and sighed.

"Oh, dear," was all she could say.

Marvin was right. She couldn't make Angel do it if she didn't want to. Lexi felt despair. Where would she end up? It looked like, as Dr Kirk had said, she was on a path of self-destruction.

"Maybe I should fly out there," she suggested to Marvin when she'd hung up.

"You'll do no such thing," Marvin said firmly. "Why don't you talk to Kenny? I know he still goes to AA meetings every week. He might advise you what to do."

"Good idea, I will," she said, dialling Kenny's number.

Kenny confirmed what Marvin had said. Angel would have to hit rock bottom and decide to want to stop for herself. Lexi could not do it for her.

"Look, I fly to LA regularly on business. If you like I'll make contact with her and see if I can talk to her."

"Thanks, Kenny. That would be great."

* * *

When Mel was still feeling ill the following day she guessed it wasn't the food but that she must have caught a tummy bug. She had no choice but to go into work as the end-of-year audit was in progress. She still had it when she Skyped Lexi on New Year's Eve to wish her a Happy New Year.

"You're looking very peaky," Lexi remarked when she saw Mel on the screen.

"I know, I've been feeling ill since Stephen's Day. I guess I've caught a tummy bug."

"It's lasting a long time. Have you been to the doctor?"

"No. The thing is, it eases up in the evening and I think it's gone and the next morning, bang, it's back."

There was a silence on the other end of the line. "You couldn't be pregnant, Mel, could you?" Lexi asked, concern in her voice.

"No, of course not," Mel laughed.

Lexi then gave her the news of Angel.

"Gosh, that's terrible. What can we do?"

"Nothing, Mel, nothing. She has to do it for herself. She won't answer her phone but Consuela is with her and keeps me informed. Kenny says he'll look her up when he goes to LA later in the month. He's a recovering alcoholic so hopefully he'll know what to do."

"That's good. I hope he can help."

Mel felt a sense of uneasiness as she came off the phone. It had been a long time since her last period. She was pretty irregular but she took out her diary to check, just in case.

"Oh my God, it's been seven weeks," she gasped aloud, shocked at the possibility of what Lexi had suggested.

She and Jack had always been careful except for that one time they hadn't used a condom. She remembered her mother's stern warnings to her of long ago.

"Once is all it takes, Mel," she used to say.

Mel sat down in shock. She felt sick to her stomach. Was it possible that she was pregnant? She remembered the day she and Jack went out on his friend's boat to that deserted island. They'd been swimming naked and had made love in the sea. It had been spontaneous, both of them overcome with passion. Neither of them considered going back on shore for a condom. She couldn't have got pregnant then, could she?

On shaky legs she walked to the local pharmacy and purchased a First Response test and also an Ept one, in case the first one wasn't conclusive. Better to be sure, she reckoned.

Getting back to her apartment she could hardly breathe as she did the first test. She had to wait three minutes for the result and they were the longest three minutes of her life. She stared at the little window and sure enough, there were two pink lines there which meant she was pregnant. To be sure, she took the second test. This time she only had to wait two minutes and this one showed a + sign in the window. There was no doubt about it: she was pregnant.

She sat down on the side of the bath, shaking with fear. She had accepted the fact some time ago that she would never be a mother, so she could barely take it in. She started to panic. What could she do? She'd seen a film about aborted foetuses and had been horrified by it. After seeing it, she'd known she could never have an abortion. But what was the alternative?

Doubts and fears assailed her. How could she raise a child on her own, without its father? What kind of a mother would she be? She knew practically nothing about babies – but then did any first-time mother? She had longed for a child but not like this. She'd wanted a family with a husband who would be a father to their child. Not to be going it alone.

She put her hand on her tummy, finding it hard to believe there was a little person growing in there. She knew she should have been overjoyed, like most women when they discovered they were going to have a baby, and she would have been, if only Jack were here to share it with her.

Chapter 28

Brenda had been dreading New Year's Eve. She'd always found it a sad time and this year would be worse than ever with so many memories of years past. At times like this she wished Lexi, Mel and Angel were here. The twins and Carly were going out to parties and Brenda had decided she would sit in and go to bed early. Jean had other ideas.

"You're not sitting in alone moping. We've always gone to the GAA club on New Year's Eve and you're not going to miss it this year just because Bob isn't around."

"What if Bob is there?"

"He wouldn't dare!"

"I don't know . . ."

"Brenda, baby, I doubt very much that he'll show up when he knows our family is there every year. I won't hear of you staying in alone. We'll pick you up in the taxi at eight."

Brenda hadn't the heart to argue with her and agreed to go. She got dressed in the red dress she'd worn at the Thanksgiving dinner and put on the beautiful red Louboutin shoes Angel had given her. She knew she looked good but she felt dead inside. However, now that she'd decided to go, she would put on a brave face.

They arrived at the hall which was hopping and alive with an air of anticipation. It was always the best night of the year. They joined her brothers and their wives at the table they'd reserved and they were all delighted to see her. They'd all rallied round when they heard what had happened and called in on her often. They had served themselves at the buffet and Brenda had just sat back down to eat when she spotted Bob and the slapper walk in.

"Oh God!" she gasped, the colour draining from her face.

Jean looked around to see what had caused her sister's distress and was furious to see Bob and his girlfriend coming into the hall.

"I don't believe it!" she exclaimed. "The nerve of him!"

Her brothers had spotted him too and were equally furious.

Brenda couldn't believe it either. As usual, Crystal was skimpily dressed with acres of skin on show. Her hair was dishevelled so obviously she had not found another good hairdresser.

"I've a good mind to go over and give him a piece of my mind," Jean declared.

"No, let me go," Conor, their youngest brother said, getting up to confront Bob.

"No, no, please, Conor. I don't want a scene. Please ignore them," Brenda beseeched him, putting her hand on his arm to stay him.

"She's right," Roy advised. "Much better to ignore them."

Brenda flashed him a grateful smile.

* * *

Bob had not wanted to come. He and Brenda had gone there

every New Year's Eve with Brenda's family which was why Crystal had kept on and on about going. Since the altercation in the hair salon she'd had it in for Brenda. All week she'd been passing snide remarks about his 'posh' wife. Bob couldn't understand it. He'd left his wife for her, hadn't he? Why couldn't she be happy with that? Why was she jealous of his ex-wife? As for Brenda being posh, that was a laugh. She was the most down-to-earth person he'd ever known.

Eventually however, he'd given in to Crystal's demands and agreed to go, figuring that Brenda would surely steer clear of the place. He hoped Jean and her husband would not be there. His wife and her sister were as thick as thieves but he had always had a love-hate relationship with his sister-in-law. Roy was a good sort, however, even though he was in the Gardaí.

Crystal had insisted they go into their local for a few drinks before the party. She'd downed three vodka-and-whites in quick succession and was quite tipsy by the time they arrived at the party. It was a shock to see Brenda sitting there surrounded by her family. He was hurt that she'd had the nerve to come when it was where they had spent every New Year together, for as long as he could remember. If Crystal hadn't insisted, he'd never have gone near the place. Bob knew that he should have been equally insistent that they go somewhere else but she was very strong-willed and he was no match for her.

He tried not to look over at Brenda as he was aware of Crystal's eagle eyes on him. She had now changed to drinking wine which frightened him as she just couldn't handle it. He was a fool to come tonight, he realised, as he saw she was getting drunk. She sat scowling, knocking back glass after glass of wine, watching Brenda with jealous eyes.

When he did sneak a glance at her, he had to admit that Brenda looked terrific. That trip to Florida had changed her.

She never looked his way once and appeared to be enjoying herself. Once the band started up she was on the floor for every dance, smiling and laughing with her partners. Huh! She didn't appear to be missing him too much, did she? She was very much in demand and was first up on the floor for every dance.

Crystal was taking in every move she made. "My God, they're Louboutin shoes she's wearing," she exclaimed.

Bob looked at Brenda's shoes. He didn't remember seeing them before but they were very pretty. "How do you know what they are?"

"Because of the red soles, dummy! How in Jesus' name did she get those? You bought them for her, didn't you?" she asked accusingly.

"I may have given her the money for them for her birthday," he replied.

"And you tell me you're broke! All I got was a measly bottle of perfume from you for Christmas. Well, if you can afford Louboutins for her, you can buy me a pair now too."

He sighed, thinking she was being very unfair. He was struggling to manage financially now and he'd spent over €100 on that bloody perfume for her. He'd never spent that much on Brenda, ever. She'd been happy with her Avon stuff.

"Who does she think she is?" Crystal demanded, looking over at Brenda who was dancing with yet another guy. "Come on, Bob, let's dance."

Bob was reluctant to get up as he never knew what Crystal might do in this mood, but she wouldn't take no for an answer. Embarrassed, he got up with her and she dragged him over to where Brenda was twirling around in a jive. Brenda had always been a terrific dancer and people used to stop dancing just to look at the two of them jiving. They'd even won a jive competition one time in Blackpool.

Crystal started gyrating in an obviously sexy manner, making very suggestive moves. She edged closer and closer to Brenda who, when she saw her coming, stopped dancing and went back to the table.

"Jean, come on to the ladies'," she said, making for the toilets. She was shaking.

"She's a tramp. Don't pay any attention to her," her sister said.

"What is she up to?" Brenda asked. "She has my husband. What more does she want?"

"She's obviously not sure of him and jealous of you, otherwise why would she do that?"

"I don't understand it," Brenda said taking deep breaths. "How could Bob be seduced by someone like that?"

"Beats me!" Jean replied, feeling really sorry for her sister.

Although it was a fast dance, Crystal, not realising that Brenda had left the room, wrapped her arms around Bob's neck and pressed her body against his. He was mortified. He tried to disengage her but she wouldn't let go and started kissing him, sticking her tongue into his mouth.

Conor had had enough. He jumped up and approached the couple. Pulling on Bob's arm, he hissed, "Get her out of here!"

"I'm sorry," Bob said, embarrassed, pulling Crystal roughly back to their table where he grabbed her bag and jacket before marching her out. She tried to resist but in her drunken state was powerless.

"How could you make a show of me like that?" he ranted, pushing her into the car.

Crystal had never seen him so angry. "She needs to be taken down a peg or two," she said sulkily.

"What is wrong with you? Isn't it enough that I've left her for you? What more do you want?"

"I don't know. I hate her!"

"Why? She's done nothing to hurt you. She's the one who's been hurt in all this."

Crystal had no answer to this.

* * *

Conor's wife came into the ladies' to tell Brenda that Bob had left.

"Are you sure?"

"Yes, they're gone. My God, what was he thinking? She's disgusting."

"Early male menopause," Jean remarked, causing them to laugh.

Brenda came back into the room with trepidation but relaxed when she saw that Bob and his slapper had really left. After that the evening took off and she put them out of her mind and enjoyed herself. At midnight, she couldn't help feeling sad and wondered what Bob was doing.

He was sleeping on the couch. After a blazing row with Crystal, she had drunk herself into oblivion and passed out before the clock struck twelve. Thinking of other years with Brenda, Bob couldn't help but think that he'd just made the biggest mistake of his life. His head in his hands, he wondered if she was thinking of him and if she missed him as much as he missed her right now.

Chapter 29

Mel was very frightened about being pregnant and alone and pondered it for a couple of days, thinking it might be a mistake. Finally, accepting that it had really happened, she needed to share the news with someone so who else but her best friends? She called Lexi first.

"Hi, how are you feeling? Have you got rid of that tummy bug yet?" Lexi asked.

"It's not a tummy bug, Lexi. You were right. I'm pregnant," Mel replied flatly.

"Oh my God, Mel. I can't believe it! How do you feel about it?"

"Terrified."

"Naturally. But you said you wanted a baby, didn't you?"

"Well, yes, but not like this."

"What are you planning to do about it?" Lexi asked, holding her breath.

"I don't have a choice, do I? I don't believe in abortion."

Lexi let out a sigh. "I'm so glad. I know it's not the way you expected it to happen but does it matter? I'm so glad you

261

don't want an abortion. It's murder and children are precious."

Her voice was sad and Mel knew she was thinking of Alessandro.

"I know. I could never do it. But how will I cope? I know nothing about babies or children either, for that matter."

"You'll be fine. You can learn. You'll make a great mother."

"Oh God, I hope you're right Lexi. I'm so scared of the whole thing."

"Don't be. We're all here to help you. Have you any idea where Jack is? He should know about it, as it's his baby."

"No," Mel said too quickly. "I'm sure he wouldn't want to know at all."

Lexi's heart went out to her. "Well, call me anytime you want," she said. "And, Mel, I just know it's all going to work out fine."

"I sure hope you're right," Mel replied without enthusiasm.

"Do call Brenda. I know she'll be thrilled for you too."

"It's too late to ring her now but I'll ring her tomorrow."

"Golly, how our lives have changed lately. You pregnant, me engaged, Brenda separated." She didn't mention Angel, obviously.

"Yeah, it's crazy. It must be the big 40 looming." Mel finally laughed.

* * *

"You're what?" Brenda cried, when Mel told her that she was pregnant with Jack's baby. "You must be thrilled, are you?"

"Thrilled isn't quite how I'd describe it. Terrified, more like, but I'm beginning to come to terms with it."

"I know it's not ideal, Mel, but isn't it better than never having a child? And it is a lovechild, Mel. You did love Jack."

"I still love him, Brenda, and I suppose if I have to be pregnant, I'm happy that it's his baby."

Brenda understood. "You remember how happy I was to be pregnant with Bob's baby even though you tried to persuade me to have an abortion?"

"Oh God, don't remind me. I'm so ashamed of that. I should never have suggested it."

"You weren't to know and thank God I didn't listen otherwise I would not have Alex."

"I was stupid. Now I know how you felt. Nothing would persuade me to have an abortion. I couldn't do it."

"I'm so glad but it won't be easy, Mel, especially on your own."

"I know that but what choice do I have? I have you and Lexi there, after all."

"What a shame that Angel is drinking again," Brenda remarked sadly.

"Yes. Lexi is very upset about it but there's nothing she, or any of us, can do. She's hopeful Kenny can help when he goes to see her."

"Let's hope so."

* * *

Brenda met with the solicitor Jean had recommended and set the ball rolling on her separation although she knew it would take years before they could divorce. When he suggested that she and Bob might try mediation, she laughed nervously.

"Oh yes, the three of us can go there. Me, my husband and his mistress. Unfortunately, as Princess Diana first said, 'there are three of us in this marriage'."

"I understand that you're bitter but I have to suggest this to you before we start these proceedings. I take it you're not interested in mediation then."

"No, I guess it's too late for that," Brenda replied softly, reality hitting her.

She was feeling low after the meeting and the New Year Eve's debacle but she knew she'd have to forget about it and get on with things. She thanked God for her job in the salon which kept her occupied although things were much quieter now than over the Christmas period. She would not have coped without it, cooped up alone in the house all day, every day. The children were making the most of their holidays and were off every day with their friends. Even so, she would miss them when they returned to college.

Bob had rung the children asking them to meet him but only Dylan agreed to do so. He didn't say much about it, just that his father didn't appear to be happy. Ryan and Carly had steadfastly refused to have anything to do with him. In a way she felt sorry for Bob. He had lost so much.

He rang her to apologise for New Year's Eve and she could tell he was embarrassed.

"I would never want to hurt you, Brenda."

Oh yeah? she thought.

He started ringing her regularly on some pretext or another. They were always civil with each other which was something but she could see no point in their talking any more. She always felt depressed after their conversations. Although he never said, she knew him well enough to know that he was not happy.

* * *

Bob was, in fact, very unhappy. Life with Crystal had become unbearable since the New Year's Eve fiasco. She had developed an obsession with Brenda which was irrational. He couldn't make her see sense and she could barely talk about anything else. They seemed to be rowing non-stop now. What had happened? Where had it gone wrong? He'd left his blameless wife and now lost his kids and for what? For this harridan with the foul mouth and bad temper. How had he been so wrong about her?

Before he'd gone to live with Crystal, she'd been so anxious to please him. He shamefully admitted to himself now that he'd been in lust with her. She had seduced him with sex, something she was expert at. He'd been an old fool, falling for her feminine wiles. The sex was thin on the ground now as she tried to punish him by refusing it.

She had constantly badgered him to get her those shoes that Brenda had been wearing on New Year's Eve. Eventually, although he was broke, he asked her how much they would cost.

"About €700 to €900," she'd replied hopefully.

He'd started laughing. "Are you serious?"

"What's so funny?" she'd screamed, lashing out at him with her fists.

He backed away trying to avoid her blows.

"If your posh bitch of a wife can have Louboutins, I want a pair too! Do you hear me?" She was shrieking now.

"Even if I had €700, I couldn't justify spending that much on a pair of shoes. But that doesn't actually matter as I don't have that much money."

"Not for me but you have it for her, don't you?" she spat out, pummelling him on the chest.

He reached out and grabbed her wrist to fend her off.

"Let me go, you bastard! I'm calling the cops to tell them you're abusing me," she yelled.

"You're not the abused one in this relationship," he said quietly. "I've had enough. I'm leaving."

He went into the bedroom and grabbed his things, stuffing them into his bag. It wasn't much. He walked out past her and she looked at him disbelievingly.

"Where are you going?" she cried. "You're going back to her, aren't you?"

"If she'll have me," he said, turning on his heel.

"Go back to her then!" she shrieked throwing her glass of wine after him. It missed the mark and splintered into a million pieces against the wall.

He let himself out never wanting to set eyes on this slapper again.

He went to his mother's house and left his things there.

"At last you've come to your senses," were his mother's terse words of welcome. "You took your time."

He rang Dylan who was due to return to college the following day and asked his son to meet him. Dylan went to meet him in the local pub and returned back home in a thoughtful mood.

"Mum, Dad wants to talk to you. Will you see him?"

"Oh, honey, I don't think we have anything much to say to each other any more."

"Please, Mum, he's in a bad way. He's terribly remorseful. Can't you at least meet with him just once? For my sake?"

Brenda looked at her son's earnest young face and couldn't refuse him. "Okay, just for you and just this once. When does he want to meet?"

"Right now is good. Ryan's on a date and so is Carly so they won't be home till late. Can I call Dad and let him know?"

She wondered what she would say to Bob as she waited nervously for him to arrive. Dylan had gone to his room. She poured a brandy for herself to give her courage but then thought better of it. The last thing she needed was to get pissed and lower her defences. She left the brandy untouched. Five minutes later she was face to face with her husband and was shocked at his appearance. He had dark circles under his eyes and he was unshaven. She felt a stab of pity for him. His clothes were crumpled and he looked unkempt. Obviously, the slapper was not looking after him.

"Hi, Brenda," he said, shuffling from foot to foot.

"Bob, come in."

He followed her into the living room and they sat down opposite each other.

"Thanks for seeing me. I appreciate it," he said and she could hear the nervousness in his voice.

"Well, I promised Dylan that I would. What is it you want, Bob?" She was amazed at how calm she felt.

"I'm so sorry, Brenda. So, so sorry for the hurt I've caused you." He was wringing his hands and looking at the floor. "I realise now that it's you I love and that I've made a dreadful mistake."

Brenda saw that he was crying, something he'd never done, not even when his father had died. Bob was not the crying type.

"Please give us another chance, Brenda. Let's try again. I love you."

He looked up at her then and she felt deeply sorry for him. She wanted to put her arms around him and tell him everything would be all right but she couldn't do that because she didn't know whether it ever would be. She didn't think she could ever trust him again and that was no recipe for a marriage.

"I don't know, Bob. You've hurt me terribly."

"I've been such a fool. It was all a stupid mistake," he said, sniffing and attempting to dry his eyes. "I've left Crystal."

She looked at him sadly.

"Where are you staying?"

"In my mother's. She's furious with me."

"I'm not surprised. Everybody is," she couldn't resist saying.

She was calm and dignified and Bob watched her in admiration. What a fool he'd been. He'd lost her, this wonderful woman who had loved him once and borne his children.

Tears rolling down his cheeks, he looked at her longingly.

"Please, Brenda, please give us another chance."

"I'll think about it, Bob. That's all I can promise. I'll think about it."

* * *

When he'd left, Brenda reached for the brandy and with a shaking hand took a big gulp of it. She was trembling and upset, wondering what she should do. It had broken her heart to see him so upset.

Dylan heard the door close and came down to find his mother crying softly.

"What is it, Mum? How did it go? Why are you crying?"

She smiled through her tears. "It's okay, son. I'm just upset. I'll be fine."

"You're not getting back with Dad then?"

"I don't know, I just don't know."

"I think he's really sorry, Mum. He knows he's been a fool. Can't you give him another chance?"

"I wish it were that easy, son."

Ryan blew up when he heard she was even thinking of taking his father back.

"Are you mad, Mum, after what he's done?" he fumed, his fists clenched.

"I said I'd think about it, Ryan. I am capable of making up my own mind, you know."

"I still think you'd be mad," he said sullenly. "Big mistake!"

To her surprise, Carly was sympathetic about it. "Mum,

you do whatever makes you happy. If you think you and Dad can be happy again, go for it. If not, we'll respect your decision."

Brenda hugged her youngest child warmly. She would miss them all when they returned to college.

* * *

Lexi was happier than she'd ever been. Marvin had moved in permanently with her and she was enjoying it much more than she'd expected to. He was very easy to live with and it was lovely having him around all the time. She still spent her mornings painting and then they lunched together and sometimes even made love afterwards. Their lovemaking had taken on a new intensity and they wanted each other more than ever.

"It's great having it on tap," she'd said laughingly to him after one post-lunch session.

"Just turn the faucet anytime," he'd replied, stroking her hair.

Another bonus to being so happy was that her joy transmitted itself on to the canvas and her paintings had become vibrant and alive again. She put away the melancholy dark work she'd done after she'd returned from LA, vowing to give up painting if she ever painted like that again.

But Marvin was worried about her as she was still suffering from fatigue and lately her appetite had disappeared. He had been trying to convince her to go and have a check-up but she persistently refused yet again.

* * *

Nothing much had changed with Angel. Lexi had left countless messages on her answering machine but it was obvious Angel didn't want to talk to her. However, she kept in touch with Consuela who reported that Angel was drinking a lot but not taking the prescription drugs she'd been taking before. That at least was something to be grateful for. Thank God for Consuela who was extremely loyal to her mistress.

* * *

Mel made an appointment to see the gynaecologist who confirmed what she already knew and gave the due date of her baby as the twentieth of August. She gave her a thorough examination and guidelines for her pregnancy. She also made an appointment for Mel's first scan. Suddenly, the reality hit her and Mel realised the enormity of what was happening to her.

She Skyped Lexi that night to tell her.

"That's great, Mel. When is your scan?"

"It's on Friday the twentieth."

"That's fantastic. I have to come to New York to see my agent about my Guatemala exhibition. I could arrange it for that day and go with you. What time is it?"

"It's 9 a.m. I'd really appreciate it if you could come with me. I wouldn't feel so nervous then."

"I wouldn't miss it for the world. I feel partially responsible for this baby, you know. After all, it was conceived in Florida." She laughed.

"Oh, Lexi, you're the best friend anyone could have," Mel said gratefully.

"You'd do the same for me."

Lexi was aware of how difficult it would be for Mel having this baby alone and was determined to be as supportive as she could be.

"Can't wait to see you." Mel blew her a kiss.

"Me too, Momma!" Lexi laughed.

Chapter 30

The phone calls started two days after Bob had been to visit Brenda and the day after the kids left for college. At all hours, and especially during the night, Brenda's phone would ring and although she knew there was someone on the other end of the line, they uttered not a word. It was very unnerving and after the third night of multiple calls which woke her up, Brenda confided in Jean.

"Well, we know who's doing this don't we? It's that silly cow, Crystal."

"I have no proof of that, Jean." Brenda was a little concerned that perhaps it was Bob. She suspected he was a little unhinged at the moment.

She left her phone on voicemail all the time now and got rid of the phone from the bedroom. At least her sleep was not disturbed any more. Then the calls started coming in to her mobile phone. That was more difficult as she needed to keep that on always in case the kids needed her but she did leave it in the kitchen overnight. This went on for over two weeks and then late one night it changed.

PAULINE LAWLESS

Her mobile rang and as usual, showed number unknown. But this time there was someone on the other end of the line. It was the slapper, and she was drunk.

"You silly bitch," she screamed. "You and your daughters think you're so fuckin' posh an' classy, dontcha? Swannin' around in Louboutins, looking down your noses at me. Well, I took youse all down a peg or two, didint I? Yeah! You're not so great, now, are youse?"

Brenda was shaking at the vehemence on the other end of the line. It was scary.

"I'll put the smile on the other side of yer faces. Youse won't look so pretty when I get thru with youse." Then she laughed, a horrible, evil laugh.

Brenda cut her off and turned off her phone. The home phone rang then but Brenda shut her ears to the crazy ranting that was being poured onto the answering machine. She yanked the cord out of the wall and sat shaking, thinking that the woman must be mad.

The following day she told Jean all about it and let her listen to the call on her mobile.

"I knew it was her. She's gone too far this time. Leave it with me. Give me your phone." Jean took it and, putting on her coat, left the salon.

"Be careful, Jean," Brenda called after her sister, afraid that she was going to confront Crystal. Instead Jean headed straight to the Garda Station and asked for Roy.

Roy listened to the ranting on Brenda's phone and looked shocked. "This is pretty nasty stuff," he said. "We can certainly find out the caller ID, although I don't think it will come as any surprise to us," he said grimly. "Will Brenda mind if I hang on to this for an hour or two."

"Not at all. Thanks, love."

An hour later Roy arrived at the salon with a colleague.

"Can you take us to hear the message on your home phone?" he asked Brenda.

"Is that okay?" she asked Jean.

"Of course, love. We're not that busy. Go ahead!"

Brenda let Roy and the other Garda hear the message.

"Make sure you don't wipe that off," Roy instructed. "She hasn't committed any crime so we can't charge her but these may come in handy as evidence in the future, if she should try anything else."

Brenda thanked them and returned to work, wondering what else they expected she might try.

Suddenly, she felt sorry for Bob. God knows what tricks the slapper used to seduce him. Brenda suspected she was capable of anything. It scared her.

* * *

The following day, Brenda had a call from Bob.

"I'm just calling to say I'm so sorry about the phone calls and threats from Crystal."

"How did you hear about it?"

"My friend at the station told me. Is it true she threatened you and the girls?"

"Yes."

"Oh my God, I'm so sorry. I never suspected she'd do anything like that. Anyway, I don't think you'll be hearing from her again. I warned her she'd be in serious trouble if she didn't stop. I'm sorry you had to go through that."

"Okay. Thanks for letting me know."

"Have you thought about what we talked about?" he asked and she could tell he was nervous.

"Yes."

"And . . .?"

"I'm still thinking about it."

* * *

Angel finally screwed up the courage to call Lexi. She rang her one morning before she'd had a drink.

"Lexi, it's me. I'm sorry." Her voice was quiet and hesitant.

Thank God she's sober, was Lexi's first thought.

"Why haven't you answered my calls, honey? I've been worried sick about you."

"I'm sorry. I didn't have the courage to tell you I'd left the clinic. I know I've let you down."

"Angel, it's not for me you were doing it, it was for yourself," Lexi said sadly.

"I'm just not strong enough. I'm a mess." Angel was near to tears.

"You're still drinking?"

"Yes, but I have it under control."

Lexi doubted it but didn't say so.

"I'm not taking any prescription drugs. I've kicked that habit," Angel said proudly.

"I'm happy to hear that."

"Now give me all the news!" Angel demanded, wanting to change the subject. "How was your Christmas?"

"Wonderful! Marvin proposed on Christmas Day and I accepted. He's moved in permanently with me now."

"Oooohh, how exciting! Congratulations!"

"Thank you. I'm very happy right now."

"Any news from Brenda and Mel?"

She was shocked to hear of Brenda's separation. "Mind you, I always did say it wouldn't last, although I never dreamt it would last as long as it did. How is she?"

"She's fine, coping well and getting on with life."

"And Mel? How is she?"

"She's great. She has some pretty special news too but I won't spoil it. I'll let her tell you herself."

"Oooohh, has she someone new in her life?" Angel asked, dying to know all about it.

"You could say that," Lexi replied cagily, smiling to herself. "By the way, Kenny sends his love. He's quite smitten with you, you know."

"Kenny? Who's Kenny?" Angel frowned, trying to recall the name.

"He's my friend and also my neighbour who was at my Thanksgiving dinner. Don't you remember him?"

"Not really. God, I was so high that night, I don't remember a lot. I wasn't very nice to him, I suppose."

"No you weren't and the poor man is constantly asking after you. You were meant to go out on his boat with him the next day and he was quite upset to find you'd flown the coop."

"Oh, God, I'm sorry. Please apologise to him for me." Angel put her head in her hands hating to hear how she'd misbehaved.

"You can do that yourself. He travels to LA regularly on business and would love to meet you," Mel said gently.

Angel had been concentrating, trying to put a face to the name. "The name rings a bell. Is he the older guy who was very sweet to me at our birthday party?"

"That's Kenny. Can I tell him that you'll meet him then?"

"Why not? It's not as though I'm being rushed off my feet by suitors. Yes, that would be nice."

*   *   *

Mel and Donna had become good friends after that Christmas Day at Donna's house and went for lunch together very often.

She was pleased to accept when Donna invited her to lunch with the family one Sunday. Lexi was arriving that week and her scan was scheduled for the following Friday. Mel was anxious about seeing her baby for the first time on the scan and so welcomed the distraction of a visit with Donna's family. She received the same warm welcome from them all as she had on Christmas Day. There were almost as many people there as had been there that day.

"Today I cook for you," Papa announced, as he hugged her.

When Mel refused a drink, Donna looked at her strangely. The meal was delicious and Mel ate her fill.

"C'mon, have some more," Papa said as he proffered the bowl of meat balls.

"No, honestly, it was all wonderful, but I couldn't eat any more."

"You didn't eat very much," Donna remarked.

"Leave her alone. It is because of the *bambino*," Mama said, beaming at Mel.

"*Bambino*? What *bambino*?" Donna asked puzzled.

"I am right, am I not?" Mama addressed Mel, patting her tummy.

"Yes," Mel blushed. "How did you know?"

"Always, I can tell from woman's eyes when she carry *bambino*."

"You're pregnant?" Donna exclaimed, as the penny dropped.

"Yes, I am," Mel replied, looking downcast.

"Congratulations! I'm thrilled for you. This is wonderful news." Donna jumped up and hugged her and then she was being hugged and congratulated by all the family as the word spread around the table.

"And here was I admiring your willpower when I saw

you'd given up cigarettes," Donna said, when they'd all resumed their seats. "I thought it was just a New Year's resolution."

"No, it's just one of the adjustments I've had to make to my life, along with giving up alcohol."

"I guess there will be a lot more to come." Donna beamed.

"No doubt," Mel replied despondently.

Everyone seemed to be thrilled that she was pregnant, except herself.

"And the father . . . or do you mind my asking?" said Donna.

"Not at all. We met in Florida but he's long gone." Afraid Donna might think that it was just a casual one-night-stand that had resulted in this pregnancy, she added. "We did love each other very much." It was only half a lie, Mel thought dryly.

Donna now understood that the change in Mel since Thanksgiving was due to love. It was so romantic. She much preferred this new softer Mel to the old hard-edged one.

* * *

Lexi arrived at JFK airport feeling exhausted. Flying was becoming more and more difficult with all the security measures now in place. She wished she didn't have to ever fly again but it was the only way to see her friends, if they couldn't come to her. However, besides the fact that she had to see her agent, it would be worth it to be there to see the first photos of Mel's baby.

A glowing Mel embraced her in the arrivals hall at JFK.

"My, but you are positively blooming," Lexi said as she surveyed the new mom-to-be.

"Blooming is right," Mel laughed, as she put her hands on her breasts.

"Pregnancy suits you! You should have done it years ago."

"You think? Better late than never, I suppose."

Lexi saw how Mel had changed. She had gained weight, not in an ugly way, but in a rounded soft way which suited her. Her hair had grown and was less severe. Everything about her had become less angular. Her skin was glowing and she looked more attractive than she ever had.

They went out for dinner and Lexi was relieved to see that Mel had given up smoking. "I'll be forever grateful to this baby for that, if nothing else, unless you go back on them after it's born."

"Good heavens, no. I wouldn't dream of smoking around my baby," Mel said, horrified at the notion.

The following morning they arrived bright and early at the clinic. Lexi held Mel's hand as the ultrasound was placed on her already rounded tummy. They watched the screen spellbound as the nurse showed them the heart beating and the tiny person that was growing inside her. Mel felt her heart contract and burst with love for this little being that she and Jack had made. It looked so helpless and tiny and was so dependent on her that all her instincts reached out to it and she knew, without a doubt, that she would love it and care for it as best she could.

"It's a miracle!" she cried, tears rolling down her cheeks.

Lexi was equally moved and felt the tears stinging her eyes as she saw this tiny creature moving around. It reminded her of her Alessandro. Pray God this baby would have a better chance at life.

Quiet but happy they left the clinic, photos of Mel's baby clutched tightly in their hands.

"Isn't it unbelievable, Lexi? I'm still pinching myself."

"You're happier now, having seen it?"

"Oh, yes, I already love this little mite," Mel smiled,

patting her tummy, and Lexi knew she was going to be okay.

"What a pity Jack isn't around to share this with you," she said wistfully.

"Well, he isn't," Mel replied matter of factly. "I'll take care of this baby and give it everything it needs all by myself." She sounded resolute.

They hailed a cab to take them to the Waldorf for a celebratory lunch.

They both had much to celebrate now.

Chapter 31

Mel called Angel when she got home and was surprised when she answered.

"Hi, Angel. I'm going to Skype you. I've got some news. Can you go online?"

"Can't you tell me over the phone?"

"No, I'd rather see your reaction in person. I want to see the look on your face."

"Okay," Angel replied, sounding not too happy.

When Mel saw how dishevelled Angel looked she understood why she didn't want her to Skype.

"How are you? You don't look well," Mel greeted her.

"And you've gained weight," Angel remarked, "but it suits you," she added hastily. "You look great and different too. I hear you have someone new in your life. Tell me all! Lexi, the meany, wouldn't tell me a thing."

"Yes, well, I have a photo here." She held up a photo of her scan to the camera.

"What's that?" Angel asked, puzzled. She squinted, coming closer to her iPad. "It's not a person. It's a scan, isn't it?"

"Yes, it's my baby's scan. I'm pregnant, Ange."

"What?" Angel shrieked. "Oh my God! When did it happen, tell me all – oh, of course, it's Jack's, isn't it? Wow! This is amazing!"

"Of course it's Jack's."

"This is just the best news. I'm so jealous. You with a baby! Imagine! How do you feel about it?"

"Well, at first I was terrified. To be honest, I wasn't too happy about it at all but after I had the scan today and saw the tiny wee thing with its heart beating, everything's changed. It won't be easy and I'll have to make big changes in my life and sacrifices, but I swear, Ange, this is the best thing that's ever happened to me. It puts everything in perspective, you know?"

"I can only guess," Angel said. "Mel, I have so much I want to say to you. I am so sorry for everything I've done to you – Simon, flirting with Jack, you know. I was a bitch, I see that now." She looked anxiously at Mel. "Can you ever forgive me?"

"I have forgiven you, sweetie. We go back too long to let anything get in the way of our friendship. I love you, honey. Now tell me how you are?"

"I'm sure Lexi has told you I did a bunk from the clinic. I couldn't take it, Mel. It was hell, or too tough or I'm too weak, whichever. Anyway, it did me some good as I'm off prescription drugs but kicking the booze is another story. Still, I am trying to cut back."

"That's good news, Angel," Mel said, feeling desperately sorry for her old friend. Alcoholism was a killer. She didn't understand it but she felt sympathy for Angel. She'd never been a strong character like the rest of them.

"Hollywood is not the best place for me, I know. I'm thinking of getting out of here," Angel confided.

"Where will you go?"

"God knows. It's just a thought."

* * *

Angel was having a tougher time than she was letting on to her friends. Her whole life seemed to have come apart at the seams. She'd been for an audition for a guest role in a well-known TV series but hadn't got the part. Her agent called her after the audition. He was very angry.

"How do you expect to land a role if you turn up drunk to an audition?" he had asked, furious with her.

"I wasn't drunk. I just had one drink before I went to give me courage." She didn't mention that it was a very big one – a full tumbler of whisky, actually.

"That's not what the studio says. They say you were drunk. Angel, sweetie, don't you know you're committing career-suicide?" He sighed. "Tinseltown is a small place and word gets around quickly. If you want to work again, you better kick the booze."

Angel was very upset after that call and downed a whole bottle of whisky that evening. Who was he to tell her how to live her life?

* * *

Brenda had given it a lot of thought and decided she owed it to their twenty-plus years of marriage to give it another chance. She rang Bob and asked him to call around that evening. He was on her doorstep at five thirty, looking hopeful yet anxious.

She offered him a beer and poured a glass of wine for herself. He thought this was a good sign.

"Well?" he asked, unable to bear the suspense another minute. "Have you decided?"

"Yes. I'm willing to give it another chance but on a trial basis and things have to change."

"I'll do anything, anything, Brenda, if we can get back together again," Bob said, wanting to hug her but afraid she might rebuff him.

"We'll give it three months, okay? If things work out then we can decide to make it permanent again. That's the best I can do," she said.

"Oh, Brenda, you won't regret it," he promised, putting down his drink and going to hug her.

"It won't be easy, Bob, but it's worth a try."

Brenda told Bob he'd have to sleep in the twins' room. She wasn't quite ready to take him back into her bed yet. She wondered would she ever be. She felt no desire for him any more. How ironic! Before they split he'd had no interest in her, now he was panting for her but she didn't want him. How the tables had turned!

So Bob moved back in later that night. He was deliriously happy and arrived laden down with a huge bouquet of flowers. He was so excited that he didn't see Crystal parked across the road, watching him as he greeted Brenda and kissed her.

The anonymous phone calls started again that night. Every hour throughout the night, the phone rang. Brenda couldn't believe it. She didn't sleep a wink and eventually came downstairs and yanked the phone out of the socket. Was that bitch starting again? She was waiting for Bob the next morning.

"Your girlfriend has started her antics again," she told him.

Bob blanched and put his head in his hands. What a terrible start to his second chance. "She's nuts, Brenda, honestly."

"Well, it's a pity you didn't discover that before you got

involved with her," Brenda said coldly. She was tired and grumpy from lack of sleep – thanks to the slapper!

* * *

Kenny had arranged to meet Angel for lunch in Providence on Melrose Avenue, which impressed her greatly. He came in carrying a beautiful bouquet of roses which he presented to her. She thought it was very sweet of him. She recognised him immediately and blushed as she recalled that she hadn't been very nice to him, claiming he was much too old for her.

He thought she was still very beautiful but the alcohol was taking its toll. As he reached forward to kiss her on the cheek he smelt the whisky. Poor girl, he thought. She ordered a glass of wine and he saw how quickly she downed it, her hand shaking as she did so. His heart went out to her. He'd been there and knew what she was going through. He never mentioned her drinking but did tell her that he was a recovering alcoholic.

"Yes, well, I'm sure Lexi told you I have a bit of a problem but I'm not an alcoholic," Angel told him.

He held his tongue although he knew the signs and could see she was. On her third glass of chardonnay, she asked him, "How did you kick the habit?"

"With great, great difficulty and a lot of help."

Angel was keen to know more about him and how he'd done it. He told her he had been an alcoholic and had lost everything, his family, his job and his home because of drink. But having hit rock bottom he had struggled to get back on his feet, mainly thanks to the support from his friends in AA, and he was now back on top again.

"Mmmm . . ." Angel murmured, thinking about what he'd said. She found his story inspiring.

"I'll be coming here to LA over the next few weeks to finalise this TV deal I'm working on. I'd be honoured if you'd have lunch with me again when I'm here?"

"I'd love that," Angel replied shyly. Kenny had given her hope for her own future. Maybe he could help her.

She'd found him to be a charming, interesting companion and was pleased she'd agreed to meet him for lunch.

* * *

Brenda's nerves were on edge. The silent phone calls continued but the Gardaí said they could do nothing about it. Then one morning, Brenda woke to find the words, POSH WHORE LIVES HERE, daubed all over her front wall. She had no proof but of course it was obvious who the culprit was. It was causing a huge strain between Brenda and Bob and not helping them get their marriage back on track. Jean was livid and advised Brenda to ask Bob to leave.

"That's just giving in to her, isn't it?" Brenda said.

"So what? Look at you! You're a nervous wreck."

That much was true. Jean was still anti-Bob and thought Brenda was crazy for taking him back. The memory of New Year's Eve was still fresh in her mind.

"I don't know," Brenda said.

She was beginning to think she'd made a mistake. Despite Bob's promises, nothing had changed very much. The distance between them hadn't been bridged and now on top of that was the spectre of Crystal. It was an impossible situation.

Bob didn't know what to do. He was terrified of what Crystal might do. He decided that placating her would be the best way to get her off their backs, so he approached her the following Friday and asked her to meet him for a drink.

She was suspicious of him but couldn't resist the

temptation to meet him. They didn't go to Ryan's, although she wanted to. He suggested O'Dwyer's which was a little further away.

After ordering two drinks for them, he took her hand in his. "I've really missed you," he said.

"Really?" she asked, raising her eyebrows.

"Yes, I think about you all the time."

"Is your posh wife not satisfying you, then?" she smirked, enjoying this conversation.

"Only you can do that," he purred, rubbing her hand.

"I knew you'd be back," she said smugly. "I'm still hot for you."

"Sexy bitch," he whispered. "You're the hottest woman on the planet." He pressed his knee against hers then reached over and kissed her. She opened her mouth for him and the kiss lasted longer than he'd intended.

Unfortunately, Bob hadn't seen Brenda's brother, Conor, sitting in the corner witnessing all of this. Infuriated, he rang Jean and told her what he'd just witnessed.

"The bastard!" Jean spat out. "I'll get Brenda and meet you there. Follow him if they leave and let me know where they go." She then dashed around to Brenda's house. Shocked, Brenda hardly believed her but agreed to go to O'Dwyer's with her.

"Come on, let's go!" Jean cried, running to her car. Brenda followed dejectedly. Would he really have gone back with Crystal after all his protestations of love?

Meanwhile back in the bar Crystal preened, running her hand through her platinum blonde hair and licking her lips. "So she's not keeping you satisfied then?"

"We're not even sleeping in the same bed," Bob assured her, which was true. "How could I want her after being with you? She's a cold fish."

"I guessed as much. Let's get out of here, I'm feeling horny," she said, throwing back her vodka-and-white.

They left, unaware that Conor had followed them out. They got into Bob's car and within seconds Crystal had lowered the passenger seat and was all over him like a rash. Bob did his best to resist but Crystal knew his weakness. It had been such a long time since he'd had sex as Brenda was still denying him. He felt justified somehow. Crystal zipped down his jeans and with her mouth quickly brought him to erection. He moaned with pleasure. Throwing off her top and underwear she pulled him under her on the seat then hiked up her miniskirt and climbed on top of him. Straddling him she guided him into her while she moved rhythmically up and down. He was lost. There was a knock on the car window which was all steamed up.

"Oh, fuck, who the hell is that?" Crystal yelled.

"Leave it," Bob cried, about to climax.

"I didn't lock the –" Crystal didn't get to finish as the car door was yanked open and the blast of cold air shocked them.

"You bastard!" Jean yelled as Conor lunged at the half-naked copulating couple.

Crystal didn't even try to cover up her big naked breasts but laughed aloud as she saw Brenda standing behind them.

Brenda said nothing. She just looked at Bob sadly and the look in her eyes devastated him more than anything she could have said.

"Please Brenda, I can explain . . ."

Without uttering a word, she turned on her heel and left. She was dimly aware of Crystal shouting obscenities after her but the roaring in her ears blocked them out.

Bob crumbled, sobbing. He had well and truly lost her now.

Chapter 32

Mel's baby bump was getting more prominent every day but she was feeling great now that the morning sickness had disappeared. Donna was turning into a great friend and her family were the family Mel had always longed for but never had. She was sixteen weeks pregnant now but she still hadn't told her parents that they were going to be grandparents. She could just imagine her mother's disapproval to hear her only daughter was going to be an unmarried mother – her mother's term for single mothers, not Mel's. She knew she'd have to tell them soon.

* * *

Angel had been turned down for another role and her agent was incensed with her.

"You don't get it, do you? You're dead in this town unless you give up the booze. Think Lindsay Lohan!"

She banged the phone down on him and called an old girlfriend of hers, Sally.

"How about a girls' night out?" she suggested.

"Great! I'll call Tiffany and Marilyn and see if they can join us."

That night they all met up in the Polo Lounge of the Beverly Hills Hotel and started with cocktails. They moved from there to Tiki Ti then on to the Viper Room ending up in Circus Disco at 2 a.m. Needless to say after numerous cocktails and shots, Angel was falling-down drunk. As she was being half-carried from Circus, the paparazzi had a field day. To add insult to injury, she fell flat on her face in front of them, blinded by the flashbulbs exploding all around them.

The following morning, as Angel was still comatose, her photo graced every tabloid and magazine in Los Angeles and even further afield. When she finally came to, she discovered over a dozen messages on her answering machine. The first one was from her agent.

"I no longer wish to represent you. Don't bother calling me back. I'm through with you."

Angel tried to remember what had happened the night before but it was all a blur. When she heard what the other messages had to say, she sent Consuela out to buy the rags.

Looking at the photos of herself, lying in the gutter, she felt deeply ashamed and humiliated. How had she let this happen? She went back to bed and pulled the covers over her head, wishing she could die.

Kenny left a message for her that afternoon.

"Hi, honey. How are you? I'm just calling to offer my support. I'm coming to LA tomorrow and would like to see you. Please call me back."

His was the only message that wasn't gloating over her downfall. She rang him back, keen to hear a kind word from someone. He was gentle and kind with her and she broke down in tears. He arranged to come to her house the following day. She couldn't face the outside world.

* * *

Kenny was worried to find Angel in a state of deep depression. He feared that she might even be suicidal. He put his arms around her as she sobbed into his chest. Gone was the glamorous star he'd first met and in her place a frightened little girl.

He sat her down and spoke firmly to her trying to impress on her the necessity to do something to stop this downhill slide.

"What can I do?" she asked. "My life is over."

"Nonsense, you have all your life ahead of you and it could be a wonderful one, if you admit your problem and seek help. I did and look at me now."

She listened to him gravely. He persuaded her to go to an AA meeting with him that very afternoon. It was the turning point for Angel.

Kenny stayed on in LA with her for the whole week and they went to AA meetings every day where she listened to the stories of others but said nothing. He stayed in her guest room, afraid to leave her alone in the house in case she might be tempted to start drinking again. He kept her busy, arranging trips every day – to the beach, to the zoo – and she found herself enjoying these simple pleasures. Every day she seemed a little stronger and finally on the fifth day, she stood up at the meeting and said,

"My name is Angel and I'm an alcoholic."

It was the breakthrough Kenny had been waiting for. That night he took her out for a wonderful meal and ordered a bottle of non-alcoholic wine.

Angel felt happy for the first time since that awful Thanksgiving night. Kenny stayed on for another two days but then had to get back to Clearwater. Angel was given an AA sponsor who would take Kenny's place. Things were looking up.

Kenny called her many times every day and was happy she was staying with the programme. He went up to visit her every week and she looked forward to his visits. She felt she owed him her life.

Lexi was thrilled to hear that she had stopped drinking and had joined AA. She was immensely grateful to Kenny. She knew it was all his doing. She was feeling so tired lately that she didn't have the energy to fly to LA even though Kenny had offered to take her in his private jet.

"Angel is like a little-girl-lost," he had confided to Lexi after his last visit. "I think what she needs more than anything is to be loved. She's been using alcohol as a crutch. It makes her feel better about herself. I've convinced her to go into therapy which will also help a lot. I have every confidence she'll come through this."

Lexi could see that he was genuinely concerned about Angel. He confirmed that she was not taking any prescription drugs either which was a relief. Lexi knew it was the combination of them and the alcohol that had caused Angel's near-fatal collapse before Christmas. Lexi wondered if Kenny really did have business in LA or was it just an excuse for him to see Angel. She sensed that he was getting very, very fond of her. If only Angel would fall for him. That would be perfect.

* * *

Brenda had called Lexi to say that she and Bob were separating for good. They'd tried to make a go of it but it hadn't worked out. Lexi wasn't surprised. Brenda didn't go into details but Lexi guessed she'd hear the whole story eventually.

* * *

Mel had been giving a lot of thought to what she was going to do. There was no way she could raise a baby while she worked such long hours. It was going to be a problem and she had to find a solution. Her life had to change.

The president of the company had called an emergency meeting of the partners and Mel was sitting mulling over her situation as she waited for him to start the meeting. She found it hard to concentrate on what he was saying as he explained that there were problems with the office in Columbus, Ohio, and that he needed one of them to relocate there for six months and find out what the hell was going on, shake them up and fix things.

Columbus, Ohio? Mel thought. Could I do it? But she knew she couldn't move there. She knew absolutely no one in that part of the world.

"And our Florida office is also showing a loss which I suspect is due to bad management and perhaps even fraud. So I need two volunteers, one for Columbus and one for Tampa, to sort out this mess."

Mel wondered was she hearing things. This was too good to be true.

"So, think it over and let me know by this afternoon," he concluded.

Before any else had a chance to do anything, Mel's hand shot up.

"Yes, Mel?"

"I'd like to volunteer for Tampa, sir, if that's okay with you."

He looked at her strangely as did all of the others. "Tampa, Mel? Am I hearing you right? I thought you were a New Yorker, through and through."

"Yes, sir, but I'd like to take on the Tampa job."

"Very well, come to my office at noon. And if anyone else is interested in taking on Columbus, let me know. There will be added perks going with the job of course."

The other partners murmured amongst themselves. This was an opportunity to shine though none of them wanted to leave New York. However, the president was due to retire in two years and something like this could catapult them into the first place as his successor. Mel had no hankering for that. She was thinking of her baby.

* * *

Mel knocked with trepidation on the door of the president's suite and his PA admitted her into her office, which was as grand as any of the partners' offices.

She then led her into her boss's grandiose room. It couldn't be called an office – more a salon, actually. It had a ninety-degree view of the city. No one entered here without a previous appointment. It was the holy-of-holies and Mel had only been here three or four times before.

"Come, my dear," the president greeted her, showing her into the dining room which was set for lunch. "I was so surprised by your offer today that I felt we should discuss it over lunch."

His butler pulled out a chair for her and she sat.

"Tell me, Mel, why do you want to take on Tampa?" he asked as she admired the lobster salad that was placed before her.

She explained that she was pregnant and that she had been thinking of asking for a transfer anyway. "And I have friends in Tampa, which will be important for me at this time."

"Well, congratulations my dear. That's wonderful news. But can you give it six months? Will you not want maternity leave?"

"Not before my baby is due, which is mid-August. I will of

course take it after he's born. That gives me plenty of time to sort out the Tampa office."

"Well, well, this has come at an opportune time for you," he chuckled. "Some people are born lucky. Guess you're one of them!"

"Yes, sir, I'm a very lucky girl," she grinned at him.

"You said 'he'. Do you know it's going to be a boy for sure?"

"No, sir, I just feel it in my bones."

He laughed and they went on to discuss the problem in the Tampa office.

"How soon can you leave?" he asked.

"I have another scan tomorrow so I'll be ready to go any time after that."

"Excellent! Let's say you start there next Monday so you'll have a few days to sort things out before you go. I'm really concerned about what's going on down there so I don't want to give them any advance warning that you're coming. Let's not give them a chance to cover up anything."

"Is it so bad?" Mel looked worried.

"I'm afraid so but I have every confidence that you'll sort them out. And who do you think should take over your job here while you're gone?"

"I've been giving it some thought, sir, and I think Donna would be more than capable of doing that. She's worked very closely with me and could step into my place tomorrow."

"Yes, I have been very impressed with her myself. Very well. Maybe you can ask her to come and see me at . . ." He buzzed his PA to see what free time he had that afternoon. "At five. Okay?"

"Yes, sir, and thank you for everything."

"I should be thanking you. You're the best employee I have and I don't want to lose you. I know you'll do a good job in Tampa. I'll brief you on Friday."

* * *

Mel couldn't contain her excitement as she dashed back to her office. She called Donna in.

"Donna, Donna, you won't believe what's happened," she cried, twirling her friend around. "I'm moving to the Tampa office for six months, to sort things out there."

Donna's face fell. "And you're happy about that?"

"Deliriously! I've been thinking of asking for a transfer as I'd like to be near Lexi and my friends there when the baby is born."

"Oh no! How will I manage here without you? What dickhead will I have as a boss now?" Most of the other senior management were male and neither of the two girls thought very much of them.

"This is the best part: you'll be taking over my job while I'm gone!"

"What?" Donna shrieked. "Are you serious?"

"Yes, the president asked who I thought should stand in for me and I said you, naturally."

"Oh Mel, thank you, thank you, thank you! I can't believe it," Donna exclaimed, hugging her.

"Believe it! He wants to see you in his office at five o'clock this evening."

"Oh, my God!" Donna cried, fanning herself with her hand. "But I'll miss you. Will you be back after the six months? Your baby is due just about then."

"I'll take maternity leave after he's born and then we'll see. In the meantime, I'm really happy about it and you can come down and visit me any weekend you want.

"That would be great," Donna said her eyes shining.

"Now back to work. We've a lot to talk about before I go."

* * *

Donna had insisted on accompanying Mel for her scan. "You shouldn't be alone at these important moments," she'd said. Mel was secretly grateful.

As she looked at the screen she was amazed at how much her baby had grown in the past few weeks. Donna was blown away. She'd never seen this before.

"Wow, this is a lively one," the sonographer remarked as she looked at the screen with them. "Do you want to know the sex of your baby?" she asked as she moved the instrument over Mel's tummy.

"Yes, but I'm sure it's a boy."

"Well, you obviously have a mother's instinct already. It is a boy, and a healthy one at that."

Mel was not at all surprised.

She couldn't wait to call Lexi. "I've been for my scan and I was right, it is a boy and everything's fine."

"That's great news."

"And I've got some even better news. The company have asked me to take over the Tampa office for six months so I'll be moving down there this weekend."

"Oh my gosh, I don't believe it!" Lexi was so surprised, she had to sit down.

"Is everything okay?" Marvin asked her solicitously, worried something was wrong.

She gave him the thumbs-up. "Better than okay," she whispered before returning to talk to Mel.

"Mel, that is fantastic news. I am thrilled. It will be so good to have you here. Will you come and stay here with us?"

"Well, I'd like to rent a house, Lexi, preferably close to you in Clearwater, but if I could stay with you for a few days till I find a house, that would be great."

"Of course. My, this is great news. And you'll have your baby here?"

"Yes. My gynaecologist will refer me to a good one there. Isn't it marvellous?"

"Better than marvellous."

* * *

Meanwhile, back in Ireland, Brenda was trying to get her life back on track after Bob's departure. She refused to speak to him any more. He'd really gone too far this time. She didn't tell any of the kids what had happened, just that she'd decided it wasn't working out. Luckily she had her job in the salon to keep her busy but that would be gone by May when Sybil, the receptionist, would be back from her maternity leave. She had also taken to bridge much better than she'd expected to. She and three others from the bridge class, all of them separated or divorced, played in each other's houses every Friday and then had supper afterwards. It was good fun. She did get lonely at times but then she'd often been lonely even when married to Bob. At least now she could come and go as she pleased. In a strange way she was happier than when he'd been around.

She'd heard Bob was drinking a lot but what he did or did not do was not her concern any more. She would never forgive him nor forget that awful night and the sight of that horrible woman, naked on top of him. The kids kept in contact with her more than ever. She was looking forward to their Easter break next which wouldn't be long now.

When Brenda got the call from Mel to say that she was moving to Tampa, she was more than a little envious. How she'd love to be there too, especially for the birth of Mel's baby in August but she knew it just wasn't possible. She did feel a bit out of the loop, being so far away from them all.

Chapter 33

Lexi hadn't mentioned anything to the girls but Marvin had finally got his way and persuaded her to see a doctor. Marvin went with her for her appointment with his doctor of twenty years who when he heard her symptoms and examined her, sent her to a gynaecologist who, in turn sent her for a blood test and a pelvic MRI. She had just returned from that and was now anxiously awaiting the results. She hoped it was something simple like an ovarian cyst – many women suffered them at some stage and they were easily treated. Whatever it was, she knew there was something wrong. Besides being fatigued and losing her appetite, she was feeling strong pressure on her abdomen. She played it down for Marvin's sake but she was secretly worried.

* * *

Her last days in New York were hectic for Mel as she packed up and made ready to move to Tampa. She thought she would feel sad leaving but instead she was buoyant, feeling that a new chapter in her life was beginning. She wasn't giving up her apartment just yet. She could have rented it out but it would have been too stressful trying to pack all her stuff away. It would be time enough to decide, when her baby was born, where they would live. She had a gut feeling that it would not be the Big Apple. In the meantime, she asked Donna if she would house-sit for her.

"Are you serious? I'd love that," was her friend's reply, excited at the prospect of having her own space and in this gorgeous Upper West-Side apartment. "You know I love my family to bits but sometimes I long for some peace and quiet. I never get that or any privacy in my parents' house. It will be great to be able to walk to work too and I promise I'll take good care of it for you."

"I know you will," Mel smiled at her, pleased that she'd thought of it. "And I'm happy knowing that you're in it."

Finally, all was done and she took a last look at the apartment before leaving for her new adventure.

* * *

Mel picked up the Lexus that the company had leased for her at the airport and drove, humming to herself, to Clearwater. Maria let her in and she ran into the house calling out hello but was stopped in her tracks when she saw Lexi, lying on the couch, looking pale and gaunt. Mel had seen on Skype that Lexi had lost more weight but was shocked now at how frail she appeared.

"Lexi, darling, what is it? Why didn't you tell me you were ill," she chided, hugging her best friend.

"I didn't want to worry you and anyway, it's probably nothing." Lexi smiled but Mel could see the fear behind her eyes. "Marvin finally insisted I go to the doctor who sent me

PAULINE LAWLESS

to see a gynaecologist. He sent me for an MRI and blood tests and we're waiting the results, so let's not jump ahead of ourselves. Now let me have a look at you? Why, you're looking marvellous!"

"Well, I've got boobs for the first time in my life. I just hope they stay that way." Mel had always been embarrassed by her flat chest and envious of Lexi and Angel's well-endowed ones.

Marvin brought them tea as they chatted and when Mel saw that Lexi was tiring, she went to unpack so as to let her rest. Later as Lexi slept, she and Marvin spoke quietly in the kitchen.

"I'm worried sick about her, Mel," he confided, tears in his eyes.

"I can understand that. I got a shock when I saw how much she's failed in just a few weeks, but let's wait until we hear from the doctors. They can work miracles these days." She patted his hand in an effort to comfort him. "If I'd known I could have stayed in a hotel till I find a place."

"Lexi wouldn't hear of that and anyway I have good news for you. Troy has bought a penthouse overlooking the marina so if you're interested you can rent my house. I'll keep the rent as low as possible."

"That's not a problem as the company is paying for it. It will be great to be right next door. When can I move in?"

"Straight away. Troy's place is finished and he's ready to move. I'll talk to him tonight."

"That's good. I wouldn't like to be a nuisance when Lexi is so ill."

"If you believe in prayer, Mel, please pray for her. I'm so scared for her."

"I will, Marvin."

* * *

300

Mel arrived at the office in Tampa at eight on Monday to find that the receptionist, a pretty young girl, was the only one there.

"Where is everyone?" Mel asked, looking around the large, empty open-plan office.

"Oh, they don't usually come in till nine or nine thirty," said the girl, smiling.

"And the manager, Mr Nesbitt, what time do you expect him?"

"Oh, he doesn't ever come in till ten or eleven. Maybe I can help you?" She smiled sweetly at Mel.

"I'm Ms O'Brien from the New York office."

The girl's face registered her shock. "Ms Mel O'Brien . . . one of the partners?"

"Correct! I'll be working here for the next few months. Now, can you please show me into Mr Nesbitt's office?"

"Certainly, Ms O'Brien. This way." The girl jumped up eagerly and led the way into the manager's office.

It didn't take Mel long to see why this branch was not functioning. There was a putting machine in the centre of the floor with a putter and some balls propped up against the desk. In the adjoining room, which was designed as a conference room, the large table had been dismantled. In its place a golf-practice facility had been erected, complete with practice net, camera and screen to focus on one's swing. Mr Nesbitt was obviously more concerned about his golf game than he was about the business. There was also a well-stocked liquor cabinet which lay open with half bottles of whisky in evidence. Well, well, thought Mel. I have my work cut out for me here.

Mel asked the young girl, who said her name was Ginny, to open up the filing cabinets for her. She took out several files and settled down to work. Things were worse than she'd anticipated.

Around an hour later, there was a knock on the door.

"Come in," Mel said, looking up to see a very flustered young man hovering on the doorstep.

"Mr Nesbitt?" she asked.

"No, I'm Donald Young, Credit Control," he introduced himself, shifting from foot to foot.

"Ah, Mr Young, I'm Mel O'Brien from the new York office."

"Yes, Ginny told me. Nice to meet you, Ms O'Brien. I've heard a lot about you," he said nervously.

"Mr Young, can you tell me what the hell has been going on in this office? These accounts don't add up." Mel pointed at the ledgers in front of her.

"Yes, well, I can't really say . . . erm . . . Mr Nesbitt would not like me to . . . erm . . ."

Mel banged the table, making him jump. "I don't give a damn what Mr Nesbitt would or would not like. I'm here to find out what's going on. Now maybe you can tell me, seeing as how Mr Nesbitt hasn't graced us with his presence yet."

"Yes, well, Monday is his golf league day. He doesn't work Mondays."

"Or Tuesday through Friday either, I guess. Now I will be working here for the foreseeable future and you will all be answerable to me, not Mr Tiger-Woods-Nesbitt. Do I make myself clear?"

"Yes, Ms O'Brien, abundantly clear."

"Good! Now I wish to interview every member of staff here, starting with you. Everything you tell me will be confidential, understand?"

* * *

By the end of the day she had the whole story. Mr Nesbitt was seldom there and the assistant manager, Mr Lundy, a horrible

302

little man who was feared by the staff, had total control and was obviously cooking the books. He was obsequious, attempting to flatter her and put the blame for the disappearance of funds on Mr Nesbitt.

She called the president on her cell phone – she had a feeling Mr Lundy might be listening in if she used the office line – and reported what she'd learnt.

"I want to fire Nesbitt and Lundy," she told him.

"Go ahead, my girl! That's what you're there for. You have my blessing."

"Thank you, sir."

Well, that was a good day's work, she thought, as she walked to her car.

* * *

She knew the moment she got home that something was wrong. Marvin was sitting holding Lexi and she could see they'd both been crying.

"What is it?" she asked, fear clutching her heart.

"It's more than a cyst, I'm afraid," Lexi told her. "I got the results of the MRI back and they found some cells that they're not happy about. I have an appointment to see an oncologist tomorrow."

"Oh, Lexi, that's awful. I'm so sorry."

"Well, maybe they're wrong," Lexi said hopefully. "No point in worrying about it till then. Maybe it's all a storm in a teacup."

Mel wasn't fooled and she could tell Marvin wasn't either. Lexi was putting on a brave face for their sake. An oncologist meant cancer and it would take a miracle to change that.

"And Mel, please don't say anything to Angel or Brenda. I don't want to worry them. Promise me you won't."

"I won't say a word, I promise."

303

"We thought we'd go out to eat in the Beachcomber tonight," Marvin said brightly. "That okay with you?"

"Would you two not prefer to go alone?" Mel asked.

"Of course not," they both said together.

"We thought we'd ask Troy to join us too. By the way, he moved his things out of the house today so after Maria gives it a good cleaning, it will be ready for you to move in tomorrow evening."

"Thanks, Marvin, I appreciate that."

Lexi tried bravely to be upbeat during the meal, of which she ate practically nothing. Troy told them all about his new pad which sounded fabulous and then Mel told them about her experiences in the Tampa office that day. Hanging over them all however, like a dark cloud, was the worry of what the oncologist would decide tomorrow. The mere word 'oncologist' drove fear into all their hearts.

Mel offered to go with her to the hospital the following day.

"No, no, I'll be fine. Marvin will take me," Lexi assured her, looking lovingly at her fiancé. "Anyway, by the sound of it, you'll be having a very busy day at the office tomorrow."

"Watch out for the Wicked Witch of the North, folks," Troy cried, as Mel swatted him.

They all laughed which lightened the atmosphere somewhat.

* * *

That night, for the first time, Mel felt her baby move. For a moment she thought she'd imagined it, but no, there it was again, a tiny flutter in her tummy. She felt the love surge through her for this tiny little being and began to understand for the first time the joy of motherhood.

* * *

Mel strode into the office the following day, determined to get proof of the fraud carried out by Lundy. She pored over the books all morning and finally she found what she was looking for. The little schemer, she thought. She called him into her office and asked him to explain the discrepancy in the accounts. He blustered, denying all knowledge of it, but she knew by him that he was lying.

She did not tell him of the off-shore account she'd unearthed into which millions of company money had been poured. She would contact the fraud squad first before alerting him that she'd discovered his scam. She would need to get those assets frozen immediately.

"Mr Lundy, I would like you to take a few days off while I look into this matter. Good day, I'll be in touch with you."

He marched cockily out of the office, certain that he had covered his traces well enough. Mel watched him go in disgust. He wouldn't be so cocky when she'd finished with him. One down, she thought as she rang Police Headquarters and got put through to the fraud squad.

* * *

Nesbitt turned out to be an overweight blusterer who she guessed had a drink problem. He was a quivering mess when he realised who she was and what she was doing there. Knowing that the game was up, he broke down in tears, begging her to give him another chance. She looked at him coldly, finding him pathetic.

"Kindly have all your golf paraphernalia removed from the conference room and your office by two o'clock this afternoon. Oh, and I would like your keys back, please, all of them." She put out her hand and he dropped them into her palm, still snivelling. Good riddance, she said to herself.

She instructed Donald Young to supervise Nesbitt to make sure he took nothing that did not belong to him and especially not any files or his computer.

Young agreed readily, knowing which side his bread was buttered on. He looked at Mel with a new respect.

She then called a removal company to come and remove everything else in his office. Next she called a painting contractor and instructed them to come and paint the office. They would come the following morning and paint it white, as she'd instructed.

* * *

Marvin called that afternoon. "The prognosis is not good, Mel. Lexi has had a PET-CT scan to discover how far advanced the tumour is. We won't have the results for a day or two."

"Can I come in and visit Lexi?" she asked.

"Better not, she's sedated now and sleeping. I think Lexi would prefer to wait until we have the results."

"Give her my love when she wakes."

"I will, of course. By the way, she says there's a chicken dish in the fridge for your supper. She told me to tell you it just needs to be reheated in the microwave."

When Mel got to the privacy of her own car, she broke down in tears. How typical of Lexi to think of her, in the midst of her own anguish. Drying her tears, Mel drove home thinking of her best friend, terrified of what they would find in her body.

* * *

When she'd eaten she took the keys that Maria had left for her and took her things over to Marvin's house, her house now. Troy had offered to help her but she didn't have that much to take. She had arranged for Donna to send some of her stuff down when she'd found a place. She looked around the beautiful airy house, thinking that she could be very happy here. And this would be the first home her son would know. She felt him move again just then, as if he understood. Somehow, it gave her comfort.

Chapter 34

Mel got the call she'd been dreading.

"Bad news, Mel. It's Stage II cancer – in the ovaries. They're starting chemotherapy right away."

* * *

The treatment was tough, very tough, and Lexi felt very ill after each session. Her first course of treatment was given intravenously, three times a week over a three-week period. She felt increasingly tired and nauseous but she was incredibly brave and uncomplaining. She wanted to live – she had everything to live for, she said – so she stayed positive which helped those around her to be positive too. They knew, as she did, that it was only a preliminary to the surgery which would hopefully rid her body of the cancer so she bore the chemo with fortitude, knowing that every treatment was giving her a better chance to survive this terrible disease. By the third week her hair had started to come out in handfuls but, as Lexi laughingly admitted, that was the least of her worries. She decided to cut it off and it was devastating for Marvin and Mel to see her glorious abundant golden curls fall to the ground.

"Now I know how Anne Hathaway felt having to chop off her locks for *Les Misérables*," Lexi joked and the others laughed, but inside their hearts were breaking.

Finally, the first block of treatment was over and they were ready to go ahead with the surgery. They all prayed that the chemotherapy had killed off some of those lethal cells.

Mel did her best to support Lexi and Marvin in any way she could, grateful that God had brought her to Tampa in this time of their need.

* * *

The day of Lexi's major surgery arrived. Mel had been in to visit her the night before and had found her stoic and brave, ready to face whatever life had in store for her. Marvin, on the other hand, was in a terrible state.

Mel felt bad lying to Brenda and Angel when she told them that Lexi had been away for a few days. Well, it wasn't actually a lie, was it?

Marvin rang Mel that morning. She could tell from his voice that he had been crying. "Lexi will be going down now shortly," he said.

"Can I talk to her?"

"Of course." He handed the phone to Lexi.

"Don't worry, sweetie, it's in God's hands now. Hopefully they've caught it in time, Mel," Lexi said, brave as ever. "Please take care of Marvin for me, Mel. He's more upset than I am about this. I hate to be worrying him so."

"I love you, Lex," Mel tried to comfort her friend, tears in her eyes. "I'll be praying for you."

"Love you too, honey."

* * *

The next five hours were the longest five hours of Mel's life as she imagined what Lexi was going through and wondered what would be the outcome of it all. Knowing she wouldn't be able to concentrate on work, she first went to an office supply company and ordered a whole new office for herself, sleek, elegant and modern.

Then she went shopping in the Countryside Mall which was quite close to the hospital. Her New York wardrobe was unsuitable for the relaxed Florida lifestyle and besides her clothes were all getting a bit tight. She bought some lovely maternity wear and to pass the time, wandered into the baby department of Macy's. She drooled over the beautiful baby clothes, unable to imagine anything so tiny. She couldn't resist the Ralph Lauren bodysuits in blue and white and bought three in different patterns. She also bought tiny romper suit in white with blue smocking.

"It's a boy then, is it?" the saleslady asked her, looking pointedly at Mel's tummy and smiling.

"Yes," Mel replied. "I can't wait."

"It's so nice to see someone buying blue and white instead of all those horrible oranges and browns and dark colours the young ones these days seem to prefer. Your first, is it?"

Mel nodded.

"Oh, I envy you. There's no feeling on earth that can compare to holding your firstborn in your arms. When are you due?"

"Mid-August," Mel replied.

"You must come in at the end of June when we have a

terrific sale. You can buy your whole layette then. And there are great bargains on nursery furniture too." She looked around to see if anyone could hear her and then whispered, "Actually, where you should go is to the Ellenton Outlet. They have fabulous baby shops there, all for next to nothing, especially at sale time."

"Thanks for that tip. I must go there," Mel said, smiling as she took her purchases.

"Don't forget to come back and see us and bring the baby too," the saleslady called after her.

Suddenly it all seemed so real to Mel. She felt like crying at the woman's kindness. She was always close to tears these days. She could cry at the drop of a hat. Hormones, the doctor explained. Her anxiety about Lexi didn't help.

She decided to have a look at the nursery furniture which was so cute that she felt like buying it on the spot. She was going to have so much fun planning it all. Her feet began to ache and she realised that shopping in heels was not such a good idea. She stopped for lunch in the Food Court but found she had no appetite and decided to go back to the hospital and wait there. On the way, she stopped off at a church – it wasn't a Catholic one but what did that matter? – and said a prayer for Lexi.

She arrived back at the hospital and, hearing that Lexi was still in surgery, went into the cafeteria where she spied Marvin sitting staring out the window.

"She's in a long time," Mel remarked.

"Yes, I don't know whether it's a good thing or bad thing."

He looked so forlorn that Mel's heart went out to him. How cruel that this should happen when they'd just found each other! "I think it's a good thing. It means they're able to do something for her." Mel tried to sound cheerful.

"Oh Mel, if anything happened to her, I don't know what I'd do."

"Lexi's a fighter, Marvin. I'm sure she'll fight this thing with all she's got."

"I should have made her go to the doctor sooner. I feel so guilty."

"You shouldn't feel guilty. You know how she feels about doctors. Brenda tried to get her to go when she was here but she steadfastly refused. She can be very stubborn, you know."

"I know," he smiled sadly.

Just then he got a call telling him Lexi was out of theatre and in the recovery room. The operation had gone well and the surgeon would meet him in an hour, in Lexi's room.

"Do you fancy having something to eat?" he asked. "I haven't eaten all day. I couldn't before but I'm ravenous now."

"Me too," she grinned at him, relieved to hear that Lexi had come through okay.

After they finished their meal they went back to Lexi's room to wait for her return. The surgeon sought them out there.

"Well, she's come through all right," he told them, "but it was quite an extensive procedure. I'm afraid we had no choice but to do a total hysterectomy. We can only hope that it has been contained and won't metastasise – spread to other organs, that is. She will need more chemotherapy of course but we'll discuss that later. Right now, she needs to rest and get her strength back before treatment can begin."

"Thank you, doctor. That means she's going to be okay?" Marvin asked, shaking the surgeon's hand vigorously.

"Only time and treatment will tell."

Lexi was wheeled in shortly afterwards, looking pale and fragile. They each held a hand as she tried to smile at them. She was very groggy so Mel kissed her and left the two of them alone together. She drove home happier than she had been driving in that morning. Lexi had survived the operation and hopefully all would be well.

Chapter 35

Brenda and Angel were shocked and saddened to hear about Lexi. It was all so sudden. Mel told them that Lexi had sworn her to secrecy until after the operation and the doctors were hopeful they'd caught it in time. She explained that Lexi would have to undergo more chemotherapy but would need to build up her strength before treatment could begin.

Brenda was upset to hear that Lexi had undergone a full hysterectomy. She knew that Lexi had secretly hoped to have a child with Marvin. However, she tried to be upbeat and look on the positive side. Hopefully they'd caught it in time before it had spread to other organs. She wished she could be with Lexi at this time, to give her support, but it just wasn't possible. She was still working in the salon. That would end soon however as the receptionist she was replacing was due to have her baby any day and would be returning to work. Brenda didn't know what she would do then. Jobs were so hard to find these days and she wasn't really qualified for anything.

* * *

Angel was shocked and deeply upset to hear of Lexi's illness. Lexi had always been her rock and if anything happened to her she didn't know what she'd do.

She called Kenny after she'd spoken to Mel. Marvin had already called with the news. Angel was crying and there was no denying how upset she was.

"I'll just die if anything happens to Lexi," Angel told him in between her tears.

"I know, honey. I know how much you care for her. A lot of people will be very upset if anything should happen to her."

Kenny and Angel had become firm friends and he was something of a rock for her too. He called her every day to see how she was and she had come to rely on his support. She admired him greatly and was determined not to let him down. He was gentle and kind and she considered him the best male friend she'd ever had. Come to think of it, she'd never actually had a male friend that she hadn't slept with before.

"I was wondering. I'll be in LA next week to finalise the TV deal. Why don't you fly back down with me to visit Lexi and I'll take you back whenever you want?"

"Are you serious?"

"Absolutely!"

"Kenny, you're an angel."

"No, honey, I thought you're the Angel." They both laughed.

"Thank you, Pops," she prayed afterwards, looking heavenwards. She just knew that her father was up there pulling the strings and had sent Kenny to her to take his place.

* * *

Mel was very pleased with her new office and was settling in well. The atmosphere had improved considerably since the departure of Nesbitt and Lundy. As a result the staff were

314

happier and performing better, all of them trying to impress the new boss. Donald Young turned out to be a gem and within a week Mel had promoted him. He was now her greatest ally, as was Ginny, the receptionist, who admired Mel greatly. She was an exceptionally bright girl and Mel suggested to her that she study law at night school, saying that the company would pay for her. Ginny was overjoyed and Mel's biggest fan after that.

Mel was extremely happy and seriously considering staying on here in Tampa rather than returning to New York. Word had spread that she was in charge of the Tampa office now and big-name clients came flocking to seek her services. The president was extremely happy with this and had even suggested that she might like to extend her time there and expand the business. It was very tempting. She had a life now with her friends close by and it would certainly be better for the baby. She started work at eight-thirty in the morning now and finished up at four-thirty every day. She didn't know herself and she began to realise just how stressed she'd been all her life in New York. Did she want to go back to that?

Her belly was getting bigger every day but she carried it proudly. The baby was very active. "A right little footballer," the gynaecologist had said at her last visit. All was going well and she was counting down the weeks with impatience.

She went in to visit Lexi every evening after work and brought her little goodies to try and tempt her to eat. By the weekend Lexi's appetite had returned and she was starting to feel much better. It was imperative that she get her strength back before she started chemotherapy. Mel kept the other girls informed of Lexi's progress.

* * *

Kenny arrived the following Wednesday to collect Angel to take her to see Lexi and they drove to the airport for the flight to Clearwater. The joy of escaping the hordes at LA airport was not lost on Angel. This was true luxury, being driven in the limo right to the steps of the plane and then being welcomed on board by the pilot. Angel admired the spacious interior of the private jet. The decor was very elegant, in bordeaux and cream. There was an office, a bedroom and luxurious bathroom on board. Way to go, Angel thought, as she smiled at Kenny.

When they had settled in, the very attractive stewardess brought a bottle of champagne on ice. Angel looked at Kenny as the stewardess opened it and poured two glasses for them.

"You know I can't drink this," Angel said.

He laughed. "Don't worry, it's non-alcoholic." He showed her the bottle. Ariel Brut, it said on the label, Non-alcoholic sparkling wine.

Angel laughed. "You nearly had me there."

He smiled at her as they toasted each other.

"I'm so proud of you," Kenny said. "Your sponsor tells me you're doing great."

"I'm actually quite proud of myself but I couldn't have done it without you," she replied.

As the jet took off she told him about the therapy and how much it was helping her.

It was the most exciting flight Angel had ever taken. When they were in the air, Kenny asked her if she had given any thought to her future. She admitted that she hadn't given it much thought.

"I'm just taking it one day at a time."

"Maybe you should," he said. "Have you ever considered moving to Tampa?"

"Well, I have thought of leaving LA, but Tampa?" She

looked at him quizzically.

"Yes. Lexi and Mel are there and I'm there too. Why not?"

"Mmmm . . . Maybe. I'll think about it."

The stewardess served them a delicious meal and opened a bottle of non-alcoholic wine to go with it.

"This wine is delicious. It's hard to believe it's non-alcoholic."

"Isn't it? I bring it with me to parties and restaurants. I'll send over a few cases to Lexi's tonight."

As they came in to land in Clearwater airport she realised that she'd had a great time and yet she was sober. It made her feel good. Now she had to face her two oldest friends. She needed more than anything to set things right with Lexi and especially Mel, after her despicable behaviour. She intended to make it up to Mel for how she'd wronged her. She didn't know how she could do this but she'd find a way. She was very excited about seeing both of them again.

Chapter 36

Lexi had come home from hospital to find the house filled with the flowers that Mel had ordered. She'd gone straight to bed to rest. Angel arrived later that evening with Kenny and went straight to Mel's as they thought it was better if she stayed there. She was delighted to see Mel was looking glowing and healthy.

Mel, after hugging her, stood back to have a look at the new Angel. Gone was the fake tan and the heavy make-up. Her hair was unstyled, held back with a hairband and she was wearing jeans, ballet pumps and a simple white T-shirt. Most importantly her blue eyes were clear and untroubled and she had an aura of calm about her that had never been there before. Mel thought she had never looked younger or more beautiful.

"You look wonderful, sweetie," she said as she hugged Angel again.

When Marvin rang to say Lexi was awake they walked next door to visit her. Angel was shocked to see how emaciated Lexi was.

Angel's reunion with them both was emotional, especially considering how they had last parted here.

"Lexi, sweetie, how are you?" Angel cried, tears in her eyes as she hugged her old friend. "You're so thin," she observed, feeling Lexi's slight frame through her dressing-gown.

"You think this is thin?" Lexi laughed. "They've been stuffing me with food in the hospital. You should have seen me last week!"

They were delighted that she hadn't lost her sense of humour and before long the three friends were nattering away like old times. Kenny had brought over a case of the Ariel Brut and a case each of the white and red non-alcoholic wine. As neither Lexi nor Mel were drinking either they were all in the same boat and Angel didn't feel like the odd-one-out. She was extremely pleased when both girls told her how proud of her they were. She hadn't heard that in a long time and it was like music to her ears.

"I've been very lucky that Kenny came into my life. I owe you thanks for that, Lexi. I also figure that my father must be up there looking out for me, to have such special people in my life."

* * *

Lexi was lying in Marvin's arms that night.

"I'm dreading this treatment now that I know what it's like," she said. "I was so sick last time."

"I know, sweetheart," he said, stroking her hair.

"It's nice to have Mel and Angel here but I really wish Brenda were here too," Lexi said wistfully. "I would feel much better about it if she was."

"You'll have a fulltime nurse with you, darling, who has experience with . . ." – he didn't want to use the word chemotherapy as Lexi froze every time she heard it – "your type of patient," he ended lamely.

"I know, but it's not the same as having your best friend with you and Brenda is so good in times of crisis."

After she fell asleep, Marvin lay awake thinking about what she'd said. He would do anything in his power if it would make this awful thing any easier for this brave woman that he loved so much.

* * *

Brenda's kids were home from college for the Easter holidays. Carly was excited that she'd been offered a job at a kids' summer camp in St Petersburg, close to Clearwater where Lexi lived.

"Have you contacted Mel about a job in New York?" Brenda asked Ryan.

"No. I've been studying so hard . . ."

She looked at him sceptically. "Don't you think it's time you started looking?" she chided him. "You've left it very late. Mel is working in Florida now but she's with the same company. Do it soon, Ryan."

That evening he contacted Mel and asked if she could get him a summer job with the firm in New York.

"Yeah, that won't be a problem, I can arrange it," she told him, knowing that Donna would fix it. "But I'm not there any more, I'm in Florida now. Why not come and work for me here in Tampa instead? We have beautiful beaches and it's much cheaper to live here than New York. Besides, there's a granny flat over the garages in my house which is lying there vacant. You'd be welcome to stay there, free of charge of course. Trust me sweetheart, rents in New York are not payable."

As she'd guessed, Ryan did not look a gift horse in the mouth. "Great, Aunt Mel, I'd love to come to Florida."

She grinned to herself. Ryan was a clever cookie and would

go far. She looked forward to getting to know him better.

"Dylan will come with me, of course."

"Of course," Mel replied, expecting that. She knew Ryan went nowhere without his twin.

"Do you think Dylan could also stay in the apartment? We don't mind sharing the floor."

Now Mel laughed outright. "Of course he can. And it does have two bedrooms."

"You're a star, Mel," he said and she noticed that he'd suddenly dropped the 'aunt'. He was quite a character.

"I'm really looking forward to touching base with you both," she said, thinking that she sounded very hip.

"Sure thing, me too," he replied.

Mel was looking forward to getting to know them, now that they were all grown up. It would be nice to have them here.

* * *

Brenda was delighted that the boys were going to Florida instead of New York. She'd been a little apprehensive about that. She knew Mel and Lexi would look out for the twins. She rang Mel to thank her. When Mel recounted the conversation, Brenda roared laughing.

"He's quite a kid, your Ryan," Mel remarked, laughing with her.

"Yes, but Dylan is very sweet," Brenda said, feeling the need to stand up for her gentle son. "He's just more of a dreamer than Ryan, who is a doer."

"He sure is. I look forward to getting to know them both."

* * *

Brenda Skyped Lexi the next day to give her this news and to see how she was doing. She said she was feeling a little better but Brenda was very concerned at how frail she looked.

"It's lovely to have Mel and Angel here although I get so tired that I'm not much company in the evenings."

"I feel so bad that I can't be there with you to help you through this," Brenda confessed.

"I wish you were here too. I'm not looking forward to this treatment. Marvin can't really take time off work to care for me so he's hiring a nurse to stay with me instead. The side effects are pretty debilitating, I believe."

"When do you start the treatment?"

"Not till May. I have to build myself up first."

"You'll be in my thoughts and prayers constantly, you know that."

* * *

That afternoon, while Lexi was resting, Marvin put the plan he'd been hatching into action. He rang Brenda and asked her if there was any way she could come over and care for Lexi once the treatment started.

"She's dreading it and very low at the moment. I know it would mean a lot to her to have you by her side."

"I'd love to come, Marvin, especially if you think I could be of any help."

"You would, Brenda. It would mean the world to Lexi. I was going to hire a nurse to be with her but I know she would much prefer to have you here."

"When do you want me to come? I'm working at the moment but I finish up my job in four weeks. Would that be okay?"

"That would be perfect. How long could you stay for?"

"As long as she needs me. I'll have nothing to keep me here. The kids will all be away working for the summer and I'll be out of a job."

"What good luck for us. Can you apply for a visa? We don't know how long this treatment will take."

"Yeah, sure."

"We'll pay for your flights naturally and I would insist that you take some payment for it. Please say you'll come."

"Oh, I couldn't possibly take payment but I'll accept the flight tickets," she replied, relieved that her savings would remain intact.

"That would be wonderful, Brenda. It will make Lexi so happy. I can't wait for her to wake up to tell her." He sounded excited.

"It's the least I can do. She's been so good to me, all of my life."

Brenda could hardly believe it. She was off to Florida again. This time there was no Bob to stop her. She would be there every step of the way with her dear friend to give her any support she could. An added bonus was that the twins would be close by too and she'd be there for the birth of Mel's baby.

* * *

Angel stayed a week in Clearwater and was good company for Lexi, keeping her amused as she'd always done. Kenny collected her every evening and they went to his local AA branch for a meeting. They were all delighted with Angel's progress and prayed it would last. They'd forgotten what a sweet person she could be without drink in her. Marvin was very busy with an upcoming exhibition and was grateful to her for keeping Lexi occupied.

Angel was very happy to be back on an even keel again with her friends and she was giving great thought to her future.

It was Kenny who finally persuaded her to move to Clearwater.

"I can't be jetting up to LA every week just to have lunch with you," he declared, laughing.

She had come to depend on him completely. She felt safe with him around and she also wanted to be a support to Lexi in her illness. So on her last night she told them that she had decided to move down here permanently. They were thrilled and Mel invited her to move in with her. Angel gratefully accepted and left the following day, in Kenny's private jet, to settle her affairs in LA. She promised Kenny she would not go a single day without attending her AA meeting. She still didn't feel strong enough to go it alone.

Angel still found it strange that she had a male friend who was just that, a friend. She hadn't tried to seduce or flirt with him and yet she knew that he liked her for herself, not for her looks or any hope of sexual favours. It was a nice feeling. It made her feel good about herself.

* * *

Angel, with the help of Consuela, packed up what she would need in Florida and put the rest of her stuff into storage. This included the more than two hundred pairs of shoes and all the evening gowns that took up two rooms of her house. She was all ready to go, three days later.

She gave Consuela a very large cheque as a parting gift. She was very sad to be saying goodbye to her loyal housekeeper who had after all saved her life. Consuela was happy to retire and spend time with her grandchildren although she was very fond of her mistress and would miss her. Angel decided to rent her house out for the moment and put it in the hands of an estate agent. She would see how she liked life in Florida before deciding to sell it. However, as she looked around the beautiful large living-room, she knew in her heart that she would never return there to live.

And so she left LA to start a new life in the Sunshine State.

Chapter 37

Brenda was on her way to Florida a month later. Lexi had been overjoyed to hear she was coming and very grateful to Marvin for arranging it. She was in better form and getting stronger every day. Mel and Angel were happy that Brenda would be there to care for Lexi as they were both quite busy, Angel with her AA meetings and therapy sessions and Mel putting the office to rights. She had finally got enough proof that Lundy had been swindling the company and had passed the information on to the fraud squad. They had charged him and Mel had taken great pleasure in firing him.

Lexi was delighted to see Brenda again and happy to have her to herself. There was something calming about her presence which she found restorative. She was less fearful with her there and every day they went for a short walk on the beach together. Lexi confided to Brenda how terribly frightened she'd been and how devastated that they'd had to do a hysterectomy.

"I haven't shared this with anyone but I had hoped that Marvin and I could try for a baby. Now that dream is gone."

"The important thing is that you're alive and have a future together."

"You're right," Lexi said, wiping the tears from her eyes. "I love him so much that I don't want to have to leave him."

"The doctors seem confident, don't they?"

"They say they think they've got it all but you never can tell with cancer which is why I have to have this treatment."

Brenda noticed that Lexi refused to use the word chemotherapy and could tell it frightened her. "Please God they're right."

* * *

Troy was overjoyed that Brenda was back. He invited them all for drinks in his new penthouse on the following Saturday. He was very excited about seeing Brenda again and she was nervous of meeting him. However, after five minutes in his company she had relaxed and wondered why she had been nervous at all. His penthouse was out of this world with spectacular views of the gulf and the marina from the floor-to-ceiling glass French doors which led onto a wrap-around terrace.

"This is so beautiful," Brenda said to him as she gazed out over the gulf. The sun was just setting and it was like something from a painting.

"Yes, it is," he replied, looking directly at her. She found herself blushing at his obvious admiration.

"Well, how have you been, Brenda? How come your husband let you out of his sight again so soon?"

"Actually, he and I have separated."

Troy was shocked. Was it possible? He had tried to forget about her, without success, and now here she was telling him she was free. "Does that mean . . .?"

She reached out and put her finger on his lip. "No, Troy," she replied quietly. "It's too soon."

He looked crestfallen but would not give up hope. He knew she was attracted to him too. "Will you come out to dinner with me some night?"

"I'm sorry, Troy. I'm here for Lexi and she's my priority at the moment. Please understand."

"I do," he said, disappointed but knowing he would respect her wishes.

* * *

Lexi was feeling tired so after an hour she and Marvin went home. Troy invited the others to dinner in the Sandpearl Restaurant.

"What did your parents say when you told them you were pregnant?" Angel asked Mel.

"Erm . . . I haven't actually told them yet."

"What?" Angel and Brenda cried at the same time.

"But you're over five months now!" said Angel.

"I know . . . I just can't screw up the courage to tell them."

"Oh, Mel, you have to," Brenda said gently. "I know it's difficult but they need to know."

"I suppose," Mel said miserably.

"Oh, fuck them," Angel cried, causing Troy to look at her askance. "It doesn't matter a damn what they think any more. As long as you're happy, that's all that matters. And they should be happy for you too. After all, you're giving them the gift of a grandchild."

"That's true," Mel agreed. "Okay, I'll call them tomorrow."

"Some mothers shouldn't be allowed to have children," Angel said bitterly.

She'd been having major therapy counselling and had come to realise that she was a love addict – as opposed to a sex addict. Delving back into her past, she came to understand that her mother's rejection of her was the underlying cause of her search for love. The therapist suggested that she seek out her mother and try and work out things between them but Angel knew it was too late for that. She could beat this thing without her mother.

* * *

They were all in Lexi's the next day for lunch when Brenda asked Mel if she'd called her parents.

"Not yet."

"Okay – now!" Angel ordered, handing her the phone.

Mel reluctantly left the room and called her parents. Ten minutes later she came back, beaming broadly.

"I don't believe it! It's a miracle! They're actually pleased about it. My mother even said she was proud of me for not opting for an abortion. Of course she had to add 'seeing as how you've been left in the lurch by the father'."

"That's great, Mel," Brenda said hugging her.

Lexi held out her hand to Mel. "We're all proud of you, aren't we, girls?"

"You bet! Absolutely! Without a doubt!" the others chorused, making Mel blush.

She was on a high after that and felt secure in this circle of friends who loved and supported her. She felt fearless and ready to face the challenge of bringing this little boy into the world.

* * *

In the meantime Troy had to settle for seeing Brenda whenever he joined in their bridge games. When Lexi had heard that

Brenda had started bridge and loved it, she was delighted and she organised a bridge game with Marvin and Troy two or three times a week. Troy was delighted to be asked and happy with the opportunity to see Brenda more often.

She was improving quickly at this difficult card game and they proposed that once Lexi was better Brenda should join the bridge club in Clearwater with Troy as her partner. He was grateful for small mercies.

* * *

It was time for Lexi's next round of treatment. This one was even more gruelling than the one she'd had before her operation. She was so brave that at times Brenda found it difficult to hold back her own tears but she had to, for Lexi's sake.

The treatment made Lexi even more ill than before but she never complained. Marvin found it almost impossible to bear and shed his tears in private. Her hair fell out completely and she took to wearing brightly coloured headscarves. "My badge of honour," she called them.

But finally, that block of treatment was done and her doctor said it was enough for the moment.

Lexi was exhausted but relieved it was over.

Having Brenda with her had helped Lexi to bear it. She had stayed by Lexi's side through it all, like a ministering angel. Mel and Angel had also been extremely supportive. They kept her spirits up and she wondered what she would have done without them. She was truly lucky to have such wonderful friends.

As for Marvin! There were no words to express her love and gratitude to him. Now she was going to concentrate on getting strong and well again and start planning their wedding. They'd set a date, the twenty-fourth of July. She was also very anxious to take up her brushes and get painting again. Life had to go on despite this awful cancer. She now had to build herself up again before the next block of treatment.

* * *

Brenda's twins had arrived in Florida the first week in June and everyone was charmed by them. Mel was pleased that Ryan settled into the job so quickly and she soon found him to be invaluable to her.

Troy and Dylan hit it off immediately and Troy offered him a job. He was a jack of all trades, some days answering the phone, others helping out with a yacht. He was very flexible and had no problem running errands or making coffee for visitors. It suited Dylan down to the ground – "Stress-free, man" – he told his twin when he asked about it. Troy was very fond of him.

Carly had also taken up her job in St Petersburg but had been met off the plane and taken directly to the camp. She loved the job, she said when she called, and would come visit on her first weekend off which would be at the end of the month.

Lexi had asked Brenda to be her maid-of-honour. Brenda was delighted to be chosen but worried that Mel and Angel might feel left out. It was her daughter, Alex, who solved the problem when she said she wouldn't dream of missing her godmother's wedding and would travel all the way from Sudan for it. She'd been very upset to hear of Lexi's cancer and wanted to support her. She had two weeks' holidays due as she had volunteered to stay on in Sudan for another year.

She had been a flower girl at Lexi's wedding to Gianni and they decided now that Alex would be her bridesmaid, so Mel and Angel needn't feel Lexi had preferred Brenda. Having her goddaughter as her bridesmaid made it even more special for Lexi.

Brenda was happy to have her children there, with the exception of Megan who was now working in Australia.

* * *

Now that Lexi was resting between treatments, Troy hoped that Brenda would at last agree to go out with him. They had become close during Lexi's chemotherapy and he had been a shoulder for Brenda to cry on when things got tough. She was also very grateful to him for taking Dylan under his wing. There was no denying the chemistry between her and Troy but Brenda was afraid of where it might lead. He was already head over heels in love with her.

Eventually, he appealed to Lexi to help him and she agreed. She could see how perfect they would be together.

"Honey, I wish you would go out and enjoy yourself now. You've been cooped up with me for far too long," she said, broaching the subject the following Saturday when the four girls were having lunch in Frenchy's. "I know Troy is very anxious to take you out. Why not go with him?"

"Oh, I don't know," Brenda replied, pushing some shrimp around her plate.

"What don't you know?" Mel demanded. "He's perfect for you. You make a lovely couple."

"Brenda, honey, anyone can see that he's crazy about you. Grab him, before some other woman does," Angel added her tuppence worth.

"I don't know . . . I suppose I'm scared of getting hurt."

"Fiddlesticks! If everyone felt like that there'd be no love in the world at all," Mel retorted.

"Troy wouldn't hurt you for the world," Lexi added. "I know he loves you very much. Life is too short, honey. Don't throw away the love of a good man."

"I suppose."

"Good, that's decided then. You're going out with him the next time he asks you," Angel said, brooking no argument.

"Or you'll have us to answer to!" Mel grinned, shaking her finger at Brenda.

"God, you're all so bossy," Brenda remarked but she was grinning too.

Lexi recounted this conversation to Troy that evening and quick as a flash he was on the phone to Brenda.

"I was wondering if you'd like to spend the day with me tomorrow? I thought you might enjoy a visit to Homosassa. It's a Wildlife Park, one of my favourite places in Florida."

She hesitated for a second and then saw Lexi looking at her sternly.

"Yes, that would be lovely, Troy. Thank you."

* * *

He picked her up at nine the next morning and Lexi and Marvin waved them off, both of them grinning broadly. Brenda felt a little nervous at first but quickly relaxed and soon both of them were laughing and joking as always. Troy slipped a CD in the player. It was Paul Simon's Graceland album.

"That's my favourite album," she exclaimed happily, humming along.

"I know. You mentioned that to me when I first met you so I bought it. I really like it too."

She was touched by his thoughtfulness. He really was the most extraordinary man.

They had a wonderful day and she agreed with him that Homosassa was a very special place. They were taken on a boat tour where they spied many of the wild animals in the park, even an enormous bear, and then went on the floating observatory to check out the manatees. Brenda had never seen one before and was fascinated by these huge but gentle creatures. She wasn't so fond of the alligators but Troy assured her that they wouldn't touch you unless you bothered them.

"Safer not to wade in the lakes here in Florida all the same," he advised.

"Don't worry, I won't!"

At lunchtime they went back to the car and Troy extracted a big coolbox out of the trunk. Going back into the park he set a blanket on the ground and proceeded to take out the delicious picnic that he'd collected from the deli that morning.

"There are picnic tables over there," Brenda pointed out to him.

"I know, but I think it's not really a picnic unless you sit on a blanket on the ground."

Brenda laughed and broke into the Billie Jo Spears song, 'Blanket on the Ground', as he set out the appetising lobster and salad and opened a bottle of chilled white wine.

"Thank you for a wonderful day. I feel so happy," he said, toasting her.

"I'm happy too. I'm having a truly fabulous time."

He had brought cheese and bread too and fruit for dessert. It was a delicious picnic.

Afterwards, they walked hand-in-hand through the park and it seemed the natural thing to do. Maybe the girls were right, she thought. If she hadn't listened to them she'd have missed this wonderful day.

On the way back, he put the car into cruise control and held her hand.

"Do you want to talk to me about why your marriage broke up?" he asked her.

"Not right now. I don't want to spoil a perfect day."

"I'd invite you back for coffee," he told her, "but I'm afraid I might not be able to control myself and then you'd never want to see me again."

Brenda laughed. She didn't say that she'd have a problem controlling herself too. Troy stopped the car outside Lexi's house and when he took her into his arms she didn't pull away but kissed him back with the all the passion she felt for him. Reluctantly, they parted, and Brenda promised to spend the following Sunday with him if Lexi had no other plans.

Brenda was relieved that Lexi and Marvin had gone to bed. She wanted to relive the day and hold on to the warm feelings she'd experienced with Troy.

Chapter 38

Angel's life was back on track in earnest. She had been nervous about the temptations of alcohol and prescription drugs that she knew she would have to face but with all the help she was getting, she was managing to stay clean. It was also a lucky break for her that neither Mel nor Lexi were drinking at the moment and Brenda had never been a big drinker so she was abstaining too. Angel suspected she was doing it to show solidarity with her.

And then there was Kenny. He was proving to be indispensable in her life – her sponsor at AA and her life support. They went to the local meetings in Clearwater where Angel found everyone to be welcoming and friendly. Stripped of all the outward trappings, people got to know the real person and this honesty was very refreshing to Angel who had been part of the fake Hollywood life for so long. People liked her for herself which still continued to amaze her.

She and Kenny had become very close and, although he obviously adored her, she kept him at arm's length. It was her therapist who had shown her that she was a love addict, always seeking the approbation of others. The one thing she was learning from these sessions was that she first had to learn to love herself, before loving anyone else. She was in the process of doing just that at the moment and she was doing fine.

* * *

The following Sunday, Brenda agreed to spend the day with Troy as she'd promised. He picked her up at eight that morning and to her surprise drove her to Clearwater airport. There they boarded an Air Key West small plane he'd chartered. Brenda clapped her hands with delight.

"Are we going to Key West?" she asked him, her eyes aglow. "I've always wanted to visit there ever since I read Hemingway's *The Old Man and the Sea*."

"I know," he grinned. "You told me that the first night I met you."

She looked at him in surprise. He really was amazing. He remembered everything she'd ever said she liked and was making it all happen. He was unbelievably thoughtful and it touched her deeply.

"Actually, we're going to be sailing back as I'm collecting a boat down there, so we have only the morning here but we will visit Hemingway's house and drink mojitos, I promise you."

He was as good as his word as he showed her around. She was fascinated with the writer's house and stood spellbound on the threshold of the room in which he had written his most famous book. They were not allowed to enter it. The room was as he'd left it, the old-fashioned typewriter sitting idle on the worn table. It was so sparse and bare and she could almost feel the great man's presence hovering there.

They strolled hand in hand down the quaint Duval Street

and Brenda loved everything about the place. The whole town was quite unique and had a buzz about it that was quite contagious. He took her to his favourite bar for lunch, the Schooner Wharf, which was an outdoor bar but with plenty of shade. There they drank mojitos and ate delicious conch fritters as they listened to the live music. Then they strolled to Mallory Square which was abuzz with various stalls and hawkers selling their wares and street entertainment.

"If you think it's lively now, you should see it at sunset. Massive crowds gather here and sit on the sea wall to watch the most glorious sunset you'll see anywhere. You can take a sailboat out and cross the path of the sun. Just like the song, Red Sails in the Sunset. It's truly magical."

"I can imagine," Brenda said, thinking how wonderful that would be.

"Unfortunately, we can't stay till sunset today but we'll come back here and stay overnight and I'll take you there," he suggested, "and we can sail into the sunset together."

"I'd love that," she smiled at him shyly.

They left around two o'clock for the long journey back to Clearwater. They sailed up the west coast of Florida and Troy pointed out the various landmarks telling her a little about each place. He had picked up a meal he had pre-ordered before leaving Key West and he dropped anchor just before sunset when they dined on fresh shrimp and scallops and sipped white wine. They stood at the rail and watched the glorious sun go down. Brenda had never felt so happy. As the sun was dipping into the ocean he pulled her to him and when he kissed her, her body thrilled to his touch and she kissed him back with passion.

"Oh, Brenda," he moaned. "I love you and I want you so much."

"I want you too," she whispered, shaking with desire.

"Are you sure?" he asked and when she nodded, he took her by the hand and led her into the master bedroom. There he made love to her, slowly and expertly, till she cried out with pleasure. Afterwards he stroked her hair lovingly as he murmured her name over and over. She felt loved and desired and it was a wonderful feeling. All fear left her and she knew she could trust this man with her heart.

Later, on deck, she pressed close to him with her arms wrapped around him as he steered the yacht back home to Clearwater. She was falling in love and it was a delicious feeling.

* * *

Mel was now as big as a house but her pregnancy was progressing well. Only eight weeks left to go! She had gone shopping for the baby's nursery and layette in the sales, as the woman in Macy's had suggested, and all was ready for him now. She couldn't wait to meet him. The only fly in the ointment was the heat. Mel found it energy-sapping, as did Lexi, but they stayed indoors in air-conditioned comfort most of the time.

Lexi had started her next course of treatment. The bad news was that the cancer was still there. This course was even tougher and the side effects more severe. She didn't think she could go through another one. They all prayed that this one would get rid of it once and for all. She stayed optimistic and still insisted on going ahead with the wedding. She'd opted for a very quiet, casual wedding in her own home and would postpone the honeymoon till she felt up to it.

* * *

She had just about recovered from the treatment in time for

her wedding. She perked up considerably when Alex arrived five days before the big day. This was the daughter Lexi had always wished she'd had. They spent many hours together and Lexi appeared more peaceful with her goddaughter by her side. Alex was a natural nurse and Brenda was happy to see how Lexi responded to her and to witness the love they had for each other.

* * *

Everyone agreed it was the nicest wedding they'd ever been to. Lexi and Marvin vowed to love, honour and cherish each other standing on the beach in front of her house, at sunset. It was intimate and casual, just what Lexi and Marvin had wanted. Lexi was so weak that she could barely stand throughout the brief ceremony.

It was a small group who gathered to share in this special moment. Besides the bride and groom there was a heavily pregnant Mel, Angel and Kenny; Troy, Brenda and her four children and Lexi's friend Sandy and her partner. The guys were dressed in shorts, as instructed, and the women wore sundresses. Lexi wore a long white linen dress and white sandals. On her head she had a white scarf underneath a large wide-brimmed white hat. Angel had made her face up expertly and they all agreed she looked so chic she could have been a model on the cover of Vogue. Marvin thought she had never looked more beautiful. Ryan and Dylan had somehow managed to find pinstripe shorts and wore bow ties with them and nothing else, which caused great merriment.

The ceremony was very moving, made all the more special by the fact that Lexi was so ill. Marvin and Lexi made their vows and when he'd kissed the bride, he scooped her up in his arms and carried her back into the garden and set her down gently on a sunbed. It was incredibly romantic and moving. They then celebrated with the lovely buffet Maria had prepared.

As the happy couple had exchanged their vows, Troy had looked over at Brenda and smiled at her. She'd been out with him many times since that day in Key West and each time their lovemaking had got better and better. He was also the most fascinating man she'd ever met and interested in many varied things. She had learnt a lot from him and he challenged her mentally. She lived for the moments they could be together and she knew he did too.

Most important of all, her children liked him and for a man with no children of his own, he was incredibly good with them. She had tried to keep their relationship a secret but it hadn't taken Alex long to suss it out.

"You're really fond of Troy, aren't you?" she asked one day as they were lying by the pool.

"He's been very kind to me," Brenda replied, blushing.

"Mum! I'm not blind. You two are crazy about each other and I think it's great."

"Really? You're not annoyed?"

"Don't be silly, Mum. Why should I be annoyed? I'm happy that you've found someone who deserves you. Dad didn't." Alex made a face showing her disgust at her father's behaviour. "I think Troy is much more suitable for you. He's really an interesting man. We all like him very much."

Brenda squeezed her daughter's hand. "I'm so glad to hear that."

It was wonderful having her eldest daughter here for two weeks and it had made Lexi very happy. Brenda could see how much Alex had matured in the year she'd been working in Sudan. She was a woman now and Brenda was very proud of her.

* * *

Mel intended working right up to the birth of her son but it was getting difficult as she was feeling enormous pressure in her abdomen. The gynaecologist told her this was perfectly normal and meant the baby was getting ready to make his debut. She had her case packed and ready to go and the nursery, with all the cute baby clothes she'd bought, was waiting to welcome her little son.

Mel had taken the ante-natal classes and knew what to expect but she was still terrified of the ordeal ahead of her. Although she hadn't voiced it to anyone she was also fearful that something might go wrong or, Lord forbid, that there would be something wrong with him. She tried not to think about it but it was always there in the back of her mind. She had been into the hospital to see where she would bring him into the world and had discussed what she wanted with her doctor.

Luckily, her medical insurance meant that she would have private care and she had booked a luxury suite in the hospital. She had insisted that she wanted her three girlfriends at the birth. This was unusual, the hospital told her, but they could be accommodated. All she had to do now was wait for him to decide when he wanted to make his entrance. She had declined to intervene artificially and wanted the most natural birth possible for this precious baby, as her mother had advised. "When the apple is ready it will fall from the tree," is what she'd said.

Amazingly, her mother had been very supportive and even offered to come over for the birth of her grandchild, even though she "detested America" as she was continually saying. Mel declined her offer knowing that her mother would try and take over everything. Instead she promised that she would bring her little son over to Ireland for Christmas. Her mother was secretly relieved at this solution and so was Mel.

341

* * *

Brenda was very sad when it came time for Alex to leave. She knew it would be another year before she saw her again.

"Don't cry, Mum, we have Skype to keep us in touch," Alex tried to comfort her as they said goodbye.

"Yes, thank God for that."

"Mum, promise me you'll be happy and follow your heart. Life is too short to not have love in it."

Brenda smiled at this wisdom from her daughter as she waved her off on her long journey back to Sudan. It had been lovely spending time with her.

* * *

Lexi had been back to see the doctor and had some more tests. The news was not good. The cancer had spread to the liver. He suggested they try another course of chemotherapy but Lexi sensed that he was not very hopeful of its efficacy. She put her foot down. No more treatment. She'd had enough. If this was to be her lot, then so be it. She just couldn't face any more. She decided not to tell any of them but bear it in silence and make the most of what time was left to her.

That night they all got together for dinner and Lexi was in such good humour that no one suspected a thing. Angel was in scintillating form and there was much laughter and fun around the table. And then Mel's waters broke!

Chapter 39

Pandemonium broke out. Mel was shocked and embarrassed, apologising to Lexi for wetting the chair and floor, Lexi was shushing her, Angel was panicking, the men were shuffling about not knowing what to do while Brenda, the only one who'd been through this herself, was calm and in control.

"Kenny, take care of Angel," she ordered, "and go next door and get Mel's case. Where is it, Mel? It's all ready, isn't it?"

"Yes, it's under my bed," Mel replied, beginning to realise that her baby had decided it was time.

Kenny took Angel, who was still shrieking, by the arm, and did as he was told. Brenda then instructed Marvin to take the car around the front so they could take Mel to the hospital.

"Lexi, would you call them and tell them Mel's on her way and that her waters have broken."

Lexi was pleased to have something to do and did as Brenda asked.

Brenda and Troy helped Mel up and out to the car and five minutes later she was on her way to the hospital, excited but

343

very apprehensive now that the time had come.

She had her first contraction as they drove to the hospital. She gasped as it hit her.

"Breathe, breathe deeply," Brenda instructed her, holding her hand.

Mel was thankful that she had taken the ante-natal classes and learnt how to breathe properly – still, nothing had prepared her for the intensity of the pain. Brenda was timing the contractions and helping her friend to ride them out. Mel was reassured to have Brenda at her side.

Marvin, who had heard stories of babies being born in taxis and cars was worried that might happen here and was thankful that Brenda was with them.

She appeared cool and in total control and was exuding a confidence which calmed them all, not least Mel. Lexi was praying that they would make the hospital in time as the contractions were coming very fast. Eventually, they arrived and Lexi and Marvin breathed a sigh of relief.

Once inside, the professionals took over but Mel clung to Brenda's hand. "Please, stay with me," she said fearfully. She was shaking, her teeth actually chattering with fear.

"May I?" Brenda asked the nurse.

The nurse, seeing how terrified Mel was and how calm Brenda appeared to be, agreed. She realised that Marvin was not the father-to-be and seeing no other man in sight guessed there was no husband or partner there to support Mel. This pleased the nurse as men were more often a hindrance than a help in the delivery room. Brenda would be a more calming influence there.

She led the two girls off as Lexi and Marvin went to the café to wait. Angel and Kenny arrived shortly afterwards with Mel's case. Angel had calmed down considerably. They handed over the case and joined the others in the café. About forty minutes later, Brenda called Lexi to say they could come up to Room 229 on the second floor. Marvin and Kenny left for home and Lexi promised to call as soon as there was news.

Lexi and Angel entered the room where Brenda was encouraging Mel to breathe deeply. Mel gave them a wan smile. "I know now why they call it labour."

"She's doing great," the nurse assured them, smiling. "This little guy is in a hurry to meet you all."

Brenda was very impressed with the comfort and luxury afforded Mel as she remembered the crowded labour ward in Holles Street where she'd given birth to her children.

In between contractions which were coming faster all the time, the girls chatted to Mel encouraging her and telling her how well she was doing. Mel had refused an epidural or any analgesics, determined to do what was best for her baby. Angel was quite horrified at the pain Mel was going through but ever the actress, didn't show it. When the contractions started coming one on top of another, they stayed quiet, holding Mel's hand or wiping her brow.

Two nurses were checking her regularly and when Brenda heard one calling for the doctor, she knew that Mel's labour was coming to an end. The other nurse wheeled Mel's bed into the next room, which was more functional for the actual delivery. Seeing the little crib there brought a lump to Lexi's throat but filled Mel with joy. The doctor arrived shortly after that, scrubbed up and ready to go. Lexi and Angel moved back to allow her space, Angel clutching Lexi's arm tightly. Brenda stayed, stroking Mel's brow. Mel was stoic, biting her tongue so as not to cry out and panting as she'd been taught to do until it was time for her to push. Within the space of ten minutes it was all over and Mel's baby boy slid into the world. He gave a lusty cry and Mel looking down at the little dark head, burst into tears.

"Oh my God," she exclaimed, smiling through her tears. "He's perfect!"

"He is indeed," the doctor said, congratulating her. The nurse whisked him away to clean him up and a minute later, wrapped in a blanket, he was placed in Mel's arms. By now all the girls were crying and crowding around her.

"My God, he's so tiny," Mel exclaimed as she clasped him to her. She had never imagined such happiness could be hers. The love she felt for this tiny being enveloped her as she kissed his dark head.

Lexi had put her finger in his hand and he grasped it with a strength that amazed her. She also felt a deep sadness as she remembered the baby she'd lost.

"He's a big baby," the doctor said smiling. "Nine-pounds-four-ounces."

"He's so beautiful. I thought all new babies were ugly and scrunched up," Angel observed.

"They usually are but this one's a beauty," the doctor remarked.

"What are you going to call him, Mel?" Brenda asked.

Mel had steadfastly refused to tell them all through her pregnancy. She'd planned on calling him Alexander but, as she gazed at him, she knew there was only one name for him.

From the first moment she'd set eyes on him and saw the way that his black hair grew in a peak, low on his forehead, saw the defined mouth that turned up at the corners, the incredibly long dark eyelashes, the dimple on his left cheek, there was only one name she could call him.

"Jack," she said, softly, smiling at them, "but he's so little, I'll call him Jacky."

It was as if she was looking at his father once more. She wished with all her heart that Jack was here to share this with her. She still loved him, she always would. Well, now she had another Jack in her life and she would love and cherish him forever.

The nurse took the baby from Mel to dress him and the girls left the room as the doctor attended to the placenta and a nurse brought Mel a cup of tea and cleaned her up. Finally, mother and baby were wheeled to her suite where each of the girls held the baby for a few minutes, marvelling at how absolutely perfect he was. The girls left then as it was now the wee small hours of the morning and Mel needed her rest. They hugged Mel and kissed little Jacky, smiling at the happy picture they made.

Mel was secretly happy to have him to herself. She looked at him intently, taking in the long eyelashes and tiny fingers with their perfectly formed nails. It was a miracle. He was her little miracle. It was the happiest day of her life. After Mel had suckled him, the nurse took him from her and settled him in his crib. Mel looked at the time. It was 3 a.m. so that meant 8 a.m. in Ireland. Her parents would be getting up now so she rang them to tell them they had a new grandson. To her amazement, her mother burst into tears and had to hand the phone over to her husband who told Mel how happy they were with the news. She had never heard her father so emotional. As he handed the phone back to her mother, he said, "I love you, Mel. Give little Jacky a kiss for me."

Mel felt the tears come to her eyes. He had never told her that before. "I love you too, Dad."

Her mother was over the moon and it was all Mel could do to dissuade her from getting on the next flight over. She wanted Jacky all to herself at the moment. She promised to send photos and to bring him to Ireland for Christmas.

Exhausted, she then lay back on the pillows, her hand resting on the crib beside her, watching her baby sleep.

* * *

Mel threw a christening party for Jacky three weeks later. Brenda and Angel mucked in and did most of the work. Lexi was too weak. Mel's happiness infected them all and there was a lot of love in the room. Jacky slept through it all and everyone marvelled at how placid he was – he hardly ever cried – and the women fought over who would hold him next.

Mel had asked Brenda, Lexi and Angel to be joint godmothers. "Just like the celebrities and royals who have six or more godparents for their babies," Angel remarked. Marvin was godfather. Mel knew she would have to watch out or her little boy would be thoroughly spoilt. So many women wanting to pet him all the time.

Donna came down from New York for the christening and Mel promised she would take Jacky up there before long to show him off to Donna's family who had sent gifts and best wishes. Carly was also there with her friend, Sarah, as they had finished at the summer camp. They were staying for a week, bunking down with the twins and then they would travel up to New Orleans where Sarah had an aunt. Ryan decided that he and Dylan would go with them. The two young girls also doted on baby Jacky.

Mel knew now that she could not return to work in New York and take Jacky away from this place where he was surrounded by people who loved him. She wasn't even sure she could drag herself away from him to go back to work in Tampa. She couldn't bear to leave him with a stranger to care for him while she worked. It was a dilemma.

* * *

Troy and Brenda were now deeply in love and spent every moment they could together. She felt she should return to Ireland but Lexi needed her and as Troy said, "Return for what?" He wanted her to move to Florida permanently and live with him. He wanted to marry her but could not until her divorce from Bob was final. He tried to persuade her that if she moved to the States she could get a divorce much sooner. It was very tempting. Besides Troy, there was Jacky. Brenda adored him and spent many hours with him. He was getting cuter by the day.

One day in early September, Mel put a proposition to her.

"Brenda, I know you'd like to stay here because of Troy and you have the three of us here too. Would you consider staying on and taking care of Jacky when I go back to work? Otherwise I'll have to give up work. I couldn't leave him with a stranger and Lexi isn't well enough to care full-time for a baby. I would pay you handsomely, of course." She looked at Brenda, her eyes pleading. "Please think about it. I need you and so does Jacky."

"I'd have to have a green card to stay longer than six months, wouldn't I?"

"That won't be a problem. I have a lot of contacts in Immigration who can pull strings. Will you consider it?"

"I'll have to think about it."

When Troy heard about this request he was delighted, hoping it would convince Brenda to move. Lexi was also very persuasive.

"I would so love to have you here. You'd have a good life with Troy, and the twins and Carly have already said they're coming back here next summer."

Brenda had to agree with what she said. The thought of being separated from Troy was unbearable so she decided to talk to her kids about it.

Alex was very enthusiastic about the idea, happy that her mother had found love again. The twins and Carly thought it was brilliant as all three of them had fallen in love with Florida and liked Troy very much. It would make no difference to Megan who would not be back in Ireland for some time anyway.

Brenda rang Jean and told her what she was thinking of doing.

"Go for it, girl! You'd be crazy not to. Don't think twice about it!" her sister ordered her.

Conor and her other brothers also advised her to stay put as Ireland was in a deep recession and no place to be at the moment. Then she received a call from her solicitor in Dublin with regard to her separation. Bob's solicitor had been in touch with her and they were ready to settle things financially. In fairness to Bob, he had been lodging money to her account every week since they had separated but now there was the house to consider. The mortgage had been paid off, thank God, so they would have to decide between them what to do. Everything seemed to be conspiring to bring her back to Florida.

It was Lexi who finally decided her.

"I've learnt how precious and short life can be, Brenda."

Brenda knew she was thinking of Gianni and Alessandro and perhaps also of her own life which seemed to be ebbing.

"I am so aware that life can be snatched away from us at any moment. So you must live it fully and treasure love because it's the most important thing."

Brenda knew she was right and it decided her. She asked Mel to sort out a green card for her. Within ten days she was called for interview but with Mel's contacts it was only a formality. Two weeks later she had her green card. Her boys were returning to Ireland the first week in October and Brenda booked herself on the same flight. She promised Lexi and Troy that she would return as soon as possible.

Chapter 40

Brenda was travelling first class as she was using the return portion of the ticket that Marvin had sent her back in May. The twins were booked into economy but the check-in girl, seeing that she was their mother, gave them an upgrade and bumped them up to first class. They were very impressed and loved every moment of the flight. Brenda laughed at their obvious enjoyment of the special treatment they received. Jean met them at Dublin airport, agog for all the news. The twins threw their eyes to heaven as the two sisters nattered on.

"How do you like your mum's new beau?" she asked the boys.

"Troy? He's cool," Ryan informed her.

"He's a really terrific guy, I like him a lot," Dylan added.

"That's good. Listen to you two! You sound American after only four months there."

They told her how much they loved Florida and that they intended going back next year.

"Well, I hope to be finding out for myself, now that your mum has decided to stay there."

"Isn't it great? We're delighted," Ryan said. Dylan agreed with him.

* * *

The weather was wet and grey and going through a cold spell and Brenda thought longingly of the blue skies and sunshine of Florida as she put on layer after layer to keep herself warm.

Carly arrived home two days later and Brenda was kept busy getting all three kids ready to return to college the following Sunday.

Brenda met with her solicitor two days after she got home who told her that Bob had offered to take out a mortgage and buy out her share of the house. This seemed like a good idea as selling the house in the current market would have been a disaster. It also meant that the kids would have a base in Dublin to come to at weekends. She guessed it was the best solution although she would feel strange not having a base for herself in Dublin. However, she couldn't have it all and Florida was where she wanted to be.

When she told the kids this they all stated that they would never live with their father again. Even Dylan had washed his hands of Bob when he heard what had occurred. This put Brenda in a quandary. The kids needed a home base. With the money she got for her share of the house, the only thing she could possibly afford to buy would be a one-bed apartment, out in the sticks.

When she spoke to Troy that evening she told him of her problem.

"We'll work something out," he said.

She missed him terribly and it seemed like he missed her just as much as he urged her to hurry back when they spoke on the phone every day. He was pleased to hear that Bob had agreed to her seeking a divorce in Florida. She couldn't wait to get back to start her new life with him.

It was agreed that she would leave all her stuff in the house until such time as Bob paid her the money for her share of it. That would probably take two to three months to finalise. She decided she would have to stay on in Ireland until then as it would cost too much to have to fly out and back then but when she told this to Troy he insisted on booking her flight back immediately. She was secretly pleased. He said she could travel over again to Ireland when the time came.

So ten days after arriving in Ireland, Brenda left again for Florida, first class naturally. She smiled to herself thinking what a globetrotter she'd become. She, who had never been further than England before, was now crossing the Atlantic in style, every few weeks. The cabin steward, who recognised her, made her feel like a treasured client.

* * *

She had forgotten just how handsome Troy was as he rushed to take her in his arms at Tampa airport.

"I've been counting the minutes," he said emotionally, as he held her tight.

She kissed him and knew with certainty that she'd made the right decision. They went to bed the moment they got in the door and their lovemaking had an urgency about it that heightened the pleasure. They stayed in bed all evening although Brenda took time out to call the girls. She told them she'd see them the next day as she was feeling tired after the flight. She didn't think they believed her.

Troy had given much thought to Brenda's problem with the house in Ireland and had come up with a solution.

"I've decided to buy a house or apartment in Dublin," he told her.

"I can't possibly let you do that."

"Why not? Your kids need a base there. You said they won't live with their father."

"Yes, but –"

"No 'buts' about it. It's perfect. I feel guilty for taking you away from them and besides you and I will want a place to stay when we go to visit. I've already been in touch with an estate agent and we'll look at places over Christmas. That is, if you'll take me to Ireland with you for Christmas."

"Of course I will," she cried, throwing her arms around his neck. "I really love you, you know that?"

"I know that," he grinned. "Now come on top of me and show me how much!"

* * *

Brenda could see that Lexi's condition had deteriorated. Angel and Mel said they hadn't noticed it but then they were with her every day. Brenda, having been away, could see the change in her. Lexi assured her she felt fine.

Mel started back at work the following Monday. It was heart-wrenching leaving Jacky but it had to be done. She felt secure knowing that it was Brenda taking care of him. Brenda had spent the past few days with her getting to know Jacky's routine. In fact he was so placid and undemanding, and Brenda so assured, that Mel was happy and content knowing that he was in good hands. Jacky smiled non-stop and she feared he would not miss her nearly as much as she'd miss him. However, she now had his future to think of, so back to work she had to go.

Brenda delighted in the little fellow who was so good. Troy often came to lunch and she smiled as he played gently with Jacky who chuckled and laughed at Troy's antics. As she watched them, Brenda reflected that Troy would have made a wonderful father. She wondered if he wanted a child. It was something they hadn't discussed. Brenda felt that she was too old for a baby, yet Mel hadn't felt that and they were the same age. Being with Jacky had made her a little broody. She guessed it was that damn biological clock. Didn't they say that most women hitting forty felt it?

Later that week as they were lying in bed having made love, she brought up the subject.

"I never wanted children until I met you," Troy confessed, honestly. "But now I don't know. I guess it wouldn't bother me if I never have children but I think I would be deliriously happy if it did happen. How about you?"

"Well, I thought five was enough but I wouldn't be averse to having another one, if it happened."

"Great! That means we can start trying right now," he said as he started caressing her nipples. He knew this was a sure-fire way to arouse her. And it worked.

* * *

Life was settling into a routine for all of them but they still got together regularly for girlie nights and met up, without fail, every Saturday for lunch. Lexi did not seem to be improving and they were all very concerned about her. They were closer than ever now and circumstances seemed to have mellowed them over the past year.

They spent Thanksgiving together at Mel's and of course their fortieth birthday was coming up.

Kenny had laughed when Angel told him how she had refused to become forty. "I realise now that I was an idiot back then," she said ruefully, but then she laughed along with him at her silliness. "Gosh, I've really changed, haven't I?"

"You certainly have. And have you changed your mind about celebrating turning forty?"

"Of course. What's another year?"

"Well, then, why don't we throw a great party for the girls to make up for it? We could have it on the yacht."

"Oh, Kenny, that would be wonderful!" she hugged him.

So, on Angel's birthday the four girls celebrated their fortieth birthday in style, on a glamorous yacht in the Gulf of Mexico.

"Who would have believed this time last year that we'd all be here again this year?" asked Lexi.

"Celebrating our fortieth," Mel remarked, "in spite of Angel!"

"I know, I was a fool back then. I'm sorry, but I have changed."

"Thank God for that!" Mel exclaimed, but she was laughing as Angel swatted her playfully.

"So much has happened to us all this past year," Brenda said.

"Yes, it's certainly been a life-changing one," Lexi agreed.

They were silent for a moment as each of them thought of the momentous year they'd each had.

"And now we're forty!"

"Aaaaagh!" Angel cried but she was joking and they all laughed.

"Forty is the new thirty, didn't you all know that?" Brenda commented.

"I hated turning thirty too!" Angel replied, making a face.

"Well, here's to our fiftieth!" Mel said.

"To our fiftieth!" they all chorused.

* * *

Lexi knew she wouldn't be around for their fiftieth. In fact she hadn't even thought she'd make their fortieth, but she had. The cancer had spread rapidly but she had hidden it from them all, even Marvin. The doctor had told her when she went for tests in October that she hadn't much time left but she'd hung on for Thanksgiving and their birthday party. She'd wanted her last weeks to be as happy as possible for everyone. The last thing she needed was sad faces and tears, so she'd put on a brave face and struggled through the pain.

The nurse who came to visit every day made sure she got all the painkillers she needed but she couldn't stop the disease. The end when it came was swift. Two days after the party Lexi collapsed and was rushed into the hospital. She lapsed into a coma that night and they were all with her two nights later when she finally slipped away. She was smiling and looked peaceful. She was with Gianni and Alessandro at last.

They were all shocked when they heard that she'd known all along that she had so little time left but had hoped to live long enough to celebrate their fortieth birthday with them. Marvin was inconsolable and the girls tried to be brave for his sake. It was what Lexi would have wanted.

They had a small private funeral for her and after her cremation they boarded Troy's yacht and sailed out into the bay. There they scattered her ashes in the Gulf of Mexico as she'd requested. Her three childhood friends threw roses on the water as they shed tears for the woman they'd loved so much, for so long.

Chapter 41

One Year Later

It was a very quiet and sombre forty-first birthday for Mel, Angel and Brenda.

Somehow birthdays would never be the same again without Lexi. The three of them went for a quiet dinner on Lexi's birthday and reminisced about her and the good times they'd spent together. It would be a year on Sunday since she passed away. They all missed her terribly, each in their own way but they'd had to go on. Things had gone so well for all three of them in the past year that they were convinced Lexi was up there pulling strings. Her spirit was with them always, in everything they did.

ANGEL:

Angel had been sober for one year, seven months, three weeks and two days. She still marked the days off on a calendar and still took it one day at a time. She and Kenny also continued to attend AA meetings regularly. She looked more beautiful than ever and Kenny still worshipped her and was extremely proud of her sobriety. He felt she was now strong enough to move on with her life but it would be important to find the right vehicle for her. He thought about it long and hard and came up with just the thing.

"How would you like to host a chat show on my TV station?" he asked her one day as they were walking along the beach.

"A chat show? Do you think I'd be able for that?" She sounded dubious.

"Of course you would. You'd be brilliant at it."

"You really think so?" she asked excitedly.

"Honey, with your personality and looks, you'd be a shoo-in. Besides, you're funny and entertaining. Everyone would love you."

The more she thought about it, the more the idea excited her. She did miss acting and was getting a little bored with just her voluntary work. So it was agreed. They'd give it a go. Kenny would be the executive producer. And so Angel was plunged back into a whirlwind of meetings and discussions and she loved every moment of it. She felt truly alive again. The show would air in September for the first time.

The media were very interested in her 'comeback', as they called it, and she was interviewed constantly in the weeks leading up to the big day. She was considered something of a celebrity in Tampa circles and as a result of all this media attention she was invited to dozens of functions. She attended very few.

Finally, the big day itself arrived and Mel, Brenda, Marvin and Troy gathered at the studios in Tampa to cheer her on. They wished Lexi could have been there to see it. She'd have been so proud of Angel.

The girls had never seen her so nervous or fearful and were afraid for her. Live television was different to making movies where one could do retake after retake. She was terrified she would mess up and was literally shaking as they wished her good luck and took their seats in the front row. Angel looked simply stunning, glamorous as ever but in a muted way, not over the top and not too much skin showing. She would leave that to her celebrity guests.

She felt her mouth go dry as she waited in the wings while her introduction music played. Kenny blew her a kiss from the control booth and gave her the thumbs-up as she walked out on stage. She waved to the audience and saw her friends, all cheering loudly in the front row. They buoyed her up and once the camera panned in on her, she smiled, relaxed, and went into orbit. She was simply wonderful and they all let out a huge sigh of relief.

She had decided to be upfront about her alcoholism from the start, knowing that if she wasn't, the media would surely find out anyway. Amazingly, people responded to her honesty and the lines were jammed with people saying how inspiring her story was. The show was a hit and earned rave reviews and garnered over a million viewers. Angel was a star once more.

In the green room after the show, she was exultant. Kenny toasted her with their non-alcoholic champagne as the rest of the guests drank the real thing.

"Well done, Ange. You were brilliant," Brenda said, hugging her tightly.

"We're so proud of you," Mel whispered as she hugged her too.

"Thanks girls, seeing you there in the front row gave me confidence. I only wish Lexi were here." She had tears in her eyes.

"She is, Angel. I feel it," Brenda assured her.

The party carried on in a local restaurant where Kenny had organised a sumptuous buffet lunch for everyone. The show was deemed a hit and Angel was once again in demand on all the national chat shows that she'd been on years before.

That night Angel made love to Kenny for the first time and was amazed at his virility and stamina. So much for thinking he was too old for me, she giggled to herself after they'd made love for the third time. She could barely keep up with him. They had become really good friends and along the way a deeper relationship had developed between them but Angel had never expected it to amount to this. She felt happy and secure as she lay in his arms. At last she had a real man, one who knew all her weaknesses and failings yet still loved her for herself. What more could a girl want?

She moved in with him shortly after that and so began the happiest time of her life. Once a week he asked her to marry him but she was in no hurry for that. She'd messed up three times before. This time she wanted to be absolutely sure.

BRENDA:
Brenda probably missed Lexi the most as they'd always had a special bond. Her children were also very upset to hear of Lexi's death, Alex in particular. She was happy, however, that she'd got to spend those precious two weeks with her godmother in July.

Brenda could not have got through that first Christmas after Lexi died if it weren't for Troy. He took her to Ireland as he'd promised and Marvin went with them. Her sisters and brothers loved Troy instantly and welcomed him with open arms, happy that Brenda had at last found someone who deserved her. She spent a quiet Christmas and New Year, still grieving for Lexi. The twins and Carly lightened her spirits as young people often do but there was never an hour went by that she didn't think of her old friend. She had taken to talking to Lexi as if she were there and somehow it helped. She felt that Lexi was with her in spirit which was a comfort.

Troy had found a beautiful penthouse apartment overlooking the canal, just off Leeson Street. It was the show apartment so it was fully furnished and Brenda loved it from the moment she saw it. They brought the kids to view it before making the final decision and were happy to be given the thumbs-up. By New Year, the deal was done and dusted.

Back in Florida Brenda's divorce went through quickly and once she was free, she and Troy were married in a quiet ceremony on the beach, much like Lexi's wedding. She was three months pregnant. Their baby son was born in September and Troy was instantly the proudest father on the planet. He flew Alex in from Sudan and Megan from Australia for the christening of their new baby brother. Ryan, Dylan and Carly had been living with Brenda for the summer and were thrilled with the little fellow. They named him Alessandro, but soon everyone was calling him Sandy.

With Marvin's blessing, Lexi had left her house to Brenda and she and Troy had moved in there the previous May. The house held too many memories for Marvin and so he bought Troy's marina apartment. He also bought himself a boat. He kept busy organising Lexi's retrospective exhibition of her Guatemalan paintings. It was a huge success and they all travelled up to New York for the opening.

Troy and Brenda planned on taking Sandy to spend his first Christmas in Ireland with her family. Brenda had never been happier and every day she talked to Lexi, feeling her presence all around her.

MEL:

Mel was also planning to travel to Ireland for Christmas and had booked on the same flight as Brenda and Troy. She had taken Jacky there the previous Christmas to meet his grandparents and it had been the best Christmas she'd ever had. Her relationship with her parents had improved greatly, thanks to Jacky, whom they adored.

"They make better grandparents than they did parents," Mel confessed to Brenda.

Her parents had even put aside their dislike of all things American to travel over to visit in May. To their surprise they loved everything about Florida and now that they were retired were considering buying a place in Dunedin so that they could spend winters close to their little grandson.

Mel had chosen to stay on in the Tampa office and was happy to have left New York. She had expanded the business there to four times its size and had turned it into the most prestigious law firm in the city. It would have been handier for her to live in Tampa itself but she wanted to be near her friends. She approached Marvin about buying his house from him and he happily sold it to her.

Jacky was a darling. An inquisitive, energetic toddler who looked more like his dad every day. His dark hair was long and curly and Mel couldn't bring herself to have it cut. He had Jack's long dark eyelashes over startling blue eyes and a dimple in his cheek when he smiled. He was adorable and everyone loved him, not least because of his sweet nature. Brenda still looked after him but since she'd had Sandy she cared for him in her own house next door. She had kept Maria and Pablo on, as Lexi had requested, so she had plenty of help with the babies and she knew they would be good company for each other when Sandy was a little older.

* * *

Brenda was sitting in the garden reading while Jacky was having his afternoon nap and Sandy was sleeping too when she heard the doorbell ring. She got up to answer it, wondering who it could be and got a huge shock when she saw Mel's Jack standing on the doorstep.

"Oh my God!" she cried, her hand flying to her throat.

"No, it's only me, Jack, I'm afraid," he grinned cheekily. "Howaya, Brenda. I was looking for Lexi."

"Come in, Jack." She stepped aside to let him in, feeling shaken. "Sit down. Can I get you a beer or something?" she asked, indicating an armchair across from her. She badly needed a drink herself.

"Great, lovely stuff. Thanks."

She asked Maria to bring them in two beers and returned to the living room.

"What are you doin' here?" Jack asked. "And where's Lexi?"

"I'm afraid Lexi died, just over a year ago."

"Oh, I'm sorry. I didn't know. What happened to her?"

"Cancer."

"Ah Gawd, that's awful. I'm sorry. Lovely woman."

Maria came in with the beers and her eyes opened wide when she saw Jack sitting there. She remembered him – Miss Mel's young man – from the parties two years ago.

"Why are you here, Jack?" Brenda asked, curious.

"I'm lookin' for Mel's address or phone number in New York. I'd like to contact her."

"Don't you have her number?"

"Nah, my phone was stolen after I left here and I had no way of contactin' her." He took a slug of his beer.

Brenda looked at him over the rim of her glass.

"Yes, you did leave in rather a hurry," she couldn't resist saying.

"I know. I was a gobshite," he replied sheepishly. "Anyway, can you give me Mel's New York number? I'd like to see her again."

"Mel's not in New York any more. She's here in Tampa."

"Jaysus! Are you serious? That's great." His eyes lit up at this news. "Can you tell me where?"

Brenda considered it. "Well, Mel may not want to see you."

"Ah, Jaysus, don't say that. I came all the way from Australia to see her again. She has to see me. I have to explain." His eyes had clouded over and he was cracking his fingers.

"Explain what?"

"That I was a fool. We had somethin' great goin' on and I blew it. I see that now. I haven't stopped thinkin' about her. I have to see her."

He appeared genuine but Brenda needed to talk to Mel first.

"Look, I'll talk to Mel. Why don't you come to the beach gate at six this evening and if she wants to see you, I'll tell her to be there."

"Does she have anyone else in her life now?" he asked, a worried frown creasing his face as the thought suddenly struck him that she might be taken.

"Well, yes, she does actually."

"Oh Christ, don't tell me I'm too late." He buried his head in his hands. "Please, Brenda, make her come. I have to see her again." He grabbed her hands and Brenda saw the sincerity in his eyes. She was again struck by Jacky's likeness to this handsome man.

"I'll do my best," Brenda said, smiling.

* * *

Just after five o'clock, Mel came in to collect Jacky. "Mommy, Mommy," he cried, running to her, wrapping his short little arms around her legs. She scooped him up in her arms and

366

smothered him with kisses. He giggled, as he always did.

"Mel, sit down," Brenda said.

Mel saw the serious look in her eyes and sat down with a worried look.

"What is it, Bren, what's wrong?"

"I had a visitor today. Jack. He came looking for your number in New York."

Mel clasped her hand to her chest and put Jacky down on the floor. "What did he say?" She was deathly pale.

"He wants to meet you. He's come all the way from Australia. He says he was a gobshite – his words – and that he was a fool and hasn't stopped thinking about you."

Mel smiled then. "That's my Jack alright – a gobshite!"

Brenda knew then that it would be okay. Mel would meet him. What happened after that was anyone's guess. "He seemed really genuine, Mel. I said if you wanted to meet him you'd be at the beach gate at six."

Mel glanced at her watch. "Oh my God, that's less than forty minutes' time. Bren, will you keep an eye on Jacky for me? Just till I talk to Jack."

"Of course. And don't worry, I'll feed him and put him to bed if you get delayed." She winked at Mel who jumped up and, kissing Jacky on the top of his head, dashed out to get ready.

Jacky whimpered a little to see his mommy leave without him but Brenda soon distracted him with a biscuit and took him on her knee to read him a story.

* * *

Mel was a bundle of nerves and her heart was hammering in her chest as she walked down the garden to the beach. She spotted him first, pacing up and down, smoking as always. He looked as gorgeous as ever. His hair was longer and he was unshaven and her stomach did a somersault as he turned to look her way. She saw the anxiety in his blue eyes as he looked at her.

"Howaya!" he greeted her, handing her his cigarette and suddenly she was smiling. Only Jack could greet someone like that after a two-year absence.

"I don't smoke any more," she told him, handing it back.

"You look beautiful," he observed, looking her up and down. "Softer, more rounded, really beautiful."

"What do you want, Jack?" she asked cautiously.

"I came to say I'm sorry, really sorry for leavin' you. I never should have. I was a gobshite. I thought once I got to Australia it would be okay but it wasn't. I thought I could forget you but I couldn't. I missed you all the time and suddenly travelling the world didn't seem so important so I came back." He looked at her and she saw he meant it.

"Oh, Jack!" She held out her hands to him and then she was in his arms and they were kissing and he was saying, "I love you, I love you so much, Mel. Please forgive me?"

And they were both crying as she replied, "I've never stopped loving you, Jack."

They sat in the sand, on that spot where they'd first made love, as he told her he was through with travelling and that he wanted to settle down, with her.

They watched the beautiful sunset as they clung to each other and she gave him all her news – well, almost all of it.

"Brenda mentioned that you have someone else now," he said, hoping that she would contradict him.

"Yes, I have. Someone wonderful. Come on, I'd like you to meet him." She stood up and pulled him to his feet.

"Oh no, I couldn't," he replied, looking devastated.

"Come on. I want you to."

Reluctantly, he allowed himself be led through the gate and up through the garden of Lexi's old house. They walked up the steps to the upper terrace where Brenda was sitting nursing Sandy. Troy was sailing a little boat in the baby pool with Jacky. The little boy saw Mel approach and came running towards her.

"Mommy, Mommy!" he cried, doing his usual dash to clasp her legs.

Jack watched in wonder as this tiny tornado dived at Mel. He saw the little face that was a mirror copy of his own when he'd been little and felt his heart constrict. He looked at Mel who had picked Jacky up in her arms.

"Mel . . . is this . . .?"

"Yes, this is the other man in my life. This is Jacky. Your son."

Jack could hardly speak as he looked at the little boy with the hair that grew in a peak on his forehead and the same long dark lashes and bright blue eyes as his own. Then Jacky smiled at him and he saw the dimple in his cheek and with tears in his eyes he reached out to take his son in his arms.

"You even called him after me," Jack said softly as he nuzzled his son's neck.

"What else could I call him when I saw what he looked like?" Mel smiled.

They hugged then, the three of them, a family at last.

Brenda watched them with tears in her eyes too. "Thank you, Lexi," she whispered, looking towards the sky.

The End

If you enjoyed
The Birthday Girls by Pauline Lawless
why not try
Behind Every Cloud also published
by Poolbeg?
Here's a sneak preview of Chapter One

Behind
Every Cloud

Chapter 1

Ellie Moran loved weddings despite the fact that she cried through most of them. She sat beside her mother now, tears rolling down her cheeks as she watched Kate Middleton walk down the aisle on her prince's arm. The new Duchess of Cambridge looked radiant and was positively glowing with happiness. Ellie dabbed at her eyes as she watched them come out of Westminster Abbey and wave to the cheering crowds. Ellie had taken the day off work from the beauty salon to watch the wedding on TV and she was loving every minute of it. Kate's dress was fabulous and, as for Pippa's – there were just no words to describe it. It was all so romantic and perfect. She sighed, reaching for another Kleenex.

Ellie had dreamed of being a bride ever since she was a little girl. Her favourite game back then had been 'getting married', when she would cajole her friends into taking turns to stand in as the groom. Ellie was always the bride, walking down the garden path, a bunch of daisies in her hand and her mother's discarded net curtains trailing behind her. She still dreamed of being a bride and had expected that she would by now have met her prince. Not a real prince like William, of course – but a dashing, handsome man who would sweep her off her feet and down the aisle for the most wonderful wedding imaginable. However, this was beginning to look more and more unlikely. She was twenty-three now and the only man in her life was David – not exactly the sweep-you-off-your-feet type!

He was an accountant and ten years older than Ellie. She'd met him in Gibneys pub in Malahide where she and her girlfriends went for a drink every Friday night. She'd noticed him there before – all the girls had. He was hard to miss with his height and dark George Clooney looks. Initially, she'd refused to go out with him thinking he was too old and mature for her, but eventually on her twentieth birthday, after far too much champagne, she'd caved in and agreed to go on a date with him.

To her surprise they got on well, although unfortunately he had none of the actor's famous sense of humour. However, he *was* very gallant and protective of her and treated her like a princess. Somehow he had grown on her and she felt comfortable with him. However, there was none of the *va-va-voom* that she had expected would happen when Mr Right came along.

She'd made it clear from the start that she did not want an exclusive relationship and that they would both be free to date others. David agreed to this and, although Ellie did go out from time to time with other guys, David stayed faithful to her alone. He was such a workaholic that she couldn't imagine how he'd find the time to date other women in any case. Most of the men she met in pubs and clubs were interested only in beer, football and sex, not necessarily in that order. Not exactly prince material! Eventually she'd given up on them and now she and David were considered a couple. She'd begun to accept that *va-va-voom* was the stuff of romantic novels and films. They'd settled into a comfortable relationship. She did, however, continue to go drinking and clubbing with the girls on a Friday night, but more for the *craic* than in the hope of meeting 'the one'.

"I do hope they'll be happy," Ellie's mother, Marie-Noelle,

said to her in French, as they watched the royal couple drive along the Mall in the magnificent carriage.

Marie-Noelle had been born to French parents who had both sadly died in an accident shortly before her marriage. They'd left France as a result of a family feud and moved to Ireland where she'd been born. She'd been raised speaking French and she in turn had always spoken French to her two daughters, wanting them to know of their heritage. She had sent them to a school run by an order of French nuns and as a result both Ellie and her sister, Sandrine, were now bi-lingual.

"Of course they'll be happy. It's all so romantic," Ellie replied, as she watched the newly married couple wave to the crowds.

Marie-Noelle looked at her youngest daughter with concern. Ellie was so trusting and soft-hearted that people often took advantage of her. She tried to please everyone and was a sucker for lost causes. As a child she'd constantly arrived home with stray kittens, dogs and even a couple of birds with broken wings. She couldn't pass a beggar or collection box without helping out. She was so naïve and such a hopeless romantic that Marie-Noelle worried about her.

The same couldn't be said of her older daughter, Sandrine, now an accountant, who had bossed poor Ellie mercilessly all her life. A hard-nosed career woman, intent on making her way in the world of finance, Sandrine had no time for such nonsense as romance and love. Marie-Noelle had no fears that anyone would try to take advantage of Sandrine. Let them just try, she often chuckled to herself. No, Ellie was the one she worried about most.

"It takes more than romance and a fairytale wedding to make a marriage work, you know," she said now.

Ellie had never thought much further than the wedding. She was in love with the *idea* of getting married. She'd never much

PAULINE LAWLESS

considered what came after the ceremony. She hoped fervently that the royal couple would live happily ever after, as they always did in fairytales, if not necessarily in real life.

"David has booked a table in Bon Appetit for this evening, to celebrate," Ellie told her mother. She'd been surprised and delighted when he'd suggested it as he'd shown absolutely no interest in the wedding up to that point.

"That's very nice of him. He'll make some girl a wonderful husband someday," Marie-Noelle remarked, looking slyly at her daughter.

"*Mmmm*," Ellie replied nonchalantly. "How about a cup of tea?" She jumped up, not wanting to continue with this conversation.

"Lovely," Marie-Noelle replied, aware that she'd hit on a touchy subject. "I have some chocolate éclairs in the fridge. Let's have them now."

When they arrived at the restaurant that evening, Ellie was surprised to find that David had ordered a bottle of champagne.

"How fabulous!" she exclaimed, pleased with this romantic gesture.

The wine waiter poured it and handed her a glass. He was grinning like a Cheshire cat and she noticed that David was beaming inanely too. As they clinked glasses she spotted something in the bottom of hers.

"I think there's something in my glass," she said, peering into it, afraid it might be a piece of broken glass.

"There is indeed," David replied, seemingly not too worried.

Ellie looked more closely and gasped aloud. She couldn't believe her eyes. There at the bottom of the glass was a glittering diamond ring. She fished it out and looked up at David enquiringly.

374

"Will you marry me, Ellie?"

She looked at him disbelievingly.

"As today was such a special day for you, I thought it might be a good time to ask you to be my wife. Please say yes."

Ellie was a great believer in fate and if this wasn't fate – being proposed to on the day of the Royal Wedding – then she didn't know what was.

She was deeply touched and her heart went out to him. He hadn't exactly swept her off her feet but she did love him, and this was so romantic. It was the most romantic thing that had ever happened to her. She burst into tears.

"Please say yes," he begged, taking her hand in his, a worried look in his dark eyes.

"Oh yes, David, yes," she answered him, smiling through her tears.

Reaching across the table, he put the ring on her finger and kissed her as the other diners in the restaurant, aware of what was happening, broke into a round of applause. She smiled back at them. She held her hand out in front of her to admire the ring. It was the biggest diamond she'd ever seen. Obviously she'd seen photographs of massive knuckledusters on celebrities like Maria Sharapova and Kim Kardashian but never one as big as this in real life. It was fabulous!

"David, it's beautiful. Exactly what I would have chosen myself," she told him, her eyes shining as she moved her hand this way and that.

"I'm glad you like it, darling."

"I can't believe it. It feels like a dream."

"It's not a dream," David replied. "Any time you doubt it, just look at your ring." He smiled at her fondly.

"It's beautiful. Thank you, David." She kissed him again, thinking how handsome he was. She knew she was a lucky girl.

David was happy that Ellie had agreed to be his wife.

They'd been together three years and he reckoned it was time they named the day. For a moment there, when she'd burst into tears, he'd been afraid that she was about to say no.

He'd been with his brother in Gibneys the first night he'd set eyes on her. She had the face of an angel and was, without doubt, the most enchanting woman he'd ever seen. She had luminous, almost translucent, skin, which glowed with freshness. Her eyes were a very unusual violet blue under long dark curly lashes and her mouth was a perfect cupid's bow which gave her a very sweet smile. Her long, dark, glossy hair swung as she spoke animatedly and he was instantly smitten and longed to get to know her.

He found himself back in Gibneys every Friday night after that and to his delight she was always there, with the same two friends. For a couple of weeks he watched her surreptitiously, wondering how best to approach her. She had an innocent and vulnerable air about her that made him long to take care of her and protect her. When eventually he screwed up the courage to ask her out, she'd turned him down. He was gutted but he persevered and finally won her over. Now this beautiful girl had agreed to marry him, making him a very happy man indeed.

Ellie was on cloud nine all the following day. Her parents were delighted for her and everyone in the beauty salon where she worked congratulated her on hearing the news. She received many envious glances from both staff and clients when they saw the stunning ring she was sporting. They all tried it on, *ooh-ing* and *aah-ing* as it sparkled in the lights. Ellie was on a high and unprepared for the avalanche of cards and engagement presents that flooded in during the following weeks. She felt like a real princess. It was all so exciting.

She couldn't wait to be a bride!